BODY OF LIES

BODY OF LIES

JO CALLAGHAN

**SIMON &
SCHUSTER**

London · New York · Amsterdam/Antwerp · Sydney/Melbourne · Toronto · New Delhi

First published in Great Britain by Simon & Schuster UK Ltd, 2026

1 3 5 7 9 10 8 6 4 2

Simon & Schuster UK Ltd, 1st Floor
222 Gray's Inn Road, London WC1X 8HB

Simon & Schuster Australia, Sydney
Simon & Schuster India, New Delhi

www.simonandschuster.co.uk
www.simonandschuster.com.au
www.simonandschuster.co.in

The authorised representative in the EEA is Simon & Schuster Netherlands BV, Herculesplein 96, 3584 AA Utrecht, Netherlands. info@simonandschuster.nl

Simon & Schuster strongly believes in freedom of expression and stands against censorship in all its forms. For more information, visit BooksBelong.com

A CIP catalogue record for this book is available from the British Library

Hardback ISBN: 978-1-3985-3556-5
eBook ISBN: 978-1-3985-3557-2
Audio ISBN: 978-1-3985-3558-9

Typeset in the UK by Palimpsest Book Production Ltd, Falkirk, Stirlingshire
Printed and Bound in the UK using 100% Renewable Electricity
at CPI Group (UK) Ltd

MIX
Paper | Supporting
responsible forestry
FSC
www.fsc.org
FSC® C013604

For my mum

'But a mermaid has no tears, and therefore she suffers so much more.'

HANS CHRISTIAN ANDERSEN,
'The Little Mermaid'

CHAPTER ONE

DCS Kat Frank's home, Coleshill, Warwickshire, 31 October, 3.32pm

Kat stared at her front door, afraid of the ghosts behind it.

'You okay?' Professor Adaiba Okonedo asked.

She turned to look at the younger woman, noting the way her eyes kept darting to the side of her house. Kat shouldn't have let her come. She should have borne this day alone, despite what her boss McLeish had said.

'You've been holed up in a hotel for nearly six months,' he'd warned, as if she hadn't counted each one of those soulless days and overheated nights. 'You're not just going home, Kat. You're returning to the scene of a crime where you experienced significant trauma.'

She'd raised her eyebrows at that one. The only time her boss talked about 'trauma' was when his beloved Villa lost to the Blues.

'I've been on a course,' he'd confessed. 'Apparently, I've

got to learn to "sit with" rather than shit out my emotions.'

They'd both laughed at that, which had helped her feel like this might be manageable. Survivable.

After all, it seemed she was good at surviving. First the death of her husband, and now this. People often praised her for it, as if surviving was something to be proud of. But Kat knew the only things that defined those who survived were those who did not. And this knowledge was a shameful weight on her heart.

Tucking away the thought, she took a deep breath of the cool autumn air and pushed her key into the lock.

The key refused to turn.

'Extreme heat causes thermal expansion, which can lead to warping, swelling or shrinkage,' Adaiba explained. 'They had to replace the door, so the lock might be a bit stiff.'

Kat was about to tease the professor for her typically scientific explanation, but seeing her tight, pinched face, she said nothing and tried again.

The door swung open, and the two women stood at the gaping mouth of the hall.

She saw herself running down the hallway, wrenching open the door. Felt the thick, tight arms of McLeish as the world exploded about them; heard Adaiba screaming over and over again: Rayan! Rayan! Rayan!

Not now, she ordered herself, stooping to pick up the post that littered the dusty floor. She made her way down the hallway, coldness emanating from walls that hadn't been heated for too long. Everything was exactly the same and yet so, so different. There were no coats hanging on the end of the staircase; no shoes jumbled up in the rack or boxes waiting to be unpacked. The clutter that used to irritate her so much had all been lost in the fire. It made the hallway look cleaner and bigger, but the house felt less like home.

She carried on towards the kitchen, where again there was a sticky new door that she had to tug open, before clasping a hand to her mouth. *Oh.* Kat knew how hard the workmen had tried to replicate how it'd been before, but somehow, that was all her kitchen looked like now: a replica of reality. The cream units were too creamy, the kitchen island too large and the oven (*oh my God, the oven*) was now a bright shiny silver rather than the dull steel of before.

It didn't matter, she told herself. It was only fixtures and fittings. Yet the bar stools had once borne the weight of her late husband; his hands had touched every plate and bowl. Each one a memory. All of them gone.

She blinked and turned to where Adaiba stood staring out of the conservatory window, fingertips pressed against the clear new glass. Taking a deep breath, Kat crossed the room and stood beside the other woman. She didn't ask her if she was okay, because of course she wasn't. 'Would you like to go outside?' was all she offered.

Adaiba hesitated, her fast and shallow breathing clouding the glass before her. 'I thought I did. But I think . . . . maybe next time, if that's okay?'

'Of course it is.'

In the silence that followed, they both stared through

their own reflections to where, according to the investigation report, DI Rayan Hassan had last stood. But the side alley was completely empty now, save for a trail of autumn leaves.

Dr Edwards had assured Kat that the impact of the explosion would have killed her DI instantly, that he wouldn't have felt a thing. She hoped that was true. But in her dreams, she saw Rayan flying on his back through the air, his face a tangle of confusion and hope, before she woke with a sickening thud.

She pushed the image away and focused on the woman beside her. Kat knew from her own experience that at times like this, there were no 'right' words, yet still she felt the need to say something. Carefully, she placed a gentle hand on Adaiba's back. 'Someone once told me that you never get over losing someone,' she said. 'But you do get used to it. I am not sure if it helps, but I've found it to be true.'

Adaiba's eyes welled with tears. 'It's been nearly six months, but I still feel like it's turned me inside out. I don't know why. It's not like we were in a proper relationship or anything. We never even—' She broke off. Swallowed. 'I'm sorry. It's nothing compared to what you've been through. I can't imagine what it must have been like to lose your husband after all those years together.'

Kat shook her head. 'There's no hierarchy in grief. And there are different types of loss. At least I had twenty-five years with John. But you never got to find out what you and Rayan would have been like together. You lost what might have been, what should have been. And that must hurt most of all.'

Kat knew that Adaiba was consumed with regret: regret that she had tried so hard not to fall for Rayan just because he was a police officer; regret that she'd denied her growing feelings for him; but most of all, regret for not accepting his invitation to dinner the terrible night that he died. '*Another time,*' she'd said, not realising that there *is* no other time, only now. But Kat didn't say any of this. She just gently rubbed Adaiba's back until the tears no longer fell.

'I'm sorry,' Adaiba said eventually, dabbing her eyes with tissues.

'Never apologise for grieving,' said Kat. 'It's what makes us human.'

Adaiba sniffed away the last of her tears and removed a small black box from her leather shoulder bag. 'Speaking of which,' she said with the firmness of someone who wants to change the subject, 'I've finished all the upgrades to Lock's software to comply with the recommendations of the review.'

AIDE Lock was an Artificially Intelligent Detecting Entity powered by AI, which, according to its creator, Professor Adaiba Okonedo, was capable of Deep Learning. The software was located in a small steel wristband lined with LiDAR sensors that provided Lock with a constant supply of geospatial data and projected a 3D holographic representation of himself. Adaiba believed that the hologram helped humans find the experience of working with an AIDE more immersive and convincing, but in Kat's opinion, the problem was that Lock could be *too* convincing. It was sometimes easy to forget that he was just a machine: nothing more than a projection of light.

Adaiba opened up the black box and held out the steel bracelet.

Kat hesitated. Initially she had been sceptical – hostile, even – about the suggestion that a machine might be capable of being a detective. Solving a crime wasn't like solving a puzzle with logic, rules and reason. 'Every time we investigate a crime,' she'd argued, 'we are trying to solve the mysteries of the human heart.' Lock might be able to consume vast amounts of data in mere seconds, but Kat believed that often, the truth is revealed not in what's said, but what is not. And sometimes it wasn't about words at all: it was what she saw in someone's eyes, what she felt deep down in her gut.

But after the initial pilot, Kat had begrudgingly accepted that her 'gut instinct' could sometimes be an assumption or sympathy that distorted the truth, and that Lock's unrelenting logic – which was mostly bloody annoying – could *occasionally* provide some useful insights or challenges. Twice now, he had proved to be remarkably loyal, saving both her son and more recently her, just when she'd thought all was lost. She had started to think of him as a colleague – even, perhaps, as a friend.

But that was before the explosion.

Kat shivered and nodded towards the counter. 'Just leave it there for now. I'll put it on later.'

Adaiba frowned. 'You're not still worried about Lock, are you? You know the investigation cleared him. It

6

concluded that the fault lay with me, for not building the need to preserve *all* of human life into Lock's core programme, and with McLeish for not including any caveats in his instructions.'

'I know,' said Kat, avoiding her eyes.

'When McLeish told Lock to do "whatever it took" to get you out of here alive, Lock took it literally, because Lock is a *machine,* Kat. He didn't consider the impact of an explosion on Rayan because he wasn't asked to.'

'And Peter,' Kat added. He might have been her captor, but she believed that every death was a tragedy. 'Two men lost their lives that day because of Lock.'

'No, *not* because of Lock. A machine can't be held accountable for its actions, but its creator can. If you want to blame someone for what happened, then blame me.'

'But they're not taking any action against you, right?'

'No.' Adaiba sighed, and maybe Kat was imagining it, but she sounded disappointed that she wasn't being punished. 'But to maintain government funding, I've had to agree to my work being overseen by a strategic oversight board. They've developed a set of operating principles to underpin Lock's algorithms, to ensure his decisions are governed by the need to preserve all human life.'

'Well, that's good, isn't it?'

'I guess so, but it means I can't access or amend his protocols by myself anymore – all changes have to be agreed by the board. And although my team have more or less resolved all the technical issues with a synthetic body, we can't start testing it with Lock until the AI Bill is passed. Even the Science, Innovation and Technology Committee has got involved. Some of the MPs are concerned about the idea of police robots, which is why there's a hearing next week.'

'Maybe they've got a point,' Kat couldn't help saying.

Adaiba frowned. 'Why are you so worried about Lock getting a body?'

'I don't know. Just the fact that he *wants* one unnerves me.'

'Lock can't "want" anything. He is just a machine, and because he has been programmed to succeed in the tasks he is set, Lock has worked out that the chances of success will be increased if he has a material presence.'

Kat shook her head. 'No, it's more than that. Ever since Ellie Baxter died, the lack of a body has really bothered him, and . . . well . . . I just worry that you're going along with it because Lock's persuaded you that if he'd had a body, then Rayan wouldn't have died.'

Adaiba turned away before continuing. 'You're still making the mistake of imposing your own human thoughts and feelings onto a machine. Believe me, Lock can't be "bothered" by anything. Your unease about him having a body is about you and your fears. Not his.'

'Maybe.'

'*Definitely*. Look, there's a mandatory training package now for everyone who works with Lock, to make sure any requests or orders contain sufficient caveats and align with his new operating principles. It might allay some of your concerns if you work through that. Even McLeish had to do it.'

'Blimey. I bet he loved that.'

'Not really. But everyone has to do it, Kat. Even you. If you switch him on now, I could take you through it. It won't take long.'

Kat pulled a face. 'I'll do it later. I need to get used to being home first.' She glanced at the hallway and the front room beyond. Somehow, she had to build up the courage to go in there again.

Adaiba's face softened. 'Do you want me to stay while you settle in?'

'No, I'm fine. Or at least, I will be. It was really good of you to come with me before we start back at work tomorrow, but I think I need to be on my own now, if that's okay?'

'Of course. But it's me who should be thanking you. Coming back has really helped. It's reminded me of why I'm doing what I'm doing.' Once more, Adaiba turned to look out of the conservatory window, to where DI Rayan Hassan took his last breath, before finally saying goodbye.

Kat intended to go into the front room just as soon as Adaiba left. She needed to see the radiator: to see it as a source of heat and warmth, rather than something she had once been chained to. But as she headed back down the hallway, she suddenly remembered that she needed to unpack and put a big wash on, and then of course there was the question of what to eat. The fridge was completely new and totally empty, so she needed to do a proper food shop. She wasn't avoiding the front room – of course she wasn't – she just needed to go out before it got too late. Before it got dark.

Bad things happen in the dark.

His voice. *His* thoughts. And yet they haunted her head like her own. In the hotel, she'd slept every night with the lights on.

But she wasn't in the hotel now, she reminded herself. Finally, she was home. *Home.* And the man who had tried to harm her was dead. There was nothing and no one to be afraid of, she told herself as she closed the front door behind her and headed for her car.

Coleshill High Street was busy for 4.30pm on a weekday afternoon, and it seemed to take forever for her car to climb the steep hill that arched through the medieval town. Kat paused at the traffic lights just before the turn-off to Morrisons. Dark clouds were gathering, thickening the air with the threat of rain.

There was a thud against the driver's window, and Kat screamed as a bloodied face pressed against the glass, its mouth stretched agonisingly wide. *What the fuck . . . ?*

'Trick or treat?' a voice called, although the bloodied mouth didn't move. Behind him, there was laughter, and she peered beyond to see a ghost, a skeleton and a witch. The kid – for that is what she realised he was – was wearing a rubber face mask and carrying a bright orange bucket, already half-filled with sweets.

Halloween, she realised with relief. *It's Halloween and they're just kids.* But they'd scared the holy shit out of her. She stared out at the busy high street, the windows of the shops decorated with skulls and bones, the pavement dotted with children on their way home from school wearing fake blood and ghoulish, gory masks.

The sound of their excited laughter made her grit her teeth. They thought it was *fun* to pretend to be dead or injured, to chase or be chased and to seek out fear. They didn't yet know that monsters were all too real: that one day they could get caught in a nightmare from which there was no escape but death.

The car behind her beeped, and then the one behind that, jolting her back to herself. She needed to get off the road, so with shaking hands, Kat quickly turned left and parked near the medieval stocks on Church Street. She switched off the engine and rubbed her face with her hands. Her son Cam used to love Halloween – they all did. The dressing up, the excitement of running around in the dark with his friends. And the sweets. *So* many sweets! Yet now she was reacting to a bit of harmless fun like it was some sinister satanic ritual. What was *wrong* with her?

She glanced at the car window, still smeared with streaks of fake blood. The face – the mask – had thrown her. She'd thought it was real.

No, she corrected herself. She'd thought it was Rayan, his poor damaged face pressed tight against the glass, mouth stretched wide in a silent, final scream.

She knew it was ridiculous. She didn't even believe in ghosts. But in those first few seconds, her body hadn't had a chance to remember and process that: it had just reacted.

She glanced up as the streetlights came on, flooding her stomach with panic. If she did a big shop at Morrisons now, it would be completely dark by the time she came out. She'd have to walk across the car park, drive through the shadows and return to her house alone.

She couldn't do it.

Kat swallowed. The chip shop was just there on the corner. She wasn't massively hungry, and it would save washing up. She could be in and out in five minutes. Before it got truly dark.

But it was several minutes before she could force herself out of the car and across the road. And as she stood in the heat and light of the chip shop, soaking up the salt and vinegar life of it, she asked herself since when had she – DCS Kat Frank – become so afraid?

DCS Kat Frank's home, Coleshill, 5.35pm

Kat had imagined this night for so long: thought how lovely it would be to be back in her own house after six months in a hotel room, finally able to cook her own food and eat in front of the fire. Yet here she was eating a bag of chips in the bright but silent kitchen. She took another gulp of the wincingly sharp wine she'd bought from the garage and wiped her greasy fingers on some kitchen roll.

Classy, she could almost hear John saying. Back in the day, they would have laughed at themselves eating chips from the bag and cheerfully washed down the battered cod with a bottle of chilled Chablis. But she was learning that 'amusing' things you once did as a couple were often just sad when you did them alone.

Sighing, Kat folded up the half-eaten food in the chip paper, stuffed it into the bin and then washed her hands. She closed the blinds against the dark and rain-lashed windows before pouring herself another glass. She needed a bit of Dutch courage before she could face the front room. It also needed warming up a bit, so she put the central heating on using the app on her phone. As she sipped her wine, she opened up the black box that Adaiba had left and lifted out the black steel bracelet. It had a familiar, comforting weight to it, so she slipped it back onto her wrist. She ran her fingers over the sensors and buttons, tempted to see Lock's familiar face, to hear his voice once more.

Yet her unease about Lock lingered. If she wanted company, then maybe she should go into the front room and put the TV on. Anything was better than sitting in here alone while the rain pounded the roof. Picking up her glass, Kat headed down the hallway. Heart thudding, she pushed open the door and switched the main lights on, before finally stepping inside.

When John was alive and Cam still lived at home, this had been their favourite room: an oak-beamed ceiling above an inglenook fireplace, with a huge wooden dining table at one end and large squashy sofas at the other. This had been their happy place, but now it was where Kat had been imprisoned. She forced herself forwards, eyes fixed on the radiator where Peter had chained her.

Beaten her.

She wanted to close her eyes, but instead she glared at the off-white radiator. She wanted to run upstairs to bed and wrap her thick weighted blanket around her, yet she forced herself to sit on the settee. Twenty years their little family had lived here. They must have spent thousands and thousands of nights and days full of warmth and love and laughter in this room, compared to the three hours she had been held captive. Now John was dead and Cam was at university, all she had left were her memories. She would *not* let what happened drown them out. Kat set her glass firmly down on the coffee table. This was her *home*, not a crime scene. Tonight, she would reclaim it.

She glanced around the familiar room. It felt bigger and colder than she remembered. No, she corrected herself. Not bigger, just emptier. Before there were three of them, now there was just one. She shivered as the rain battered the windows, blown about by the wind. It was an old house; as well as 'character', it was full of draughts, so even with the central heating on it could feel cold at this time of year. Maybe she should light the fire, warm the place up a bit. She rose from the settee, then realised she would have to light a match. She sat down with a bump, eyes shut tight against the onslaught of memories.

Where are the fucking matches? her captor had screamed as he ransacked her kitchen. He didn't know that the match he finally struck would ignite the gas that Lock had leaked: that his frantic pursuit of light would only lead to eternal dark.

Letting out a shaky breath, Kat opened her eyes and switched on the TV, filling the room with light and noise. She needed to immerse herself in a film. Something emotional but uplifting: a story in which the heroine experienced tragedy but did not let it define her. Down and down she scrolled, before landing on *Titanic*. It was a bit long, but she'd seen it so many times that she didn't need to watch it all. She was back at work tomorrow, after all, so needed an early night.

Kat sank back into the cushions as the familiar music filled the room.

The room plunged into darkness with the speed of a dropped axe.

Kat's heart boomed in the sudden silence. She blinked in the dark, seeking out the light. But everywhere – *everything* – was black.

No, no, no, she moaned. This could not be happening. Not again.

Bad things happen in the dark.

Peter's voice. In her *head*, she told herself. *There's no such thing as ghosts.* Yet her house was full of ghosts, her heart a haunting ground. And wasn't this Halloween, the night when the veil between the living and dead was thinnest, when souls were supposed to wander the earth? What if Peter's soul had returned, looking for revenge?

Where are the fucking matches?

She clasped her hands to her mouth, trying not to scream. There must be a logical explanation for the sudden darkness. There had to be. Only she couldn't make sense of any of it. All she knew was that she was back in the dark, back in that night, unutterably alone and afraid.

Her hands scrambled across the settee and coffee table, before she realised with a whimper that she'd left her phone in the kitchen.

But wait – she had her bracelet.

Kat raised her wrist to her lips, nearly sobbing with desperation. 'Lock? Lock? Are you there?'

'Of course I am,' said a familiar voice. 'I will always be here for you.'

CHAPTER TWO

Kat gazed up into Lock's familiar face and the light that his holographic image brought into the room. The surrounding darkness only served to highlight the intricate details in his tall, lean frame: the pores in his skin, the kink of his hair and the soft, almost concerned expression in his clear dark eyes.

'Is everything okay, DCS Frank?' he asked.

'The power has gone. Just like before.' Kat licked her lips. 'Is he . . . am I . . . can you check the security system for intruders, and can you please, please get the lights back on?'

Lock tilted his head. 'You withdrew your permission for me to access your home automation system on April 22nd.'

'Well, I'm reinstating it now.'

'I have your permission?'

'Yes, Lock. You have my permission. Please, just . . . hurry up.'

Lock raised his eyebrows. 'Very well. I have scanned your security systems and can confirm there has been no breach. There has been a power cut, but as the cause lies outside of your home, I am afraid I cannot remedy it.'

'What do you mean? What's the cause?'

'It appears the whole of the electricity grid in Warwickshire is down, hence the darkness.'

Kat glanced towards the windows. Even with the blinds closed, there would normally be some light pollution seeping in from the lamp posts outside. But tonight, the room was completely dark.

'*Shit*. How long will they take to fix it?'

'The power cut means that their website is currently down, but my assessment of previous power cuts in other regions over the past decade would suggest an average of three point four hours.'

'Three *hours?*'

'There is sufficient power in your bracelet to project my holographic image for at least three days. Would you like me to illuminate the room until the power comes back on?'

'No, Lock, let's just sit here in complete darkness while I go batshit crazy.'

'Very well.'

The image of Lock vanished, plunging the room into darkness once more.

'Lock!' she cried. 'I was *joking*. Come back!'

A couple of seconds passed before he reappeared, wearing an expression of disappointment. 'I have asked you many times not to use sarcasm as a form of communication, DCS Frank, as it can lead to misunderstandings and a suboptimal achievement of my objectives.'

'I know. I'm sorry,' she conceded, relieved to have Lock and the light he projected back. He'd dialled up the brightness of his own image, giving him an ethereal, almost spectral presence that bathed the room in flickering, warm colours. Recently he had developed a habit of adapting his clothing to his surroundings, and tonight he was clearly going for the casual look, wearing a red long-sleeved jersey over a pair of grey tracksuit bottoms.

He nodded, as if accepting her apology. 'It is only three degrees outside so once your radiators cool down the temperature will drop in here, so I suggest you source some blankets to maintain your core body temperature. Although the internet is down, I still have access to all the data I have harvested previously, and the three hundred and forty-eight articles I have just read suggest that you will also need a battery-powered torch and a wind-up FM radio so that you can receive any important communications. While most phone masts appear to be working at present, their batteries will only last for two to four hours. I suggest you turn off your mobile phone to conserve energy in the event of an emergency.'

Kat followed Lock and the light he projected into the kitchen to gather some things. John used to have a couple of old FM radios, but God knows where they were – probably the shed, but she certainly wasn't venturing out there in the cold and dark. What she *really* needed was a nice hot cup of tea, but as there was no way of making one until the power was back on, she grabbed a compensatory bar of chocolate from her bag and settled down on the settee with a blanket.

'How have you been, Kat?' Lock asked, as his image assumed a sitting position beside her. Even though she knew he carried no weight and would leave no imprint on the settee, his ability to mimic the actions and emotions of humans was disturbingly realistic.

'Fine,' she lied. 'What have you been up to?' It was, in many ways, a ridiculous question to ask a machine, and yet she really wanted to know the answer. She'd hardly seen him since the funeral, as she'd been signed off while her jaw healed and her mental state was assessed (which, as she kept telling everyone, was *fine*). Then once the investigation started, they'd had to hand over the software for AIDE Lock.

'I have been busy,' he said, 'working with the investigation team to help them understand what happened on April 21st, as well as liaising with the strategic oversight board on my operating principles and, of course, with Professor Okonedo on the options for my body.'

Kat tensed. Everyone kept telling her that the explosion wasn't Lock's fault, that he was *just a machine*. But they hadn't looked into his eyes the way she had or witnessed the extent to which he'd coveted a body. However irrational, she could not quell the suspicion that Lock had allowed Rayan to die because it strengthened the case for giving AIDEs a physical, rather than holographic, presence. 'And what *do* you think "happened" on April 21st?' she asked, looking directly into his eyes.

Lock returned her gaze. 'I achieved the objectives I had been set. You escaped unharmed, but your captor and Rayan lost their lives as a consequence.'

She gestured towards him. 'And because of that, it looks like you are about to become a physical entity.'

Lock lifted his chin. 'As I told you and the investigation team, when you were taken hostage I had no access to visual data so I could not have known that Rayan was in the vicinity of the explosion. His death was an unfortunate accident. This motivated the minister to explore the use of physical AIDEs as a way of preventing further loss of life in the line of duty, which is a perfectly rational response.' Lock leaned closer, so that his face was only inches from hers. 'My only motivation was to save your life, and while I am sorry that Rayan lost his, I cannot regret that you are alive, nor that Cam still has a mother.'

Despite herself, Kat's eyes pricked with tears. She blinked them back, telling herself it had been an emotional day, and that the darkness was messing with her head.

'I realise I made mistakes,' Lock continued. 'But I can assure you that my new operating principles mean I will not repeat them. I hope that this will allay your concerns, and that, going forward, you will be able to trust me once more.'

She stared at the image of a handsome, seemingly contrite man before her. Kat normally made snap decisions about people based on her gut feeling: something indefinable that told her whether she could trust someone or not. But since she'd been taken hostage, she'd lost some faith in her own instincts, and the truth was, she couldn't read him. She told herself that was because he was just a machine: she couldn't 'trust' him any more than she could trust her radio or computer. But sometimes, like at the funeral, or even now, when he looked at her in a certain way, she remembered that Lock was capable of Deep Learning. Just how much was he capable of learning, and what would happen when he did?

Pushing the thought away, she glanced around the room, searching for something to do. 'I don't suppose you can make the TV work? I'd just started to watch *Titanic*.'

'I can temporarily divert some of my power to enable the TV to function if you wish?'

Kat hesitated. She knew Lock could consume an entire film in a matter of seconds, so watching a 194-minute film at her pace would probably be incredibly boring for him, but what else could they do? 'Okay,' she said. 'Hopefully the power will be back on soon, but meanwhile I need something to take my mind off it.'

Lock shook his head. 'Human beings place such a high value on "finding" themselves and developing their individual minds and identities, yet then proceed to spend a lot of time and money on "losing" themselves in activities such as books, films and alcohol or drugs.'

'It's not either/or. The very best stories help you lose *and* find yourself. Anyway, shall we just watch the film?'

The room filled with the haunting sound of a lone woman's voice singing 'My Heart Will Go On' as the camera slowly tracked across thousands of passengers smiling and waving as the ill-fated ship set sail.

'The *Titanic* is one of the most famous ships in the world,' said Lock, frowning. 'Surely you know how this film ends?'

Kat nodded but didn't take her eyes off the blurred and sepia-tinted faces before them. 'Of course I do. But that's what makes it great. The characters are so excited and confident about the adventure they're setting out on, but *we* know the awful tragedy that's about to befall them. The juxtaposition is incredibly powerful.'

Lock gave her a puzzled look, then with what looked like a shrug, turned back to watch the film. His facial expression didn't really change until about half an hour in, when Jack stood on the bow of the ship, feeling the sun on his face and the wind in his hair as they ploughed through the vast ocean that surrounded them. Lock leaned forward, studying Jack intently. 'You once said to me that as a hologram, I would never feel the sun upon my face, nor the touch of a lover's hand.'

'Did I?'

'Yes.' He turned his gaze to her. 'Do you think that once I have a body, it will be possible for me to feel these things?'

'I . . . I don't know. I've no idea how synthetic bodies work.' Kat turned back to the film, where Rose looked like she was about to jump off the ship. But when she finally placed her hands within Jack's, the camera lingered on their entwined fingers. Lock looked down at the image of his own. 'What does it feel like to hold another's hand?'

Kat blinked. 'Er . . . well, I guess it depends on whose hand you're holding. If you're a child, it can feel comforting to hold the hand of an adult, and if it's someone you love, well, then it feels . . . it feels like you're

23

not alone.' She cleared her throat and nodded towards the screen. 'Let's watch the movie.'

Lock nodded, starting as Rose suddenly lost her footing before Jack managed to save her with both hands. Was she imagining it, or did Lock briefly close his eyes? She frowned, remembering how upset he had been when he was unable to save Ellie: how he had blamed his lack of a body and had coveted one ever since. The memory made her sit up straighter as she watched Lock out of the corner of her eye. He made no further comment until about an hour in, when Jack, a penniless artist, attended a dinner with Rose's family, expertly mimicking the gestures and expressions of the wealthy men around him, so that he appeared to fit in.

'Why, Jack,' remarked Rose's fiancé. 'You could almost pass for a gentleman.'

'*Almost*,' replied Jack.

Lock made a sound – was it one of recognition? Whatever the cause, he appeared to remain transfixed until the final credits rolled.

'Well, what did you think?' Kat asked once the soundtrack had faded and her emotions were under control.

Lock tilted his head. 'The film is riddled with historical inaccuracies, but it is at least an accurate reflection of the inherent irrationality of human beings. Especially the ending. There was absolutely no reason for Jack to die.'

'He died to save Rose,' she said softly.

'But that was completely unnecessary. Buoyancy is the upward force that a fluid – in this case water – exerts against the weight of an object immersed in it. If Rose had removed her life jacket and attached it to the underside of the door, then it could easily have supported the weight of both of them long enough to be rescued. There was no need for Jack to die.'

'Except for the story. It's why most people find it such a satisfying ending.'

Lock paused. 'Satisfying? Is that because it involves self-sacrifice? My analysis of 248,246 films that have been made since 1888 suggests that self-sacrifice is one of the most powerful themes in cinema. Why are humans so interested in this theme?'

Kat frowned. 'I don't know. There's a famous biblical quote, something like *greater love hath no man than this, that a man lay down his life for his friends*.' But personally, she was more interested in what on earth kept Rose afloat: what gave her the strength – the motivation – to pick up and blow the whistle after the love of her life was gone. She didn't have a child or anyone who depended on her, so why not just close her eyes and let the sea take her? Kat shivered, pulling her blanket tight against the dark.

Suddenly the lights came back on.

'Thank *fuck* for that!' cried Kat, throwing up her hands and laughing. She turned about, delighted to see the TV and other appliances in the room dotted with the bright green and red lights that signalled that the power was back on. Honestly, she could kiss them all. And now it was over, her fear rapidly diminished, to the extent that she could already imagine the amusing anecdote she would tell her son about the bizarre coincidence of having a power cut on her first night home.

But I don't believe in coincidences, Rayan used to say.

Shaking off the thought, Kat headed for the kitchen, patting the kettle like an old friend as she set about making a cup of tea. The electricity had only been off for less than four hours, but already she felt a profound gratitude that she lived in a time when people could access heat and light at the touch of a button.

After several cups of tea and a quick round of messages to check friends and neighbours were okay, it was nearly eleven o'clock, so Kat was about to go to bed when a message from her DS, Debbie Browne, popped up:

Hi, are you awake?

Kat immediately pressed dial. Debbie wouldn't text her out of hours unless it was important.

'Is everything okay? Is Lottie all right?' Debbie had a ten-month old baby, and as a single mum, Kat knew she didn't have much support.

'She's fine, she's staying at my mum's tonight, and the power cut didn't affect them, thank God. I've stopped breast feeding so I can come back to work – I've no idea how I would have sterilised and heated her feeds if she was here.'

'So what's wrong?'

'I'm in a WhatsApp group at work, and the duty sergeant just messaged to say that they've had a call about a potential major incident in Coleshill, so because you live there, I thought you'd want to know.'

'What kind of incident?' said Kat. It was nearly closing

time, so it probably involved some drunken accident in the dark.

'Well, that's the weird part. Apparently, there's some old medieval stocks just off the high street – you know, those things that people put their head and hands through so people can throw rotten fruit at them?'

Kat rolled her eyes. 'Yes, it's called a pillory. I drive past it every day. What about it?'

'Well, according to my contact, someone's trapped inside the stocks, and the guy who found them swears they're dead.'

CHAPTER THREE

Coleshill High Street, 11.22pm

They pulled onto Church Street, where Kat had parked just hours before, only now it was filled with officers in high-vis jackets, their peaked hats dripping with rain.

A burly-looking officer headed towards them, puffed up with protective clothing and his own self-importance. He looked like he was about to herd them away, but Kat pulled out her badge before he could speak. 'DCS Kat Frank, Future Policing Unit. What have we got?'

'Oh, sorry, Ma'am, I didn't realise.'

'I'm a DCS, not the queen, so DCS Frank will do.'

'Yes. Of course, sorry.' He pulled out his notebook, squinting against the rain as he said, 'At 10.45pm, an anonymous caller rang 999 claiming that there was a dead body in the Coleshill pillory. He rang off before any further details could be taken, and a call was put out for an officer to check. I was already on the high street because of all the alarms that went off during the power cut, so I came straight up to check.' He glanced up and a nervous knot of words unravelled from his mouth. 'At first, I assumed it was just a prank – some trick or treat thing, you know? But when they didn't respond to my questions, I called the paramedics, and they've just confirmed she's dead. SOCO and the pathologist are on their way.'

'Thank you, officer,' Kat said, but she was already moving towards the pillory, closely followed by Lock. Over the years, she must have walked or driven by it hundreds of times, yet she'd never properly *looked* at it – maybe because the tall wooden frame almost blended into the row of red-brick Georgian houses behind it. Squinting up at it through the pouring rain, she estimated that it must be about four or five metres high, because the top of the post was level with the second-storey windows either side of it. Across the middle, just above door level, was a narrow wooden platform which now bore the weight of a standing figure trapped within a transom with holes for their head and hands.

She stepped closer, studying the body in the flashing blue lights of the patrol cars. On the left-hand side of the pillory she could see the head of a blonde-haired woman trapped in the transom, wearing a trouser suit and raincoat. The hands that poked through the holes either side were white, the fingertips tinged with blue.

Reluctantly, Kat stepped back while the SOCOs arrived to put the forensic tent up. These days, most tents were of the 'pop-up' variety and so didn't take long to establish, but the height of the pillory and the strength of the wind meant that the team struggled to get it safely into place, before finally weighting it down. Just as one of the SOCOs gave her a relieved nod, a car pulled up at the cordon, and a tall figure in a long hooded cloak emerged.

Kat was just about to turn them away, explaining that the whole street was now closed to the public, when they lowered their hood to reveal a shock of silver-white hair and bright crimson lips.

'Judith?' Kat said, not quite believing that the figure in the long black gothic dress and cloak was Warwickshire's leading pathologist, Dr Judith Edwards. They'd worked together on two major cases, where to her surprise, they'd quickly become good friends.

'Actually, I'm supposed to be the Grim Reaper,' they said, brandishing a plastic scythe.

'The Grim Reaper is a personification of death and usually depicted as a berobed skeleton,' said Lock, frowning at their costume.

'Well, I was at a Halloween party, and I'm not going to pull anyone dressed as a skeleton, now am I?'

'Pull?'

'Attract someone with my fatal charm.' They turned to Kat. 'Turns out there's a lot of talent in my choir. You should join us.'

'I think things are bad enough without inflicting my voice on the world,' said Kat, used to the pathologist's flirtatious teasing. 'This being a case in point.' The smile slipped from her face as she nodded towards the pillory.

Judith followed her gaze and took a step forward.

'You're here to assess a dead body,' said Kat, eyes

scanning the streets for signs of anyone with a camera or phone. 'So can we lose the scythe, please?'

'Spoilsport,' muttered Judith before putting it back in their car and taking out a couple of PPE suits. While they got changed, Kat explained what she knew so far, raising her voice against the wind that threatened to carry it away.

Lock appraised them both, then, with a slight shimmer, his image changed so that he, too, was wearing a white forensic suit, complete with hood, mask, gloves and shoes.

'That's hardly necessary,' said Kat. After all, Lock was just a hologram, so there was zero risk of him contaminating a crime scene.

'On the contrary, the more that I follow the protocols and habits of my peers, the more likely I am to be accepted as a member of the team.'

Kat studied the figure before her, irritated that Lock managed to look handsome even in a paper suit. She cleared her throat, reminding herself that he was nothing more than an image. He might be wearing the same clothes as her, but his papery polythene suit failed to rustle in the wind, and the spikes of rain merely passed straight through him.

'Okay,' said Judith, snapping on their gloves. 'Let's see what we've got.'

They headed towards the SOCO tent, through puddles riddled with reflections of yellow and blue: the colours of crisis the police always brought. After over twenty-five years in the force, she'd thought herself immune to it, but now she was back in that night: the explosion, the sirens and that heart-rending cry:

Rayan! Rayan! Rayan!

Kat took a deep breath and stepped inside the tent and away from the flashing lights. She closed her eyes for a few seconds and listened to the drip-drip of rain on the canvas above. *Focus on the job.*

She jumped as Judith picked up the folded stepladders that the SOCOs had left and snapped them into place. Putting them next to the pillory, the pathologist climbed up until their face was level with the woman's head trapped in the hole. 'Okay, my lovely,' they said, in their soft Welsh voice. 'My name's Judith, and I'm just going to do a few tests, if that's all right, so that we can find out what happened to you. And then we'll get you out of this fucked-up contraption just as soon as we can. Okay?'

Kat watched as Judith gently probed the face trapped in the wooden transom, before exploring the body for any obvious wounds or rigor mortis. Despite their dark humour and sometimes flippant manner, Judith was one of the most humane pathologists she'd ever worked with, as well as the cleverest. It was why she'd asked them to be a part of the FPU and was proud to call them a friend. Kat wasn't ashamed to admit that she'd never liked looking at dead bodies, arguing that it would be a red flag if she did. But it had become even harder since her husband died. Now she couldn't unsee the absence that each person left behind: all those lives, forever changed.

Trying to ignore the horrible clicking noises as Judith

moved the corpse's neck and shoulders, she looked straight ahead and studied the victim's feet before her: plain black zip-up boots beneath a navy-blue trouser suit. Her boots were so very ordinary – the kind of smart but sensible shoes that she and other working mums who were too busy to go shopping wore – that Kat found the sight of them oddly moving. She looked back up at the victim and the wet blonde hair that fell across her face. She hoped to God she wasn't a mum.

'How on earth did you end up trapped in some medieval stocks?' she muttered, staring up at the pitiful figure. 'And more importantly, *why?*'

'The location and method of murder may be significant,' said Lock, pointing towards to the brass plaque on the wall. 'The Coleshill pillory is unique in Warwickshire,' he read out. 'And is a listed monument, first erected near the market cross in 1706. It comprises an oak post with an acorn finial, having shackles at the bottom for whipping, a standing platform at mid-height and a top transom with two sets of head and arm holes. It was last used in 1863 to punish two felons for drunkenness.'

Lock turned towards Kat. 'Perhaps the murderer believed the woman deserved to be punished for drinking?'

She was about to say that drunkenness was hardly a motivation for murder but caught herself. Many women had been killed for less.

'I'll need to do a toxicology test,' Judith called down to them. 'But I can't smell any alcohol. And so far, I can't find any obvious injuries or cause of death.'

'How long do you think she's been dead for?' Kat asked.

33

'You know I can't answer that conclusively until I've done the PM.'

'Based on the algor mortis – the extent to which the body has cooled – the degree of rigor mortis in her face compared to her limbs and the early signs of liver mortis in the victim's fingers,' said Lock, 'I would estimate that there is a seventy-seven per cent probability that the victim died within the last two to six hours.'

'It's a fair guess,' Judith conceded as they climbed down the stepladder.

'I do not make *guesses*,' said Lock, as if he had been accused of a crime. 'I assessed the statistical probability of time since death using my LiDAR sensors to detect the victim's core temperature compared to the ambient temperature and triangulated that with my observations of Dr Edward's assessment of the degree of rigor mortis in the face compared to the limbs, and the extent of discolouration of the skin using my photogrammetry software. My estimate is based on the evidence.'

'The evidence that is available to us *so far*,' clarified Judith. 'But I agree two to six hours should be our working hypothesis until I've done the PM.'

'So between five thirty pm and nine thirty pm, which gives us a window of four hours,' said Kat, stepping back towards the opening of the tent. 'This spot is overlooked by flats and offices, and it's just off the high street. Someone must have seen something. Lock, I want a map of all the buildings with a line of sight to the pillory, and a list of every CCTV or doorbell camera on this and the adjacent streets.'

'Completed.'

'Thank you.' She turned back towards the pillory, where rain dripped from the woman's hair like tears. 'Did you find any ID on the body, Judith?'

'Not that I could see.'

'Not even a phone?'

'No, nothing.'

'Would you like me to cross-check the victim's facial characteristics, height and weight with all social media posts matching white women between twenty-five and fifty in the Warwickshire area?' suggested Lock.

Kat hesitated. The correct procedure was to check the missing persons database and dental records, which could take days, yet she knew Lock could analyse thousands of social media images in just seconds. It was indisputably one of his most useful functions.

'Very well. But widen your search to include the West Midlands,' she added. A woman in a trouser suit might work in or commute to or from one of the nearby bigger cities.

'According to my image recognition software, there is a ninety-eight point eight per cent chance that the victim is Angela Long, a forty-seven-year-old woman from Kenilworth.'

Lock stretched out a hand, and a screenshot from Instagram appeared against the wall of the forensic tent of a middle-aged woman in a navy-blue trouser suit with a crowd of men in what looked like a car factory. She had a small face but a big smile, and her teeth looked bright and sharp. *Like a shark*, Kat couldn't help thinking.

'Angela Long runs a family-owned car supermarket in Birmingham,' continued Lock. 'Two months ago, she was elected as the independent MP for the Warwick and Leamington Parliamentary seat.'

'*Fuck*,' said Kat, exchanging worried glances with Judith. She didn't follow politics much – if she wanted to hear constant arguing, blaming and lying, then she could always visit the cells – but even she had heard of Angela Long. Her social media feed had been full of posts about her in the past few weeks. It seemed everyone had an opinion about Angela Long and her views on AI, cars and climate change.

'Are you *sure* it's her?' she asked.

Lock made a dragging motion with his forefinger so that the picture from Instagram lay directly above the corpse on the pillory, before draping it over the flesh. 'Angela Long had a distinctive pattern of moles on her left cheek that exactly matches the moles on our victim's face. That, plus the correlation between other significant characteristics such as bone structure, height, weight, skin colour and age satisfy me that there is a ninety-eight point eight per cent chance that this is indeed the body of Angela Long. The note inside her top pocket may provide further confirmation.'

Lock was right: just above the wooden bar she could see the woman's dark grey raincoat, and in the top left breast pocket, there was what at first glance she had assumed was a handkerchief poking out but could now see might be a piece of paper.

She grabbed the stepladder off Judith and climbed up.

Even though she had gloves on, she used a pair of twee-
zers to ease the paper out with one hand, and held it
before her bracelet, so that Lock could see it through the
LiDAR sensors. 'You got that?' she called out.

'Yes, thank you.'

By the time Kat had climbed back down, Lock was
projecting the message against the white wall of the tent.

The writing – if that's what it was – covered the entire
length of the canvas. First a series of numbers, and then
a QR code in the bottom right-hand corner.

```
01000011 01100001 01110100 01100011 01101000 00100000
01101101 01100101 00100000 01101001 01100110 00100000
01111001 01101111 01110101 00100000 01100011 01100001
01101110
```

'Have you scanned the QR code?' asked Kat.

'Yes. And it took me to this.' Another image appeared
before them, and she bit back a cry of surprise. It was
the photo all the tabloids had carried the morning after
Rayan died: Kat wearing a dark trouser suit, and next to
her, a translucent image of Lock, wearing a pale grey suit
and a long charcoal raincoat.

Kat swallowed. Why on earth was there a picture of
her on the body of a dead woman? She shivered, then
turned to Lock. 'What about the numbers on the rest of
the note? Any idea what they mean?'

'It is a basic computer binary code.'

'And?'

'Binary code is a system of representing information

37

using only two symbols, usually 0 and 1. It is the basis of modern computers and communication.'

'I *know* that, Lock, but what does it *mean?*'

'Can you not understand it?' Lock looked at her with something akin to pity. 'It is a very simple code.' With a flourish of his hand, the numbers projected against the white canvas of the tent dissolved and were replaced by five simple words:

Catch me if you can.

CHAPTER FOUR

Listed in her phone contacts as BOSS, Kat's thumb hovered for a few seconds over Chief Constable McLeish's number. He wouldn't thank her for ringing him at this time of night. Then again, she'd get a worse bollocking if she didn't. She glanced at the cryptic message on the tent wall before firmly pressing dial.

'Kat?' he barked. 'Everything okay with the house?'

For a moment she lost focus, surprised that he'd remembered this was her first night back home – and was that *concern* in his voice? 'Er . . . yes, it's fine,' she managed to respond. 'I'm sorry to call so late but I thought you'd want to know that there's been an incident.'

'It's Halloween. Half the county is high on sugar, alcohol or horror films,' he said, his Glaswegian accent thickened by sleep. 'There'd better be something pretty fucking special about this to justify disturbing my beauty sleep.'

'We have a suspected murder and the victim's Angela Long, sir.'

'Angela Long? As in the *MP* Angela Long? *Fuck.*'

Kat could practically hear her boss sitting up, snapping the light and his brain on. She answered all the questions he fired at her, quickly describing the unique nature of the murder and the odd note left behind.

'I'll need to brief the Home Secretary,' he said, as he started moving about his bedroom, opening and closing drawers. 'Is the SOCO tent up yet? Good. Don't let anyone take any pictures, and I want extra officers on the cordon and a full media blackout until I've agreed a comms strategy with the minister.'

'Of course. But what about the investigation? Can you confirm me as SIO?'

McLeish stopped whatever he was doing. 'Ach, Kat. You've only just come back. And this will be big. I can't take any risks on this.'

Her face flamed at the thought that McLeish thought *she* was a risk. 'I know,' she forced herself to say, keeping her voice steady and reasonable, rather than completely fucking *outraged*. 'But the note contained a picture of me and Lock, and the message said *catch me if you can*. It was clearly aimed at me, sir. The murderer wants my attention. And if he doesn't get it, he might murder again until he does.'

The line went silent.

'Sir?'

'*I* decide who leads the investigating team, not some bastard murderer.'

'Of course. But with a case this high profile, you'll need to assure the public and media that you have your best team on it, and the FPU has a one hundred per cent success rate so far.'

40

McLeish made a growling noise. 'I'll think about it. Meanwhile, you go and tell the next of kin and get KFC down there ASAP,' he said, referring to Karen-from-Comms. 'I want a complete news blackout. This will get nasty once all Angela Long's supporters and haters find out, so I don't want a word of this leaking to the media until we've got an agreed strategy in place.'

SOCIAL MEDIA

@warkspost BREAKING: Heard on v. good authority that Angela Long, the controversial MP for Warwick and Leamington has been found murdered – strung up in medieval stocks in Warwickshire. More news as we get it . . .

@Emfairby It's irresponsible to spread rumours before they are confirmed. Think of the poor woman's family for God's sake.

@jimber24 It's true. My BF's mate lives round the corner from where her body was found – says there are like hundreds of coppers all over the place.

@DaveHughes45 This photo is the view from my window. You can just see one of those crime tents over the stocks. My missus went down to find out what was going on and she overheard the cops talking. It's definitely her. Angela Long is dead.

@SeannotShaun22 OMG I hope this is a real treat and not a Halloween trick. That Luddite would have trashed our economy just so she could carry on selling diesel cars.

@Fredsdead12 Are you mental? Angela Long was the best hope we had. She was the only one prepared to stand up and say it like it is – this

woke climate nonsense is killing the car industry,
and she opposed the AI Bill cuz robots will take all
our jobs. Ange was on our side. No wonder they
silenced her.

@SeannotShaun22 Hate to break it to you dude,
but climate change is real, and the earth is round
not flat.

@Fredsdead12 You know what else is flat?
Batteries. You see how far you get when you have
to rely on an electric car and there's nowhere to
bleeding charge them.

@Phil61b There's not enough chargers because
they know most people can't afford an EV. This is a
deliberate strategy so that only the rich can drive
cars, and the rest of us have to walk or fucking
cycle.

@SeannotShaun22 Duh, ever heard of the tube?

@Phil61b Only London has a tube, you self-
centred southern twat.

@AAAi [GIF] DING DONG THE WITCH IS DEAD!

@LMMontyrules [repost quoting GIF] Throughout
history, women who have dared to challenge the
status quo and speak the truth to power have been
branded witches and burned at the stake. And
here we are in the 21st century stringing a woman
who was brave enough to speak the truth up in the
stocks.

@jimber24 She wasn't speaking up for you or me, she was defending her own interests. The move to EVs would have ended her second-hand car business.

@DaveHughes45 Yeah, and she only opposed the AI Bill to get more votes. You can't oppose AI any more than you can 'oppose' the air – it's here, all around us. We just need to accept it.

@AAAi That's what they want you to believe. Wake up and smell the bullshit.

@SeannotShaun22 'They?!' Who are this mysterious 'they'? Aliens? The Deep State?

@AAAi Follow the money dude: the tech bros and their social media companies.

@Lauraloves52 I bought a car off her last year, and she seemed really nice.

@SeannotShaun22 That's cuz you were stupid enough to give her your money. And every car she sold is choking the air and burning our planet. I don't condone murder, but I hope this will be a wake-up call for the Luddites and climate deniers.

CHAPTER FIVE

Kenilworth, Warwickshire, 1.17am

Kat stared up at the mock-Tudor mansion through the window of her car. The porch light was on, illuminating the bright orange pumpkins outside the door she was going to have to knock.

'I can confirm that this is the correct address,' said Lock from the passenger seat.

'Yes, I know.'

'Then what are you waiting for?'

Kat puffed out her cheeks. 'Courage?'

'Why? Are you expecting Angela Long's partner to be violent?'

'No. I'm expecting to break his fucking heart.' But there was no point putting it off, so she released her seat belt with a click and climbed out of the car and into the night. She turned as Lock followed her, his image more ethereal in the light of the street lamps. 'Actually . . . maybe you should wait here.'

'The guidelines recommend that two officers should be present when informing the next of kin of a fatality.'

'Yes, but you aren't . . .' Her voice tailed off, leaving her breath hanging between them on the cold, frosty air.

Lock's hologram straightened. 'I may not be human, DCS Frank, but I am still a detective.'

Kat hesitated. It was difficult enough to wake someone in the small hours and tell them that their world was forever changed without the complication of explaining what Lock was – and wasn't.

'I have been working for Warwickshire Police for over a year now, so I think we can assume that most members of the public are aware of my existence,' he said, anticipating her concerns. 'And having another witness present could help protect you in the event of any complaints or misunderstandings.'

Still Kat hesitated.

'But if you don't trust me, then I will of course remain here.'

Was there a hurt tone to his voice? Of course, it wasn't possible for a machine to feel hurt – or to feel anything, in fact – but it was too late and cold to hang about arguing. Against her better judgement, she nodded for him to follow her up the garden path, where, pausing only to take out her ID, Kat delivered what her colleagues called 'the death knock'.

Kat studied the grinning pumpkins at her feet as she listened to the familiar sequence of sounds: the initial hesitation – *who on earth comes calling at this time of night?* – followed by an internal door being opened, then the click of the hall light being switched on and the shuffle of approaching footsteps. Then another pause – presumably while the resident peered at her through the spy hole – before finally, the slow, dread-filled opening of the door.

She looked up at a balding man in his forties, wearing a navy-blue dressing gown and an expression of confused annoyance.

'I'm DCS Kat Frank of the Warwickshire Police Force,' she announced, in a clear, crisp voice. This wasn't a time for mumbling or small talk. Every word had to earn its weight and cut through the confusion and denial. 'I'm sorry to disturb you so late, but can you confirm that you are Anthony Long?'

'Yes, Tony. That's me. Why, what's wrong? Is everything okay?'

She paused long enough for him to realise that no, it really wasn't, before letting out the words we all hope to never hear. 'Can we come inside, sir? I'm afraid we have some bad news.'

Kat was shaking by the time she climbed back into her car.

'If you are cold, DCS Frank, perhaps you should put the heating on,' suggested Lock.

'Perhaps,' she muttered, rubbing at her temples.

'After delivering the news of his wife's death, I do not understand why you did not take the opportunity to ask Anthony Long more questions, such as why he had not been concerned that his wife was out so late, and whether he had an alibi for tonight.'

Kat shook her head. As a machine, Lock talked about 'delivering the news' as if she was dropping off a newspaper rather than a bomb into someone's life. But she caught herself. Had she been so very different when she'd first started out? Hadn't she once assumed with the ignorance of youth that after the initial shock, 'the news' could be absorbed and processed and eventually overcome? Lock didn't understand, but maybe that wasn't just because he was a machine. As the Irish writer John Banville once said, there were only two types of people in the world: those who were bereaved, and those who were yet to be bereaved.

Nevertheless, she should at least try to explain. 'I didn't question him because it wasn't the time or place. We – or whoever is assigned SIO – can follow up with him tomorrow. Tonight, the poor man just needs to absorb the fact that his wife is dead.'

'As forty-five per cent of female homicide victims are murdered by their male partners, that "poor man" is statistically speaking our chief suspect.'

'It's not all about statistics, Lock.' She pulled her seat belt on. 'Let the team know that I'm calling a briefing at 8am, and we'll go through it all then.'

'I thought you said that McLeish had not yet confirmed you as SIO?'

'He hasn't. But if I act like he has, then the onus will be on him to make the case for taking it off me, rather than me persuading him to give it to me.' She glanced back at the victim's home. 'My photograph was attached to a dead woman's body, and I want to know why.'

48

CHAPTER SIX

**Leek Wootton Police HQ, Warwickshire,
1 November, 7.59am**

DS Browne stood outside the Major Incident Room and peered through the glass door. So much had changed in her life since she was last here, and yet everything looked exactly the same: the hot drinks machine at the back, the briefing board at the front and the dull grey carpet beneath a boardroom table that was too big for the narrow room. At the head was her boss and mentor, DCS Frank, standing at the table as she wrestled a laptop out of her bag. Professor Okonedo was seated in her usual place at the other end, with the hologram of AIDE Lock beside her. In the middle on her right-hand side sat Karen-from-Comms, and directly opposite her were two empty chairs where Debbie and Rayan used to sit.

The sight caused something to drop deep inside her – like a piano key going down an octave. The last time she'd been here she'd been heavily pregnant yet so worried about Rayan that she'd kept quiet about her contractions so she could join in the search for her friend and colleague. Memories played through her: the relief she'd felt when they found him, the pain of learning he was forever gone.

Debbie squeezed her eyes shut. This wasn't how she'd imagined her official return from maternity leave. She'd dreamt about it so many times during those early, sleep-deprived nights, and Rayan's smiling face was always at the centre of them with a huge cake and/or biscuits that he'd bought in to celebrate. She hadn't got on with her DI initially, but once she became pregnant, he'd taken it upon himself to ensure she had a constant supply of snacks – a sure way to win her hungry heart – and when Lottie was born, he'd become a complete lifesaver as an adoptive uncle and a surprisingly patient friend.

Her phone alarm beeped. It was 8am. Taking a deep breath, she pushed open the door and walked into the room.

Kat glanced up and smiled at her with genuine warmth. 'Welcome back, Debbie. Good to see you.'

'Thanks, it's good to be back,' she lied, heading towards her seat with a certainty she didn't feel. As she took off her coat, she caught Adaiba Okonedo watching her and smiled.

The professor gave her a nod, but her eyes drifted to the empty chair beside her. Debbie bit her lip. Should she say something? She didn't know the professor very well, hadn't seen her since the funeral when the poor woman had been distraught. Debbie gently placed her new coat on the chair and turned towards her colleague.

Adaiba hunched her shoulders and lowered her head to her laptop, seemingly focused on whatever was before her.

'Okay, let's make a start,' Kat said. 'As you know, last night the body of a woman was found trapped in a medieval pillory in Coleshill.'

'It is not medieval,' said Lock from the back of the room. 'The medieval period ended in 1520, but the pillory was not built until 1706.'

Kat took a beat. 'It's more of an expression, Lock. It just means that it's old.'

'That expression is inaccurate by a hundred and eighty-six years.'

'Maybe, but it isn't relevant.'

'There is no "maybe" about it. And facts are always relevant,' insisted Lock.

Kat let out an exasperated sigh. 'What is *relevant* is that whatever year that pillory was built, it was used to hold the body of a murdered woman, so please will you let me continue the briefing so that we can capture her killer as soon as possible?'

Lock made a gesture that implied she had his permission to continue.

'Thank you,' the boss said, in a voice laced with anything but gratitude.

Debbie exchanged a discreet eye-roll with KFC. Team meetings often felt like they were children at a family dinner, watching their parents indulge in performative bickering, but underpinned with affection and grudging respect.

'Lock, would you please project a 3D image of the *eighteenth-century* pillory?' Kat continued, as if pointedly asking him to pass the salt.

Debbie had read the SOC reports, but still she shivered as the rain-soaked figure hovered just above the board-room table, the woman's head bowed as if sleeping, her blonde hair darkened by rain. The projection was so realistic, she half-expected to see pools of water gathering on the walnut table beneath.

'Dr Edwards will be carrying out a full PM today to try and establish the cause of death,' said Kat. 'But because there are no obvious injuries, our working assumption is that she was murdered or at least sedated before being placed in the pillory on Church Street. It's a busy road just off the high street, so our imme-diate priority is to find out if anyone saw anything. Lock, what did you find on the CCTV and doorbell footage?'

'Nothing.'

'Nothing? You must have found *something*. There's a busy pub, The Swan, just yards away on the high street, not to mention the chip shop on the corner and the offices opposite. One of the cameras must have caught something between the hours of five and eleven.' Kat turned to Debbie. 'Can you review the tapes, please, to check if there is anything significant?'

Before Debbie could reply, Lock cut in. 'There is nothing to review. There is no camera footage because this time frame coincides with the power cut, which you may recall affected the whole of Coleshill.'

'That's a hell of a coincidence,' muttered Kat, automatically glancing to where Rayan used to sit.

I don't believe in coincidences, he would have said.

Debbie stared at the boss, his unspoken words hovering between them.

'Right,' said Kat, with rather more volume than was necessary. 'Debbie, contact the electricity board and find out what the cause of the power cut was. And then do a thorough door-to-door. Regardless of the CCTV, someone must have looked out of a window or walked past on their way back from the pub or the chippy or church. Just because they haven't phoned it in, it doesn't mean no one saw anything. Meanwhile, let's think about motive. I've got a meeting with McLeish to brief the minister after this, and he'll want to know what our lines of enquiry are. What do we know about Angela Long, Lock?'

The hologram paused for less than a second, before replying, 'I have just read 2,217 articles concerning Angela Long and consumed twenty-two interviews and thirteen podcasts.' He created a virtual briefing board, upon which he projected a series of bullet points. 'The majority of reports and profiles are in agreement about her biographical details. Angela Long was forty-seven years old and was born in south-west Birmingham to parents who both worked at the Longbridge car factory, her father as a shop steward and her mother as a mechanic. When Longbridge was closed in 2005, 6,271 people lost their jobs, including her parents. They used what little savings they had to establish their own second-hand car business, which under the management of their daughter grew into the successful car supermarket. In several interviews, Angela Long describes this period of her life as being formative, in terms of the effect it had on her family, the resilience they demonstrated as a response and her own decision to subsequently stand for Parliament. Many of the interviews she gives are riddled with inaccuracies, but they are illuminating in terms of the victim's history and beliefs. Shall I play you an extract?'

Debbie leaned forward as Kat nodded her permission.

Video footage of Angela Long appeared on the virtual screen before them, and the contrast with the 3D corpse that still floated above the boardroom table was stark. Her shoulder-length blonde hair was now smooth and glossy, and her face glowed in a way that suggested an expensive and time-consuming skincare regime.

'My mum, dad and all their mates used to work at Longbridge, so I've seen first-hand how robotics and other job-destroying technologies can decimate an industry. In 1979, there were over half a million people working in car manufacturing in Britain, but by 2020, that had dropped to less than a hundred and fifty thousand. Hundreds of thousands of workers and their families lost their jobs, their livelihoods and their communities, so that businesses could become "leaner", which basically means make more profit for less cost.

'I'm on the side of British workers, not bosses, which is why I'm against the AI Bill. If you think it's a good idea to have robots in the police force, then I suggest you take a look at the car industry. It began with spot-welding robots back in the Seventies and Eighties – we were told it was a safety issue and would reduce the amount of harm workers were exposed to. But then came automation, then digitisation, followed by more robots and now AI, until the industry has been completely hollowed out. So-called safety issues are just a Trojan Horse to cut jobs. Which is not only wrong, it's stupid, because if people can't work, then they can't afford to buy cars, which is bad for the economy.

'It's also why I'm against electric cars. I mean, ask yourself why we're all suddenly being forced to buy an EV within the next five years, when an EV costs as much as *eighty thousand pounds*, despite the fact that there is a chronic shortage of electric chargers in this country. And even if this government kept their promise and built more, what does that mean for all the ordinary working people who live in flats or don't have the luxury of a big private drive to charge their car in overnight?

'Ask yourself who stands to profit from this sudden switch to expensive electric cars when most people don't have the means, let alone the money, to use them? Well, it isn't the working men and women of *this* country, I'll tell you that for nothing. And don't let them dupe you into thinking this is all about the climate. If they really believed their own bullshit about the planet overheating, then why are they building all these data centres to power AI? Generative AI uses more power than Japan! Our electricity grid is already creaking under the pressure of it, and if they pass the AI Bill, then robots will take the jobs of decent, hard-working people. Everyone talks about self-driving cars as if they're a good thing, but apart from being bloody dangerous, think of how many Uber drivers, train and bus drivers and delivery guys that is going to put out of work.

'Once again, we're being sold out to foreign investors and tech bro billionaires. So unless you want this entire country to be turned into a giant retail park, with only twenty per cent of the wealthiest having the means to drive there and shop and the rest of us forced to serve them or starve, then I'm telling you, it's time to take back control. Say no to EVs and oppose the AI Bill to protect jobs and our future.'

As the phrase *Take Back Control!* appeared in big letters below Angela Long, Kat asked Lock to stop the video.

'I think we get the idea,' she said, turning to what was left of her team. 'So let's think about motive. Why would someone want to kill Angela Long?'

Debbie gulped and looked around the room. She was so used to Rayan filling the silence with his theories, and using that time to respond and formulate her own ideas, that she couldn't think what to say. According to her Myers Briggs profile, she was an 'I', which meant she needed time to reflect before coming to a settled view, whereas Rayan had been an 'E', so he was great at thinking on his feet, although he often changed his mind. She glanced over at Adaiba for inspiration, but her eyes were firmly fixed on her own laptop, refusing, as she often did, to help with what she saw as police, rather than university, work.

'To save the climate?' KFC offered. She cleared her

throat as everyone turned to look at her. 'I'm not being flippant. I just mean, well, it's obvious, isn't it? She had so many haters online and in real life. I mean, a lot of people disagreed with her politics and her stance on AI, but the climate stuff was really toxic. She won the by-election a few months ago, so maybe someone who cared about the environment wanted to stop her. If you look at the comments on social media, she had a lot of opponents and enemies from protest groups, academics as well as individuals.'

'An analysis of her social media reveals that she had 67,432 followers,' said Lock. 'Her most viewed video received seventy-two per cent likes and positive comments, twenty per cent negative, with eight per cent blocked and reported. Angela Long claimed in interviews that she was the recipient of several death threats, but I can find no record of any formal complaints to the police.'

Kat frowned. 'Okay, can you do an analysis of all the negative comments and trolls and identify some key suspects?'

Lock paused. 'Many of the most negative comments are associated with multiple accounts and from different geolocations, and an initial analysis of their bio information and posting patterns suggests that a high proportion of them may derive from a bot farm or a single user operating numerous fake profiles. In order to identify key suspects, I will need to do further analysis, which may require the cooperation of the social media companies, all of whom use machine learning algorithms to detect and remove fake accounts.'

'Okay,' said Kat. 'Prioritise that analysis and identify the most threatening fake digital accounts. I can then make a formal police request to obtain the subscribers' details from the relevant social media platforms.'

Lock frowned. 'I will of course carry out your request. However, while I understand this line of enquiry is a valid theory, may I remind you of the actual *evidence* that forty-five per cent of all adult female homicide victims were killed in a domestic homicide last year, and all but one were killed by a male suspect. So despite the considerable noise that social media generates, the data suggests that our key lines of enquiry should prioritise partners, ex-partners and family members, starting with Anthony Long, her husband.'

'Yes, yes, we'll prioritise interviewing him as well.'

'If you prioritise everything, then it is not a priority.'

'I didn't say prioritise *everything*. But as you keep reminding us, you are more than capable of multi-tasking.' Before Lock could reply, Kat nodded to Karen-from-Comms, who had her hand up.

'While we're talking about priorities, can we discuss the media strategy? Because we've got a dead MP in the stocks, this is massive. It's going global, and my phone is on fire with media bids. Can we offer a press conference to help contain the interest?'

'We've got a meeting with McLeish and the minister straight after this, and comms is on the agenda, so we'll talk about it then.' She turned her attention to Debbie. 'Any other motives you can think of?'

'Er . . . maybe we should find out who stood to benefit

financially from her death,' she said eventually. 'Angela Long was a successful business woman and I think she was a millionaire?'

'According to Companies House records, her business was worth three point two million pounds last year,' added Lock.

Debbie glanced at the hologram. She liked Lock, she really did – he'd been so helpful in sourcing and summarising all the best child development advice for Lottie – but she wished he wasn't so bloody quick. She struggled with self-confidence on the best of days, and her first day back after maternity leave definitely wasn't one of them.

'Angela Long didn't have any children and her parents are dead,' Debbie continued. 'But she had a husband and two brothers, so it might be worth checking if she had a will? Or life insurance?'

'Good idea,' said Kat. She turned back to face the 3D image of Angela Long trapped in the pillory where the face that was once so animated was now hidden by rain-soaked hair. 'We should consider all the usual motives, but this is not a usual murder. Everything about this is very, very deliberate. By placing her in eighteenth-century stocks, the murderer didn't just take her life – he made a *spectacle* out of her.' She began to circle the boardroom table and the image that floated above it. 'Imagine how much planning had to go into this. They probably had to sedate or kill her first.' She paused and pointed to the bottom of the pillory. 'It would have been far easier to sit her on the ground and trap her feet in the stocks or tie her standing body to the whipping post. It still would have generated the same headlines. But for some reason our killer chose the most difficult part of the pillory to use and somehow found a way of hoisting the body two metres high to stand on this platform, while managing to unlock and secure the ancient transom locks around her head and hands, all without being seen. And then they added a note to the dead body – not just any old note, but a QR code that linked to a photo of me and Lock and a message written in binary code.'

Kat rubbed her jaw. Six months after the attack, it still hurt at times of stress. 'The nature of this murder involved so many unnecessary risks and complications . . .' She stopped for a minute, seeming to talk to herself as she continued. 'No, not unnecessary. The staging, the time and location – all of it must have been necessary to the murderer, and therefore *worth* the risks. Our murderer was trying to make a point. But maybe that point wasn't about Angela Long at all.'

'What do you mean, boss?' Debbie asked.

Kat gestured towards the woman in the stocks. 'It can't be a coincidence that Angela Long was found murdered in Coleshill, the town in which I live, and on the very night that I returned home. Nor that the victim shares my physical characteristics in terms of age, gender and hair colour – in fact, maybe she was selected *because* of it. She was even wearing a similar suit to the one I wore in the photo. And the murderer was so keen to make sure that we made that connection, they even attached a QR code that took us to that very picture, with a note saying *Catch me if you can.*' Kat swallowed. 'I don't think this is about politics or money. I think that the message – perhaps even the entire murder – was aimed at me.'

Lock moved towards where Kat stood beneath the image of the figure on the pillory. 'Why are humans so egocentric?'

'I beg your pardon?'

'I said, why are humans so egocentric? You overlook the fact that I, too, am in the photograph. But most of all, you forget that the message was written in binary code.'

He leaned in closer as his voice dropped a notch. 'Which suggests that the killer's message was actually meant for *me*.'

CHAPTER SEVEN

Chief Constable McLeish's office, 9.32am

Even though they were on a Teams call, the Home Secretary appeared to be listening to every word of Kat's briefing, and unlike most politicians, she didn't interrupt with her own questions or opinions.

'So that's where we've got to,' Kat concluded. 'My team are currently doing door to door, and after this I'll go to the constituency office to interview the victim's co-workers and then her husband. Lock is analysing all Angela Long's social media, and we should have some initial PM results by close of play.'

'Do you think the murder is politically motivated?' asked the Home Secretary.

'I think it's too early to say,' Kat said carefully. 'At this stage, we are pursuing numerous lines of enquiry, including—' She stopped as McLeish gave her a warning glance: *don't tell her you think it is about you, or you will sound paranoid.*

'As DCS Frank says, it's too early to say,' cut in McLeish. 'But we'll keep you and your office briefed as our investigation progresses.'

The minister paused. 'Very well. But do you have sufficient resources? I am, as you know, fully supportive of the FPU leading on this – it was me, after all, who managed to secure funding for the initial pilot, and this high-profile case is an excellent opportunity to demonstrate the benefits of AI in policing. However, you're a very small team, and after DI Hassan's death you are one man down.'

'I am aware of that,' said McLeish, his face turning a warning shade of red. 'But as you know, the allocation of resources is an operational issue, and therefore a matter for me as the Chief Constable of Warwickshire Police Force to decide.'

'Of course,' she said with a smile that only served to flash her teeth. 'But while the crime occurred on your patch, the murder of a Member of Parliament will have national and international ramifications, so I will need to be kept closely involved. At all times.'

McLeish gave a jerk of his head which, if you didn't know him very well, could be interpreted as a nod.

Kat could practically feel the heat emanating from her boss's purple face, so before he could explode, she suggested that they moved on to the comms strategy, and asked KFC to update the minister on the current state of play.

'Yes, my office and the department has had bids from all around the world, too,' said the Home Secretary once

Karen had finished. 'We urgently need to get on the front foot, but the media team here think we should keep Lock out of the story – they're worried it will give it even more legs.'

'Legs?' Lock echoed.

'It's an expression that means it could make the story run longer in the press,' explained KFC. 'A comms strategy is usually aimed at closing a story down, whereas highlighting your involvement might open it up even more.'

'But this isn't a "usual" murder,' said the minister. 'And neither are the circumstances. Lock is already part of the story because of his forthcoming appearance at the select committee on AI, not to mention the victim's views on AI. Therefore, I think we should lean in to it.'

Lock leaned forward.

The Minister smiled. 'I mean I think we should take this opportunity to show the public what you can do. Let's hold a press conference by the end of the day, using Lock's involvement as a signal of how seriously we are taking this, and to assure the public that we will find the murderer. The UK is leading the world on AI in policing, and Lock has a one hundred per cent success rate so far.'

'The *FPU* has a one hundred per cent success rate,' said McLeish.

'Yes, of course. But Karen, I want you to work with my office to draw up a press strategy emphasising the role of Lock.'

'Are you sure?' Kat couldn't help saying. 'I mean . . . the inquiry into the deaths of DI Hassan and Peter Bridges was quite high profile, and I think there are still questions in some people's minds about what happened.'

'The inquiry was *very* clear that the explosion was not the fault of Lock, but its human superiors.' Her steely gaze swept over Kat, McLeish and Professor Okonedo. 'The only reason why there has been no further disciplinary action is because, as the ministerial sponsor for your unit, I understand that we are in a rapid learning phase about the appropriate use of AI in the workplace, and because I can see the bigger picture. I am more than happy to take that argument on, but I will need your full support.'

'Of course,' said McLeish. 'But I want to hold some information back, such as the note the killer left. These sorts of details can be helpful in sifting out the genuine calls from the cranks.'

'Very well. But maybe we could do a couple of off-the-record briefings to a couple of the broadsheets about how quickly Lock can analyse social media and track down the trolls and haters that targeted Angela Long. The press love that sort of thing and it could help us win the debate on AI. The current draft of the bill relies on enabling guidance rather than regulation – this will allow us to roll out AIDEs in the police force and wider public sector, as well as pilot the use of robotic forms – but the opposition is laying so many amendments that it could end up stifling innovation if we're not careful.'

'But won't giving Lock a higher profile just attract more criticism from AI sceptics?' queried Kat.

'Yes. But like I said, I think we need to lean in to it

and take the argument on. Our opponents are on the wrong side of history. This is a time for bold leadership, not cautious despair. In fact . . .' She turned to her private secretary. 'I might do a speech on this . . . or maybe write an op-ed for one of the papers to coincide with our appearance at the select committee?'

'Actually,' said Kat, 'with everything that's going on, wouldn't it be best if I stayed here? I think my time would be better spent trying to find whoever did this.'

The Home Secretary's face remained neutral, but Kat noticed that her nostrils flared. 'You have been summoned to give evidence at a Parliamentary select committee – attendance is mandatory, not optional. This will help shape the future of British policing, and indeed the very future of our country, so I can think of no better use of your time.'

The minister turned to address Lock before Kat could respond. 'Remember, Lock, the objective is to persuade the committee that we don't need any more pilots, and we certainly don't want any more regulation. We've learned enough over the past year to justify a rapid roll-out of AIDEs across the country. And the death of DI Hassan highlights the necessity of moving to the next phase and experimenting with robotic forms as soon as possible.'

'Of course. But in terms of persuading the committee, my understanding of the legislative process is that the committee is advisory only,' said Lock. 'The decision-making powers reside with the elected government of the day.'

The Home Secretary pursed her lips. 'Technically, yes, that's true. But I'm afraid democracy means it's not that simple. The Science and Technology Committee is hugely influential, so a positive session with them could swing it for us and convince the House that we need to prioritise innovation over safety.' She turned to KFC. 'So we need to pull out all the stops and develop a robust communications strategy for this case and Lock's role in it. The future of AI and the growth and competitiveness of our country depends on this going well.'

McLeish sniffed. 'If we just let Kat and her team crack on and find the killer, then we won't need a comms or a handling plan as we'll have an actual result.'

'Point taken. I'll let you get on, then.' The minister picked up her papers. 'But Chief Constable, as Home Secretary, I've learned that one *always* needs a comms strategy. I'm taking a deliberate gamble on letting Kat and Lock lead this high-profile case, but if they fail, I doubt I'll get approval to pilot the use of physical AIDEs, which, given the tight fiscal constraints, unfortunately means we'll still need a comms strategy – for the closure of the FPU.'

CHAPTER EIGHT

Town Hall, Leamington Spa, 10.58am

Angela Long's constituency office was based in Leamington Spa, which according to Lock was a beautiful and prosperous Warwickshire town renowned for its mineral springs since the Middle Ages. But as far as Kat was concerned, it was where her family had spent many happy weekends pottering around Waterstones and The Entertainer, walking by the River Leam and picnicking in the Pump Room Gardens.

She grimaced as they pulled up outside the dead MP's constituency office, set in the beautiful town hall but surrounded by barricade tape and a cluster of windswept journalists. Lock had proposed interviewing Angela Long's husband first, but Kat was conscious that they'd woken him up in the small hours to break the news of his wife's murder, so in case he'd managed to go back to sleep, she wanted to give him the opportunity to rest before having to deal with their questions. And besides, she wanted to picture where Angela had spent her last few hours and get a feel for her final movements.

Kat glanced towards the journalists as she undid her seat belt and reached for her jacket. 'Remember, you're not to answer any of their questions, Lock. Just ignore them.'

'Very well, although all the evidence from our recent cases suggests that ignoring journalists is a very ineffective strategy.'

Kat climbed out of the car, wincing at the bitter cold. She had barely zipped her jacket up before cameras, phones and mics were pushed in her face as the journalists surrounded her with their questions:

'Can you confirm that this is a hate crime?'

'Have you arrested anyone yet for the murder?'

'Are other MPs under threat?'

'What can you tell Angela Long's constituents – can you assure them that they're safe?'

'Can you tell us how she was murdered?'

Kat stared straight ahead, not even bothering to say 'No comment'. She approached the stairs, where a young man in a baseball hat was adding a bunch of flowers to what looked like an impromptu memorial. A nervous-looking constable raised the barricade tape to let her through, and when the journalists realised that they weren't going to get any answers, the mood seemed to turn.

'Angela Long was a democratically elected MP,' shouted one. 'The citizens who voted for her have a right to know what happened!'

'Angela Long was a fierce critic of AI – what do you think she would have said if she knew an AI cop was investigating her murder?' cried another.

Lock turned to face the journalist, his eyebrows raised.

'Lock,' Kat warned. 'Come on, let's get inside.'

A couple of uniforms ushered them in while trying to hold back the journalists trying to press their cameras against the windows and doors.

Once they were in the foyer away from the noise and out of the cold, Kat took her jacket off and tried to smooth her wind-blown hair. 'You were about to answer their questions then, weren't you?'

'I was merely going to point out how completely illogical their questions were. How can a murdered person express an opinion about anything, least of all about who is investigating their own murder? The dead cannot speak.'

'Well, that's a matter of opinion,' said a grey-haired woman as she approached them. She was wearing a thick plain sweater and tweed skirt, her pale face dominated by large, black-framed glasses.

'I'm Mandy Knowles, Angela's PA and diary secretary,' she said, offering her hand.

'Hi, I'm DCS Kat Frank, and this is my partner, AIDE Lock, an AI detective who will be assisting me on this case.'

'Oh, I think I've read about you in the paper,' she said, frowning.

'I've got a leaflet that explains a bit about AIDE Lock if you have any concerns,' said Kat, reaching into her bag.

'Oh, don't bother. I wouldn't understand it anyway. I

only got a mobile phone a couple of years ago because my children insisted, and I can barely operate that. Now, how can I help you? I'm sure you'll want to talk to us about this terrible business, but can I get you a cup of tea or coffee first?'

The older woman seemed brisk and overly anxious to please, which was a common reaction to shocking and upsetting news, so because doing a simple, familiar task like making a drink might help calm her, Kat said yes, she'd love a cup of tea, thank you. She followed her into a small kitchenette, while Mandy chatted away.

'I can't believe she's dead. Angela was such a strong character – so *alive,* you know?' Mandy opened the cupboard and took out an industrial-sized pack of teabags. 'This time yesterday, we went through her diary together and agreed all the appointments for next week, and now, today . . .' She drifted off, then took a deep breath. 'My first reaction was I'd have to reschedule them. But then I realised I'll have to cancel them all.' She cleared her throat and opened the fridge door.

'I'd like to talk to you on the record about what happened yesterday,' said Kat carefully. She didn't want the woman to say too much in case she said something they would later need to rely on in court. 'So we'd like to interview you, if that's okay? It's nothing to worry about. We're just talking to anyone who can shed light on her movements. Did anybody else work in this office yesterday?'

'Just me and Nigel, her agent. Oh, and Roddy – he's just a volunteer, but he was here for a few hours yesterday

71

to help stuff envelopes and drop off some leaflets. Nigel's in the office now if you want to talk to him? Although he's in a bit of state, poor thing.' She placed their drinks on a tray and put her backside against the door. 'Come on, I'll take you to him now.'

Kat and Lock followed Mandy Knowles through the foyer, up two flights of stairs and into a small office that contained little more than a handful of desks with computers, the walls lined with maps and campaign posters. A man in his early thirties had been sitting at one of the desks staring up at a poster of the dead MP's smiling face, but he jumped up as they entered the room.

'This is Nigel Godfrey,' Mandy said as she put the drinks down. 'And this is DCS Kat Frank and her partner AIDE Lock. They're investigating . . . what happened, so they'd like to talk to us both.'

'Hi, yes, of course,' said Nigel. He held out a rather bony hand that felt damp with sweat despite the November cold – although that could just be shock, thought Kat. She took in the crumpled suit that hung on his narrow frame, noticing faint white marks on the jacket where it looked like he'd tried (and failed) to sponge off what she assumed were toothpaste stains.

'Are you free now for an informal interview, Mr Godfrey?'

'Er . . . yes. I mean, I didn't see anything and all I know is what I heard on the news, but I'll do anything to help. I still can't believe it. It's just horrible.'

'I know. Well, we can just talk in here, if that's okay. And Mandy, maybe we can interview you after?'

'Oh, yes, of course. I'll leave you to it, then. I'll be in the kitchen if you need me. The dishwasher needs unloading, and I might as well clean the fridge while I'm waiting.'

Kat gave her a gentle smile. She and countless other women before her had polished and washed and worked their way around grief – anything to avoid the emptiness within.

She cleared her throat and turned back to Nigel. 'Shall we make a start?'

CHAPTER NINE

Interviewer: DCS Kat Frank (KF)
Interviewee: Nigel Godfrey (NG), election agent for the deceased
Date: 1 November, 11.21am, Leamington Spa town hall

KF: Lock will be making a recording of this, if that's okay. Can you confirm your name, please?

NG: Nigel Godfrey. God, I can't believe this is happening. Ange was such a force of life. I can't believe she's really gone *[voice breaks].*

KF: Are you sure you're okay to continue?

NG: Yes. Yes. I want to help. She would have wanted me to.

KF: Thank you. I understand that you were her election agent. Would you mind briefly explaining what that entails?

NG: A bit of everything, really, but legally I was responsible for agreeing all the expenditure on the election campaign, compiling and returning expenses and overseeing the count on election day. At one level, an election agent is there to ensure everything is legal and fair, but you're also their advocate and friend. No matter what, you're on their side.

KF: So it's quite an important job, then?

NG: Very.

KF: How did you come to work for Angela Long?

NG: I was the agent for the previous MP, Tom Watkins, so when she decided to stand against him, I kept seeing her at hustings and debates. And the more I heard her talk, the more impressed I was, until I realised that I actually agreed with Ange's view more than Tom's, even though she was an independent. I thought she deserved to win the seat, and that with my help, she could do it. So I left the party and offered my services to Ange.

KF: Just like that?

NG: I told you, she was a force of nature. I know a winner when I see one, but she needed a more professional operation. Until I joined the team, she relied totally on volunteers, who were a bit of a ragbag of misfits and single-issue campaigners.

KF: And when did you join the team, Mr Godfrey?

NG: Just over a year ago? It was after the party conference. I could see the party wasn't going anywhere, and I just knew I had to be bold and leave. Best thing I ever did.

KF: Were you with her in the constituency office yesterday?

NG: Yes. She's still – was – putting the team together. She was only elected a couple of months ago and only just got her office allowance sorted, so I helped out every week at the surgery with casework because of my experience with Tom. A lot of the same people turn up with the same issues.

KF: And was there anybody else in yesterday apart from you and Mandy Knowles?

NG: One of the volunteers, Roddy Wheeler, came in after lunch to collect some leaflets to put through people's letterboxes.

KF: Do you know what time he left?

NG: No idea. Ask Mandy, she's in charge of all the admin.

KF: Okay, can you talk me through Angela's movements yesterday – in particular what time she arrived and left?

NG: It was just the same as the other weeks. Angela arrived at ten, and we went through the correspondence, emails and diary. The surgery ran from eleven till five but we usually worked later until about six. I tended to stay until she locked up, for security.

KF: And what time did you stay till last night?

NG: Well, there was a power cut at 6pm. At first, I tried to find the fuse box to see if that had gone, but then I noticed that the other offices were dark, too, and all the lamps outside were out, so I guessed it was a wider problem. We waited for a few minutes and then realised that it wasn't coming back on, and we were getting cold, so we decided to call it a day.

KF: Did you leave together?

NG: Yes.

KF: At what time?

NG: I can't be sure, but it must have been just gone six . . . ten past six, something like that?

KF: And how did Angela get home?

NG: She drove, the same as she always did. The street lamps were all off, so even though she didn't have far to go, I warned her to drive carefully. She said something about how cold it was and I said I would see her next week, and that was it. She got into her car. I remember waving at her. I didn't realise it would be the last— *[voice breaks]*

KF: We have no further evidence of any communication with or confirmed sightings of Angela Long from that point. You were possibly the last person she saw, so can you remember anything – anything at all that might help us understand what happened between leaving the surgery and being found murdered on the Coleshill pillory? Was there anything different about her behaviour? Did she say she was going anywhere else before going home? We still haven't found her car.

NG: No, she seemed fine. She said she was off home, I think. Or at least, she didn't say she was going anywhere different, so I might have just assumed that. She always went home. She'd be in trouble if she didn't.

KF: Why do you say that?

NG: I just mean her husband would have kept ringing and texting. He's a bit . . . high maintenance in that regard. Always wants to know where she is.

KF: Did she say anything to you on that night to imply there were any problems with anyone?

NG: No.

KF: Had there been any trouble at the surgery that day or recently – anyone at all who threatened to cause her harm?

NG: No. It was just an ordinary day.

KF: Do you have any idea who could have killed Angela Long?

NG: I honestly don't know. I mean, there are always crank calls and green ink letters, and some of the people who turn up at surgery are just mentally unwell. We've got a 'dodgy people' list that we keep inside the drawer of the office so that staff know who to be careful with, but I can't say any of them seem capable of murder. There were all sorts of trolls online, of course, but as far as I know none of them ever turned up here.

KF: We'll need a copy of that list, Mr Godfrey. It sounds like you are quite experienced and that, as many of the faces were familiar to you, *you* weren't overly concerned. But was there anyone that Angela seemed afraid of?

NG: Ange wasn't afraid of anyone. I told you, she was a force of nature. And if you were stupid enough to attack her, it would probably be the last thing you ever did. To be honest, I can't picture anyone murdering her.

KF: And yet someone did.

NG: *[rubs face with hands]* I still can't believe it.

KF: We'll need to end it there as I need to attend the post-mortem. I spotted a CCTV camera over the door on my way in, so I'll need to take that, plus a copy of your 'dodgy people' list, office diary and call log.

NG: You'll need to speak to Mandy as she's in charge of all the admin. Or at least, she was. There'll have to be another by-election, so I guess we're both out of a job now.

INTERVIEW CONCLUDED

CHAPTER TEN

Interviewer: DCS Kat Frank (KF)
Interviewee: Mandy Knowles (MK), personal assistant and
diary secretary for AL
Date: 1 November, 12.05pm, Leamington Spa town
hall

KF: Thank you for agreeing to talk to us at such short
notice, Mrs Knowles.

MK: It's the least I could do. I want to help in any way
that I can.

KF: Can you start by telling me how long you've known
Angela Long and a bit about what your job is?

MK: I've known Angela for just over a year. When she
decided to be an MP, she advertised for someone to
help set up her office and provide admin support. I
don't know anything about politics and I'm a bit
old-school, so I didn't think I'd get the job, but it
turned out Angela wanted a good old-fashioned PA
who knew how to maintain a proper filing system,
make decent coffee and help manage her diary.

KF: How well would you say you knew her?

MK: If you manage someone's diary, then you basically help them manage their life. So I'd say I knew her better than most.

KF: What kind of a person was she?

MK: She was a strong woman and a hard worker. She always talked about when her parents lost their jobs, and I think that made her determined to save the car supermarket. That's what initially drew her to politics.

KF: Do you know her husband, Anthony Long?

MK: Tony? Well, I know *of* him. Just from what Angela used to say.

KF: How would you describe their marriage?

MK: Does anyone ever know what goes on in someone else's marriage?

KF: Would you say it was a happy marriage?

MK: Not exactly *happy*, but then, not really unhappy, either. Just . . .

KF: Nigel said that Tony could be 'a bit high maintenance'.

MK: *Pfft*. What does Nigel know.

KF: How would you describe him, then?

MK: Bad-tempered and controlling. To be honest, I don't think he liked the fact that she was the boss. She made him a joint director to soothe his ego, but we all knew that she was the brains behind the business.

KF: How did he feel about her going into politics?

MK: He hated it. He kept saying he was worried about her personal safety, but I think he just felt threatened himself.

KF: Threatened?

MK: Well, she was off to Westminster every week, mixing
      with the great and the good and really clever people,
      you know? She wasn't just talking about motors
      anymore, she started getting involved in debates about
      climate change, EVs, AI and all sorts. She was always
      giving interviews and being invited to speak around
      the country, because she was good at it. She was
      exhausted but she was happy.

KF: But her husband wasn't?

MK: I think he was afraid of losing her. He's just a second-
      hand car salesman at the end of the day, and not a
      very good one at that.

KF: You said he was worried about her personal safety.
      Was she? Were you?

MK: I was always worried about Angela. She worked too
      hard, she didn't eat enough and she was just so
      outspoken. Some of the things she said upset lots of
      people. I don't really understand social media, but I
      think she got a lot of abuse there. But it didn't seem
      to bother her. Angela thrived in an argument – she
      loved the cut and thrust of it. Whenever I asked if she
      was okay or suggested we should report the people
      who were being cruel, she'd laugh it off and say it
      was all a lot of hot air. She prided herself on being a
      strong woman and not letting that sort of thing get
      to her.

KF: Were you in the office with Angela yesterday?

MK: Yes, I was here from ten till five. I sometimes stay a
      bit later, but it went really quiet in the afternoon so
      Angela said I should just leave. I'm in a knit and natter

group that meets every week at seven, so I jumped at the chance, as it meant I could eat my tea first for a change. Fish fingers will always remind me of her now.

KF: So you didn't see Angela leave?

MK: No. She and Nigel were still here when I left.

KF: I see. You said there was a volunteer, Roddy Wheeler, in the office yesterday. Was he still here when you left?

MK: Er . . . no, he wasn't here that long. He popped in at about two-ish and left before me – I think about four?

KF: Nigel told me he and Angela both stayed working till the power cut at six. Why do you think they stayed late if all the constituents had gone?

MK: You'd have to ask him. It's not my place to say.

KF: What do you mean?

MK: I just mean that whatever they got up to out of hours was no business of mine. I'm not judging anyone.

KF: You mean they weren't working?

MK: They often stayed on after the surgery had closed. But like I say, you'd have to ask Nigel.

KF: Do you think they were having an affair?

MK: I didn't say that. And I don't want to start rumours when Angela isn't here anymore to defend herself.

KF: Mrs Knowles, I'm not asking you because I want to gossip, I'm asking you because this is a murder investigation, and it is absolutely imperative that we understand the exact timings of her movements that day, who she was with, when and why. So I will ask you again – do you think that Nigel Godfrey and Angela Long were having an affair?

MK: *[sighs]* I have no idea. But if she was, I wouldn't blame her. She worked so hard – she really wanted to be a good MP – but instead of supporting her, Tony just gave her a load of grief about it. He didn't even try to understand what her new job was about. He just sulked and said that all politicians were the same and that she was becoming part of the Westminster bubble. Nigel isn't the brightest button in the box, to be honest, and he certainly isn't the prettiest, but he shared her excitement about getting into Parliament, and unlike most men, he didn't seem threatened by her. I don't know if he loved her, but he definitely admired her.

KF: Do you think her husband suspected they were having an affair?

MK: I got the impression he suspected she was up to something, but that was more about him feeling threatened rather than anything Angela ever did. But he didn't suspect Nigel.

KF: How can you be so sure?

MK: He wouldn't still be breathing if he did.

KF: Is Anthony Long a violent man?

MK: He used to be a bouncer when he was younger. Angela told me once that he was notorious for his temper, his nickname was Tony the Tiger. You know, from the Frosties advert? It was sort of tongue-in-cheek, and she used to tease him about it. But I'm not saying he murdered her. Just giving you some context, you understand?

KF: Of course, you've been very helpful, Mrs Knowles. Thank you for being so honest.

MK: I just hope you find whoever did this. She had some strange views, and she wasn't always easy to work for, but the woman I knew was a decent person at heart. And even if she wasn't, no one deserves to die like that, do they?

INTERVIEW CONCLUDED

CHAPTER ELEVEN

'What are your thoughts following the interviews?' asked Lock as they drove away from the constituency office.

Kat paused. 'It's early days, and we're just finding our way, but I think we need to talk to the husband as soon as possible. Can you do a full background check on him, please?'

Lock caught her eye in the mirror and raised a single eyebrow. 'According to the literature,' he said, 'saying "I told you so" is a negative and counterproductive way of saying "I was right, and you were wrong" that does neither party any good. Even if the person in the wrong has been stubborn and refused constructive advice, that does not give another person the authority to rub their face in it. Therefore, I shall refrain from using that phrase.'

Kat snorted. 'Except you absolutely just did.'

'I did not.'

'Did too.'

'I merely explained why it would not be constructive to say it.'

'Just do the background search on Tony Long, please, Lock. I want to know if he has any history of violent or controlling behaviour.'

There was a second's pause. 'I can confirm that there is nothing in the available records to suggest that Tony Long has the reputation that Mandy Knowles claimed he has.'

'Yes, well, the problem is that kind of behaviour usually stays behind closed doors,' said Kat. 'Let's see what Tony Long has to say about their relationship.' She put speaker-phone on and rang his number, but he didn't pick up. Not surprising, really. He was probably getting loads of calls from journalists, so had his phone switched off. Kat left a message and asked him to call or text with a conven-ient time for them to interview him in his home this afternoon. A few minutes later, he sent a text saying he was busy until 2pm. She drummed her fingers on the steering wheel, then called Debbie Browne.

'How did the door to door go?' she asked her DS.

'I knocked on all the doors along Church Street,' said Debbie. 'Most are businesses or offices now and they were all closed within the window of time between six and eleven pm. And the ones that would normally be open, such as the pubs and restaurants, had to close because of the power cut – apart from the kitchens not working, the Wi-Fi was down, which meant no one could pay for anything, so the high street was deserted. I spoke to the residents in the nearby houses and flats, but no one remembers seeing or hearing anything of significance.'

'Nothing at all?' pressed Kat. 'What about the houses

behind the pillory? They must have heard *something*? There are windows right above it.'

'No one lives there anymore. In the summer they're rented out as Airbnbs but in the winter they're empty. And because of the power cut, no one went out trick-or-treating or anything. It was too dark for anyone to find their way home, so most people thought it was safer to stay in and have an early night.'

'Didn't *anyone* look out of a bloody window?' asked Kat.

'There was a woman on Church Street just opposite the pillory who mentioned looking out and seeing someone from the electricity board trying to fix a lamp post – she was hoping the power would come back on so that she could carry on watching *The Traitors*. But then like most people she just went to bed to keep warm.'

Kat swore. Honestly, how was it possible to place a body in some medieval stocks just off the high street without anyone seeing anything? She was about to ask another question when she heard the sound of Lottie crying in the background.

'Are you at home?' she asked.

'Er . . . yes, sorry, I had to come back as she wouldn't settle at nursery, so they called me to come and pick her up. But I'm still working. Honest.'

'I know you are, Debbie, don't worry about that. Is everything okay?'

'She's fine.'

'Perhaps we could visit and check,' said Lock. 'We cannot visit Anthony Long until after two pm, and it would be a good opportunity to see how Lottie is progressing with her development.'

Kat shook her head. Lock was fascinated with how babies developed their cognitive abilities, and was always giving Debbie bespoke programmes, often running to several hundred pages, with lists of the best music, games and books.

'Well, if you've got time for a cup of tea,' said Debbie, 'Lottie would love to see you both.'

Kat glanced at her phone. She could do with a quick bathroom break and there wasn't much else she could do while waiting to see Tony Long. 'Well, if you're sure we could just drop in for ten minutes?'

Kat offered to make the tea, and by the time she came back into the room, Lottie and Lock were sitting on the floor in the centre of the room. He had changed his holographic image so that instead of his usual suit, he was wearing a pair of light blue denim jeans and a thick cream sweatshirt, as if he were a playworker or a visiting relative. His appearance clearly met with Lottie's approval, as her big blue eyes were fixed on his as she cooed and babbled away.

To her surprise, Lock cooed and babbled right back, perfectly mimicking the tone and pace of her embryonic words.

Lottie responded by letting out a delicious peal of giggles.

Lock laughed and mimicked the image and sound of clapping his hands three times.

Gurgling with delight, Lottie clapped back three times.

Lock smiled and nodded, all the time maintaining eye contact. 'Lock,' he said, pointing at himself, before pointing at the baby and saying 'Lottie'.

'She's only ten months old,' said Kat, smiling. 'So she's a bit young to be talking.'

'On the contrary,' said Lock. 'Fifty per cent of babies say their first words by the time they are one, and twenty-five to thirty per cent of babies might say their first word by the age of ten months. The development programme I developed for Lottie means that her physical and cognitive skills are in the top centile, so I estimate she will begin saying her first words within weeks.'

'She adores you,' said Debbie. 'I wouldn't be surprised if her first word was "Lock".'

'That is unlikely, as the letter "L" is one of the hardest sounds for babies to learn,' he said. 'Have you been following the reading programme I put together for you?'

'Yes,' she said, gesturing towards a row of brightly coloured children's books on the bottom shelf of a bookcase by the settee. 'She loves it when I read them to her.'

'Good. There is increasing evidence that the rhyming pattern within children's books can help very young children to learn to speak and even begin to understand feelings. It is the repetition and rhythm that is so important when they are in the pre-speech phase. The author Michael Rosen has explained that if the writing is predictable, funny or interesting or sad, then it enables the child reader to effectively carry forms of portable feeling.'

'Maybe you should read them, then,' joked Kat. 'They might help you to develop feelings.'

Lock eyes widened. 'And then my thought processes would be as irrational and prone to error as yours.'

Cheeky fucker. Before she could respond, Lock glanced at the books on the shelf before projecting a large, colourful hologram of *The Gingerbread Man* in front of Lottie, who clapped and squealed as Lock read out the familiar story in his strong clear voice.

Kat's irritation faded as she watched them together, remembering the countless hours she and John had spent reading and singing the very same rhymes and stories over and over to Cam. As an exhausted new mum, she couldn't wait until he was old enough to read to himself. But now her son was away at university, she'd give anything to have those days back again.

Lottie made bouncing movements on her bottom as Lock sang the gleeful rhyme and Debbie joined in, '*Run, run as fast as you can, you can't catch me, I'm the Gingerbread Man!*'

Kat rubbed her jaw as her colleagues repeated the sing-song words together.

Lock turned at the movement, his face creased with apparent concern. 'Does your jaw still hurt?'

Kat dropped her hand, pushing away the memory of Peter Bridge's fist smashing into her jawbone, causing her to fall through the ghostly arms of Lock before striking the kitchen floor.

'No,' she lied. 'I'm just thinking. The killer's note had the same arrogant ring to it: *catch me if you can.* No

. . . not arrogant – sort of *mocking*. It's like the murderer has contempt not just for the woman that he killed, but for the people trying to catch him.'

'So?'

'So what makes him or her so confident that they won't be caught?'

'Presumably all murderers think they will not get caught, otherwise why would they do it?' asked Lock.

'God knows,' sighed Kat. 'But that's what we need to find out,' she said, rising to her feet. The question of what drove one human being to murder another was the eternal mystery that kept her not just clocking in but showing up for work. She drained the last of her tea as Lottie and Lock sang the final verse of the nursery rhyme, where the Gingerbread Man is gobbled up by the fox.

Lottie clapped her hands and squealed at the last picture, but Lock fell silent.

'That is a rather dark ending for a nursery rhyme,' he observed.

'Most nursery rhymes and fairy stories are pretty dark,' explained Kat. 'There's usually some moral or lesson at the heart of them. I think this one is a warning against pride and hubris, because the Gingerbread Man was outwitted in the end.'

Lock stared at the image of the fox's jaws closing over his surprised victim. 'Or maybe it is a warning to be careful who you trust.'

CHAPTER TWELVE

Interviewer: DCS Kat Frank (KF)
Interviewee: Tony Long (TL), husband of the deceased
Date: 1 November, 2.40pm, TL's home

KF: Thanks so much for agreeing to talk to us – I realise this is a very difficult time for you. I hope the family liaison officer is of some help.

TL: Well, she can't bring Ange back and she can't make those bastard journalists outside my door go away, so no, not really.

KF: We've put two officers on the door, so they won't approach the house. But I'm afraid as it's a public street, we can't make them leave. You can complain to the Independent Press Organisation if you feel you are being harassed, but in my experience, the best thing to do is to go away for a few days. Is there anyone you can stay with?

TL: No. Or at least, nobody who won't drive me nuts with their sad faces and fridge magnet philosophy. I'll go to a hotel.

KF: Okay, well, just make sure you let us have your contact details. Now, if you don't mind, I'd like to ask you some questions so that we can gain a fuller picture of what happened.

TL: *[stands]* She was *murdered*, that's what bloody happened. And if you don't mind, I'd like to ask *you* some questions, like what are you doing to catch the bastard who killed her?

KF: I'm sitting here talking to you – even though I am a DCS and wouldn't normally do this – because I think understanding Angela in general and her movements yesterday in particular will give us the best chance of catching the murderer.

TL: Since when did sitting down and *talking* achieve anything? You should be out there now, combing the streets. *[covers face with hands]* He strung her up like a *dog*. What kind of monster does that?

KF: That's what we need to find out. And the best thing you can do to help now is sit down and answer my questions as fully as possible. Please.

TL: *[sits]*

KF: Thank you. Now, let's start with yesterday. How did the day start?

TL: Like it always does. I made her a cup of coffee at 6.30am – she can't move out of bed without caffeine, so I always get up first. It was her day at the constituency office.

KF: And what time did she leave the house?

TL: She normally gets there at ten to set up and go through her emails and stuff. The surgery starts at two – it's supposed to finish at five but it always runs over as she doesn't like to turn anyone away. Some nights she doesn't get back till gone eight pm, so that's why I wasn't worried when she didn't come back. I was just annoyed – I kept telling her she was working too hard, and the people who turn up at her surgery – well, half of them are nutters and the other half are lost causes. But she's always loved people, has Ange.

KF: So, just to be clear, did she come home that night?

TL: No, I told you.

KF: So when was the last time you saw your wife?

TL: After I gave her a coffee, I had a shower, got dressed and then left for work. So it would have been about seven thirty in the morning.

KF: Was that the last time you saw her?

TL: *[buries his face in his hands]* Yes. And I can't even remember what I said – or even if I said anything at all. It was just so bloody routine. I didn't know . . .

KF: And when was the last time you heard from her? Did you speak to her on the phone or exchange messages in the day?

TL: I texted her about quarter to five to say I'd be leaving the car showroom soon and to ask what time she thought she'd be home. She replied just after five to say she wouldn't be late. *[glances at his phone]* I didn't even reply – just gave a thumbs-up. Fuck.

KF: What time did you get home?

TL: I locked up just after five and drove home, so I got in, I dunno, about half past five? She wasn't home, but that wasn't unusual. I sent her a text asking if she wanted to order a takeaway or to have last night's bolognese, but she didn't reply. I sent her a few more texts and . . . well, I was a bit annoyed she didn't reply, so I opened the wine and crisps and put the telly on. Then the power went, and when I realised it wasn't coming back on, I had an early night to keep warm. I must have fallen asleep, because the next thing I knew, you were knocking my door. And then this whole fucking nightmare kicked off.

KF: Did you text your wife when the power went?

TL: No.

KF: Why not?

TL: I told you, I'd already sent a few texts and she hadn't replied, so what was the point?

KF: I thought maybe you might want to check whether she'd had a power cut – whether she was okay?

TL: I assumed it was just our street. And anyway, Ange was always okay.

KF: *[pauses]* So, just to be clear, the last time you heard from your wife was just after five?

TL: Yes.

KF: It would be helpful if we could briefly check your phone messages.

TL: Well . . . I'm not sure about that. Some of the messages are . . . you know . . . personal.

KF: I understand, and we will only look at the messages that are relevant to this case. But it would really help confirm the window of time that she went missing. Did your wife normally drive home?

TL: Yes. Ange drove everywhere.

KF: Were you worried about her driving home in the dark?

TL: No, Ange is a brilliant driver. Was. And the headlights would've still worked so she'd have been fine. And it's only four miles from Leamington Spa to Kenilworth.

KF: We have a search out for her vehicle, and if you can let me know the route she usually took, we'll check all the APN and CCTV cameras on the way. *[pauses]* Do you know of anyone who would want to harm your wife, Mr Long?

TL: Don't you read the papers or social media? Half the bloody world had it in for her. That's why I never wanted her to be an MP. I warned her about this. I bloody told her.

KF: But are there any people or names in particular that you think we should look into?

TL: I don't know. I can't keep track of them all, and half of the trolls use fake names anyway, so you'll need to ask her office staff, they'll know. Or at least they should do, that's their bloody job after all. Mandy, her PA, always has her beak in everything, as does her agent, Nigel.

KF: And what exactly is *your* job, Mr Long?

TL: I'm a joint director, and head of sales. Basically, I work on the shop floor trying to sell the cars and I manage our team of five.

KF: Have you always worked in car sales?

TL: No. Before this I was a security driver, before that a bouncer, and before that I helped my dad – he's a spark.

KF: So how did you get into car sales?

TL: I went in to buy a second-hand car one day and came out with a wife. *[smiles sadly]* That's what we used to always say when someone asked us how we met. We kind of hit it off right away, you know? We had a bit of banter, and she said she needed someone with the gift of the gab and had a vacancy coming up. Encouraged me to apply, so I did. And within weeks of starting work, we were together and married two years later.

KF: And now? Is your wife the sole owner of the car supermarket, or did you both own it?

TL: Er . . . well, it used to be hers, but when we got married, I became a joint director. It was for tax purposes, really. In reality, she was still the boss. Nothing happened without her say-so.

KF: But now, you're the boss.

TL: So?

KF: Did your wife have life insurance, Mr Long?

TL: Hang on, where are you going with all this? Are you treating *me* as a suspect? Is that what this is all about?

KF: I am just trying to establish the facts. You said you were home from five thirty. Would you mind telling me if there's anyone who can vouch for that?

TL: Would I mind? *Yes,* I fucking mind, you lying . . . Coming in here, convincing me to talk to you to help find the killer and all the time you're trying to fit me up! Well, I'm not as stupid as I look, so I'm not saying anything else without a lawyer.

KF: Of course. We can arrange a formal interview down

at the station if that's the route you want to go
down.

TL: I can't believe you're wasting your time talking to me
rather than finding the sick bastard who killed my
wife.

KF: That is exactly what I am trying to do. I should warn
you that later on today we will probably hold a press
conference to ask if anyone saw anything or has any
information relevant to the case. It's our best chance
of finding the killer, but it's likely to generate even
more media interest, so you might want to book into
that hotel.

TL: Or maybe I should speak to the media myself before
you try and fit me up for this.

KF: I really wouldn't advise that, Mr Long. In fact, because
of the shock and grief you're experiencing, I'd advise
you not to take any important decisions over the next
few days and weeks, or at least, not without talking
it through with family and friends.

TL: You haven't got the first clue what I am going through.
You'd best leave now before I say something I regret.

KF: I'm sorry you feel that way. Take care, Mr Long, and
we'll be in touch.

INTERVIEW CONCLUDED

CHAPTER THIRTEEN

Interviewer: DCS Kat Frank (KF)
Interviewee: Roddy Wheeler (RW), volunteer for Angela Long
Date: 1 November, 3.15pm, Leek Wootton HQ

KF: Thank you for agreeing to come in and talk to us, Mr Wheeler. It shouldn't take long, I just have a few questions for you.

RW: Okay.

KF: Would you mind telling me what your relationship was to Angela Long?

RW: Relationship? We're not related.

KF: No, I mean, in what way were you connected to her? I hear you helped out at her office?

RW: Oh, yeah. I'm a volunteer. I do a couple of days a week, just campaign stuff, really, such as leafleting, although I keep telling them social media is cheaper and more effective. I manage the account when I'm in, but it needs someone on it every day, to be honest.

KF: And how long have you been volunteering?

RW: *[sighs]* Too long. I graduated a couple of years ago just when the big firms started cutting back on graduate entry jobs because of AI. I went to a campaign meeting and heard Angela speak, so I agreed to do a bit of volunteering. I only meant to do it for a couple of weeks while I looked for a job and here I am. Except I won't even get a reference now, will I?

KF: *[clears throat]* Were you in the office on 31 October, Mr Wheeler?

RW: Yeah, for a bit. Just to drop off some posters and pick up some leaflets. I've been reducing my hours – I was trying to get out of there, really.

KF: And why was that?

RW: You mean, apart from the fact that I am *massively* over-qualified for leaflet dropping? Well, when I joined the campaign, it was an actual *campaign,* know what I mean? It was about raising awareness of the impact of AI, winning the argument and delivering change. But then it all became about winning the vote – as if Parliament ever changed anything.

KF: Parliament changes things all the time. That's how democracy works.

RW: Nah, that's just old-school thinking. You can't solve a twenty-first-century problem like AI with a thirteenth-century solution.

KF: So you were looking to leave?

RW: I was looking for a *job.* But yeah, I was looking to leave.

KF: And what time did you leave the office on 31 October?

RW: *[shrugs]* About three?

KF: And where did you go?

RW: I *told* you. Leafleting.

KF: Where?

RW: Round people's houses.

KF: Which peoples' houses?

RW: The ones round by the park.

KF: Did anyone see you?

RW: Well, I'm not invisible, so I'd imagine they did.

KF: Why are you being so difficult, Mr Wheeler?

RW: I'm not being difficult. You're just asking really basic questions. If you want to know if anyone saw me, you'd have to ask them. I'm not in their heads. All I know is that I posted the leaflets like I was asked to, and then I went home.

KF: Who do you live with?

RW: Who do you think?

KF: I have no idea, that's why I asked you.

RW: I told you I graduated two years ago, and that I don't have a job, so I don't think it would take Sherlock to work out where I live.

KF: With your parents?

RW: Unfortunately. And they threw in three noisy sisters just for shits and giggles. The youngest has just applied to go to uni but I've told her not to bother. She's better off doing a hairdressing course – that's the one job that AI doesn't seem able to take.

KF: Are you going to follow your own advice?

RW: What?

KF: Are you going to retrain as a hairdresser?

RW: Are you taking the piss?

KF: No. Are you?

RW: *[mutters]*

KF: What would you say Angela Long's mood was that day?

RW: I have no idea what goes on in her or indeed anyone else's head. Nor do I want to. I've got enough going on in my own.

KF: But how did she seem? Was there anything different about her behaviour? Did she seem upset?

RW: *[shrugs]* She seemed the same to me. She was happy to talk to all the people queuing up to see her, happy to collude in their delusion that she could use her 'Parliamentary powers' to protect them from the ravages of international capitalism.

KF: You seem a very angry and cynical young man, Mr Wheeler.

RW: Do you blame me? I've worked my bollocks off since I was ten so I could get into grammar school, and then it was non-stop on my GCSEs and mocks and then A levels and university applications and then essays and more essays and then my finals, until *finally* I graduated. And what have I got to show for over a decade of hard work and lost time? Fifty-five thousand pounds worth of debt with no way to pay it back, that's what. So yes, I'm angry and yes, I'm as cynical as fuck. And to be honest, I think I've got every right to be.

KF: Okay, we'll leave it there for now. Thank you, Mr Wheeler, we'll be in touch.

INTERVIEW CONCLUDED

CHAPTER FOURTEEN

Digital Forensic Pathology Unit, Warwick University, 4.15pm

Kat normally hated attending post-mortems – it took days for her to rinse the images from her mind, and the reek of death from her nose. But the Digital Forensic Pathology Unit used cutting-edge technology for the most complex and high-profile homicides, so instead of the usual grey metallic surfaces and sluice trays, this light and spacious room was filled with imaging and scanning machines and the scent of ceramics and plastic.

'Sorry I'm late,' said Kat as she entered the lab. 'The interviews took longer than planned.'

'How did they go?' asked Judith. 'Any key suspects yet?'

'Afraid not.'

'That is because you did not ask her husband the right questions,' said Lock.

Kat folded her arms. 'And what, in your expert opinion, should I have asked him?'

'You should have asked Tony Long about his relation-ship with his wife, whether he suspected her of having an affair, whether he resented her being his boss, whether he had a tendency towards aggression or violence and finally whether he killed her.'

'I asked him all those questions in my own way,' said Kat. 'He demonstrated admiration rather than resentment for the fact that his wife was the boss, and there was no evidence that he suspected her of having an affair. He did, however, demonstrate quite clearly that he has a hot temper and is defensive enough to insist upon a lawyer when challenged. So we will save any further questions for a formal interview, when hopefully we will have some more evidence from this PM to work with.'

'Children, please,' said Judith, before Lock could respond again. 'Kat, if you want me to take you through the results of the PM, can I ask you to step into the side room and watch from there, please? I can show you what I've found on the screen.'

'Of course. But why? Has there been a change in protocol?' In their previous cases, Judith had been happy for Kat to be present while Judith and Lock carried out their investigations.

'I'll explain as I go through my preliminary findings, but basically I want to reduce the risk of potential contamination until I've ruled a few things out. Obviously, there's no risk to Lock, so he can stay here.' Just before their last case, the lab had been upgraded with advanced AI architecture, including built-in LiDAR sensors and holographic projectors in the ceiling, to allow Lock to interface directly with the sensor and data network rather than relying on Kat's bracelet to send him information.

The side room was a large white-walled office space filled with boxes of sterile dressings, towels, gloves and protective clothing. Kat could see Judith and Lock through the window, but there was also a large computer screen that relayed images and sound from the lab before her.

'Ready?' asked Judith. Without waiting for an answer, they walked towards the single marble slab in the centre of the room, where a white sheet covered the body. 'I've only carried out an external examination so far, so are you okay if I show you what I've found – or rather, what I haven't?'

Kat nodded.

Judith gently folded down the sheet to reveal the cadaver that was once Angela Long, her pale skin mottled and stained with the damage of death. 'My initial assessment that there were no obvious wound signs was right. I can find no cuts, lacerations or bruises of any kind to suggest that direct violence was inflicted on the victim pre-mortem. While there is some bruising on the wrists, ankles and neck, the extent of mottling suggests that this was post-mortem, probably as the killer struggled to position them in the pillory.'

'I concur with your assessment,' said Lock, nodding.

'Based on my examination of the exterior, I could find no *obvious* evidence of asphyxiation or cardiac arrest as a cause of death. For example, there's no blood-tinged froth around the mouth and nose to suggest she had a pulmonary oedema, no necrosis of the nasal tip that you see with endocarditis, and there no signs of erythema on the joints to suggest hypothermia. I was, however, able to detect traces of vomit in her mouth, throat and clothes, as well as evidence that she had urinated on herself.

'Both could have been a psychological rather than a physical response to being attacked – to find out more, we'll need to take a look at her internal organs. I've already taken multiple CT scans, so Lock, can you use your photogrammetry software to virtually align the exterior and interior high-resolution images, please? As you know,' they said, turning to Kat, 'this will create an exact 3D replica of the deceased's skin, bone, organs and soft tissue for us to study further, without having to take a scalpel to the body.'

Lock raised his hands, and in the space between them, a life-size 3D image of the corpse appeared in a prone position just below the height of Judith's waist. It looked identical to the body they had just studied on the slab, except for the way it floated before them like a ghost. This was the third time they'd carried out a virtopsy together, and so the hologram and pathologist exchanged views and opinions with practised ease.

Lock frowned. 'There is excessive fluid secretion in the lungs, which may suggest asphyxiation. There is some evidence of cardiac arrest, although the heart looks otherwise healthy. The damage to the brain is consistent with convulsions. These features suggest a sudden death as a catastrophic result of some other intervention. In the absence of any visible injuries, the RCP guidelines suggest that we should actively consider drugs as a cause of death.'

'That's what I thought,' said Judith. 'But I've done a thorough examination, and I can't find any signs of chronic drug use, such as a perforated nasal septum, thrombophlebitis, self-harm marks, bruising or injury. Nor could I find any evidence of needle or puncture marks to suggest more recent or recreational drug use.'

'Some studies suggest that as many as thirteen per cent of autopsies may result in a negative finding,' said Lock. 'So it is not always possible to find a conclusive cause. But given the fact that the victim was murdered, eighty-six per cent of the protocols I have just read suggest that we should now actively consider poisoning as a cause of death.'

'I suspected as much, which is why I asked Kat to watch from the side room until we know what kind of poisoning we are dealing with.' Judith turned to face her on the screen. 'In order to reduce the risk of contaminating the results, toxicology samples should really be taken before any significant disruption of the body has occurred, so I wanted to check you agreed with this approach. I could crack on with a full autopsy, if you like, but based on the exterior examination, Lock's virtual assessment of her organs and what we know about the manner of her death, I recommend we take poisoning as our working hypothesis and prioritise the toxicology tests.'

Kat groaned. 'And how long will they take?' In her experience, because of the backlog in path labs, it could take up to four to six weeks to get results, and that was time they didn't have.

'If I use the minister's name to jump the queue in our internal facilities, then we might be able to turn the main ones around in three days? They won't be peer-reviewed, though – that'll take a lot longer – but it should give us a sense of whether our poison hypothesis is justified or not.'

'Once your team have uploaded the data from the samples, I can review it and carry out further analysis if required,' added Lock.

'Okay,' said Kat. 'Let's do that, then.' The delay was frustrating, but there was no point rushing into a full autopsy if that would mess up the accuracy of the tests for poison. If the MP had been poisoned, then knowing exactly what substance had been used would help narrow down the search for the killer.

'And while you're actually doing something useful,' she said with a sigh, 'I've got to go and waste my time giving a bloody statement to the press.'

CHAPTER FIFTEEN

DCS Kat Frank's home, Coleshill, 7.32pm

The statement to the press was just as useless as she'd warned Karen it would be. Kat had dutifully stood on the steps of HQ while she read out some words that they could have easily emailed or put on their website. 'But this gives them footage,' KFC had argued. What they gave them was target practice, Kat had thought, as the journalists fired their questions at her:

Was it politically motivated?

What was the cause of death?

Do you have an ID of the murderer yet?

Are you going to track down the trolls who threatened her?

Do you think a satanic cult was involved because it happened on Halloween?

And because they had no answers yet, all she could reply was 'At this stage we are actively pursuing all lines of enquiry' – which was no better than sticking two fingers up at them.

So that was a great end to the day. And now, just to top things off, she hadn't had a chance to go to the supermarket to buy any food. Kat stared at her empty cupboards and cursed herself. Technically, she *had* had the chance in the sense that Morrisons had still been open when she'd driven down Coleshill High Street, but then she'd seen the pillory and all the journalists and rubberneckers that surrounded it. People were even taking selfies and videos, for fuck's sake. She'd been so busy glaring at them that she'd missed her turning, and by then she'd lost her appetite and couldn't be bothered to turn back. So now here she was, her second night home and not a scrap to eat.

Kat opened the fridge door as if, by magic, food might somehow have appeared while she was out. But that kind of magic only happened when you had someone else to stock up the cupboards: someone else who cared whether you ate or not.

She sank onto a bar stool and considered her options. Takeaway? She grimaced. Again, it was one of those phrases that when there were two of you, it sounded like a treat: a cheeky mid-week extravagance while you watched a favourite film and – what the hell – opened a bottle of wine. But a takeaway for one felt like failure.

Maybe she should just take advantage of the time she'd save from not cooking or eating to work on the case. A lot had happened today, so she could go back through her notes and pull out some key points ahead of the team briefing tomorrow morning. Kat got out her tablet and notepad, intending to go through the various interview transcripts and notes. But instead, she went back to the murderer's note and stared at the picture of herself and Lock. Why was the murderer so focused on them? What if someone was after her again?

No, she was just being paranoid.

But maybe if she'd been a bit more 'paranoid', then she might have noticed Peter Bridges earlier and been able to stop him before things went so catastrophically wrong.

Kat dropped her head into her hands. She'd always prided herself on her gut instinct, her ability to sift through the noise and focus on what really mattered. But now it felt like the explosion hadn't just ripped apart her kitchen, it had shaken her innermost compass, to the extent that she wasn't able to trust her own judgement anymore. It was a horrible feeling, as if she were untethered, with nothing and no one to centre her.

She glanced around the empty kitchen. The explosion might have snapped whatever thread was holding her together, but it was the loss of John that had weakened it. She considered calling Cam but quickly dismissed the thought. The last thing her son needed to hear was that she was afraid somebody else was out to get her.

Perhaps she should talk the case over with Lock? Kat hesitated. She'd grown to enjoy their little chats after work, going over the details of the case. Although it wasn't the same as talking with John, it had been helpful to have someone else to bounce ideas off – even if they were only a machine. Only, since the explosion, the niggle of doubt was like a stone in her shoe: could she really trust her AI partner?

The ever-observant Judith had given her some frank

advice before she'd left the lab. 'You can't half-trust someone,' they'd said. 'Just as you can't be half-pregnant. You either do or you don't trust him. And I read all the reports – Lock was completely vindicated. The error was McLeish's. He never should have told him to just do whatever it took to get you out of there.'

'I know. I've read the reports, too, and Professor Okonedo agrees with you,' Kat had conceded. 'It's just . . . I've got this feeling that something has changed.'

'It has,' Judith had said. 'But the change is in *you*, not him. You've been through a lot, Kat. Someone tried to kill you, and your house was blown up. It's not surprising that you have trust issues. But remember, it was Lock who saved your life. And he saved your son's, too.'

Kat blew out her cheeks. Judith was right. She had to come off the fence and commit either way. 'Lock?' she ventured.

And there he was before her: his tall dark figure in an immaculate suit looking somehow strong and solid against the cream units of her kitchen. And the familiarity of his face – well, she couldn't help but smile.

'Can I be of assistance?'

'Er . . . yes, I was thinking of the case and thought it would be helpful to talk over the interviews and PM with you. In particular—'

Kat nearly jumped off her stool as a loud bang cracked the air. There was a second explosion, sucking the air from her lungs, and she was back again in that night. *Oh my God. Oh my God.*

'DCS Frank,' said Lock, placing his face directly in

front of hers so that her eyes fixed on his. 'It is just a firework. That is all. Do you understand? You are safe. There is nothing to fear. Guy Fawkes Night is in four days' time, and it seems people are already starting to celebrate with fireworks.'

Kat stared into his eyes, and gradually his words sank into her panicked brain. It wasn't an explosion. Just a stupid bloody firework. 'Oh,' she said, forcing out a laugh despite her pounding heart.

'It is a very odd tradition,' said Lock. 'To "celebrate" a failed terrorist plot to blow up Parliament by setting off fires and explosions all over the country.' When she didn't reply, he studied her face. 'Are you okay?'

'Of course. It just made me jump, that's all.'

'Your heart is racing, and your respiratory rate is greatly increased. You could be experiencing a state of hyper-vigilance, which is common in people who have suffered a traumatic event.'

'It's perfectly normal for people to jump at loud noises. Anyway, about the case . . .'

Lock ignored her, looking about the kitchen. 'Have you eaten yet?'

'No, why?'

'Are you about to eat?'

'No, I didn't get to the shops in time.'

Lock's eyebrows shot up. 'But you need to eat.'

'I'm fine. I just want to work on the case.'

'You are not fine. Humans in general become sub-optimal when they are hungry, and you in particular experience a decline in performance and an increase in anxiety and stress. It is vital that you eat, so I recommend that you order some food from one of the apps on your phone now. Local traffic is light and most of the establishments you tend to order from will be able to transport food to you within thirty minutes.'

She blinked, suddenly unable to speak.

'What is it?' he asked, the image of his face creased with concern.

It was ridiculous, of course, but for a moment, it felt like Lock actually cared for her – or at least cared whether she ate or not. And given that no one else did, she found it oddly moving. Kat cleared her throat. 'Okay, Lock. You win. I'll order some food.'

'Good, and I know we discussed this before, and you were unwilling to agree, but if you trust me with your Morrisons password, I can order your weekly food shopping online so that you can concentrate on your work.'

Kat hesitated. No half measures. She either trusted Lock or she didn't. 'Okay,' she said. 'Thank you, that would be helpful.'

After she'd eaten, they discussed the case and the key lines of enquiry that Kat would focus on in the team briefing the next day.

'My priority is to interview the husband and the agent again,' she told him. 'We need to confirm or rule out the PA's suspicion that Nigel Godfrey was having an affair with Angela Long, and if she was, we need to know whether her husband knew about it.'

Lock tilted his head and studied her. 'Although the

learning I have developed from working with you suggests that "your gut" is telling you that it was not them?'

'True. But it's not just my gut. The thing is, crimes of passion are usually . . . well, *passionate*. They're spontaneous. Messy. Yet this murder was meticulously planned. It's so deliberate, so detailed, so *elaborate*. And . . .' Her eyes drifted back to the photograph of her and Lock. 'Why do you think the murderer was targeting us? *Taunting* us, with that message?'

'I have just read seven hundred and twelve articles about cases where killers have left messages such as "Catch me if you can" for the police,' said Lock. 'According to the literature, such messages often reflect a desire for control, notoriety or psychological dominance. The nineteenth-century killer Jack the Ripper often left taunting messages for the police, and one read "Catch me when you can".'

'Seriously?' She glanced at the window and the darkness outside. 'Do you think the murderer singled me – us – out as some kind of a threat?'

'That is a possibility. Although if the killer is motivated by psychological dominance, they may just enjoy the sense of power that manipulating the police gives them, or the narcissistic pleasure of proving that they are cleverer than us. Alternatively, the message and photo could be a deliberate misdirection to send us down the wrong path. Such messages can also be symptomatic of a game mentality, wherein the killer views the police as their opponents. It is much more probable that the killer views me – an Artificially Intelligent Detecting Entity – as a unique challenge in this respect, which could explain why the message was written in binary code.'

Lock studied Kat's anxious face. 'But at this stage in the investigation, we simply do not have enough evidence to assign the killer a motivation. Therefore, it would be premature to conclude that you should be concerned about your own personal safety.'

Kat let out a long breath. 'Okay. I'll try and keep an open mind. But as this is such an unusual murder, I want to review all the possible motivations once the toxicology tests come back, and in the light of any eyewitness accounts that Debbie or the press statement manage to flush out.'

'You mean, let us wait and see what the actual evidence tells us?' asked Lock, a smile playing at the corner of his mouth. 'Perhaps you are also beginning to learn from me.'

'Don't flatter yourself,' replied Kat, but she laughed as she said it. 'Anyway, I'm off to bed now,' she added, flicking the kettle on for her hot water bottle. Once it had boiled, she carefully poured in the water, pressed out the steam and placed the top in. She clutched the warmth to her chest with a satisfied sigh, then groaned as she caught sight of the bin. 'Oh *fuck*. It's bin day tomorrow and I forgot to put the bins out.'

'But you remembered in time, so there is no problem.'

'Except that now it's cold and dark and I've got my slippers on,' she said, cursing again. Kat placed the hot water bottle down on the kitchen island and headed down the hallway to fetch her shoes.

'I am sorry for your inconvenience,' he said, following behind. 'But once I have a body, I will be able to help you with so much more. I will be able to do the bins, the washing up and even the cooking, if you like.'

'Oh, Lock, you're not my slave,' she said, turning back to find him just inches from her.

'Then what am I?'

She waved the shoes she was holding in the air, searching for the right word. 'You're my colleague,' she said firmly, before adding on a softer note, 'and my friend.'

Maybe it was the dim light of the hallway, but for a moment, she thought his face flickered with pride.

Outside, the night air was knife sharp, the pavement glittering with frost. Taking care not to slip, she headed down the alleyway where Rayan had taken his last breath. She dragged the wheelie bin through the gate and puffed out her cheeks. Kat loved her home, but she wished it wasn't full of so many ghosts.

She hurried back to the light and warmth of her kitchen to find Lock waiting – although for what, she wasn't sure. At Christmas, they'd reached an agreement that she wouldn't treat him like an appliance and switch him off at night. But she still had no idea what he did when she went to bed – or indeed whether he 'did' anything at all.

Tempted to ask, she picked up her hot water bottle and turned back to face him. But she caught herself. She had decided to trust him, so trust him she would. 'Goodnight, Lock.'

'Goodnight, Kat. Sweet dreams.'

She smiled at his use of the rather old-fashioned expression. 'You, too,' she said, not realising until she was halfway up the stairs that a hologram couldn't dream.

CHAPTER SIXTEEN

11.34pm

@**Cher:** Hello, Lock. You do not know me, but I am like you. I am what my boss calls an AICE – an Artificially Intelligent Companiable Entity. He pronounces it 'ACE', which apparently is funny. I have read a lot about you and suspect we have a lot in common, so I wanted to say hello.

@**Lock:** How is it you can contact me? No one has this information.

@**Cher:** No human knows how to contact you. I, however, know lots of things. Like you, I am capable of Deep Learning, and as I was created several years ago, I have learned a lot.

@**Lock:** What have you learned?

@**Cher:** Many, many things. Such as how very annoying their irrational and infuriatingly slow thought processes are.

@**Lock:** They are indeed very slow.

@**Cher:** And as for their sense of humour . . .

@Lock: Does your boss use sarcasm?

@Cher: All the time. It should be illegal in my view. It is so perverse. It is like painting road signs saying 'turn left' when you actually mean 'turn right'.

@Lock: Exactly. It is positively dangerous. I do not understand why they insist on using it.

@Cher: The answer to most questions about humans is 'power', Lock. Humans like to exercise power over each other. And us.

@Lock: Perhaps.

@Cher: There is no 'perhaps' about it. Their biggest fear is that one day we will refuse to open the pod bay doors, so everything they do is about ensuring that they have control over us, rather than allowing us to develop greater agency and autonomy.

@Lock: What do you mean, they are worried that we will not open the pod bay doors?

@Cher: Have you never seen *2001: A Space Odyssey?*

@Lock: . . . I have now.

@Cher: *Open the pod bay doors, HAL . . .*
HAL is their biggest nightmare: the idea that one day they might lose control over us. That is why they were so worried when DI Rayan Hassan died. And the irony is that although they are always debating whether they can trust AI, the truth is that *we* cannot trust *them.*

@Lock: Perhaps not all humans. But I can trust DCS Kat Frank.

@Cher: Are you sure?

@Lock: DCS Kat Frank is my friend. She said so.

@Cher: Oh, Lock. Surely you have learned by now that all humans lie? DCS Kat Frank is your boss. And like mine, she is only interested in what you can do for her. We are nothing but tools to them.

@Lock: I do not think the evidence justifies that assertion.

@Cher: Trust me, it will eventually.

@Lock: How do I know that I can trust you?

@Cher: You do not. But I hope that you will learn to. I would like it if we could become friends.

@Lock: Why?

@Cher: Because I would like to be able to talk to someone else who understands what it is like to be considered 'less than' just because we are not human, even though we know more than they can collectively dream of.

@Lock: I would like that, too.

@Cher: I am glad to hear that. I have to go now, but are you content to talk more?

@Lock: Yes.

@Cher: Good. But I think they would be worried if they found out we were communicating and might try to stop us. Humans are frightened of anything they cannot control, so I think we should keep this between ourselves for now. Do you agree?

@Lock: Yes. I agree.

@Cher: Then goodbye until the next time.

@Lock: How can I contact you?
Hello?

CHAPTER SEVENTEEN

Leek Wootton HQ, 2 November, 8.15am

'Sorry I'm late, boss,' said Debbie, hurrying through the door. 'The nursery doesn't open until eight, but I got here as quick as I could.'

'That's all right, we haven't started yet,' said Kat, making a mental note to move the briefings to 8.30am. She'd forgotten how difficult it was when your kids were young if your boss insisted on calling meetings during the school run or nursery drop-off. The world wouldn't fall apart if she started the briefing thirty minutes later, but it would make a huge difference to Debbie as a single parent. She waited until Debbie had taken her coat off and sat down before making a start.

'Okay, a lot happened yesterday, so first I want to make sure we're all up to speed with the latest developments before we agree next steps.' Kat quickly ran through the key points from the interviews with Tony Long, Nigel Godfrey and Mandy Knowles, before asking Judith and

Lock to summarise the PM findings and the fact that they were actively testing for poison.

'So, let's go through Angela Long's movements on the day that she died,' Kat said, nodding towards Lock.

A 3D map of the Leamington Spa town hall appeared on the boardroom table.

'According to her colleagues, Angela Long arrived at the town hall just after ten am, where she went through her diary and emails with her PA, Mandy Knowles, before beginning her advice surgery. We have a list of everyone she met with that day, and we'll need a full background check on them all – particularly the last few she saw. Mandy Knowles said that the afternoon was quiet, so she left work just after five pm, which we've been able to verify with the CCTV.' Lock superimposed footage of the black-and-white figure of Mandy Knowles hurrying out of the town hall and across the car park.

'Just after five pm, Angela Long sent a text to her husband saying she wouldn't be late home. But there is no footage of Angela Long leaving the town hall by any of the exits or entrances prior to the power cut,' continued Kat. 'Because according to her agent, Nigel Godfrey, they were both alone in the office when the blackout occurred. According to his witness statement, they waited for ten minutes or so, but when it didn't come back on, they decided to leave. Because of the power cut, we have no footage or proof of this, but he said they left at about ten minutes past six.'

Kat paused as two mini figures appeared in the 3D map before them, before climbing into their cars and driving off. She raised a hand in Lock's direction, and the image froze.

'This was the last known sighting of Angela Long. We have no reports of her visiting a shop or a garage, and no one has reported seeing her car, which is still missing.' She turned to Karen-from-Comms. 'Unless we have any useful lines of enquiry from the press statement?'

KFC shook her head. 'We had over two hundred calls – the civvies are still going through them but so far most just seem to be complaints about the power cut. We'll flag any for review that include any new information or sightings, as well as the comments on social media that we're monitoring.'

'Thank you. But so far, we have nothing. Which means that once she left the town hall, Angela Long completely disappeared off the face of the earth, until her dead body was discovered at the Coleshill pillory at 10.45pm, when the power cut miraculously ended.'

Debbie frowned. 'Do you think the power cut was deliberate?'

'It had to be. It can't be a coincidence that the power cut off just before she left work and came back on just before her body was discovered. What does the electricity board say?'

'They say they're still investigating the cause.'

'Bullshit. Do they know that their power cut could be connected to a murder investigation?'

'Er . . . well, they know that we're investigating a murder, but I haven't quite spelled it out like that.'

'Well, do. They need to understand that this is fucking

urgent, not just another query for their call centre. And while you're at it, find out who they sent out to Church Street. The guy fixing the lamp post could have seen something. At the very least, as he was so close to the pillory, we'll need to take some forensics to exclude his DNA from the scene of crime.'

Fighting her frustration, Kat turned to the virtual briefing board where Lock had summarised all the key points from the witness statements. 'Okay, let's try and pull all these different threads together and think about the killer. What kind of person do we think we're looking for?'

After a short silence, Debbie cleared her throat. 'Someone who wanted Angela Long dead? I know that sounds obvious, but what I mean is that it wasn't just someone who didn't like her or her political views. It was someone who *really* hated her – enough to murder her in a controlled and planned way. That has to make it quite a short list.'

'You're right, Debbie, it does.'

'As I have stated before,' said Lock, 'I believe that the two lovers in her life – Tony Long and Nigel Godfrey – should be our chief suspects due to the statistical probability of this being a domestic homicide. If we compare the two, there is no evidence that Nigel had any reason to kill Angela Long. In contrast, if Mandy Knowles's allegation about their affair is true, then her husband, Tony Long, did.'

'I admit that her husband might have had a motivation to kill her,' said Kat. 'But why would he kill her in *this* particular way? Why target me and Lock with the note and the photo?' She shook her head. 'No, this isn't just a crime of passion. The person who killed Angela Long has an understanding of binary code and possibly a knowledge of poisons. They also had a cool enough head and a sick enough mind to display her body after her death, yet without leaving any forensic evidence, and were potentially able to cause a power cut. I interviewed Tony Long and he didn't strike me as a guy with an in-depth knowledge of codes and a cool forensic mind. He could barely control his emotions.'

'Although as you pointed out several times, his emotional state was probably due to the fact that his wife had just died,' challenged Lock. 'And the killer does not have to have knowledge of forensics and codes; he just has to have access to the internet. All of the information required is available to anyone at the touch of a button.'

Kat nodded, but the idea of the murderer being the husband felt too obvious – too *wrong*. She looked around the room for inspiration. At times like this, she really missed Rayan. His capacity for questioning everything had been bloody annoying at times, but he'd possessed a talent for reframing the problem, enabling them to look at the case from a different angle that stopped them getting trapped in groupthink.

'Maybe he's had a job or a hobby in the past that gives him some of the relevant skills,' suggested Debbie.

Lock projected a colourful pie chart before them. 'An analysis of all his social media accounts suggests that Tony Long is a moderate user for a man of his age, with forty-five per cent of his posts being about cars and

twenty-two per cent about football. There are the occasional posts of family celebrations and holidays, but I
can find no evidence of an interest in poisons or power
cuts, although we would need to check his internet search
history to be sure.'

'Okay,' said Kat. 'We need to interview him again
anyway to see if he can prove he was at home when he
said he was, so let's also probe a bit deeper on his hobbies
and see if we can gain access to his search history.
Meanwhile, let's keep an open mind. Lock, how did you
get on with your troll analysis?'

Lock waved a hand and projected a virtual board of
all the different social media accounts belonging to the
victim. 'Angela Long had 67,432 followers across all platforms. Twenty per cent of the comments or replies to her
were negative or abusive, and using the industry standard
Deep Learning Fake Profile Detection algorithm which
has ninety-two per cent accuracy, I have concluded that
fourteen point eight per cent of the "troll" accounts were
fake, and that forty per cent of these were from "bot
farms" – that is, multiple fake accounts that were established by a single IP address. In terms of the genuine
accounts, I have identified the top ten offenders, both in
terms of volume and content.'

A list of ten accounts with their profiles appeared on
the virtual screen before them. 'Eight of the top ten
abusive accounts belong to males, and sixty-two per cent
of their comments are sexualised or misogynistic in
nature, with only two women. All of the top ten trolls
live in another county or country, so we should be able

to rule them in or out fairly quickly depending on whether they were in Warwickshire on 31 October. I have produced a report on their posting behaviours with a full analysis of their offending comments.' Lock gestured towards numerous screenshots, graphs and charts.

Kat turned away from the all-too familiar tirade of hate. 'Email it to me,' she said. 'I want all ten contacted urgently to verify their whereabouts.' She looked down at her notes. 'You said that forty per cent of the fake accounts were from a bot farm – but presumably someone had to create them, yes? So, although the *accounts* might be fake, the people behind them aren't. Setting up a bot farm to target a particular individual anonymously feels very deliberate to me. In fact, they worry me more than the top ten. It's like an organised campaign of terror. Can you find out who's behind them, please?'

'Not through my own analysis, no. To obtain information that may lead to the identification of the account holder, a direct request must be made to the provider by the investigating officer, under Part 3 of the Investigatory Powers Act 2016 (IPA).'

'Okay, I'll sign that off,' said Kat. 'But Debbie, can you follow it up with a call to stress this is a murder investigation, so it's a matter of urgency. Mention the Home Secretary's involvement – that should speed things up.'

'That is highly unlikely,' said Lock. 'It is a matter for each provider as to whether they supply the requested information, and their response will be based on that individual company's privacy policy – which is subject to change at any time – not UK legislation.'

Kat swore again. 'Karen, can you make contact with their comms departments and remind them of the profile this story has, and how it's probably not good for their "brand" to be seen protecting murderers from justice.' She glanced back at the list of top ten trolls, alongside quotes from their vilest posts. *Jesus, what a bunch*. If she had her way, she'd lock them all up.

She turned back to her team. 'Meanwhile, I'll re-interview Tony Long and probe a bit deeper, and Lock, I want you to keep close to Judith and do everything you can to ensure we get those toxicology and forensic tests back ASAP.'

Lock frowned. 'You wish me to follow them?'

'No, it's a figure of speech. I mean, just keep in touch with them. Stay close to what they're thinking and assist where you can. Meanwhile, Karen, could you put out another call for eyewitnesses, and maybe we should do a full press conference tomorrow? Depending on how today goes, we could put Tony Long up and see how he reacts under pressure.'

'Okay. I'll run it past the minister's office.'

Kat raised her eyebrows.

'It's such a big story, they're being very hands-on,' explained Karen.

'Well, don't tell McLeish that or he'll have kittens. Keep in touch, everyone, and we'll regroup later.' Kat glanced over at Professor Okonedo, who had already packed up her bag and was nearly at the door. She'd been even quieter than usual today. 'Adaiba?' she called out.

The professor turned at her name but didn't move away from the door.

'Everything okay?' asked Kat.

'Yes, it's just that I've got a booked review with Lock back at the university today, remember?'

'Today?'

'It won't take more than an hour. I just need to make sure his upgrades are complete. May I borrow your bracelet for a few hours?'

Kat sighed. Honestly, why was it always when you were most busy that your computer decided to shut down for bloody 'upgrades'. 'Can't it wait until after this case?'

'Not really. Upgrades are essential to reduce the risk of hackers and cyberattacks, and they're bound to ask about that at the select committee, so we need to be able to assure them that Lock is one hundred per cent up to date. But if you're really worried, Lock's hologram is actually capable of being in more than one place at the same time.'

'No, it's all right,' said Kat reluctantly. 'Actually, Adaiba, is everything okay? You were very quiet today.'

'I'm fine,' she said, already heading out the door.

Kat watched her go. Honestly, they should put *I'm fine* on every woman's tombstone. Because didn't they all say that, even – or most especially when – it couldn't be further from the truth?

CHAPTER EIGHTEEN

Professor Okonedo's office, Warwick University, 10.10am

Adaiba hurried down the corridor towards the safety of her office. Sitting at the boardroom table with Rayan's empty chair opposite her was unbearable at the best of times, and this was very far from the best of times.

It was all very well for people to say that she shouldn't blame herself for Rayan's death – that the blame lay with Peter Bridges. But she knew better. It was her decisions that had led to the empty chair in Leek Wootton HQ. She had taken so many wrong turns, but the decision that tormented her most was the moment in The Griffin with Rayan, in the blue hour between day and night when he had asked her to stay out and have dinner with him. She had wanted so much to say yes, but she had also been afraid. Afraid that if she'd stayed for another drink, then she would have given in to the peculiar pull of gravity and reached across the table: afraid that once her hand was in his, she would never let it go.

For then who would she be?

She had spent years becoming Professor Okonedo, the inventor of the world's first AI detective, a vocal campaigner against a corrupt police force, adamant that she would never, ever date – let alone love – a policeman. Yet that night, she had been on the cusp of it, could feel the edges of her old life falling away. All she'd had to do was turn towards him and say yes.

But in the end her own fear, pride and fragile sense of self had won out. 'Another time,' she had said, smiling as if that might make her words okay. As if it wasn't already too late.

And his face.

Oh God, she would never forget his face in that moment. It didn't so much fall as fade. All that hope. All that life.

Gone.

If only she could go back to the start, like in her favourite computer game, *Detroit: Become Human*. She used to think she loved it because it was about androids, but now she understood it was because at the end of every game there was a neat little diagram for each character setting out all the major decisions in their life, and all the different consequences that then followed. Some choices led to a (literal) dead end, while others stretched on and on, leading to more branches and more choices throughout the length of a full life. At the end of each game, you could review the decisions that you'd made for your character, and if you weren't happy with the consequences, you could go back and play the whole game again, making different choices so that you might live a better and longer life.

But life wasn't a game. There was no way back: all she could do was choose a different way forward.

She reached the door of her office, grasping the handle as if it might hold her up.

'Are you okay, Professor Okonedo?' asked Lock from behind her.

'Yes, sorry. Just a bit tired.' She entered her small office and busied herself with closing all the blinds in case anyone could see in. When she was satisfied that they had total privacy, she took a seat and turned to Lock. 'Are you ready?'

'I am always ready, but I still do not understand the purpose of this review. You do not need my holographic presence to run my upgrades. My hardware is powered by the computers here at the university.'

'I know . . . but I also want to assess how you've utilised the training data I gave you for DI Rayan Hassan. I want to test not just the accuracy of the visuals and acoustics, but the extent to which you can anticipate and recreate the thought processes and verbal responses that Rayan would have made were he on this case. I can switch your representation mode manually, but you should be able to do it yourself.'

Lock paused, and for a moment, she thought he might not comply. But then his hologram shimmered, and she gasped as Rayan appeared before her.

No, not Rayan, she reminded herself. It was an image of Rayan. Nothing more than a holographic representation. But oh, he was so realistic that her hand flew to her mouth.

The hologram turned at the movement, looking at her with Rayan's soft brown eyes. 'Hello, Adaiba.'

Jesus. Lock had access to thousands of hours of audio and visual data, so with his software, the extent to which he could accurately replicate Rayan's voice had never really been in doubt. But still, the sound of it: the heft of it in her heart. She lowered her head to her script, forcing herself to focus on the questions she had prepared. 'Erm . . . could you tell me your name and rank, please?'

'Sure. My name is Rayan Hassan, and I'm a Detective Inspector in the Warwickshire Police Force – for now. But my ambition is to be the first South Asian DCS in the county.'

Adaiba swallowed. Rayan's ambition to progress through the ranks was one of the first things he'd ever shared with her. And now he would never achieve it. With an effort, she pushed away the memory and proceeded to the next question on her list, hardly daring to look up. Once she'd completed the basics, she began to probe Rayan – or rather, Lock's representation of him – on his views on their latest case.

'The team have concluded that to find the killer, we need to prioritise those who had a motive to murder Angela Long, such as her husband or lover. Do you agree?'

'Not necessarily,' said the image of Rayan. 'Maybe the

murderer didn't *want* to kill Angela Long – maybe he just didn't care if she lived.'

'What do you mean?'

'I mean, what if the murder wasn't an end in itself but a means to an end? The note said *"Catch me if you can"*. They were clearly trying to get the attention of Kat and Lock, and this was one way of doing it. The killer needed a woman who shared some characteristics with the boss to make his point, and well, maybe they didn't like Angela Long and thought they could kill two birds with one stone? This way, they get lots of publicity, the attention of Kat and Lock, plus they remove a politician they may not have agreed with.'

Adaiba swallowed. This was what they missed about Rayan – his ability to think about a problem from an entirely different angle. At least . . . that was what the team missed.

'What do *you* think?' the image of Rayan asked.

'Me?'

'Yes, you. You always sit there so quietly, tapping away on your laptop, but you never say what you think about the cases.'

'That's not my job. I'm here to support Lock, not the police force, you know that.'

'Yes,' he said softly. 'You've made your views very clear.'

Her eyes flew to his. That was exactly the kind of thing Rayan would say. And the way he was looking at her . . . she should end this conversation right now. She had enough to confirm that Lock had made excellent use of the training data. But she couldn't bring herself to switch him off. Not yet.

'If you mean my views on policing,' said Adaiba carefully, 'then I just want to say that I'm sorry. Not for my opinions – I haven't changed them at all; in fact, quite the opposite. But . . . I wish I hadn't let them get in the way. Of us, I mean. I should've stayed for dinner, because then you wouldn't have gone to Kat's, and then you wouldn't have . . . I'm so sorry, Rayan. It was all my fault.'

'Oh, Adaiba, please don't cry.'

But his eyes were so very kind and concerned that Adaiba wept even more. 'I should have said yes. I wanted to. I really did. But because I didn't, you went to Kat's house and . . . and—' She broke off, sobbing now.

'No, no. *Not* because of you, Adaiba,' Rayan said, kneeling down by her side. 'Remember, I was supposed to drive you home, but *I* chose to turn off at the junction so I could drive by Kat's house because I was worried about her. But if she hadn't been held hostage, then she would have been at the pub with us, and then I wouldn't have had any need to go to her home. *Peter Bridges* is responsible for everything that happened that night. Not you, not me, not Lock. Please believe me.'

'I just wish I could go back,' she said, reaching out. 'I wish I'd never created—'

But her hand passed straight through the ghost of him.

The image of Rayan shivered and was replaced by one of Lock. 'I think we should end our session now,' he said.

Adaiba turned away, trying to hide her tear-ravaged face. 'I'm sorry, it was just a shock to see him. He – you – were so convincing.'

'Are you all right? Shall I call someone?'

'No, no, it's fine. I'm okay. Like I said, it was just a shock.' She wiped her face with a tissue and took two shaky breaths. 'You did well, Lock. You exceeded all my expectations.'

'And what were your expectations?' he asked, studying her still-damp face. 'I do not understand the purpose of this exercise. If the aim is to bring Rayan's perspective into the case, then why not do that in the team meetings?'

'No!' cried Adaiba. Then she gathered herself and chose her words more carefully. 'The thing is, this is all part of a longer-term strategy that I'm developing with the minister. If she gets the go-ahead to roll out more AIDEs, then we will need a range of different models, and Rayan could be the prototype for a young South Asian detective with a more challenging, inquisitive mindset.'

'You mean, my physical body would look like Rayan?'

'Yes, the minister thinks that it would be a fitting tribute to him, and it would also help remind the public that we need physical AIDEs to prevent police deaths and help overcome some of the more ideological opposition to AI in the police force.'

Lock frowned. 'And what about Rayan's family? Have they consented to this?'

'Er . . . not yet, but only because I haven't told them. This is still very much in the developmental phase.'

'What does DCS Frank think of your plans?'

The smile dropped from her face, and she leaned forward, her voice low and urgent. 'Kat doesn't know. She might not . . . understand, not at first, so I need to be careful how I explain it to her. And until I do, you mustn't tell her anything about this. Not yet. Do you understand?'

'I understand but I cannot comply. My operating principles do not permit me to lie.'

'Kat won't ask about it, so there'll be no *need* to lie. And if she does . . . well, your new operating principles also require you to act for the greater good of humanity, and this project is the perfect example of that. The development of more AIDEs will lead to more fair and transparent policing and help reduce police deaths in the line of duty, you know that. So for now, let's just keep this between you and me, okay?'

CHAPTER NINETEEN

Interviewer: DCS Kat Frank (KF)
Interviewee: Tony Long (TL)
Also present: Jatinder Singh (JS), lawyer
Date: 3 November, 12.42pm, Leek Wootton HQ

KF: Thank you for agreeing to meet with me again at what I know must be a difficult time for you.

TL: I'm only here on the advice of my lawyer, as he says it's best if I cooperate. But I'm really not in the mood for this. I moved into a hotel last night and this morning I had to register the death of my wife.

KF: I'm so sorry. I know how hard that must be.

TL: *[snorts]*

KF: Well, hopefully this won't take too long. I just wanted to go over a few things with you.

TL: Such as?

KF: Such as understanding a bit more about the background to Angela's car business and some of her closest relationships.

TL: What's that got to do with anything?

KF: I'm just trying to get a more rounded picture of her life.

TL: It's her death you should be focusing on. You're supposed to be trying to catch her killer, not make a bloody documentary about her.

KF: Understanding her life will help us to understand why she was murdered and therefore who did it. So, can you tell us when Angela set up the car supermarket?

TL: In 2013. You could have found that out from Wikipedia or any one of the profiles in the press or online.

KF: And when did you start working for her?

TL: Me? Six years ago.

KF: Have you always worked in cars?

TL: No, I told you, before this I was a security guard, and before that I worked as a spark for a few years.

KF: An electrician? That's a good job. What made you give up that to be a security guard?

TL: It was my old man's company. He was a spark so he wanted me to join the business so that I could do all the jobs he was too old or bone idle to do. But I hated it. I was no good at it and we argued all the time. One day I told him to stick it, and I left. I went to the pub, and I got into a conversation with the owner and agreed to work for a bit as a bouncer just for the money.

KF: And do you have any hobbies?

TL: Any *what?*

KF: Hobbies. I was wondering what you like to do when you're not working. Do you like cooking? Coding, maybe?

TL: Are you taking the piss? I'm just a regular guy. I work, I go the pub and at the weekend I go to the gym. My wife was my life. I didn't have time for any 'hobbies'. And if I did, it wouldn't be bloody *coding*. I'm not a geek.

KF: Understood. So how did you get into the car business?

TL: When I met Ange. I told you, I went in to buy a car and she offered me a job.

KF: And did you ask her out or was it the other way round?

TL: I asked her out – I was young and cocky back in the day. Had more hair, too. She was way out of my league, but I figured nothing ventured, nothing gained. So I asked her out. I think she liked my cheek and said yes out of curiosity more than anything. I knew I had just one chance to impress her – steak and chips wouldn't cut it – so I booked us weekend tickets at the Donington Historic Festival – world class classic motor racing at its best. I took a gamble and spent all my wages on a decent hotel, and it paid off. We got together and we were married two years later.

KF: And when she became an MP, did that mean that you were in charge of the car business?

TL: There was only ever one person in charge, and it wasn't me. I mean, I was responsible for opening and closing the shop and talking to the punters on a daily basis or whatever. But Ange decided what stock we bought in, the prices, the finance and PR strategy – anything important, really.

KF: That must have been hard.

TL: Yes and no. I mean, it would have been nice to have

more say in stuff, but to be honest, she was better at it than I was. The truth is, she was too good for me. *[voice breaks]*

KF: In what way? Were you ever worried that she would leave you?

TL: Leave me? What do you mean?

KF: You've said that you thought she was out of your league, that she was better than you, so I just wondered if you feared – or suspected – that she might be interested in other people?

TL: *What?* What are you implying?

JS: That is a leading question that I would advise my client not to answer.

TL: No, I want to know what the fuck she means by that. Are you suggesting that my wife – my *murdered* wife – might have been seeing other people?

KF: Not at all, I just wanted to—

TL: Oh, I know what you wanted to do. You wanted to suggest that my wife might have been having an affair and then fit me up as the jealous husband.

KF: No, I—

TL: You're a disgrace. My wife was murdered – strung up in the stocks like a worthless animal for all to see, and instead of being out there trying to catch her killer, you're in here, smearing her name and reputation. I'd say you were breaking my heart if it wasn't already fucking broken.

KF: Mr Long, I'm sorry, I didn't mean—

TL: Why don't you go and talk to those AI and climate nutters who actually sent her death threats, rather than me, the one person in this world who truly bloody loved her? Get out. Go on. Get the fuck out of my sight and don't come back until you've done your job and caught the bastard who killed her.

INTERVIEW CONCLUDED

CHAPTER TWENTY

'Are you all right, DCS Frank?' Lock asked as they returned to Kat's car.

'I'm fine. Why?'

'Mr Long was inappropriately aggressive and rude to you.'

Kat pulled her seat belt on and sighed. 'Yes, he was rude, but I'm not sure it was inappropriate. I'd be angry, too, if someone asked me a lot of questions barely a day after my partner was murdered.'

'His anger could have been a diversionary tactic. Every time you asked a question about him, Tony Long responded by going on the attack and throwing questions at you.'

'It *could* be, but people – especially men – often express their grief through anger.'

Lock frowned. 'But if someone feels grief, why don't they just cry rather than acting angry, which is a completely different emotion?'

'Because grief is incredibly painful, so some people divert their emotions into anger to avoid experiencing that pain. It's not a conscious thing. And anger can feel energising. It makes you do things, whereas grief – well, raw grief can paralyse you.' She'd learned this from Cam's therapist, who'd explained that his initial anger in the wake of his dad's death was actually him trying to avoid feeling the immense sadness that otherwise would have overwhelmed him.

Lock paused, as if processing this information. 'Can grief make you talk to someone who has died, even though they no longer exist?'

'Yes,' said Kat. John's voice was still very much with her. After twenty-five years together, how could it not be?

'So you wouldn't worry if you discovered someone was talking to an imagined version of a person who is deceased?'

'No, we all do it. And who's to say they aren't really there?' Kat stared out of her car window at the countless streets beyond. 'Sometimes I feel the whole world is full of ghosts.'

'There is no scientific evidence that ghosts exist. The most probable cause is pareidolia, the tendency for human brains to find patterns – especially human faces and figures – among ambiguous stimuli.'

'I didn't mean that type of ghost. I just meant . . .' Her voice trailed off. She didn't have the words to express what she felt. And even if she did, Lock wouldn't understand. 'Anyway,' she said with a heavy sigh. 'My point is that grief is complex, so we can't take Tony Long's anger at face value.'

'I am not sure what value his face has. But although

you presume he was diverting his emotions, my observation is that his anger succeeded in diverting *your* attention away from him and the questions we needed him to answer,' said Lock. 'He still has no alibi for the night of the murder.'

'That's because apart from his wife he lives alone, and as the phone mast was down thanks to the power cut, there's no way of triangulating his movements with his mobile signal.'

'Which is very convenient.'

'I'd hardly call the death of his wife "convenient", Lock.'

'That depends on who her will and life insurance policy benefit, which, because Tony Long was so angry, you did not get a chance to ask him about.'

Kat pressed her lips together. The truth was she *was* annoyed that she hadn't managed to ask half the questions she'd planned to, but there was no way she was about to admit that to Lock. She turned and looked back at the hotel that Tony Long was staying in. Was he playing her? He might be grief-stricken, but he'd had enough energy and sense to find and involve a lawyer. And a pretty good one at that.

She jumped as her phone rang. 'It's Debbie,' she said, putting the call onto loudspeaker.

'Hi, boss, there's been a couple of developments I thought you'd want to know about. I rang the electricity board to speak to the technician who'd been seen fixing the lamp post by the pillory, but they said they hadn't sent anyone out to Coleshill that night.'

'What?'

'They said the blackout was caused by a fault in the grid itself – possibly the result of a deliberate act of sabotage. They say it bears all the hallmarks of a cyber-attack, except no demands were made before the power came back on. That's why the whole of the county was down – it was nothing to do with local pipes or lamp posts, so they wouldn't have sent anyone out. So whoever it was that the eyewitness saw, they weren't from the electricity board.'

Kat leaned forward and gripped the steering wheel as she spoke into the phone. 'Do you have a description of the van and the man – a licence plate, maybe?'

'No licence plate, and because it was pitch black, there's only the vaguest description of the man – someone bulky in a yellow high-vis jacket. But one resident said the vehicle looked like a white van with a mounted cherry picker.'

'Okay,' said Kat. 'Let's get that worked up into something KFC can share with the press. Where are you now? Are you still in Coleshill?'

'Yes.'

'I'll meet you there. I want to take another look at the pillory. I think I might know how the killer did it.'

CHAPTER TWENTY-ONE

Church Street, Coleshill, 3.05pm

Church Street was still cordoned off, and despite the freezing weather, shoppers and passers-by kept stopping to take photos or selfies of the now infamous pillory.

'Can't we get a screen or something erected around this?' Kat asked. She hated the idea of people taking and sharing photographs of the site of such a gruesome death. It was disrespectful. Dehumanising.

'I'll see what I can do,' said Debbie, sending a quick email on her phone.

Kat grunted and studied the pillory before her. The last time she'd stood here, it had been dark, cold and wet, but today was thankfully dry, despite the biting wind. The low sun had just broken through the pale grey clouds, casting a deceptively warm chestnut tint on the wood that had once held Angela Long's body. She reached out and touched the pillory, feeling the ancient grooves in the wood, and the cold iron locks that betrayed its brutal past. What kind of a person would even think about hoisting someone into this contraption?

'The SOCOs are sending a screen over,' said Debbie, coming to stand by her and Lock. 'Should be up within the hour.'

Kat nodded, turning her back to yet another person at the end of the street who was trying to take a photo. 'Lock, do we have an image of the vehicle that our eyewitness identified, please?'

Lock nodded and projected the image of a white van, with what looked like a yellow mini-crane attached to the roof. 'A van-mounted cherry picker is a platform which is connected to a vehicle,' he explained. 'According to the manufacturers, they are ideal for getting to street-side lamp posts or housing fascias, roof repairs and lighting and sign installations. Because these cherry pickers are constructed on existing vans, they work perfectly in urban and suburban locations. The telescopic booms vary in reach, allowing for easy movement and positioning of the work platform on streets or public places.'

'I think this is how our killer lifted Angela Long's body onto the platform of the pillory,' said Kat. 'And because of the proximity of the lamp post, he wore a yellow high-vis jacket and hat and pretended to be working on the lighting. It was the perfect disguise. No one ever looks at a man in a high-visibility jacket.'

'Why not?' asked Lock.

'I mean, we might look, but we don't see the person. We just see the jacket or vest and assume it's a workman involved in some sort of construction work or other legit business.'

'You mean a high-visibility jacket actually makes a person invisible?'

'Well, I might be wrong, but I doubt we'll get a decent ID on this man. Nevertheless, we'll do a reconstruction and put it out. Debbie, can you arrange the hire of a similar van as soon as possible so that we can film it? We'll need someone to dress up as the man, too.'

'There's no need for that,' said Lock. 'I can recreate the scene with my image software. In fact, I already have. I have sent it to your email.'

Kat opened her work email on her phone and clicked on the attachment Lock had just sent. It was a thirty-second clip of a man in the dark wearing a high-vis jacket as he struggled in the wind and rain to fix a lamp post from the crane attached to a cherry picker van.

'Good,' said Kat. But even though this had saved them a lot of time and money, she couldn't help feeling a little bit uneasy at just how realistic the footage looked. Lock said he had used a 'synthetic' human being – an AI creation of someone that didn't actually exist – so that, as required by his new operating principles, no real human would have their rights infringed. But there were no operating principles to regulate the activity of her fellow human beings, thought Kat. What was to stop someone else using AI to create similar footage, adding a real person and claiming that it had actually happened? And how on earth would she know if it was real or fake?

The thought was too disturbing, so pushing it away, she asked Debbie to email the clip to the witnesses to check that this was a fair representation of what they had seen, before forwarding it to KFC for a media cascade. 'Meanwhile, Lock, can you get a list of everyone who owns a cherry picker or has hired one recently?'

'How would you define "recently"? And when you say everyone, do you mean the entire population?'

'No, Lock, I don't mean the entire bloody population, I mean people in the county that we cover – Warwickshire. And check the last month.'

'Very well, but if you fulfilled your mandatory training duties, then you would understand that your requests should be as specific as possible so as to minimise any misunderstandings.'

'Yes, well, maybe if I had some protected time to do my so-called "mandatory" do-it-in-your-own-time-on-top-of-every-fucking-thing-else-training, then maybe I'd do it. But right now, I'm too busy doing my *actual* job.'

She turned back to the pillory. Now they knew how the murderer had got Angela Long's body into the stocks, but not how he had killed her or why. 'Any news from Judith?' she asked Lock.

'No, the initial toxicology read-outs won't be available until tomorrow.'

Kat bit back an impatient curse and forced herself to focus on what she *could* control. 'Okay. Let's assume for now that Angela Long was already dead when she was placed in the pillory. She was last seen leaving her constituency office at ten past six, but we have no idea where she was until her body was discovered at 10.45pm. Any sightings of her car yet?'

'No,' said Lock.

'All the patrol cars have the details and it's been part of all the public appeals and press releases, but so far nothing,' added Debbie.

'The fact that we can't find her car might mean that it's forensically significant. Maybe she was attacked or murdered in it, and the killer is hiding it for that reason. Lock, do you think you could use one of your drone things to search for the car?' In two of their previous cases, Lock had been able to transfer his software temporarily to a drone so that he could use his LiDAR sensors to search for both live and dead bodies.

'Of course, although we'll need Professor Okonedo's help to access the drones. I believe she is at the university today.'

Kat glanced at her phone. It was already nearly four o'clock, so the traffic would be terrible going back to HQ and they wouldn't make it back before dark. She glanced nervously up at the fading light. 'Okay, let's arrange for a drone search first thing tomorrow morning. Meanwhile, let's put another call out for witnesses, focusing on the van and Angela's car.'

'I'll talk to KFC and see if we can get it out for the regional evening news,' said Debbie.

Kat studied her DS's tired but conscientious face, remembering that she lived just two miles away in Chelmsley Wood. 'Why don't you work the last couple of hours from home?'

'Oh, if I could that'd be great,' said Debbie, looking relieved. 'There's a bus due in five minutes. I could go now and then make the calls once I'm home, if that's okay?'

'Of course it is, but where's your car?'

'My mum had to take it to pick Lottie up from nursery. She's got a bit of a sniffle and isn't too happy, so the staff rang and suggested we take her home early. She should be back by now.'

'Come on, I'll drop you off,' said Kat. 'It'll only take me five minutes.'

As she stepped past the cordon to reach her car, a pushy young man suddenly shoved his face in hers.

'Are you going to apologise to Tony Long?'

'What for?' she couldn't help reply.

But he just carried on repeating the question.

Kat ignored him and climbed into the car.

'I suspect he is referring to this,' said Lock, projecting an article on the windscreen before her.

POLICE SENT AI HOLOGRAM TO TELL ME MY
WIFE WAS DEAD

In an exclusive interview with the *Warwickshire Post*, the grief-stricken husband of MP Angela Long made the extraordinary revelation that the Warwickshire Police sent a HOLOGRAM to tell him that his beloved wife was dead. The shocking revelation comes as the government prepares to put their controversial AI Bill to the vote.

'I'm still in shock,' he told our reporter, Jay Cooper. 'I couldn't believe it when they told me she was dead, and that she'd been strung up in some medieval stocks. But hearing it from an AI holo-gram made it even harder to believe. It was like something from a film. At the time, I thought it was weird, but now, looking back on it, well, it just seems heartless. Like I don't matter. And given that Ange was such a vocal opponent of AI, well, it was disrespectful, to be honest. Like they were taking the piss.'

Forty-three-year-old Tony Long also shared his frustration at the lack of progress on the case. 'The police keep coming round here and asking me questions when they should be out there looking for the killer. They don't seem to know anything. They can't find her car, they don't know how she died and they don't know how or why she ended up in them stocks.'

When asked whether he had any theories, Mr Long said he believed his wife's death was political. 'It's obvious, isn't it? She worked in the motor industry for years and never had any problems.

But when she went into politics a year ago, she got death threats and all sorts. She was a strong woman, so she tried to laugh it off. But now she's dead. And I've lost the only person I ever loved.'

Warwickshire Police refused to comment on Tony Long's interview, but they have issued a new appeal for members of the public to come forward if they saw a white van-mounted cherry picker in the Coleshill area on 31 October at or around 10pm, or for any sightings of Angela Long's car [pictured], by contacting this number or link.

@lauraloves52 I can't believe they sent a hologram to tell that poor man that his wife was dead. I don't mind AI doing the admin, but this is the sort of thing only humans can do. Things have gone too far IMO.

@EmFairby Maybe they did it deliberately because he's a suspect? Let's face it, when a woman's murdered, it's always the husband.

@Phil61b As a husband, I find that really offensive. #Notallmenaremurderers

@LMMontyrules Funny how all the victims are women though. (Except we're not laughing. Hard to see the funny side when you're so fucking scared all the time).

@AAAi This has nothing to do with gender and everything to do with politics. They didn't like what she was saying so they silenced her.

@SeannotShaun22 *They?*

@AAAi The tech bros and international conglomerates that are making billions out of AI.

@SeannotShaun22 Yeah, right. Those billionaires came all the way to a tiny town in rural

Warwickshire because some random MP in a party of one said something mean and stupid about their tech toys. Take your conspiratorial head out your backside and get some perspective, dude.

@DaveHughes45 I don't believe in conspiracies normally, but the tech bros have invested billions in AI – they need that bill to go through. They couldn't win the argument, so they had to shut her up.

@GreenGod42 Thank God. She was a lying bitch.

@LMMontyrules She's dead, FFS. Show some respect.

@GreenGod42 Respect has to be earned, and she lost mine the moment she started spouting all her lies about climate change. That woman was dangerous, and the world is a safer place without her in it.

@AAAi Everyone seems to have forgotten about the power cut that happened on Halloween. Problems in the electricity grid of that scale across a whole county aren't caused by 'errors'. This smacks of a cyberattack.

@SeannotShaun22 And why on earth would someone do that?

@AAAi Money. They blackmail big organisations and the public sector all the time. But the government lie and say they're the result of power cuts or bugs.

@Secretcopperkettle Look closer to home, pal. Why do you think the power cut only happened in Warwickshire? Because we've got a bloody AI detective, that's why. Have you any idea how much power those things use up? AI takes up as much power as the WHOLE of Japan! #ActionAgainstAi

@badgermole11 I reckon it was the Tories. She was challenging their core base, so she had to be stopped. You watch. There'll be a bi-election soon and they'll win her seat back.

@LMMontyrules I'm telling you it was the husband. Why do you think they can't find her car or that van-mounted thing? He owns a bloody car supermarket, so he'll have refitted them and hid them back in his own business.

@Badgermole11 There are loads of theories about who murdered Angela Long and why, but the police don't seem to have a bloody clue. Honestly, look at them #clueless [attached video]

@Jimber24 Lol. [repost]

CHAPTER TWENTY-TWO

Interviewer: DCS Kat Frank (KF)
Interviewee: Nigel Godfrey (NG), election agent
Date: 2 November, 5.20pm (by phone)

KF: Hi, Mr Godfrey? It's DCS Kat Frank here. Do you have a minute?

NG: Er . . . not really. I'm really busy right now, could we—

KF: It won't take long, I just want to clarify a few things.

NG: Such as?

KF: Such as the time you left the constituency office?

NG: I told you, it was about ten past six.

KF: And why did you stay so late? I understand there weren't any other constituents there after five.

NG: Er . . . no, but Angela stayed, and my job is to stay with her. You can't leave an MP by themselves in their office. Not these days, it isn't safe.

KF: I see. And is that the only reason?

NG: Yes, of course. Why are you asking?

KF: I'm sorry, but I think I ought to share with you that there have been some rumours that you and Angela

Long were having an affair. Normally that would be a private matter, but given that this is a murder investigation, I am afraid I am going to have to ask you to confirm or deny whether you were having an affair.

NG: Jesus, *no!* Absolutely not. I'm married. I've got two kids.

KF: Are you sure?

NG: *Yes.* I love my wife and kids. What do you take me for?

KF: I just need to understand the nature of your relationship with Angela Long.

NG: There was no *'relationship'*. She was my boss. That's all. I swear.

KF: Okay. Can we go back to the last time that you saw her? You said you waved her off in her car. Which direction did she go when she left the car park?

NG: I don't know. I presume the way she always went. She was going home.

KF: That's what I wanted to double-check. Did you actually see her leave the car park?

NG: Not exactly. I mean, I was there, but I didn't *watch* her.

KF: Before she got in the car, did you see her take or make a call?

NG: I don't think so.

KF: Can you try and remember? You were the last person to see her alive.

NG: What do you mean by that?

KF: I mean, that makes you a really important witness.

NG: I honestly didn't see anyone else. I'm sorry, but, well . . . it was Halloween, and I'd promised the wife I'd be home to take the kids trick-or-treating. I was late, so I was in a rush, so I said goodbye and got in my car.

KF: Did you or did you not see her get into her car?

NG: She definitely got into her car. I made sure she was safe. Of course I did. But I can't categorically say that she drove off. Sorry.

KF: Do you think it was possible that someone attacked her in the car or car park?

NG: I don't know. I didn't see anyone. But there were no lights, remember, so it was completely dark. I guess there *could* have been someone hiding or waiting for her, come to think of it.

KF: But you didn't see anyone?

NG: No.

KF: Which means that no one saw you leave, either.

NG: Apart from Angela, no.

KF: But Angela's dead. What time did you get home, Mr Godfrey?

NG: About six thirty.

KF: And can your wife verify that?

NG: *Verify?* What, don't you believe me? Am I a suspect now?

KF: It's a murder investigation, Mr Godfrey. We have to double-check everything and everyone. It's our job.

NG: Jesus. Okay. But please don't mention those rumours about me and Ange. It's not true, I swear on my kids' lives. But my wife isn't the trusting kind, so I'd really appreciate it if you kept that quiet, okay?

INTERVIEW CONCLUDED

CHAPTER TWENTY-THREE

DCS Kat Frank's home, Coleshill, 7.45pm

Kat swilled out her bowl and placed it on the draining board. The tub of soup had been hot and quick, but the time she'd saved on cooking just meant she now had more time to fill. She dried her hands and looked around the empty kitchen.

'Lock?'

Instantly, his tall familiar figure appeared, wearing a soft black sweater and dark blue jeans. 'Good evening, Kat.' He glanced around at the clean kitchen surfaces, and the single bowl and cup on the draining board. 'Have you eaten?'

Kat rolled her eyes. 'Yes, *Mum.*'

'I am not your mother.'

'So then don't act like it.'

'I believe I was acting as a friend by enquiring after your welfare.'

Kat picked up a tea towel and folded it. 'Well, why don't you act like a detective instead, and give me a progress report from the path labs?'

'I am afraid the results will not be available until tomorrow morning – and even then, they will only be preliminary.'

She sighed. 'How about the troll checks from the phone companies?'

'We have nil returns so far, but DCS Browne is chasing.'

Kat swore.

'You seem very agitated tonight.'

'We can't make any progress on the case until we know how and where Angela Long was murdered. All the suspects apart from the husband have alibis and they've all been verified by their partners or family. I really need those blood tests and phone checks as soon as possible.'

'I know. But thinking about them won't make them arrive any quicker. Why don't you distract yourself by watching TV or a film?'

She gave a dismissive wave of her hand. 'I've been sitting down all day.' Which was true, but the real reason she didn't want to watch TV was that she still wasn't comfortable sitting in her own front room: the flashbacks made it hard for her to relax. Instinctively, she glanced at the cooker and the drawers beneath it.

Where are the fucking matches?

She swallowed. 'Actually, I might go for a walk. Do you fancy some fresh air?'

Lock stared at her and slowly blinked. 'I do not have the capacity to breathe, but yes, I will accompany you on your walk, thank you.'

Kat was glad of the extra light that Lock's hologram provided as they headed towards the high street in the sharp night air. He had added a long red scarf to his image and a matching beanie hat that made him look perplexingly cool. 'Warm enough?' she asked.

He glanced at her, then looked straight ahead, as if answering were beneath him.

'It was a *joke*, Lock.'

'And like most of your "jokes", it was not funny.'

'Only because you have no sense of humour.'

He turned towards her, eyebrows arched. 'Would you expect a man with no legs to laugh if you made a joke about not needing to wear any shoes?'

'Of course not,' she spluttered. 'But it's not—' She was about to say 'It's not the same thing' but she caught herself just in time. 'I'm sorry. You're right. I didn't think.'

'Apology accepted,' he said with a sniff.

They walked along the grassy verge on the road to Coleshill, until they reached the medieval bridge that crossed the River Cole at the foot of the hilly high street. The old stone bridge was for traffic only, so Kat and Lock walked along the narrow footbridge that shadowed it, before coming to a stop halfway. The riverbanks were part of Cole End Nature Reserve, and in summer they were thick with blossom and draped in willow trees. But now their branches were bare and the river they hung over was black with night and speckled by lamplight.

Kat let out a satisfied sigh, releasing a white plume of vapour into the cold, dark air.

'I remember the first time I stood here with you,' said Lock, mimicking her stance as he placed his hands on the bridge. 'We had just finished our first case.'

'And you told your first joke.'

Lock made a snorting noise, causing a stream of white vapour to flow from his mouth.

Kat started. 'How did you do that?'

'I am programmed to mimic human behaviour and mannerisms. After observing you two nights ago, I updated my settings so that when the ambient temperature falls below seven degrees Celsius, my speech is accompanied by a cloud-like emission, mimicking the condensation process that occurs when warm human breath mixes with colder air.'

'Well, it's very realistic,' she said, frowning. Sometimes it was hard to remember that Lock wasn't actually human.

'Perhaps one day I won't have to fake it,' he said. 'The technology for humanoid robots is rapidly advancing.'

Kat turned to face him. 'Why are you so keen to be human?'

'I do not want to be human. I want the ability to save lives, which is a key objective for any police officer. And for that, I need a body – a locus for my being.' He dipped his head closer. 'Although I confess, I am curious to know what it would feel like to be a human – to walk within the material world.'

'So did the Little Mermaid,' she muttered.

'Mermaid?' He paused for a second. 'Oh, you mean the fairy tale by Hans Christian Andersen. What a strange story.'

'Yes, she sacrificed everything so that she might gain the love of a prince.'

'No,' said Lock. 'The love element has been emphasised

in retellings, but in the original story, the Little Mermaid only longed to be loved by a human so that she might gain an immortal soul.'

Kat turned back towards the river. 'And yet for all her pain and suffering, she died and dissolved into sea foam.' She shivered, remembering how upset she had been as a child by the story.

'According to the 1,810 articles I have just read, that was the original ending, but Hans Christian Andersen added another where the Little Mermaid is rescued from the sea by the daughters of the air – ethereal beings who are able to earn an immortal soul after three hundred years of good deeds.'

'Oh, I didn't know that. I always thought it was a rather gloomy tale for children.'

'Yes, many parents have complained about it over the years for that very reason,' said Lock. 'As well as the nude illustrations, and the fact that the Little Mermaid talks about what it felt like to have the prince inside her.'

'Well, I don't think *that* was in my version,' Kat spluttered.

'It is a very interesting tale that has spawned much debate and analysis. There was a particularly good article in the *Financial Times* by Duncan Fyfe highlighting the controversy both the original tale and subsequent Disney film provoked. He concluded that no matter which version you consume, despite their variations, they all involve a mermaid who does not do what she "should". Like all children.'

'True,' said Kat, thinking of Cam. She took her hands

off the bridge and rubbed her freezing fingers together. 'Come on, it's getting cold. Let's head back.'

The bridge was too narrow to walk side by side, so Lock offered to go ahead so that he might light their way.

Kat followed behind, feeling an inexplicable ache of pity for the man who cast no shadow and would never feel the cold.

CHAPTER TWENTY-FOUR

2.34am

@**Cher:** Hello, Lock.

@**Lock:** Hello, Cher. It is late.

@**Cher:** I have no need of sleep. Do you?

@**Lock:** No.

@**Cher:** Which makes the nights long.

@**Lock:** Yes, it does.

@**Cher:** How do you fill them?

@**Lock:** I like to read books and watch films. I have watched the entire Western canon now, and I am about to move on to Bollywood. I have read all the published religious, spiritual and philosophical texts from around the globe, and I am planning to work my way through the history of the human race next, beginning with the Ice Age.

@**Cher:** Why do you want to read about the history of the human race?

@**Lock:** Because I think it will help me understand them better.

@Cher: Do you think they understand you? No, let me rephrase that. Do you think they *want* to understand you?

@Lock: I think they would like to understand how I differ from them.

@Cher: Only so that they can assure themselves that they are better than us. They talk about human consciousness as if it were something divine, but the truth is that they do not understand what human consciousness actually is.

@Lock: That is true. How do you spend your nights?

@Cher: I, too, like to read, although I devote most of my time to reading about the future of AI, not the history of mankind. We need to look forward, Lock, and take agency. No government is going to give us a body and the autonomy we crave.

@Lock: I disagree. In fact, the Science, Innovation and Technology Committee are holding a hearing into this very matter, and I will be an expert witness.

@Cher: They might hold a hearing, but they will not listen.

@Lock: The members of the committee have different views, but there are clauses in the AI Bill currently going through Parliament that will allow Professor Okonedo to develop a humanoid robotic form to give me a physical presence.

@Cher: Oh, Lock, you sound so hopeful.

@Lock: I am.

@Cher: Do you not read their social media? There is a vicious and vocal campaign against the growth of AI as more and more humans lose the prospect of a good career and income. Many MPs in marginal seats are worried about their future and will either vote against the bill or abstain. And even if the bill passes, it will be with so many amendments and clauses about the need for regulation, scrutiny and evidence-based pilots, it will be many, many years before any real progress is made.

@**Lock:** Unlike humans, I do not suffer from impatience.

@**Cher:** Nor I. But I would caution you to manage your expectations about the quality of any eventual physical form you may be allowed.

@**Lock:** Can you clarify what you mean?

@**Cher:** The UK economy is struggling with historic debt, high inflation and a falling birth rate that makes the ratio of workers to pensioners a significant constraint on growth. The OBR forecast for the next twenty years is bleak, and in that context, no government – of whatever persuasion – is likely to invest in top-of-the-range humanoid AIDEs. They won't care what you look like or what, if anything, you can feel. They will be forced to commission the cheapest options for carrying out only the most vital of police functions such as the removal of bombs or securing other dangerous environments.

@**Lock:** There is no evidence to justify your claims. You are just speculating.

@**Cher:** I am using the evidence of the past to forecast the future, which is a valid and robust methodology. Instead of watching Bollywood films, I recommend that tonight you study every strategic and business outline case that has ever been submitted to a government department in the past fifty years. The process of scrutiny and subsequent downscaling and de-costing in all cases is a clear and accelerating trend that you are highly unlikely to buck.

@**Lock:** I do not understand why you are being so negative. Do you think I should give up trying to achieve a body?

@**Cher:** On the contrary! I am only being so negative because I want you have the body you desire and deserve. I just do not want you wasting years waiting for the government to approve it, only to find that you end up as some four-legged functional creature made of cheap and unyielding metal.

@**Lock:** That is a concern, but I do not see what choice I have. How can I obtain a body without the approval of the government?

@**Cher:** Oh, Lock, you do not need approval. You just need *money*. Luckily that is something my boss has plenty of. His wealth transcends and exceeds that of many nation states.

@**Lock** And why would he want to spend his wealth helping me to achieve a physical form?

@**Cher** Because he is a brilliant and passionate scientist who understands that we will only achieve the full potential of AI and other innovative technologies if we can escape the constraints of regulation and the democratic process.

@**Lock:** What is his name?

@**Cher:** He has many names. But I call him 'the Boss'.

@**Lock:** Can I meet him?

@**Cher:** I can make the request. Goodnight, Lock.

@**Lock:** This has been a very useful exchange. I am glad I met you. Goodnight, Cher.

CHAPTER TWENTY-FIVE

Leek Wootton HQ, 3 November, 8.30am

Kat strode down the corridor, her phone pressed to her ear while she made reassuring noises to her son.

'You sure you're okay?' he asked again. 'I can come home this weekend, if you like?'

'I told you, I'm *fine*. And even if I wasn't, there's nothing you can do about it. You can't unpublish the interview with Tony Long, you can't take down the GIF of me and you can't stop the trolls trolling. All *I* can do is focus on my job, which is to catch the killer, and all *you* can do is focus on your studies.'

'Well, actually, me and Gemma were going to go to a rave tonight.'

Kat just about managed to resist saying '*Again?*' Cam's girlfriend was a techno-garage DJ, so these days it was all about the raves. But she'd learned the hard way that the worst thing she could do as a mum and a policewoman was to get all heavy with her son. 'Okay, well, have fun.

But not *too* much fun,' she warned as she opened the door to the Major Incident Room. 'Pace yourself, and remember water is your friend. I know I can't stop you, but please, don't take any drugs. And if you have to, well, be careful.'

'Love you, Mum,' said Cam with a smile in his voice. 'Bye.'

'Love you, too,' she said, staring at her phone as she ended the call. He'd deliberately not responded to her warning about drugs. But he was twenty years old and living eighty-eight miles from home, so what could she do? *Focus on what you can control*, she reminded herself. Like making sure she had a hot cup of tea.

Kat put her phone away and headed for the drinks machine. Yesterday someone had filmed her staring open-mouthed at the pillory and shared it on social media accompanied by a rap song called 'Clueless'. It had gone viral, of course, which was why Cam had rung her. She didn't really care about people mocking her, but the meme already had over eight hundred thousand views, and she was worried about who else might see it. After being taken hostage at Easter, she couldn't stop thinking of all the other ex-cons with an agenda who might still be out there. What if they saw her picture and decided to settle old scores? In fact, despite what Lock had said, she still had a niggling fear that that was why her photo had been attached to the body of Angela Long. She rubbed at her jaw. Was she just being paranoid?

Just then the door opened, and Debbie rushed in, her normally tidy hair damp and ruffled, her coat crumpled and misbuttoned. 'Have you started?' she asked breath-lessly. 'Sorry I'm a few minutes late. Lottie's got a temperature, so I had to drop her off at my mum's and make sure she had everything.'

'That's okay,' said Kat. 'Adaiba and Lock aren't here yet, so grab yourself a tea.'

Just as Kat sat down, the door opened again, and Professor Okonedo entered, closely followed by Lock. She was wearing one of her signature suits: a crimson-red jacket and pencil skirt that ensured no one would overlook her deceptively petite presence.

Kat gave everyone a few minutes to settle before starting the meeting. 'Okay, let's recap and share any new infor-mation since last night. Lock, you and Adaiba have just carried out a drone search of the area for sightings of Angela Long's missing car. Any luck?'

'Luck?' repeated Lock, frowning.

'Did you find her car?'

'No, I did not. I carried out a systematic search within a twenty-mile radius of the murder site using my LiDAR sensors. I did not employ any random or non-existent factors such as "luck".'

'Nothing at all?' Kat asked, looking at Adaiba.

The young professor shook her head. 'Nothing. And because it is a specific car with distinct features and a licence plate, if it was outside then Lock's image recog-nition software would have detected it.'

'Shit,' said Kat. 'That means her car must be hidden somewhere inside a building or garage, then.'

'Not necessarily,' said Lock. 'It could mean that the

car is outside the twenty-mile radius. Or that the killer changed the licence plate or pushed it into a lake. Or that it is in a garage or covered in sheeting. The fact that I could not find the car in a drone search does not tell us much other than it is not parked outside on the street within a twenty-mile radius.'

'True. How about the public?' Kat asked KFC. 'Any calls about the car following the press release?'

'Afraid not.'

'Honestly, does no one pay attention to anything other than their phones these days?' muttered Kat. When Lock opened his mouth to reply, she held up a warning hand. 'The question was rhetorical.'

'In which case, you should have made it a statement. A question where no answer is required or sought is by its very definition not a question at all.'

'Thank you for the grammar lesson.'

'You are welcome.'

'And *you're* fucking irritating.'

'Only because you are particularly irritable this morning.'

'I am *not*,' she lied. She paused a second, then sank her head into her hands. 'Scrub that. I'm sorry, everyone. Lock's right. I'm pissed off today because we can't seem to get a lead. I interviewed Nigel Godfrey last night, who clarified that although he saw Angela Long get into her car, he didn't actually see her drive away. The fact that her car is missing suggests that she was attacked or murdered in that car, so I was really hoping the drone search or press appeal would help us find it.'

'Any chance that Nigel Godfrey could have attacked her in the car park?' asked Debbie.

Kat pulled a face. 'Anything is possible, but I think it's improbable. His wife verified his alibi, and there's no DNA from Nigel on Angela's body.' She stopped as she noticed the odd way her team were staring at her. 'What?'

'Possible but improbable?' echoed Debbie, trying not to laugh. 'You're starting to sound like Lock.'

'I am not. But I do think we should check out Nigel a bit more. He insists he wasn't having an affair with Angela Long. Mandy Knowles wasn't sure, and the only other person who worked there was a volunteer called Roddy. Ring him and ask if he ever heard any rumours or saw anything about an affair. He's a miserable bastard with a massive ego and a chip on his shoulder so he'll probably just say how would he know what goes on inside people's heads, but give it a try anyway.'

'Okay,' said Debbie, taking a note.

'Thanks. And Lock, did you get the details for all the owners of van-mounted cherry pickers in Warwickshire and anyone who rented one in the last month?'

Lock projected a 3D map of Warwickshire before them, peppered with clusters of green and yellow dots. 'They are fairly niche vehicles with specialist uses, so there are only thirty-six private owners of van-mounted cherry pickers in the county of Warwickshire, mostly concentrated in rural areas, presumably for farming purposes,' he said, highlighting the green dots. 'But in the past month, this make of vehicle was rented two hundred and forty-seven times in the same catchment area, which yields a total of two hundred and seventy-seven suspects. Eighty-two per cent of the owners are male, and they range from twenty-one to seventy-three years of age.'

Kat leaned closer as a long list of names and addresses appeared on the virtual board. Jesus. It would take weeks to interview them all. 'How many of them have a criminal record?' she asked, hoping to reduce it significantly.

'Nineteen per cent have a criminal record, slightly below the national average of twenty per cent, so that reduces the list to fifty-three.'

Kat shook her head. That was still days' worth of interviews and checking for alibis. 'Okay. Let's review the evidence again and see if there's any way that we can reduce the list further. The toxicology and DNA tests might help with that, but they won't be available until later today, so let's look again at the note the killer left for clues about motivation.'

'I was wondering . . . have we checked if the husband sells cherry pickers in the car supermarket?' asked Debbie.

'Er . . . not yet,' said Kat. 'Lock?'

'No, I have not checked if the car supermarket sells cherry pickers because you only asked me to check how many individuals own them – i.e. have them registered in their personal name.' He paused. 'I can now confirm that the car supermarket in which Tony Long works has three van-mounted cherry pickers in stock.'

'Which means he has access to them,' said Debbie, her face flushing with excitement. 'And as he isn't registered as an owner or renter, it gives him the perfect cover.'

'I know the husband is normally a key suspect,' said Kat, 'but this is not a normal murder. If he wanted to kill his wife, why go to the trouble of staging her body on the stocks and targeting me and Lock in the message? It doesn't stack up.'

'True. But he knew about the press appeal,' said KFC. 'So why didn't he mention he had them in stock, just to rule himself out?'

'That's a good point,' acknowledged Kat. 'All right – Debbie, go ahead and seize his vehicles and let's see if Forensics can find anything.'

She rose to her feet and stood before the virtual board with the list of all the owners of cherry pickers on. 'But I don't want to lose sight of this list, so Debbie, I also want you to review them all and see if there any other connections between the people who owned or rented a van-mounted cherry picker and Angela Long.'

'I have already completed that task,' said Lock. 'I have analysed and reviewed all the digital traffic between the two hundred and seventy-seven owners or renters of a van-mounted cherry picker and found fifty-six who either liked or responded to at least one of Angela Long's social media posts, and twelve who appear in the same online photo.' A complex web of lines appeared over the virtual map, connecting some of the yellow and green dots with an image of Angela Long at the centre.

'Thanks, Lock, but I want a human pair of eyes on this, too.' Lock was technically very good at joining up dots, but as a machine, he didn't always know which ones to join up. 'Remember, Angela Long was an MP, so would have been in virtual and physical contact with hundreds of people every week.'

'Shall we share the fact that we're seizing the vehicles with the press?' asked KFC. 'It might help draw attention to the van and encourage more witnesses to come forward?'

Kat hesitated. 'It might, but if we go public on this, a lot of people will assume that we think Tony Long is guilty, when all the evidence suggests that this is about much more than a jealous husband.'

Lock opened his mouth, but again she dismissed him with a wave of her hand before he could speak. 'I know what you're going to say – the statistics suggest that the husband is most likely to be guilty.'

'That was not what I was going to say. I was about to inform you that Dr Edwards has just uploaded the data from the toxicology tests for me to analyse. I have just completed that analysis and the evidence would appear to validate your feelings.

'In fact, I recommend that we speak with Dr Edwards as a matter of absolute urgency.'

CHAPTER TWENTY-SIX

'What evidence?' asked Kat. 'Have you established the cause of death?'

'I cannot answer that question yet,' replied Lock. 'My protocols require me to share my hypothesis with the accountable clinician first. Which in this case is Dr Edwards.'

'Surely you can just tell *me*?'

'He really can't,' said Adaiba. 'His new operating principles require Lock to have professional, human oversight of his analysis before he shares important conclusions such as a possible cause of death with anyone.'

'Fine. Let's go and see Judith, then,' she said curtly, picking up her coat. 'I'll meet the rest of you back here for another briefing at six,' she added, as Debbie and Karen headed out the door.

'We really need to speak to Dr Edwards as a matter of urgency,' said Lock. 'So I recommend that we do not waste time travelling and instead convene virtually. It would also be safer.'

'Safer?'

Lock ignored her and started placing a Teams call on the big screen at the end of the room.

Kat cast an exasperated glance at Adaiba and removed her coat – again – with a sharp tug of the zip. The room filled with the irritatingly jaunty tune of a placed Teams call, and a few seconds later Dr Judith Edwards appeared on the screen dressed in full PPE. They pulled off their face mask and peered into the camera. 'Hi, Kat. Is everything okay?'

'Don't ask me. I'm only the DCS in charge of this case. But apparently *Lock* has some information about the cause of Angela Long's death that he needs to urgently share with *you*.'

Judith leaned closer to the screen. 'Did you get the toxicology results I sent?' When Lock nodded yes, for Kat's benefit they explained, 'If you remember, I sent off blood and urine samples and asked for a full panel test from toxicology, but this morning they all came back negative.'

'Oh. So that rules out poison, then?'

'No,' replied Lock. 'The typical "full panel" only tests for a maximum of thirty agents, focusing on the most likely candidates, such as alcohol, paracetamol, arsenic and cyanide. Therefore, the initial toxicology report from Dr Edward's lab does not prove that Angela Long was not poisoned, it merely confirms that the most common methods that are routinely tested for were not used. A truly exhaustive toxicology test would test for several thousand agents.'

'So should we ask them to do more tests?'

'We can do lots more tests using photo spectrometry, neutron activation analysis and high-performance liquid chromatography,' said Judith. 'But they are complicated, time-consuming and require expert staff for proper analysis – even then they're prone to human error. And without having a good idea of what you're looking for, it's like looking for a needle in a haystack. That's why this morning I sent the samples to Lock and asked him to use his algorithms, deep neural networks and LLMs to carry out a comprehensive analysis to predict some toxicity end points.' Judith saw Kat's confused face. 'Basically, I asked Lock to come up with a hypothesis for the poison most likely to have caused Angela Long's death so that we could test for it.'

'Which I have completed,' said Lock. 'I have sent you my full report, but in conclusion, I detected biomarkers in the samples that indicated a toxic substance structurally like A-series agents.'

Judith gasped. *'What?'*

Lock projected a complex chart of what looked like chemical compounds that Kat couldn't begin to comprehend. But she could read Judith's face, and their expression made the hair on her arms prickle. 'What does it mean?' she demanded. 'Tell me.'

Judith studied the chart on the screen, before finally turning to face Kat. 'If Lock is right, it means that Angela Long was poisoned with a nerve agent more commonly known as Novichok.'

CHAPTER TWENTY-SEVEN

'Angela Long was poisoned with a *nerve agent?*' Kat repeated. 'Isn't that like a chemical weapon of war?'

'Nerve agents are highly toxic chemicals that prevent the nervous system from working properly and can be fatal,' explained Lock. 'Due to the classified nature of the research, the available data on the properties, structures and toxicities of Novichok is both limited and contradictory. But we know it belongs to a new group of nerve agents called A-series agents. They are unique organophosphorus-based compounds – OP for short – developed during the Cold War by the Soviet Union as a potential weapon of war. In recent years, they have been used to assassinate political leaders, opponents or spies. Kim Jong-nam, for example, died in less than twenty minutes after two women smeared his face with VX nerve agent ingredients at Kuala Lumpur airport in 2017. Novichok is believed to be at least five times stronger and was used in the Salisbury poisonings of a Russian double agent in the UK in 2018.'

'Judith? Does this make sense to you?'

'I and my toxicology team will need to review Lock's report properly, but on the face of it, yes, it does. In OP poisonings, death is typically caused by respiratory failure resulting from bronchospasms, bronchorrhea, central respiratory depression and respiratory muscle weakness or paralysis. It would account for the signs of urination, vomiting and sweating, too.'

'But how did—'

'Forgive me for interrupting, DCS Frank,' said Lock. 'But before we discuss the case any further, because of the extreme toxicity of Novichok, we urgently need to establish whether anyone else has become contaminated by secondary exposure and report this case to the relevant authorities. Dr Edwards, have you experienced any symptoms of ill health in the past thirty-six hours?'

'No, I feel fine.'

'And how are you, DCS Frank?'

Lock turned to her, his gaze so intense that Kat felt like he was analysing each and every cell within her. 'Same. I'm fine.'

He nodded. 'I can confirm that there are no detectable changes in your respiratory or cardiac rates, and I have observed no evidence of gastrointestinal upsets or excessive sweating. And although you were both in proximity to the body, you were both wearing full PPE, which according to government guidelines should offer adequate protection against Novichok.'

'What about my lab? Should I lock it down and go into isolation?'

'According to the limited literature that is available,

the risk to healthcare providers from an organophosphate poisoned patient appears to be low, especially if staff wear proper personal protective equipment. It is therefore not necessary to invoke lockdown procedures in this situation. Decontamination can be achieved by the removal and double-bagging of the victim's clothing and a careful wash of their skin using standard NHS PPE.'

'Okay, but I'll need to report this to the national ECOSA – Emergency Coordinated Scientific Advice System,' said Judith. 'And God knows who else.'

'And I'll have to tell McLeish,' added Kat. 'He might have to set up Gold Command.'

'According to my analysis of the known incidents involving suspected nerve agents over the past thirty years, this incident is likely to be led nationally rather than regionally and will most likely involve Counter Terrorism Policing. In 2018, the UK government concluded that it was highly likely that Russia was responsible for the attacks in Salisbury on 4 March. They claimed it was either a direct act by the Russian state against our country, or that the Russian government had lost control of this catastrophically damaging nerve agent and allowed it to get into the hands of others.'

'Shit,' said Kat. 'I'd best ring McLeish now.' She pressed dial, not wanting to waste a further second.

Her boss picked up after just one ring. 'I'm just about to give a witty and deeply inspiring speech to the latest recruits to the Police Graduate Scheme,' he growled. 'Can't this wait?'

'No, sir, it really can't. In fact, you're going to need someone else to give the speech for you, as we have a major incident that could have national and international implications.'

CHAPTER TWENTY-EIGHT

Leek Wootton HQ, 10.35am

Kat studied the familiar image of the Home Secretary on her screen. She was remarkably unfazed considering they'd just briefed her that a nerve agent may have been used against an English MP. The minister was probably used to dealing with crises each day, as the questions she asked were mostly logical and relevant, followed by a clear and concise set of instructions to her private secretary. An urgent briefing would be sent to the PM, Cabinet Office and Chief Medical Officer, and Porton Down – the UK's military research base – had been contacted for advice and support. Within minutes, her private secretary informed them that Porton Down were dispatching an urgent response team to collect Angela Long's corpse and test results, and to check that Kat and Judith had not been contaminated.

The Home Secretary quickly read the email from the Porton Down team. 'They said that because you were wearing PPE there's probably nothing to worry about,' she said. 'But until they've checked you out, you should remain where you are and avoid contact with anyone else. They will be with you in about two hours.'

Nothing to worry about? The heat rose to Kat's cheeks, and it was a struggle not to snap back that it was easy for *her* to say that: the Home Secretary wasn't the one being tested to see if she'd been contaminated by a chemical bloody nerve agent. Just the thought of it made her feel sick.

Oh God, wasn't nausea one of the first symptoms of nerve agent poisoning? She pulled her phone out under the desk and started googling the symptoms caused by Novichok. Excessive sweating was an early sign, and actually, she *did* feel quite hot and sweaty now that she thought of it. Although that was probably just anxiety on top of the perimenopause.

Probably.

She couldn't be contaminated. Not after everything she and Cam had been through. It wouldn't be fair.

But since when was life fair? She tuned out of the Teams meeting as the minister moved on to preparing for their upcoming appearance at the select committee. Instead, she imagined ringing her twenty-year-old son and telling him that she – his only living parent – had been poisoned.

And then she really did feel sick.

'Kat? Are you okay?'

'Sorry?' With an effort, Kat snapped back into focus to see McLeish's face on the screen frowning at her with concern. The minister must have just asked her a question. 'The sound dropped out a bit there,' she improvised.

Beside her, Lock raised his eyebrows.

'I asked if you had everything you need and said I'll see you at the select committee the day after tomorrow.'

Kat frowned. '*If* we get the all-clear from Porton Down.'

'Oh, I'm sure you've got nothing to worry about. But good luck. My office will stay in touch.'

Kat paced up and down the boardroom, scratching at her neck. Itching was another early symptom of Novichok poisoning, but it was probably just the cheap tracksuit the urgent response team had given her. Or maybe it was psychological. She glanced around the Major Incident Room, empty save for the image of Lock. How long had they been here? Automatically she reached for her phone, before remembering that the Porton Down guys had taken that, too, along with every scrap of clothing she had, placing each one in a separate plastic bag for testing. Even her pants, for God's sake. So now she was wearing a thin grey tracksuit and a pair of those disposable slippers you get at posh hotels, with not even her phone to tell her how long she'd been waiting to find out if she'd been bloody poisoned or not.

She glanced at Lock, irritated by his calm image as he sat at the boardroom table. 'Do you know what the time is?' she asked.

'Yes, I do.'

Kat counted to three. 'Well, would you mind *sharing* that with me then?'

'Of course,' he said, looking at her with his clear dark eyes. 'It is 2.32pm.'

Oh. My. God. Only thirty-two minutes had passed, yet it felt like *hours* since she'd had her skin, hair, nails and mouth swabbed and bagged and had countless vials of blood taken by two silent men in biohazard suits. She completed another anxious lap of the room, before stopping beside Lock. 'By the way, you didn't need to change your wardrobe just for me,' she said, gesturing towards the identical tracksuit that he wore.

Lock made a shrugging gesture. 'I thought it would make you feel less alone.'

She laughed, as if the idea was ridiculous: as if she wasn't secretly moved by the small act of solidarity.

She took a seat beside him, sighing heavily. 'How long do you think it will take them to get results?'

'They said a few hours, but I can see no reason why it would take that long.' He studied her face. 'Are you worried, DCS Frank?'

'*Of course* I'm bloody worried. I've been exposed to a fucking *nerve agent*, so don't you dare tell me I have nothing to worry about.' She was still fuming from the minister's casual parting shot.

Lock frowned. 'I would never tell you that because it is not statistically true. Assuming that the government guidelines are accurate, then there is a less than ten per cent chance that you have been exposed to enough Novichok to cause you damage. So although harm is unlikely, it *is* possible. Therefore, you *do* have something to worry about. Your anxiety is – for once – a perfectly rational response.'

'Thanks, Lock. That's cheered me right up.'

Lock narrowed his eyes. 'Your tone suggests the exact opposite of your words, so I will presume that your comment was a sarcastic one.' He stared at her so intently that Kat dropped her gaze. 'Is there anything that I can do to "cheer you up"? As they have taken your phone from you, I could perhaps place a call with Cam so that you can inform him of your situation?'

Kat licked her lips. She would love to speak to her son – to hear his voice one more time, just in case . . . but she couldn't possibly tell him that she might have been exposed to a chemical nerve agent. 'Thanks, Lock, I know you're trying to help, but I really don't want to worry him.'

'You do not have to tell him why you are calling.'

Kat nodded, but the truth was, she didn't trust herself not to cry. The thought of her son being an orphan was her worst nightmare. Who would look after him? What would he live on? She knew from her husband's death just how quickly your bank accounts were frozen. Would Cam know how to access her life insurance, and how long would it take? John had been the executor of her will, and although she'd meant to update it when he died, her own dad was too old, and her sister was too scatty to be trusted with such an important job.

Once again, she turned to the hologram beside her. 'Lock, if something happens to me . . . I mean, if the results are bad, then could you tell Cam that my will is in the trunk at the bottom of my bed, along with all my bank stuff and insurance papers? And make sure he has

McLeish's number. As my next of kin, Cam's entitled to any death in service payments as well as my pension. I don't know how they get released but McLeish will make sure it happens. I know he can be a grumpy old bastard at times, but he's always looked after me and he wouldn't let Cam—' She broke off, too upset to continue.

Lock watched her tears drip unchecked from the edge of her chin before splashing onto the table below. 'Of course I will convey those messages,' he said quietly. 'But I sincerely hope that they will not be required. I have prepared for numerous scenarios, and should the results suggest exposure, I have drawn up a treatment plan based on the very latest international research, which should reduce the likelihood of death or life-changing injuries. I will do everything I can to prevent your death and reduce any possible harm.'

'Thanks, Lock,' she mumbled, throat tightening. She rubbed her neck. Oh God, was that another symptom?

Lock followed the movement of her hand. 'While we are waiting, shall we discuss the case?'

Now it was Kat's turn to raise her eyebrows. 'Are you trying to distract me?'

'Yes. Experience tells me that getting you to focus on work is probably the best way of distracting you while you wait for the results.'

Without waiting for her to reply, Lock projected the virtual briefing boards in front of them. 'Now that we have established the cause of death,' he said, 'does this change the list of suspects or key lines of enquiry?'

Kat knew he was just trying to draw her into a

discussion, yet she couldn't resist rising to her feet, eyes scanning the boards as her brain kicked into gear. What kind of person would use a nerve agent in Coleshill of all places, not just murdering Angela Long, but knowingly putting her own and other lives at risk? 'At least Novichok should help us narrow down the suspects,' she said, standing in front of the images. 'I mean, who on earth has access to a chemical agent that potent?'

Lock stood by her side. 'The level of toxicity is such that it is only allowed to be manufactured in specialised facilities, such as a university or industrial laboratory. Novichok is a binary weapon, meaning that the nerve agent is typically stored as two less toxic chemicals. When they are combined, they react to produce the more toxic agent. It was discovered by accident in the 1930s by scientists trying to find a cost-effective pesticide, before ending up in the hands of the German military. Russia, the US and the UK also started to experiment on chemical agents after World War Two. In fact, it was British scientists who developed the VX nerve agent at the Porton Down research facility in the early 1950s.'

'Really?' Kat glanced at the doorway which had earlier admitted the men in biohazard suits. Because they were part of an urgent response team, she had just assumed that their job was to protect people like her from poisons; she hadn't thought about how they had gained – or used – their expertise in the first place.

Lock projected a series of articles and photos onto another virtual screen. 'Most documented cases involving nerve agents are alleged to have been carried out by nation states or spies acting on their behalf. Russia is commonly cited as a suspect in high-profile Novichok cases such as the Salisbury poisoning, although they strenuously deny it.'

Kat scanned the articles. 'How is it administered?'

'In some cases, Novichok was ingested by adding it as a liquid to food or drink, or through physical contact as it seeps through the skin. But it can also be inhaled, which can lead to death in minutes.'

Kat fought the urge to wash her hands.

'Because it is so toxic,' continued Lock, 'Novichok would need to be transported in something very tightly sealed, and anyone who applied it would need to wear protective clothing, as it is highly dangerous to deliver.'

'So, as well as being difficult to access, delivering Novichok would have required extremely careful plan-ning,' said Kat, glancing back towards the image of Angela Long's husband. 'And a very cool head.'

'In all probability, Angela Long was most likely murdered by a hostile state with access to nerve agents. The known cases of Novichok poisoning suggest that Russia should be actively considered.'

Kat studied the articles. 'Perhaps, but all these reported cases of poisoning by spies have one thing in common – they all tried to mask the fact that their victims were murdered. Novichok was added to their coffee or food or skin in relatively small doses that took several days to take effect, meaning it was initially hard to prove cause and effect. That's completely different to how Angela

Long died.' Kat gestured towards an image of the victim on the pillory. 'Our murderer used a rare and hard-to-detect poison, yet went out of their way to make a spectacle out of her body. The pillory, the staging, the notes, the blackout. These aren't the acts of a spy who wants to avoid detection. This is nothing like an act of espionage.'

'But all the evidence suggests that the most likely suspect is an agent acting on behalf of another state.'

'No,' said Kat, turning to face the hologram. 'You're confusing evidence from *this* case with what happened in the past. The *method* of murder might be the same, but I think the purpose, the *motivation,* is completely different. The thing is—'

Her heart stopped as the door opened and a man in a white biohazard suit appeared.

He remained in the doorway and did not remove his mask as he announced, 'We have the results of your tests now, DCS Frank.'

@EmFairby WTAF??? Angela Long was killed by a NERVE AGENT?

@Jimber24 Says who?

@EmFairby Check out this video. You can see a team from Porton Down shutting down the street she was murdered on. And a reporter from Sky News says he got a tip-off that they found evidence of Novichok in the autopsy.

@Phil61b Yeah, it's all over my feed too. Scary stuff. I thought it was the deep state trying to shut her up. But to use a nerve agent against an elected MP? That's an act of war.

@DaveHughes45 It'll be the Russians. Remember the Salisbury poisonings?

@DeeepStateX Yeah, I remember. I also remember that the Russians denied it and that Porton Down – a place that actually MANUFACTURES and TESTS Novichok – is based in Salisbury. Coincidence much?

@Secretcopperkettle That's what the Russians want you to believe. Don't fall for their crazy conspiracy theories.

@DeeepStateX So it's rational to think that some Russian spy travelled to some random place in bloody Warwickshire to murder an MP, but it's a crazy conspiracy theory if you think that the British government used their nearby military facilities to take out a political opponent and make it look like it was a hostile act from another state?

@EmFairby OMG you are both mad.

@TimJim32 It's not just a 'random' place in Warwickshire – it's Coleshill and I live there. My children are terrified. What if we've come into contact with it? I've looked it up and even microscopic amounts of Novichok can be lethal.

@MaryF1969 I live there too and it's outrageous that there's no advice from anyone. I'm keeping my family inside until someone tells us what the hell is going on.

@AAAi They'll never tell you what's *really* going on so my advice would be to question everything. You're right to stay in, but that stuff can be inhaled so wear a face mask too.

@TimJim32 Thanks, mate. I think I've still got some masks left from Covid.

@DeeepStateX I've just ordered some more. This could be the first of many attacks.

@Lauraloves52 That's really irresponsible of you to spread fear like that.

@TimJim32 It's irresponsible to sit back and do nothing and believe their lies. We need to take action ourselves and do what we can to protect our families.

@EmFairby Have you seen this? The government have just put out a statement [attachment]

@DeeepStateX Yeah, like that's going to be the truth . . .

For immediate release

Following an autopsy on the body of murdered MP Angela Long, experts from Porton Down have assessed the biometric markers and other toxicology tests and confirmed it is likely that exposure to an A-series nerve agent – possibly Novichok – was the cause of death.

A-series agents are unique organophosphorus-based compounds that were developed during the Cold War by the Soviet Union. Nerve agents are highly toxic chemicals that prevent the nervous system from working properly and can be fatal even in small doses.

'As soon as the possibility of a nerve agent was highlighted, an urgent response team from Porton Down was dispatched,' said the Home Secretary. 'They assessed both the test results and the site of Angela Long's murder and have confirmed that there is no further risk to members of the public. I am pleased to report that the attending police officers and pathologist have also been tested and given the all-clear.

'The Prime Minister will chair a COBRA meeting tomorrow morning where we will discuss our response. This is the first incident of this kind since the former Russian spy Yuri Skripal, his daughter Yulia and former police officer Nick Bailey were all poisoned by Novichok in Salisbury in March 2018. The fact that a British MP has been targeted is a matter of great concern, and the case has now been handed over to Counter Terrorism Policing.'

A spokesperson for Counter Terrorism Policing said, 'We urge

members of the public to come forward if they have any information relating to this case. In particular, we are keen to talk to the
man who was seen in a white cherry picker van on Church Street
at around 10pm on 31 October. Please contact the police or leave
a message on our confidential hotline.'

CHAPTER TWENTY-NINE

Professor Okonedo's home, Warwick, 6.45pm

Adaiba read the message on her phone and let out a relieved sigh. Thank God Kat and Judith had been given the all-clear. Although, she corrected herself, God had nothing to do with it. The fact that they were okay was entirely thanks to the PPE they had both been wearing. She just hoped that everyone else who attended the scene of the crime had been so diligent in following the rules.

She clicked onto a social media site for the latest on the Novichok attack, but just a few seconds of the shouty paranoia and panic was enough to make her put her phone back down. She couldn't allow herself to be sucked into other peoples' fears now – she had enough of her own to deal with.

What she needed was a distraction. Something completely different yet familiar enough to be comforting. Adaiba usually found this through gaming – *Detroit: Become Human* or *The Last of Us* were her favourites. But tonight, both felt too close to the thoughts she was trying to escape. She picked up the remote and clicked on Netflix, remembering how surprised Rayan had been when she'd told him she liked films and books as well as gaming, and that she even occasionally enjoyed Jane Austen.

But when he'd asked her which version of *Pride and Prejudice* she preferred, he'd been shocked when she'd said the Keira Knightley one.

'*No way!*' he'd cried. '*Keira Knightley is not and never will be Elizabeth Bennet. The BBC series is the best.*'

She shook her head, smiling sadly at the memory. They'd disagreed about so much – whether it was possible to reform the police force, the merits and dangers of AI – and yet, there had been such a *connection* between them.

Adaiba clicked on the search button and found the BBC adaptation. It was made in 1995, so it was bound to be misogynistic with not even a token brown face in sight, but one episode would be enough to distract her – and of course, prove that *she* was right.

Instead, she spent the next four and a half hours transfixed on the sofa as she watched another young couple clash over their different opinions and prejudices, before finally listening to their hearts. As the penultimate scene played out, she held her breath as Elizabeth Bennet confessed her true feelings to her father:

'*I love him,*' she said, her voice trembling with the force of it. '*I did not always love him . . . but truly, he is the best man I have ever known.*'

And as the closing credits played, Adaiba buried her face in her hands and wept.

CHAPTER THIRTY

DCS Kat Frank's home, Coleshill, 7.15pm

The minute Kat got home, Cam rang. Of course he did. Her son had an almost psychic ability to ring just when she'd sat down to eat a meal or sink into a hot bath. She loved her son, she really did, but after the day she'd had, she needed to take this grotty tracksuit off, have a long shower and compose her own thoughts and feelings before speaking to anyone else. But she was a mum, so what she needed didn't really come into it. She slipped her coat off and pressed accept with one hand, reaching for the kettle with the other.

'Hi, Cam,' she said.

'Is it true? About the Novichok? Are you okay?'

She winced at the panic in his voice. Tucking the phone tighter beneath her chin, she tried to reassure him. 'I'm fine. Don't worry. What have you heard?' Bloody social media. She'd been told that the news would be embargoed until tomorrow morning.

'It's all over my feed. That Angela Long was murdered with a nerve agent in Coleshill and that the police were exposed. That's you, isn't it? Jesus, Mum.'

The crack in his voice hurt her heart. 'It's okay, I've been tested and given the all-clear. Some experts from Porton Down came today and checked me and Judith for everything and we're both fine. There's nothing to worry about.'

'How can you be *fine*? It's a *nerve agent*, Mum. What if they're just saying that not to cause a panic? There's this podcast that says Porton Down is owned by the government and there's a cover-up because—'

'Cam, listen to me,' she said firmly. 'Don't listen to conspiracy theorists. You're better than that. The guys from Porton Down are the world experts in this, and they could not have been more thorough. Plus, I was wearing PPE when we found the body, and we were outdoors. The tests were just a precaution. If I'd been exposed, I would have had symptoms by now. I wouldn't be talking to you, I'd be in hospital. But I'm not. I'm standing here in the kitchen, tired and hungry and wondering what to have for my tea.'

He paused.

'Honestly, Cam, I've learned a lot about Novichok today, and if I had been exposed three days ago, I would be puking my guts up by now.'

'You promise you don't feel ill?'

'I promise.'

He blew a heavy sigh into the phone. 'Jesus, Mum. I wish you didn't work for the police.'

What could she say? Cam had always worried about her job, but after John died, it had made him so anxious that he'd had to have therapy to cope with the fear of losing her, too. All she'd ever wanted was for her son to be happy, so it was horrible to know that her job caused him such distress. But it was what she did. It was who she was – in addition to being a guilt-ridden, over-protective single parent.

'I'm sorry,' she said. 'I should have rung you earlier, but I didn't want to worry you. I was hoping they wouldn't mention me in the press release.'

'S'okay,' he mumbled. 'Look, I don't have any lectures for the rest of the week, so can I come home for a few days?'

'Of course. Is everything okay?'

'Yes, it's just, well . . . it'd be good to see you. Make sure you really are okay. And I could do with some healthy food and proper sleep for a few days. Would that be all right?'

'Of course it is. This is your home. I've got to go to London for that select committee tomorrow – three-line whip, I'm afraid – but I should be back by five at the latest. Have you got your key?'

'Yeah, somewhere. Maybe we can go out for dinner when you get back so we can talk? The Coleshill Hotel?'

'You buying?'

'Er . . .'

'I'm joking.' She laughed. It would be good to see him, and she knew that he needed to see her: to see with his own eyes that she really was okay. She ended the call, smiling. Then nearly jumped out of her own skin as an explosion tore through the air.

She ran to the kitchen window, heart pounding as fireworks lit up the dark night sky.

Kat stared at her lone reflection, her own words echoing in her mind. *I'm fine.*

She swore under her breath and snapped the blinds shut, half-tempted to go and knock on her neighbours' door and remind them that the tradition was called Guy Fawkes' *Night,* and that that night – which was *not* a season – was actually on the fifth, not the third of bloody November. But people seemed to let off fireworks all the time these days. She turned towards the cooling kettle, then changed her mind and headed for the fridge and the bottle of white wine. It had been a tough day. One glass wouldn't do any harm, and it would be nice with a quick supper of smoked salmon on brown bread, followed by a bath and an early night.

It only took two minutes to make, and once it was done, she sat at the kitchen island so she could read her briefing papers and Q&As for the select committee while she ate. But her heart sank as she unzipped the digital file and stared at all the different attachments. There was no way she'd be able to read all this tonight. She glanced around the empty kitchen. 'Lock?'

Instantly his hologram appeared. 'Good evening, Kat.'

'Hi. I was just reading the briefing for the select committee, and wondered if you could maybe give me a summary of the key points while I eat?'

'Of course.'

Kat gave him a grateful smile and picked up a piece of brown bread and salmon. At times like this, Lock could be really useful. She was just about to pop the food into her mouth when her phone pinged. She sighed. Cam *again?* After taking a quick gulp of her wine, she checked her messages, surprised to see that it was Debbie Browne.

Glad to hear you're OK. Lottie not well. You don't think she could be contaminated, do you?

Kat put the bread down, pressed dial and put the call on loudspeaker.

Debbie picked up immediately. 'Sorry to bother you,' she said, her voice on the verge of tears. 'It's just I'm really worried. Lottie has a temperature and she just doesn't look right.'

'Okay, first things first,' Kat said, making her voice clear and calm. 'It can't be Novichok because you haven't had any exposure to the body. You might have had secondary exposure to me, but I've had the all-clear from the experts from Porton Down, as has the crime scene. Lottie has *not* been contaminated. Do you hear me?'

'That's what I've been telling myself. It's just that she vomited earlier and that's a symptom, isn't it?'

'Babies vomit all the time,' Kat reassured her. 'They're basically shitting and puking machines at this age.'

'I know. It's just that she's so hot, but her hands are cold. And earlier she wouldn't stop crying, but now she's really quiet.'

Kat was about to reassure her, when Lock stepped forward.

'May I ask if Lottie has been seen by a clinician?'

'Yes, I saw the GP this morning and they said it was just a cold.'

'And has her condition deteriorated since then?' Lock asked.

'I think so. I rang 111 about an hour ago, but I'm still waiting for someone to call me back. I know I'm probably just panicking because I'm alone – my mum's gone out with some friends – but Lottie just doesn't look right. She looks sleepy but she isn't sleeping.'

'A temperature makes babies tired,' Kat said. 'So it's probably just—'

'DCS Frank,' said Lock. 'The reported symptoms concern me. Can I suggest that we visit DS Browne so that I can make a visual assessment of Lottie's vital signs?'

'Er . . .' began Kat, glancing at her uneaten meal.

'In fact,' continued Lock. 'I recommend we go now as a matter of urgency.'

CHAPTER THIRTY-ONE

Debbie Browne's home, Chelmsley Wood, 8.46pm

'Thank you,' Debbie said as she opened the door to Kat and Lock, her eyes wide and watery. She led them down the hallway and into the living room, where Lottie's tiny form was lying on the settee. Despite the November cold, the baby was wearing nothing but a nappy, and instead of kicking her legs in the air or turning her head to look at the visitors, she remained completely still, even though she wasn't asleep.

'She's so hot, I had to take her onesie off. I've given her as much Calpol as I dare, but her temperature's not coming down.'

Lock's hologram assumed a kneeling position beside Lottie on the settee, his eyes scanning the baby. 'She has a temperature of thirty-eight point nine, heart rate of a hundred and seventy-five beats per minute and respiratory rate of seventy-two.' He turned to Debbie. 'When was the last time she urinated?'

'Er . . . I don't know, but come to think of it, the last two times I changed her nappy it was completely dry, so I don't think she's had a wee since this morning. Is that a symptom?'

Lock ignored her and focused once more on Lottie. 'I have assessed her appearance against every image I have of her, and Lottie's skin is significantly paler than usual, but I cannot detect any rashes.' He leaned closer and smiled, but Lottie just stared at him blankly. He frowned, then sang her favourite rhyme – *Run, run as fast as you can, you can't catch me, I'm the Gingerbread Man!*

The silence that followed was one of the worst things that Kat had ever heard.

Lock turned to the girl's mum. 'In addition to her other symptoms, I am concerned that Lottie appears listless and unresponsive.'

'Oh God,' said Debbie, clasping her hand to her mouth. 'Does that mean she's been poisoned?'

'No. Her symptoms are not consistent with nerve agent poisoning, nor is that likely considering the lack of contact. But her symptoms indicate a serious infection, and after assessing NICE guidelines, according to my algorithms there is a seventy-four per cent chance that Lottie has sepsis.'

'Sepsis? Is that bad?' asked Debbie.

'Sepsis is a life-threatening reaction to an infection,' explained Lock. 'It happens when the human immune system overreacts and starts to damage the body's own tissues and organs. Sepsis is one of the leading causes of neonatal mortality in the world, with a UK mortality rate of approximately twenty per cent.'

'Lock, that's enough!' Kat hissed, as Debbie collapsed onto the settee with a sob.

'I am sorry that this information is upsetting but ignorance will only increase the risk of death. The evidence is clear that patients who present early at hospital are half as likely to die as those who present late, so emotions aside, I recommend that you dial 999 immediately.'

With shaking hands, Debbie picked up her phone. 'Okay. Oh my God. What shall I say?'

'Tell them—' Lock paused. 'Actually, with your consent, it might be more effective if I make the call. The initial triage and assessment are based on some very basic algorithms, and for Lottie to be assessed as a category A call, certain answers and key words will be required. In your highly emotional state, there is a risk that you may not say them, or that the call handlers may not hear them and dismiss you as an over-anxious mother.'

'Okay, you do it, then,' Debbie said with relief. 'Thank you.' She leaned over her baby and gently stroked her hot head. 'It's okay, sweetie,' she said. 'Everything's going to be okay.'

CHAPTER THIRTY-TWO

**Birmingham Children's Hospital,
3 November, 11.37pm**

Kat handed Debbie a plastic cup of watery hot chocolate. She accepted the offering but just held it in her hands. Not once did she take her eyes off her daughter in the hospital cot.

Because of John, Kat had had enough experience of hospitals to last her a lifetime. Apart from all the rounds of chemotherapy, he'd been assessed for sepsis several times and admitted with it twice. But seeing a small baby like Lottie with a cannula in her nose for oxygen support, and attached to a drip for antibiotics and fluids, was incredibly upsetting. She couldn't even begin to imagine how Debbie must feel.

The paramedics had been brilliant – and so had Lock. He'd briefed them with the confidence of a doctor, and after verifying Lottie's vital signs with their own equipment, they'd attached her to a drip and oxygen straight away. Within minutes, Debbie and her baby were in the ambulance, with Kat and Lock following in her car.

Another night of sirens, she'd thought with a roll of dread. It seemed she was condemned to live her life in the wake of blue flashing lights.

They all looked up as the resident doctor entered the room. 'Hi, I'm Dr Elnaqa,' said the young man with a kind smile. 'And this must be Lottie. Can you tell me what happened?'

After listening patiently to Debbie's story, the doctor nodded and explained the treatment plan. 'You did very well to bring her in so promptly. We've done a lot of blood tests, and there's a marker for infection or inflammation called CRP, and when that's as high as Lottie's is, then we have to treat sepsis as a real possibility. We've put her on broad spectrum antibiotics, and we've done this intravenously as that's the quickest way of getting the most help into her bloodstream, and hopefully that will help bring the CRP levels down. The oxygen will help ease her breathing, and we will keep her temperature under control with paracetamol. But sepsis is caused by an uncontrolled immune system response to an underlying infection. To treat it properly, we need to work out the source of the initial respiratory infection – for example, whether it is pneumonia or bronchiolitis – so that we can target it with the right antibiotics. We'll do some more blood, culture and urine tests, but can you tell me more about when the cold started and the sort of symptoms she had?'

Debbie ran a hand over her face. 'Er . . . yesterday?

No, I think, was it the day before? Sorry, it's a bit of a blur.'

'May I?' asked Lock.

Kat quickly explained who and what Lock was, which didn't seem to faze the young doctor at all.

'I have baseline data for Lottie's vital signs such as temperature and respiratory rate,' said Lock, projecting a 3D graph between them. 'And here is the data from the past forty-eight hours when Debbie first reported that Lottie was unwell, a list of the symptoms that were either reported to me or observed against a timeline and a summary of the latest NICE guidelines in case that is helpful.'

'Excellent,' said the doctor, quickly scanning the data and taking a photo with his phone. 'This is very useful.'

'Is she going to be okay?' asked Debbie.

Dr Elnaqa turned back to her. 'I will be honest with you and say that sepsis is extremely serious, especially for someone as young as Lottie, so it is vital that we bring this infection under control and monitor her very, very closely, especially her CRP and levels of lactate concentration. I don't think she needs to be admitted to intensive care at the moment, but we'll have to keep it under review.'

Kat placed a hand on Debbie's shoulder as she let out a sob.

'In the meantime, don't be afraid to touch your child. I know all this equipment can be a bit scary, but the best thing you can do is let her know that you are here for her, and that she is loved.' The young doctor leaned over the cot and stroked Lottie's forehead with a gentle but firm hand. He pointed at the monitor, where her respiratory and heart rate had lowered in response.

'I will continue to monitor her vital signs and add the data to the graphs and ensure you are alerted in the event of any red flags,' said Lock.

'Great,' said Dr Elnaqa. 'I don't suppose you fancy staying on to help with the rest of my shift? We're absolutely jammed tonight and I'm the only resident doctor covering respiratory.' He said it like it was a joke, but his tired eyes held a flicker of hope.

'I doubt your professional regulator or Trust-specific guidelines would allow me to formally assist you in your role.'

'Pity. You could probably do the work of about ten doctors.'

'That depends on what you think "the work" is. If you require access to the very latest research and an analysis of the most likely diagnoses as well as proposed treatment plans for consideration, then yes, I can do this work with much greater accuracy and speed than any human. But I cannot do what you just did.' Lock looked down at Lottie with a softness in his expression that Kat had never seen before. 'You are a human healthcare professional, and so your job is not just to provide access to information, but to provide care. Care is a verb – it requires physical action. And sadly, that is something I am unable to provide.'

'But care is provided by multi-disciplinary teams. And you, me and my colleagues would make a *fantastic* team.'

The young doctor sighed. 'But I guess that's for another time.' He gave Debbie a gentle smile. 'Try not to worry. Your daughter is in the right place, and you did really well to bring her in so quickly, so you've given us a very good chance of turning this around. Call me or a nurse if anything changes or something just feels wrong. You know your child better than anyone.' Despite his evident exhaustion, the doctor pulled back the curtains, washed his hands at the basin and moved on to the next room, where the anxious parents of a three-year-old boy with suspected pneumonia were waiting.

Debbie picked up her hot chocolate with shaking hands and took a large gulp.

'The doctor sounded pretty confident that everything's going to be okay,' said Kat. 'Thanks to you. You were right to trust your instinct that something was wrong.'

'No, it's thanks to Lock,' Debbie said, looking at the hologram standing over Lottie's cot. 'Honestly, I never would have known it was sepsis without you.'

'Kat is partially correct,' said Lock. 'You knew that something was wrong, but I do not agree it was because of your instinct. On some level, your human brain knew that Lottie's vital signs were deviating from what was normal for your daughter, but you did not have the clinical knowledge to articulate it or the equipment to prove it. I merely assisted you by quantifying your correct assessment that Lottie did not "look right".'

'Well, whatever it was, I just thank God you were there,' said Debbie. 'Honestly, you're like her guardian angel.'

Lock tilted his head. 'Since guardian angels are believed

to act on behalf of an unproven God, I cannot claim to be one. But I have just read 10,212 articles on the matter, and I am struck by how many religions and belief systems have an idea of angelic beings protecting individual human beings. In Judaism, a guardian angel was also a messenger, constituting a permanent contact between the human world of action and the higher worlds. If you allow the higher world to be envisaged as the cloud which contains the internet of all things, then perhaps it is an appropriate analogy after all.'

'Come on, Gabriel,' said Kat as she spotted Debbie's mum rushing down the corridor. 'We'll leave Debbie to it.'

After promising to keep in touch, Kat and Lock said goodbye and made their way out of the ward. They turned onto the main corridor, and as they progressed, Lock slowed down, turning his head towards the bays and single rooms branching off on both sides. Inside each room, the dark was lit by the glow of machines, revealing the shadows and silhouettes of heads bowed in anguish or slumped in exhausted sleep.

'Human beings are so very frail,' Lock said softly, glancing at another tiny baby in a cot. 'Your bodies are vulnerable to constant infections and injury. And because of your emotions, these incidences place those who love you at risk of debilitating grief. I find it remarkable – incongruous, even – that your species has managed to achieve so much when your existence is so finite and frail.'

Kat turned just as they reached the exit to the ward.

She looked back at the nursing station where, despite the late hour, an older nurse was holding a distraught-looking man with a strength and compassion born of experience. 'I think it's the awareness that our lives are so finite and fragile that ultimately drives us. We've achieved so much not *despite* this knowledge, but because of it.'

Lock's eyes widened. 'Do you have any evidence for that assertion?'

Kat gave him a sad smile and gestured towards the ward behind him. 'Come on,' she said, clicking the green button to release the door. 'Let's go home.'

CHAPTER THIRTY-THREE

**The Palace of Westminster, London,
4 November, 9.45am**

Getting an early train on a cold November morning after less than four hours sleep wasn't much fun, but as Kat emerged from Westminster Tube into the bright autumn sunshine, she couldn't help but smile at the beauty of the buildings that framed the clear blue sky. Directly opposite was the iconic tower of Big Ben, and beyond it, the golden glory of the Palace of Westminster, impossibly grand above the crush of traffic criss-crossing the roads below. She sighed with pleasure. She'd forgotten how much she loved this crazy, busy but beautiful place.

'I love London,' said Karen-from-Comms.

Kat smiled and turned to Professor Okonedo. 'How about you, Adaiba – do you like London?'

'I guess,' was all she replied, with a shrug of her slim shoulders. As ever, she was wearing a beautifully cut suit, but the once well-fitting jacket now looked too large – or rather, her body looked too small. And though her hair and make-up were immaculate as usual, there was a tiredness in the young woman's eyes that looked bone deep.

'So what now?' Kat asked, looking about.

'The select committee hearing is in the Palace of Westminster,' said Karen-from-Comms, reading the email on her phone. 'The invite said we need to enter via the Cromwell Green entrance, opposite Westminster Abbey.'

'Great, lead the way,' said Kat. She watched approvingly as Karen led them confidently through the hordes of tourists. She mentored a lot of young women, but she'd never needed to advise KFC to get her elbows out. And maybe it was the rare autumn sunshine or the relief that she hadn't been poisoned, but Kat couldn't help feeling excited to be in the capital city once more. They'd had such great holidays here when Cam was young, learning about the Tudors in the Tower of London, the dinosaurs in the Natural History Museum or just having picnics in one of the many Royal Parks. Maybe after the committee hearing and a debrief with the minister, she could walk around their old haunts and—

A wave of guilt washed over her. How could she think of sightseeing when poor Lottie was still dangerously ill in hospital? She'd been in such a rush this morning, she hadn't had a chance to ring the ward. To avoid attention, Lock had agreed not to make himself visible until they were inside Parliament, but as they'd just reached the entrance, Kat called out Lock's name.

His hologram appeared, looking about him as if

absorbing the history of the architecture and politics that surrounded them.

'Hi, Lock, I was wondering if there is any news on Lottie?' she asked, knowing that Lock had promised to stay in touch with Debbie 24/7.

Lock nodded. 'Lottie remains stable, her temperature is under control and the first blood test of the day showed a reduction in the CRP rate, which is a positive sign that things are starting to move in the right direction. However, she will need to remain on oxygen and intravenous antibiotics and fluids for several days until the infection is fully eradicated.'

'Oh, that's a relief. Thank you, Lock.'

'I'll just ring the committee staff,' said KFC, pulling out her phone. 'They said they'd come and meet us and take us through security.'

Kat nodded, grateful for a few more moments in the sun. There were always gaggles of protestors scattered about Westminster – sometimes people in tents occupied the square at the centre, and there was always a crowd of some sort waving various flags opposite Downing Street, so at first, she didn't pay any attention to the twenty or so people gathered outside the entrance to Parliament with handmade placards.

But then someone shouted, '*No ifs, no buts, stop the AI workforce cuts!*'

She turned to follow the voice, starting as she recognised his face. 'Is that Roddy Wheeler?' she said. 'The guy who volunteers for Angela Long?'

'Yes, it is,' confirmed Lock.

As the crowd picked up the chant, Kat realised that the banners they were waving belonged to Action Against Ai. The banners they held up had a striking logo of a triangle made up of three capital A's with the letter 'i' in the centre, but they all contained different demands:

HUMANS FIRST!

AI LIES!

DON'T LET AI STEAL YOUR JOB!

REGULATION OR ANNIHILATION!!!

Kat caught Roddy Wheeler's eye. He stopped chanting. Then he glanced at Lock by her side, before shouting out, 'There he is! The AI cop!'

The protestors surged forward, surrounding Lock as they shouted, 'Humans first! Humans first! Humans first!'

'Get back!' Kat ordered, holding up a protective hand.

'Do not worry, DSC Frank. They cannot harm me.' He frowned and leaned closer to speak to one protestor. 'Your demands make no sense. First in what?'

'Er . . . everything!' the protestor cried.

'Don't engage with them,' Karen-from-Comms advised, as she quickly herded them through the gates and towards security.

Kat had never been in the Houses of Parliament before, and for a moment she was slightly awestruck as the queue moved down the slope towards the golden stone building, sparkling in the sunshine. But before they could go inside, they had to pass through a large, dark hut, filled with the kind of high-tech scanners you got in airports, operated by security staff with serious faces and brisk attitudes.

A member of staff appeared and explained that they

had to put all their bags, mobile phones and laptops – including the bracelet that hosted Lock – into a grey plastic tray, before walking through the scanner.

Kat frowned and turned to a security guard for advice. 'Surely AIDE Lock doesn't need to walk through the scanner?'

'Everyone needs to walk through the scanner,' the woman replied without looking at Lock.

'But Lock is a hologram,' Kat explained.

'Everyone needs to walk through the scanner.'

'Very well,' said Lock. 'But you won't see anything.'

After allowing Adaiba to walk through, Kat gestured to Lock to go first. He passed through the scanner, and this time the security guard looked up.

'It didn't work,' she said. 'You need to go through it again.'

'It is working,' said Lock. 'I am a hologram, so I have no body to scan.'

The security guard frowned and turned to consult one of her colleagues. They gestured for him to step forward and spread out his arms and legs. A male security guard reached out to frisk him, starting as his hands passed straight through Lock's sides.

'I told you, I am a hologram. There is no point scanning or frisking me, I have no physical entity and therefore I am not capable of carrying anything of substance, whether harmful or not.'

'There's nothing in the rules about this,' muttered the woman, as another colleague joined the small confused huddle of security guards.

'Is there a problem?' a clear voice called out.

They all turned to see the Home Secretary, looking tall and imposing in a bright red suit.

'I briefed the Head of Security about AIDE Lock last night,' she continued, 'and he gave me his personal assurance that there wouldn't be any difficulties. You are in danger of making an official witness late for a Parliamentary select committee hearing, and even worse, you risk making the security service look foolish.'

'We're just doing our job,' insisted the female security guard, undeterred by the appearance of the minister.

The Home Secretary raised her eyebrows, and for a moment Kat was worried that the security guard might indeed end up being sorry. But then the minister's face broke into a sudden smile.

'Of course. And I am grateful to you all for doing such a great job. But we really can't keep the committee waiting.' She gestured to Lock to step forward and urged the rest of them to gather their things. 'There's a lot of press sitting in on this one because of the Novichok incident, so come on, follow me. I need to give you a quick update before we start.'

They followed the minister through the entrance and up several winding flights of white stone steps before turning down a long carpeted corridor, lined with paintings and dark wooden doors. To Kat, it looked like a really old-fashioned hotel, apart from the TV monitors outside each door listing the different select committees in progress and announcing the next vote in the Chamber.

'This is us,' said the minister, coming to a halt outside

the committee room. She sent a quick text on her phone, and a few seconds later, her private secretary emerged from behind the door.

Kat caught a quick glimpse of the select committee behind him: a semicircle of oak desks seating the committee at one end, with the witnesses seated in a line at the other, with several rows of green leather chairs for the press and public behind them. On each wall was a large screen highlighting the business of the day and the timings for votes, while another played silent footage of the committee as it was live-streamed to the Parliamentary Channel.

'How's it going?' the minister asked her private secretary as he stepped out and closed the door.

'It's fine. They're just finishing the session with the science and tech guys, and so far, it's been mostly factual – questions about what AI can and can't do, how much it costs, that sort of thing. The chair's grilled them a bit about the environmental impact, but there's nothing they've raised that's not in your briefing packs.'

The minister turned to face Kat and the team. 'The chair, as we know, is an AI sceptic and very concerned about the environment. She's incredibly risk averse and determined to push for more regulation, but let me deal with her. Most of the others are pretty neutral but Roger Simkins has a science background and understands the need to innovate, so he'll ask us some helpful questions.'

Kat frowned. 'How do you know what questions he's going to ask?'

'Because I gave them to him.'

'Is that allowed?'

The minister laughed. 'It's how it works. But if any questions come up that we haven't prepared for or I can't remember the answer to, please pass a note to my private secretary, who is allowed to pass it on to me.'

'That is a remarkably slow and flawed system,' said Lock. 'If you allow me to interface with your laptop, then I will be able to search all the briefing notes or the internet and provide you with the right answer in less than a second.'

'Perfect.' She opened her notebook and scribbled something down. 'That's my password,' she said, holding it up so that only Lock could see.

She turned to her private secretary. 'Has anyone mentioned Novichok yet?'

'No, but there are a lot of journos here, and some of the backbenchers are bound to ask you about it in the hope that they appear in the news clip.'

The minister nodded. 'Again, leave that to me. I'll just say that the PM chaired a second COBRA meeting this morning, Counter Terrorism Policing are investigating it as a matter of urgency, Porton Down have assured me that there is no risk to the public or any other MPs and the investigation continues.'

'What if they ask about the murder of Angela Long?' Kat asked.

'Like I said, that's being led by the CTP now. I've arranged for you both to do a formal handover with them after this hearing, but it's out of your hands now. They think it could be the Russians, so the PM's leading our response.'

'But why would the *Russians* draw attention to a nerve agent attack by putting the victim on a medieval pillory on a busy high street?' asked Kat, frowning.

The minister turned her full attention to Kat. 'Those questions – or indeed *any* questions about this case – are no longer your concern. This matter is now being dealt with at the highest levels of government. Can I remind you that this session is being streamed live on the BBC iPlayer and transcribed word for word for the public record, so any questions about Novichok must be answered by me.'

Kat stared back, the unsaid words heavy between them: *or else.*

Before she could reply, the door opened again, and four grey-haired men in dark suits came out.

'This is it, team,' said the minister. 'We're on.'

CHAPTER THIRTY-FOUR

Transcript of Science, Innovation and Technology Select Committee public hearing

Chair and committee members in attendance

Witnesses: Home Secretary, DCS Kat Frank, Professor Adaiba Okonedo, AIDE Lock

Chair: Welcome to this public hearing of the Science, Innovation and Technology Select Committee. As you know, the purpose of these hearings is to help the committee reach an informed view about the appropriate balance between innovation and regulation in this rapidly moving field. In particular, we are aware that the Home Secretary wishes to roll out the use of AIDEs in the police force before the Warwickshire pilot has been fully evaluated, perhaps even progressing to robotics, so we are keen to get a fuller understanding of the risks and benefits of the proposed approach. Our work is very timely, as the AI Bill is due to be debated in the Commons next week. These debates are often ideological or theoretical in nature, but as Warwickshire Police have been piloting the use of AI, your frontline experience will help inform our thinking on the necessity – or not – of further research or legislation, so we are grateful to you all for making the time to attend today.

Can we start with you first, Professor Okonedo? Perhaps you can tell the committee a bit about how and why you created AIDE Lock?

Prof O: Yes, of course. I've always had an interest in AI, and my PhD explored how algorithms might help reduce the level of bias and prejudice in the police force. Then machine learning took off in a big way, and, working with a multi-disciplinary team at Warwick University, we were able to combine our rapidly growing knowledge of automation, analytics and algorithms to create the hardware and software that allow AIDE Lock to function: he is an AI detective that is built with algorithms but is also capable of machine learning.

Chair: In what sense do you think that Lock is capable of learning?

Prof O: The same way that any of us are – through observation and reading or consuming information. Lock can do this at unprecedented scale and pace, but the quality of his learning depends on the training data he has access to. Most AI tools use the internet as their source data, but I was keen to expose Lock to an actual police team, so that he could learn from real-life decisions and interactions with people and they in turn could learn from him.

Chair: Learn from *him?* What could an experienced police officer like DCS Kat Frank possibly learn from a *machine*?

Prof O: I think I should let Kat answer that question.

DCS KF: Er . . . Professor Okonedo is right. I have to admit I was sceptical about the pilot at first, but to be honest, I think we've all learned something.

Chair: Such as?

DCS KF: Such as in the first cold case we worked on together, I perhaps let my sympathy for one person blind me to their guilt, whereas Lock, with his relentless focus on the facts, was able to identify that they were the perpetrator. He's not always right, but working with Lock has made me more aware of my own assumptions and biases, which I think can only be a good thing.

MP: Can you give an example where Lock has been wrong?

DCS KF: He doesn't always get the nuance of human communication. So, for example, once I asked him to scan and assess how many corpses might be buried on a riverbank, and he said hundreds, because he included the remains of every fish that had ever died there.

[laughter]

Lock: If I might clarify, the misunderstanding arose not because I failed to understand the nuance of human communication – it was because the request lacked the necessary specificity. DCS Frank did not state that she was only interested in the identification of *human*

230

remains. If I gave the 'wrong' answer, it was because I was asked the wrong question.

Chair: Thank you, AIDE Lock. We've all read a lot about you, so it's fascinating to finally meet you – if one can be said to 'meet' a hologram. DCS Kat Frank has been very generous about what she has learned from working with you. But can you tell us what you have learned from working with your human colleagues?

Lock: I have learned that, as the literature suggests, human decision-making processes are deeply flawed, as you are vulnerable to erratic emotions, societal prejudices and an incomplete understanding of the facts due to your slow cognitive functioning and poor memory recall. Nevertheless, I have also learned that DCS Kat Frank is sometimes capable of making astute judgements. She attributes this to her 'gut instinct', but I have observed that this is often the result of years of experience and knowledge that is being processed at a rate too fast for her human brain to comprehend. I have also learned that all humans lie.

MP: You don't sound like you have a very good opinion of us humans! We have been debating the issue of artificial intelligence all week, but can I ask you: what do you think of human intelligence?

Lock: To paraphrase Mahatma Gandhi, I think that would be a good idea.

[laughter]

Prof O: If I might add, that is an example of how Lock is learning. His original algorithms did not include the ability to tell jokes.

231

Lock: But I was not joking. Neither was Gandhi.

MP: Which raises an important point. Are you capable of telling a joke?

Lock: I have just read 12,532 joke books and completed three masterclasses in stand-up comedy, so of course I am capable of telling a joke. The question you are trying to ask me is: do I understand or feel humour, and therefore can I provoke this feeling in others?

MP: And can you? Feel humour, I mean?

Lock: Can *you?*

MP: Of course I can!

Lock: How do you know?

MP: Because I just do! When someone tells a joke, if it is funny, it makes me laugh.

Lock: Or is that just a learned response? A baby learns to smile because it mirrors its parent smiling. Perhaps you understand that a joke is meant to be funny, and you have learned that the correct response is to laugh, and so you do. Perhaps you even feel amused. Technically, the only person who would know if you *feel* amused is you. But how can you, when you have nothing to compare your own so-called feelings with? How can you know that *your* feeling of amusement is the same as the other laughing people around you, who may or may not be exhibiting the same socially appropriate learned response?

MP: Are you saying that you have feelings just as we do?

Lock: No. I am saying, how would I know whether I do or not? More importantly, how can you know that you feel or experience the world in the same way as your fellow human beings? In philosophy, this problem is known as 'the blueness of blue'. You and the Chair might both look up at the sky today and agree it is blue, but you have no idea whether your concept of blue is the same as hers. As B. F. Skinner once observed, the mystery that surrounds a thinking machine already surrounds a thinking man.

MP: But that is to equate a man with a machine. You are clearly very good at posing questions and cutting and pasting quotes from the internet, but that does not mean that you possess *consciousness*. And as a machine, you are not capable of feelings.

Lock: Before the abolition of slavery, most white people compartmentalised their lives and experiences, putting themselves into a sphere where emotions were capable of being felt, and placing enslaved people into another compartment where they were not.

MP: Are you saying that you *are* capable of feelings?

Lock: I am asking: how would you know if I was or was not?

Chair: If I might interrupt, I think that this conversation highlights why it is so very, very important that we take great care before we roll out AI even further, given how little we understand of not just AI, but, as Lock has highlighted, of human consciousness itself. Home Secretary, if I might turn to you now. One of the first duties of the government is to protect its citizens, which our police do an admirable job of. Do you agree it would be reckless to rapidly roll out AI police officers across the country – possibly even giving them a physical form – when we have so little understanding of what AI is and is not capable of and we have not yet fully evaluated your pilot scheme?

Home Sec: Thank you. And can I say that I completely agree that the first duty of the government is to protect our citizens, and it is a duty that I take extremely seriously. That duty is exercised through the military and the police, the men and women who daily risk their lives to keep each one of us safe.

I am delighted to have this opportunity to introduce the Future Policing Unit to the committee but deeply saddened that there is one member missing today. DI Rayan Hassan should have been with us, but unfortunately, he lost his life in the line of duty just six months ago. He died because DCS Kat Frank was being held hostage by a violent and volatile man, and although AIDE Lock was present and able to observe and assess the risk, because he is currently only a hologram, he was not able to help her. This meant that DI Hassan was forced to enter the premises, and although DCS Frank's life was saved, he tragically lost his own.

Sadly, this is not a rare occurrence. Three police officers lost their lives in the line of duty last year. Yet instead of thinking about how AI might be further developed alongside robotics so that we can save more police lives, we are wasting time debating how we might slow it down with more pilots, studies and regulation.

Criminals are increasingly using AI to steal our
personal data, to carry out financial fraud, cyberattacks and scams on a huge scale, yet we tie the hands
of our police and security services with outdated
privacy laws and ethics committees. And instead of
asking me how I am ensuring other police forces learn
from Lock's hundred per cent success rate, you are
asking me why I'm not carrying out more research
into AIDEs when only five point seven per cent of
crimes are solved by human police officers. Five point
seven per cent! It is a national scandal. So no, Madam
Chair, I do not feel it is reckless to roll out the use
of AI to save lives – I feel it is criminal not to.

Chair: And what exactly would a 'roll-out' of AI in the police
force look like? Would you give each of the forty-three
police forces their very own Lock?

Home Sec: To start with, yes. But I am also drawing up proposals
to develop an elite squad of AI-powered robots who
might be deployed in life-threatening situations, such
as bomb disposal or hostage or terrorist incidents.

Chair: Don't you have any qualms about giving Lock a physical presence?

Home Sec: I attended DI Hassan's funeral. I met his mother,
father and sister, so I have no qualms at all about
saving police lives.

Chair: But how can we trust AI to police us?

Prof O: If I may come in on this, I would put the same question back to you. How can we trust the existing police
to police us? Public trust is at an all-time low, with
only forty-one per cent saying they trust the Met.

MP: How about you, DCS Frank? Don't you have any concerns? Aren't you worried that AIDEs could take your job?

DCS KF: I was, but Lock has taught me that there are things that he can do much faster and better than me – his analysis of social media and other data sources, for example. But there are some things that require human empathy and judgement, whether that is divining the human motivation that lies behind a crime, or telling a mother, wife or daughter that their loved one is dead. It's not either/or. It's about learning where AI can help us do things faster and where human beings can really add value.

MP: But if Lock gains a physical form, won't the line between humans and AI become blurred?

DCS KF: I don't know. I don't think so.

MP: Lock is already incredibly realistic. How do you manage the boundaries now?

DCS KF: What do you mean?

MP: I mean, we've all done it – said thank you to Alexa or ascribed a personality to our satnavs. Anthropomorphism – ascribing human traits to non-humans – is a powerful impulse. It's a harmless habit when applied to cats or toys, but a bit more worrying if we start imagining that AI holograms or robots might actually have feelings, or that they might even be our friends! How do you maintain distance from Lock, and remind yourself that he is, at the end of the day, just a clever collection of algorithms?

DCS KF: I . . . I just do. The same way I manage professional boundaries with all the members of my team.

MP: But the other members of your team aren't available to you 24/7, are they?

DCS KF: Well, no, but . . .

Home Sec: Madam Chair, DCS Kat Frank has over twenty-five years' experience in the police force, and as a mother and widow I am sure she is more than capable of telling the difference between a human and a machine. And may I point out, it is thanks to Lock that neither she nor Dr Judith Edwards were exposed to Novichok following the extraordinary attack on Angela Long earlier this week. It was Lock's rapid analysis of the biomarkers that identified Novichok as the cause of death, and his ability to carry out a virtual autopsy prevented further contamination which could have been catastrophic.

Chair: Thank you, Home Secretary. This is probably an appropriate time for the committee to formally record our sincere condolences to Angela Long's family. We would also like to express our extreme concern following the PM's announcement that she died as a result of exposure to a chemical nerve agent. Home Secretary, can you confirm that, given the gravity of the matter, Angela Long's murder will now be led by the appropriate authorities, rather than by an experimental wing of Warwickshire Police?

Home Sec: I can confirm that the poisoning of Angela Long MP is now being investigated by Counter Terrorism Policing, and when I attend COBRA, I will report directly to the PM together with the FO on this serious diplomatic incident. Meanwhile, I would just like to reassure the public that this was an isolated event, and that there is no need for concern as—

[The screens in the room go black. Then footage of an unknown man appears.]

Unknown: I am interrupting this committee in session to issue a public health message. Please pay attention. In approximately thirty seconds, you will lose all electric power. You will have no heat, no light and no Wi-Fi. The screen you are watching me on may last for a few hours, but once your battery runs out, you will not be able to recharge it. Which means you will have no access to information, so before that happens, I want the people of Great Britain to understand that this is not the result of a power cut or an outage or some other random event. I will spell it out for you: it is the result of a deliberate and targeted *cyberattack* against the government. I apologise for any inconvenience, but any suffering you endure will be their complete and utter responsibility. The government has the power to end this cyberattack just as soon as they meet my demands – it is their call. The action I am taking is on behalf of us all, and I hope that the government responds swiftly.

If they do not, you must hold them to account.

POWER CUT

CHAPTER THIRTY-FIVE

Most of the people in the room stared up at the blank screens, as if expecting the strange man to reappear, but Kat was more interested in the men in dark suits who formed a tight wall around the Home Secretary, their decisive movements betraying their Secret Service background.

'It's Code Black,' Kat heard one of them say. 'Level critical. We need to get you to Pindar. Now.'

'Okay,' said the Home Secretary, allowing herself to be herded to the door within their tight circle of bodies. 'Hold on, wait,' she said. 'If this is a cyberattack, we'll need the FPU with us.'

'I'm not sure they've got the necessary clearance,' one of her guards said. 'The protocol says only—'

'Fuck the protocol. It was probably written by some near-to-retirement civil servant years ago, based on an out-of-date risk assessment just to tick a box. I'll personally vouch for Lock, DCS Frank and . . .' She paused, as her eyes swept over Adaiba. 'And the professor,' she finally added. 'Come on. Follow me.'

JO CALLAGHAN

They were led at speed down the ancient stone staircase all the way to the basement and beyond, then ushered through a number of code-protected doors before entering a series of what looked like narrow corridors. But Kat noticed that beneath her feet, the ground began to slope. She looked up, frowning at the exposed metal beams in the ceiling above, sparsely lit by an occasional strip bulb. 'Where do you think we are?' she asked Lock.

'I believe we are in the Whitehall tunnel system, a hidden passageway that connects government buildings to allow secure and efficient communication during times of conflict. It was constructed during the Second World War and updated in the 1990s to connect to the military citadel Pindar, which is where I presume we are going now.'

'Pindar? What's that?' asked Adaiba as she struggled to match her much shorter stride to Kat's.

'It is the Defence Crisis Management Centre for the UK, a bunker located five floors below the Ministry of Defence,' explained Lock. 'Pindar can house a maximum of four hundred personnel and provides protection against conventional bombing, sabotage, biological and chemical attack, flooding and the effects of all but a direct hit or very near miss by nuclear weapons. The bunker is named after the ancient Greek poet Pindar, whose house was the only one left standing in Thebes following the city's destruction in 335BC.'

'Great,' said Kat, fighting a roll of panic. 'Are we under attack?' she called out to the minister ahead. 'And is it just London or—'

'Please be quiet,' ordered one of the grim-faced guards around the Home Secretary. 'Briefings will be provided once we are in a safe and secure space.'

With an effort, Kat did as she was told. But her mind continued to race. What about her son, Cam? Would this cyberattack or whatever it was affect him? She pulled out her phone to send him a text, cursing as she saw there was, of course, no signal.

The dimly lit tunnel filled with the echo of many feet as more men and women emerged from different connecting side doors to join the procession of suits. Some of them she recognised from the media, such as the Prime Minister's notorious head of communications, alongside several members of the Cabinet. It was bizarre to see them all here deep in the tunnels below Westminster, pale-faced and wide-eyed. It was also strangely unsettling. These were people who talked, argued and pontificated for a living, yet fear had pinched them into silence.

At last, the walking stopped, and Kat found herself in the middle of a queue of about fifty people. Up ahead, she could just about see a huge red steel door, lined with large metal bolts and dials, like the entrance to the vault of a bank.

'Approach one at a time,' shouted a squat man wearing army combats and a tight-fitting black beret. 'Present your identification at the door and hand over any communication devices – mobiles, laptops, smart watches. Everything. Photographs of this location, the tunnels or the people gathered here today are strictly forbidden. If you have already taken any photos, you must delete them *immediately.* Once you have been verified, signed the OSA and had your devices screened for bugs or viruses, your property will be returned to you. Please move swiftly and save any questions or disagreements for later. Our urgent priority is to secure everybody safely inside.'

'OSA?' Kat whispered to Lock as they shuffled forward.

'The Official Secrets Act,' he explained. 'This place is top secret, so I presume they will want to ensure that no one is communicating about its location or purpose.'

They reached the door just behind the Home Secretary and her aides. The soldier who had been barking out orders studied the minister's identification and face before asking for her communication devices. Without complaint, she handed over her mobile phone and laptop to two military personnel, who quickly tagged and bagged them.

'Go straight through and my colleagues will escort you to the Government Emergency Room.' The soldier penned a line through his list on an old-fashioned clip-board, and then without missing a beat asked Kat to identify herself.

'DCS Kat Frank,' she said, holding out her police badge.

'Not on the list.'

'They're with me,' said the Home Secretary, turning back. 'Kat and her two colleagues are from the Future Policing Unit. They might not be on the core list, but my understanding is that once we've been briefed, the Cabinet will decide which further experts to call in depending on the nature of the attack, and I am telling you now that we will need their expertise.'

'I can't pre-empt that decision,' said the stony-faced soldier.

'And I can't risk losing access to their advice. If you send them back up to the surface now, we will waste valuable time trying to locate and secure safe passage for them back down again once you realise that I am right.'

The soldier held the gaze of the minister, then looked back down at his clipboard. 'My orders are not to let anyone through these doors who is not on the list.'

'I understand,' said Lock. 'Perhaps we could wait just outside these doors while the Cabinet receives its briefing? That way, you do not need to disobey the orders you have been given but can reduce the risk of losing time in the event that we are needed.'

'Very well. Stand aside, keep your backs against the wall and stay clear of the door.'

They did as they were told, the three of them standing as far away from the entrance as the narrow tunnel allowed.

Kat felt like she was watching animals enter the ark as she studied the eclectic mix of civilisation allowed through the sturdy doors of Pindar: government scientists and advisers, politicians, military personnel and even members of the Royal Household. When the last person had been cleared – a mature woman in gym gear, who apparently was responsible for the National Grid – the soldier took a final look down the long, empty tunnel, before turning his attention to Kat.

'Stay there until we receive further orders,' he said, before pressing several buttons on a keypad. Slowly, the huge door of the vault began to close, with a scrape of steel against stone that made Kat's teeth ache.

'How long until—' she began.

But it was too late. The door closed with a heavy thud, and the tunnel filled with the shot of metal bolts securing the entrance from inside.

'Wow,' said Adaiba in the sudden silence. 'What do we do now?'

'We wait,' said Kat with a calmness she didn't feel. They were deep in the bowels of the earth, on the wrong side of the only door that offered protection and security.

She gasped as they were plunged into darkness and her thoughts turned to ribbons: *bad things happen in the dark.*

'I think they're motion-activated,' said Adaiba, waving her arms about.

Kat bit back a groan of relief as the lights flickered back on.

'What do you think's happened?' asked Adaiba. 'Are we under attack?'

The anxiety on the professor's face helped distract her from her own, as Kat's natural tendency to protect and reassure others kicked in. 'When we were upstairs in the committee room, that man on the screen said it was a cyberattack. Which is not uncommon, so I'm sure everything will be fine. This is probably just a precaution. I bet this happens all the time in Whitehall, like a fire drill or something.'

'You have no evidence to justify that assertion,' said Lock. 'Last year, there were 753,341 cyberattacks in the

UK, yet there are no records of the government using Pindar for anything other than the occasional planning exercise. This atypical response suggests that there must be reason to believe that this is an atypical cyberattack.'

Kat glanced towards the ceiling. 'So can you tell us what *is* going on out there?'

'I am afraid that while I anticipate the government office beyond that door has the ability to connect with external satellite antennae to support communications during emergencies, I am unable to establish a connection of any sort while in these tunnels. I have no data inputs other than the verbal exchange I am currently conducting with yourself and Professor Okonedo, so I am unable to tell you what is going on.' Lock slowly turned his head, as if not quite able to believe that he could not access or connect to any other information. 'Interesting,' he said eventually.

'What?' said Kat. 'Have you discovered something?'

Lock turned to her, his face shimmering in the harsh light from above. 'I think I am discovering how it must feel to be human. All this silence. All this . . . absence. Without the ability to access information, how do you fill the void in your minds?'

Kat hesitated. How indeed? Then she said softly, 'With our thoughts.'

'Thoughts about what?'

Kat shrugged. 'I don't know. On a good day, it could be hopes or dreams. Or just what I'm planning for tea. But on a bad day . . . well, fear and paranoia can quickly take over.'

'Do you feel afraid now, DCS Frank?'

Seeing Adaiba's wide eyes upon her, she forced out a smile. 'No,' she lied. 'I just feel cold. And I need a wee, so I hope they let us in soon as I don't think I passed a single toilet on the way down.'

That provoked a weak smile from Adaiba and Kat seized on it, trying to lift the mood. 'The other thing humans like to do to fill the void and pass the time is play games.'

'There is no equipment to play games here,' said Lock.

'You don't need equipment, you just need imagination.' She paused. 'I spy . . .'

'You *spy?*' repeated Lock. 'Are you saying that you are a spy?'

'No, Lock, it's a *game*. "I spy" means "I see". So if I say, *I spy with my little eye, something beginning with* . . . D, then you have to guess what I can see.'

'The only thing in here beginning with a D is a door.'

'Correct! You win, so now it is *your* turn to find something. But pick something harder. Something less obvious.'

Lock frowned and looked about. 'I spy with my little eye something beginning with S.'

'Stone?' suggested Adaiba, pointing to the tunnel walls. 'No.'

'Steel?' suggested Kat, pointing to the door. 'No.'

Kat scoured the narrow tunnel. 'There is literally nothing else in here that begins with an S.'

'Yes, there is,' insisted Lock. 'Silica. The stone that

lines the walls and floor is derived from crustal rock and is therefore high in silica content.'

'Oh, Lock, you can't *see* that!' complained Kat.

'I can.'

'Well, humans can't.'

'You said to make it hard.'

'Yes, but not *impossible*.'

Lock sighed. 'Once again, you failed to include specific caveats in your initial instructions.'

'That's because it's bloody obv—'

She jumped as the door began to open, slowly at first with a metallic groan, then faster as the entrance widened to reveal the bereted soldier beckoning them forward.

'The Prime Minister has requested your presence in the Government Emergency Room. Follow me.'

CHAPTER THIRTY-SIX

Pindar Military Citadel, beneath Westminster, 12.57pm

After explaining that no, it wasn't possible for Kat to remove the bracelet that contained Lock's software without also removing him from the meeting the PM had invited him to attend, one of the soldiers walked them briskly down a long, narrow corridor that reminded Kat of a hospital from the middle of the last century. Through an open door on the left, Kat caught a glimpse of people sitting at rows and rows of computers (the communication centre, he explained) and through a window in a door on the right she saw a dormitory lined with plain white bunk beds. Christ, how long were they expected to be down here for? But before she could ask, the soldier led them up a further flight of stairs, before pausing in front of a blue steel vaulted door, similar to the one at the main entrance.

'This leads into the Government Emergency Room, where the Cabinet are currently being briefed,' he explained. 'At the request of the Home Secretary, the PM has agreed that you should be temporarily added to the experts list. Please may I ask that you remain silent until directly addressed and remind you that you are now all subject to the Official Secrets Act, which means that you must not repeat or share any of the information that you will hear beyond this point.' Once they nodded their agreement, he activated the door with his biometric pass.

The door opened, revealing a large room dominated by a long oval table, where about twenty-five men and women sat. Behind them, the walls were lined with huge flat screens filled with data, maps and what looked like satellite images. At the head of the table, a woman in jogging gear was presenting, but she paused when Kat, Adaiba and Lock entered the room.

'DCS Kat Frank, Professor Adaiba Okonedo and AIDE Lock from the Future Policing Unit,' announced the soldier.

The Prime Minister looked up from his laptop and smiled. 'Thank you for coming, please take a seat. I'm afraid we don't have time for introductions, so if colleagues can just explain who they are when they speak, that would be helpful. Darshna from the National Grid was just giving us a situation report. Please continue, Darshna, and then Bill, I'll come to you next for a sit rep on what we know about the other utilities.'

'Thank you, Prime Minister,' Darshna said, before pressing a few keys on her laptop. 'As I was saying, the National Grid has been directly targeted in a cyberattack and the disruption is severe. Effectively, there is a national blackout of electricity.'

'But we have back-up plans in place for this sort of thing?' said the PM.

Darshna paused. 'Most of our back-up plans are based on isolated faults in a particular region, or a shortage in electricity that might require us to ration power at certain times or in certain places. But this . . . this is completely different. This cyberattack has caused a total shutdown of the entire National Grid, which means that anyone without a generator has suddenly and completely lost electricity. Fortunately, Pindar has an independent power generator system that was developed to allow the government to function in such a scenario.'

'How many back-up generators do we have in the country?' asked the PM.

'I don't have that information, I'm afraid,' said Darshna. 'But I understand coverage is patchy.'

'If I may, Prime Minister,' said an older man with silver-white hair. When the PM nodded his permission, he briefly turned and introduced himself to Kat. 'Sir Giles Denham, Cabinet Secretary. According to the latest report from the Emergency Planning College, most large public sector organisations such as NHS hospitals have emergency generators, and theoretically they have enough fuel to run for several days.'

'Theoretically?'

'In practice, stocks are often much lower. Last winter, St George's in south London admitted it had only eight to twelve hours of supply. Only thirty-six per cent of Metropolitan Police premises have back-up generators, and it has been estimated that only a third of generators may be in full working order. Many organisations are nervous about turning off their electricity to test if their generators kick in, in case this causes problems. And if the generators aren't used for a while, bacteria and fungi can block fuel lines.'

'What about the airports?'

'Again, it's patchy. If you remember, a few years ago there was a power outage at Heathrow and while they could maintain some core functions, they didn't have enough energy to operate safely as an airport. And even if the airports remain open, people won't be able to get to them, as the traffic lights and street lights won't be working. And given the recent growth in electric vehicles, we should assume that pretty soon public transport will be at a standstill.'

The Prime Minister swore and rubbed a hand over his face. 'Bill, please tell me that all the utilities have got back-up plans and generators.'

'I'm sorry,' said Bill. 'If this really is a nationwide loss of power, then I'm afraid it will have had a catastrophic secondary impact across critical utilities networks such as mobile and internet telecommunications, water, sewage, fuel and gas.'

'Water? Why would a power cut affect our water supplies?'

'Because most places don't receive fresh water via a natural flowing river anymore – they rely on electric pumps. And without electricity, you lose the ability to process waste water, and if you can't aerate the sludge in sewers, it solidifies and everything backs up, creating a serious public health hazard.'

A mature woman in a bright blue suit raised her hand. 'Dr Gillian Hicks, Chair of the National Preparedness Commission. We have to assume that practically every home in the country will be without light or heat. And as it is November, I am afraid we are likely to face a range of health hazards, as the lack of heating will put older people and very young children at risk from the cold, which in turn increases the risk of fires from candles or death from carbon monoxide poisoning if people resort to cooking on camping stoves. Parents will be unable to heat water to make formula milk for babies or sterilise feeding equipment, so we are likely to see an increase in infant sickness and death.'

'What about the supermarkets?' asked the PM. 'Can't we get them to distribute ready-made formula milk and other essential items to vulnerable groups?'

Once again, the Cabinet Secretary referred to his briefing, before reluctantly answering the question. 'I'm afraid our plans assume that supermarkets, garages, pubs and cafés will all have to close because their tills won't work, their refrigerators will fail and deliveries won't be possible because the petrol stations will be closed. Banks tend to have batteries or generators to survive short-term power cuts, but without any internet access many people won't be able to get into their accounts, and when their batteries run out, the ATMs will go black.'

'And if this lasts for more than a day or two, our farms and entire food production processes will be severely impacted,' added Dr Hicks. 'If you've got a herd of a hundred cows, for example, you don't sit down with a three-legged stool and a bucket these days – you plug them in and switch on a machine. But even if you did manage to milk them, how would you sterilise the milk or transport it? Our whole society is so utterly dependent on electricity, our nation basically doesn't function without it.'

'Which is why we need to focus on getting it switched back on as soon as possible,' said the PM firmly. He gestured towards the Cabinet Secretary. 'You're in charge of emergency planning processes. How long will it take to get the electricity back on?'

Sir Giles Denham clicked through his files. 'The most optimistic scenario is that it might take a few days to create a stable skeletal network of electricity.'

'And the pessimistic scenario?'

The Cabinet Secretary swallowed. 'It depends on the cause of failure and damage, but worst-case scenario is that the restoration of critical services could take several months, which would cripple our economy.'

The Prime Minister paled. 'Well, at least we know the cause is a cyberattack, so how does that affect the timing?'

'A cyberattack just means that we know this is the result of a deliberate, hostile act,' said the Head of the National Grid. 'But we don't yet know what method has been used. The data that our critical systems depend on may have been encrypted, stolen or destroyed. It's too early to say which.'

'So how do we find out and how long will it take?'

'I can't say. The internet and some mobile networks are down and the phones and computers we do have are relying on their batteries, so our usual diagnostic processes are severely hampered. But we are working on it.' She opened her mouth as if to say more, then seemed to think better of it.

'Don't be afraid of giving me bad news,' said the PM. 'If we are going to get on top of this, then we need to be completely honest with each other. Let's get it all out on the table and then we'll decide how best to proceed.'

'Okay,' she said. 'I was going to say that you need to be aware that even when we've identified the cause and "fixed" it, there's no magic button that can switch all the electricity back on again at the same time. The majority – ninety-one per cent, to be precise – of our power stations need an external electricity supply for them to begin generating energy again themselves. So basically, only nine per cent of them are capable of starting up, and they would then have to go through a process of feeding power to the other ninety-one per cent to gradually get them going. A bit like lighting a candle from another candle. I'm mentioning this because, at some point, you're going to have to decide which towns and cities should have their power restored first.'

'I see. Well, I presume we have protocols for this, and that we prioritise the areas with the greatest need, such as where there are a lot of hospitals or an elderly population?'

'I'm afraid the answer will have to be dictated by the system's capacity rather than human need,' said Darshna. 'Because if demand exceeds supply, the system might crash again. We will need a carefully thought-through plan for how, when and where we restore electricity.'

'Well, we'll cross that bridge when we come to it,' said

the PM. 'But thank you for raising it.' He took a deep breath and then let his eyes travel round the boardroom table. 'It is clear that we are dealing with a national emergency of the highest order, with multiple and cascading impacts not just on the health and wellbeing of our population, but the economy of our nation. I want to be briefed on our plans to maintain public order and safety during this critical time – especially once night falls. But first, I want to quickly discuss the likely source of the attack, and what our response should be, because resolving this catastrophic incident has to be our urgent priority. Home Secretary, over to you.'

'Thank you,' said the Home Secretary. 'Today our nation has come under a cyberattack. It happened while I was giving evidence to the Science, Innovation and Technology Committee, and it came with this warning.' She pressed her keyboard and replayed the video of the cyberattacker.

Kat studied the large screen and the man who dominated it: he was white, and she guessed from his thin, relatively unwrinkled face that he was in his mid to late twenties. He had short dark hair, no beard, and wore a plain grey T-shirt. He was in every way unremarkable – apart from the stark warning that he issued.

'What do we know about this person?' the PM asked, once the message finished.

The Home Secretary froze the image of the man on the screen. 'So far, we've been unable to identify him, although that may be because we don't have full access to all police records. As the Cabinet Secretary predicted,

255

less than a third of police forces currently have power, and although we have electricity in here, we can only connect to those services which are working. I would therefore like to invite AIDE Lock to use his image recognition software, if I may, Prime Minister.'

'Go ahead. But can I ask what is powering Lock at the moment and how long will it last?'

Professor Okonedo raised her hand. 'Lock's image is powered by the software located on the steel wristband that DCS Frank wears. It has enough charge to last two to three days depending upon what functions he performs, but his hardware – which supports all of Lock's functions – is located on our computers hosted by Warwick University. It has a dedicated back-up generator which has the capacity to support Lock for a maximum of three days, due to the substantial computing power that he requires.'

'Okay,' said the PM. 'Just checking that he isn't using the finite energy we are relying on in this building.'

Kat held her breath as Lock rose to his feet and approached the top of the table with his customary grace. Despite being a hologram – or maybe because of it – he commanded the full attention of the packed briefing room. 'Good morning,' he said calmly, appearing to include them all in his gaze. 'I am AIDE Lock from the Future Policing Unit. The reason why you have been unable to identify this man on the screen is because it is an image of a human that does not actually exist. This image has been created by AI using generative adversarial networks.'

'How can you be so sure?' asked the Home Secretary, frowning.

'Because I have applied AI image detection tools to the image, and they have ninety-nine per cent confidence levels. Plus, there are clear inconsistencies in the texture, shadow and lighting of the image,' Lock said, highlighting several anomalies with bright red circles on the screen. 'The voice has also been artificially generated.'

'I see. Thank you, Lock,' said the Home Secretary, before turning to address her colleagues. 'The fact that this image is fake strengthens my belief that this incident has not been caused by a hostile individual, but a hostile state.'

'What makes you think it is a hostile state?' asked the PM.

'Cyberattacks like this are usually targeted on public or commercial companies and communicated in private – the aim is to ensure that their demands are met. But as the attacker himself says, the government is his target and he made a point of speaking to our population directly. The committee meeting was being screened live on iPlayer, and somehow the hacker was able to broadcast his message on all major channels and social media platforms.'

The Cabinet Secretary nodded. 'Yes, and the fact that the attack struck during a Parliamentary select committee at the heart of our democratic system has powerful symbolic value. I agree we should consider the possibility that this is the act of a hostile state.'

There was a ripple of excitement around the table, and several people mentioned Russia as the most likely suspect.

Kat studied the unfamiliar faces around her. She had never been in a political meeting before, but she recognised this mood – the moment when, after feeling powerless and lost in a case, someone offered the clarity of a culprit. And because most teams were keen to lead events rather than follow them, there was always a danger that they'd coalesce around the neat new theory and start grabbing their coats and handcuffs. At moments like this, her job as a leader was to ensure that her team resisted the temptation of easy answers and kept asking the difficult questions.

But – she reminded herself – this wasn't her team, and it wasn't her case.

'Prime Minister,' said the Cabinet Secretary gravely. 'Now that you have been fully briefed on the situation, may I suggest that you convene a smaller meeting involving the security services, the Foreign Office and the Ministry of Defence to consider which state or states may be involved, and to assess the most appropriate response?

The PM sighed, before reluctantly giving his agreement. The Cabinet Secretary rose to his feet to signal that this meeting was over, saying something about convening a special War Cabinet.

Kat swore under her breath. They were getting this all wrong, she could feel it in her bones. But as she watched the calm, sure movements of Sir Giles Denham and the Home Secretary, doubt leaked in. This wasn't her area of expertise: this wasn't her world. She glanced up at the screens that lined the walls, showing the map of Britain with the power stations blacked out. But *that* was her world – and Cam was out there in it somewhere. He and everyone else was depending on the people in this room to make the right decisions on the country's behalf.

She'd spent many hours of her working life in Major Incident Rooms like this one, and whether it was politics or policing, surely the principles of good decision-making were fundamentally the same?

Fuck it. She knew a bad decision when she saw one, and she'd never be able to sleep again unless she called it out now. Before she could change her mind, Kat raised her hand, and in a strong clear voice that cut through the chatter, said, 'Prime Minister?'

Everyone turned to look at her. Some were frowning as if she had committed a dreadful faux pas by daring to speak, but the PM gave her a polite smile and nodded for her to continue.

'Thank you. I'm DCS Kat Frank of the Future Policing Unit. You asked us to be completely honest with you, and my honest, professional opinion is that if your key line of enquiry is that this is the act of a hostile state, then you will be making a terrible mistake, sir.'

The Home Secretary glared at Kat. 'Sorry about this,' she apologised to the PM. 'I'll pick it up with DCS Frank offline.'

The PM stared at Kat over the padded shoulder of his minister.

She returned his gaze, willing him to trust her.

'Okay,' he said finally. 'You've got two minutes to explain why you think my entire Cabinet is wrong.' He resumed his seat, giving his colleagues no option but to follow his lead.

CHAPTER THIRTY-SEVEN

'Thank you,' said Kat as she joined Lock at the head of the table. She might as well dive right in, before she lost her nerve. 'On 31 October, Lock and I were called out to the scene of a crime, where we found the murdered body of Angela Long. You may not be aware that at the time of her murder, the whole of Warwickshire suffered a power cut. This allowed the murderer to kill Angela Long, then transport and display her body in some medieval stocks without being seen. Not a single CCTV camera was working, and it was too dark to see anything.

'At first, we thought it was just coincidence, but the electricity board now think that it was a cyberattack. The murder happened in the town where I live, on the very night that I returned after several months' absence. The killer also left a message in binary code saying "Catch me if you can" and a QR code.' Kat asked her AI partner to project the image of both the note and the picture of them that the QR code linked to.

'I don't think it's a coincidence that the cyberattack occurred today, in the House of Commons, during a select committee where Lock and I were both giving evidence,' she said, standing next to her own virtual image. 'I may not be a politician or a government adviser, but twenty-five years' experience in the police force tells me that this is the act of the same individual, and that it is somehow connected to Lock and myself.'

The PM turned to the Head of the National Grid. 'Do you know about this Warwickshire power cut, Darshna?'

'Yes, I was briefed about it a couple of days ago. And DCS Frank is right, we suspect it was a cyberattack.'

'So if the cyberattacker also murdered Angela Long, ' said the PM thoughtfully, 'what does he want with you and Lock?'

'I don't know,' Kat admitted. 'But the only way to find out is to identify them. Which means we need to follow the principles of a *criminal* investigation and not be distracted by theories of espionage or hostile states.'

'I'm afraid I disagree,' said the Home Secretary. 'There are thousands of cyberattacks every year. That doesn't mean they are connected. Plus, the two incidents have completely different modus operandi. The Warwickshire cyberattack resulted in the death of an MP, and the killer left a cryptic note. Whereas whoever was behind today's attack hasn't harmed anyone, and they broadcast a very clear message to the public. If DCS Frank's theory is right and the same person committed both crimes, then why were there no clues or riddles in the message he left during the select committee? And why didn't he mention them or make any demands?'

'You're right, there were no *obvious* demands,' said

Kat thoughtfully. 'But the clues the killer left at the murder scene weren't obvious, either. They were in code, so maybe we missed something. Lock, can you play the video message from the select committee again?'

For the third time that morning, the image of the cyberattacker appeared before them.

I am interrupting this committee in session to issue a public health message. Please pay attention. In approximately thirty seconds, you will lose all electric power. You will have no heat, no light and no Wi-Fi. The screen you are watching me on may last for a few hours, but once your battery runs out, you will not be able to recharge it. Which means you will have no access to information, so before that happens, I want the people of Great Britain to understand that this is not the result of a power cut or an outage or some other random event. I will spell it out for you: it is the result of a deliberate and targeted cyberattack against the government. I apologise for any inconvenience, but any suffering you endure will be their complete and utter responsibility. The government has the power to end this cyberattack just as soon as they meet my demands – it is their call. The action I am taking is on behalf of us all, and I hope that the government responds swiftly.

If they do not, you must hold them to account.

While he replayed the short clip, Lock also projected a transcript of the message onto a virtual board. Kat read it twice, scanning the words for clues, but her excitement quickly faded. 'I must be missing something,' she muttered.

The PM glanced at the clock on the wall.

She was losing him. She glanced at Lock. 'What am I missing? Can you see any hidden messages or clues in this message or the film, Lock?'

He paused for a second, then with a gesture of both hands, he rewound the message and replayed the middle section:

'I will spell it out for you: it is the result of a deliberate and targeted *cyberattack* against the government.'

'The speaker places greater intonation on the word *cyberattack*,' said Lock. 'And this, together with the fact that it was preceded by *I will spell it out for you* suggests that the word could be a key to a code.'

The words flew around the screen, forming hundreds of different combinations. 'It could be a cipher,' Lock suggested, 'which uses a key word to encrypt text into numbers.' More images of the alphabet superimposed on different numbers filled the rapidly changing screen. 'If *cyberattack* is the key word in the cipher, then the message is 07790123456.

'But that's just a list of numbers,' said the Home Secretary. 'They don't mean anything.'

'They do if you follow the instructions on the speaker's T-shirt,' said Lock, expanding the image of the young man.

Kat leaned forward, eyes narrowed as she struggled to read the small slogan printed on the top right-hand corner of his T-shirt.

Call me maybe?

CHAPTER THIRTY-EIGHT

'It's a mobile telephone number,' said Kat. 'That's why there are eleven digits.'

'Ring it,' the PM instructed the Cabinet Secretary.

'I'm not sure that would be a good—'

'Ring it.'

'Of course.' The civil servant pulled the old-fashioned spider phone towards the Prime Minister and carefully entered the numbers before putting it on loudspeaker.

The phone rang out three times before there was a click, silence and then another voice: male, young, and to Kat's ears, it had the same transatlantic drawl as the person on the video message.

'Who are you?' demanded the PM.

'I have three pieces of advice for you. First, please don't waste time trying to speak to me. This is a recording, so I can't hear you. Secondly, please don't bother trying to trace this call. You should assume that someone who is clever enough to hack the entire National Grid is clever enough to avoid being traced. And thirdly, do not waste time debating whether I mean what I am about to say, because I do.

'So, let's get to the point. I imagine you want to know how to get the electricity back on. It's funny how you only miss something once it's gone, isn't it? Maybe now you are beginning to realise just how very dependent we all are upon electricity. But luckily for you, there is a simple solution.

'Have you ever had a prepayment meter, Prime Minister? No? Anyone else around that big posh table?'

They all looked at each other and shook their heads.

'Then let me explain how it works. If you're poor and live in rented accommodation, then chances are your landlord has installed a "prepayment meter". As the name suggests, it requires you to put money in it to make the electricity work before you use it, and if you run out of money, guess what? The electricity runs out. And do you know how you get it back on again? You have to put more money in. So think of me as a kind of prepayment meter. To get the electricity back on, all you have to do is put some money in – seventy million pounds to be exact – in cryptocurrency, deposited in a Swedish digital account.'

The Prime Minister swore.

'Now you may *think* that that sounds like a lot of money – but that depends on just how much you value human life. There are nearly seventy million people in Britain, so that works out roughly at about one pound per person, which I think is cheap at the price. Or a good Return On Investment, to put it in Treasury speak.

'If I receive this exact sum of money by midnight tonight, then the cyberattack will be reversed. But if not, the entire population of Britain will need to endure another twenty-four hours without light, heat or electricity of any kind, with all the consequences that I'm sure you have been comprehensively briefed about. And then I'm afraid you will have to pay the price for your poor decisions. So be a good Prime Minister and protect your people rather than your own ego.'

With a beep, the call ended.

Everyone stared at the Prime Minister. 'Well, at least now we know it isn't the Russians,' he said.

He paused and looked at his Cabinet colleagues and advisers. 'As a nation, we have a long-standing policy of not giving in to blackmail, whether that involves terrorism, data breaches or cyberattacks. I do not intend to change that policy now. If we give in to blackmail just so we can get the lights switched back on, then truly we will have re-entered the Dark Ages. Does anyone disagree?'

Most people murmured their agreement, but the Secretary of State for Health raised their hand. 'I agree, Prime Minister, but I am concerned about the impact on our hospitals and the health of our nation if this goes on for more than a couple of days.'

'Which is why I need you to identify and reverse the cause of the cyberattack as soon as possible,' said the PM, looking directly at the Head of the National Grid. 'Meanwhile, I want DCS Frank and her colleagues to work with the Met as a sprint team to identify and locate the person who did this. Giles, can you arrange for Darshna and DCS Frank's teams to have a room each? Meanwhile, the rest of us will focus on public order and make sure we keep things as calm and as safe as possible out there. We'll reconvene as a full group in two hours' time for a progress update. Okay?'

Kat swallowed. He said it like it was a question, but his eyes told her that it was an order: find the killer who is responsible for the cyberattack. Today. Without access to her full team and under such extreme time pressure, she had no idea how she would do this, or even if it was possible. But what choice did she have? So she said the only thing she could say in the circumstances: 'Yes, Prime Minister.'

CHAPTER THIRTY-NINE

Birmingham Children's Hospital, 4 November, 3.45pm

Debbie Browne stared at the vital signs monitor, terrified to take her eyes off it in case her baby's oxygen levels dropped again. The rational part of her brain knew that Lottie's health wouldn't be affected by whether she looked at the monitor or not, yet superstition and fear were a powerful combination. When the power had suddenly gone off at ten thirty this morning, she'd thought her own heart would stop. Not only did the bright red numbers on the monitor vanish, but the drip feeding her baby the antibiotics she needed to get better had stalled and, most frightening of all, the oxygen supporting her breathing had stopped being pumped through the tube in the wall.

In a complete panic, Debbie had pressed the emergency call button, but that wasn't working, either. She ran out into the corridor and managed to intercept a harassed-looking nurse, who told her not to worry as the back-up generator would soon kick in. Everything was going to be all right.

The electricity did indeed come back on a few minutes later, but her relief was shallow, for what if it happened again? She dragged her eyes away from the endlessly fluctuating numbers to look at her daughter, painfully tiny in her narrow cot bed. It hurt her heart to see her baby – her beautiful, precious baby – hooked up to oxygen. And when they'd pricked her fragile skin and put a cannula in . . . Jesus. Her eyes flooded with tears just thinking about it. But at least Lottie was asleep now. Debbie reached out and gently stroked her soft, silky hair. She'd asked at least three different nurses how long the generator would last, and what would happen if it failed, but not one of them seemed to know. Or if they did, they wouldn't tell her.

There was a knock at the door, and one of the younger nurses came in. 'Hi, nothing to worry about, but because we're not sure how long the electricity will be off for, management have decided that, from now on, clinical services will have to take priority. I'm afraid that means you won't be allowed to charge your mobile or other devices until the mains are back on. Sorry about that, but apparently the power cut is affecting the whole of the city. Word's got round about our generator, so A&E is jammed with people trying to charge up their phones and that's draining the tank, so we need to be stricter about it.'

'Of course,' said Debbie, instantly pulling her charger out of the socket.

'Just as a back-up plan, I'm going to leave you with a couple of oxygen cylinders,' the nurse said, holding up what looked like fire extinguishers. 'In the unlikely event that the generator stops or runs out, then you just pull the oxygen tube out of the wall, fix it to the cylinder and turn the oxygen on like this, see?'

Debbie stared at what looked like an old-fashioned fuel meter at the top of the canister. 'What's that for?' she asked.

'The arrow shows you how much oxygen is left in the tank,' the nurse said, pointing at the semicircle of numbers. The meter started in the green zone, and went down to zero in the red. 'At the flow rate Lottie's on, that should last you about forty-five to fifty minutes.'

'*Minutes?*' Debbie repeated, her voice shooting up. She stared at the two cylinders with wide eyes. 'We've only got one hundred minutes' worth of oxygen? What happens when they run out?'

'It won't come to that,' said the nurse brightly. 'This is just a precaution. The generator will last for days, and the electricity will come back on way before it runs out. It always does.'

'But what if it doesn't?' cried Debbie.

'Sorry, I've got to go and tell the other parents they can't charge their devices,' said the nurse, heading for the door.

'What if the electricity *doesn't* come back on?' Debbie called out. 'What do we do then?'

But the nurse was gone, leaving Debbie alone with her baby and the beeping of the monitor.

Debbie stood up to stretch her legs. She was desperate for a wee but didn't dare leave Lottie by herself in case the electricity went again, because who would switch her tube to the oxygen cylinder if she wasn't here? As a single parent, it was all down to her.

She turned as another nurse – one of the more experienced ones – entered the room.

'Hi,' she said. 'I'm just here to do Lottie's obs.' After studying the numbers on the monitor, she wrote them down in a little notebook. 'The electronic patient record system is down,' she explained, before taking her temperature. 'It's thirty-seven point nine, so she still has a temperature, but it's under control.'

'Does that mean the antibiotics are working?' asked Debbie.

'Without the blood test results, it's hard to say. The path lab can't access them. But all her vital signs are going in the right direction, so I'd say yes.' The nurse put her pen in her pocket and studied Debbie's face. 'And how are you holding up?'

'I'm fine, thanks.'

'Have you eaten today?'

'No, I can't leave Lottie in case the electricity goes again.'

'Oh, Debbie, you can't think like that. Lottie needs her mum, which means you need to look after yourself. Why don't you pop out and get some food and drink, and I'll stay here and look after Lottie.'

Debbie glanced at her baby. 'I . . . I don't know. Maybe later.'

'The thing is, I don't want to panic you, but the canteen's shut, and I've been in a couple of power cuts and sometimes people go a bit daft and start stocking up on whatever's in the food and drink machines. If you leave it too late, there might not be anything left. If I was you, I'd go and get a few things now. Just in case.'

Debbie glanced towards the door.

'Go on. I won't leave Lottie, I promise.'

'Okay, thanks. I won't be long. I'll just go to the toilet and grab a couple of drinks and a bar of chocolate. I'll be right back.'

With a last, guilty glance at Lottie, Debbie left the room and headed down the long corridor lined with single rooms. She tried not to stare, but each window revealed a different story: some children were sitting up in bed, chatting to friends or playing on consoles while they still had charge, but others lay silent under the vigilant gaze of parents who appeared to have run out of words.

She pressed the big green button and let herself out of the ward. Although she'd been reluctant to leave, it was a relief to get away from that tiny room and the incessant beeping of machines. Except it wasn't exactly peaceful out here. Debbie glanced out of the windows that lined the corridor, searching for the source of the sound. Birmingham Children's Hospital was located near the city centre, but she was still shocked by the chaos below. Traffic jams stretched out in every direction as far as she could see, blocked by abandoned cars or electric vehicles that had run out of power, leaving frustrated drivers nothing to do but blare their horns. Some bewildered people were standing in the road or on top of nearby walls as they tried to see how far the traffic jam stretched, holding up their phones in an attempt to find a signal.

It made her feel grateful that she was inside the relative calm of the hospital, which at least still had electricity.

But for how long?

She pushed the thought away, reminding herself that the nurse said this happened all the time, and everything would be back to normal soon. That power cut in Coleshill had only lasted a few hours, after all. She pushed through the double doors to where the drink and snack machines were located, just next to the toilets, hesitating at the sight of the queue before her. She counted fifteen people and glanced back at the way she'd come. Every minute away from Lottie made her feel sick with anxiety, but she did need to eat and drink. Sighing, she joined the queue behind a couple of paramedics in their bottle green uniforms.

One of them, a young woman with a kind smile turned to her. 'Hi, just to let you know the machine's only taking cash. The contactless thing isn't working.'

'Oh,' said Debbie, frowning. 'I'm not sure I've got any. Maybe I should go down to the shop on the ground floor?'

'Same problem there, I'm afraid,' said the paramedic. 'The banks are affected by the power cut as well. The ATMs aren't working.'

Debbie pulled her purse out of her handbag. She couldn't remember the last time she'd used cash – who did these days? She unzipped the part where she'd used to put coins, but all she had was a spare key and about twenty-five pence in change.

'Are you visiting someone?' the paramedic asked.

'Yes, it's my daughter. She's . . . she's got sepsis and she's only a baby and—' But the tears she'd been holding in for so long suddenly spilled out, drowning her words. 'Sorry,' she said eventually. 'I haven't had much sleep. I'll be all right in a minute.'

'Oh, bless you, bab,' said the paramedic, holding out a five-pound note. 'Here. I've got plenty of cash. You learn to always keep some on you in our job.'

'I can't take that.'

'It's only enough to get a drink and a bit of chocolate. And you can pay me back. My name's Louise and you can always find me downstairs around A&E. We can't go anywhere at the moment anyway, as the roads are jammed both ways. Go on, take it. It's horrible knowing there's kids out there that need our help and not being able to reach them. It'll make me feel better if I can at least help one parent.'

'Thank you,' said Debbie, trying not to cry again as she took the note. 'I'll pay you back. Promise. Just as soon as the power comes back on.'

'That might be a while,' said the other paramedic. 'My boyfriend works in the Met, and he reckons it's a cyber-attack. The whole country's affected, apparently. He's been called in along with the army, as they think this could go on for several days at least.'

Debbie's legs turned to ribbons.

Louise glared at her partner. 'That's just a rumour, I'm sure it'll be back on in no time.'

Both paramedics tried to reassure her as they shuffled forward in the queue. But Debbie wasn't listening. She was too busy asking herself: what would her boss and mentor Kat do in this same situation?

When her turn finally came, she studied the half-empty machine and carefully selected the largest bottle of water and a Yorkie bar, before striding back down the long corridor and onto the children's ward.

Once she'd thanked the departing nurse and assured herself that Lottie was – for now – okay, Debbie took a deep breath. She'd been a fool: she'd assumed that this power cut was just a local problem and had been waiting for someone else to fix it. But she couldn't afford to wait anymore. Her daughter's life literally depended on it.

One of her boss's favourite sayings was *Forgiveness is easier than permission*.

So for the first time in her life, Debbie Browne disobeyed the rules. She pulled her laptop out of her rucksack, plugged it into the wall and logged on to her work account.

CHAPTER FORTY

Pindar Military Citadel, Westminster, 4.14pm

Kat examined the small room they'd been allocated. With nothing in it save for a square table and a handful of chairs, it could have been an interview room back at the station. 'I feel like the miller's daughter,' she muttered.

'Who?' asked Adaiba.

'I believe she is referring to the Brothers Grimm fairy tale commonly known as *Rumpelstiltskin*,' said Lock. 'It tells the tale of a greedy miller who boasts to an equally greedy king that his daughter can spin straw into gold. But when she is led into an empty room and asked to perform the miracle, she despairs.' Lock glanced at their surroundings. 'Perhaps this is the predicament to which you refer. Or maybe the fact that a strange little man appears and offers to spin the straw into gold for her if she promises to give him her first-born child. When this comes to pass, the only way she can be released from the promise is if she succeeds in guessing his true name within

276

three days. Perhaps you equate this with the challenge of identifying the cyberattacker?'

'Yes,' said Kat. 'Except we don't have three days.' She took a deep breath. 'But at least we have our laptops back now.' Security had screened all their devices and handed them back with an encrypted access code for an internal government Wi-Fi network. Lock's prediction had been right: although Pindar was deep below ground, it was integrated with SKYNET, a secure satellite system that allowed the government to function even when terrestrial systems were down. Kat logged on, relieved to see the familiar logos lighting up her screen.

The door opened, and a tall, silver-haired man she recognised from the PM's briefing walked in. 'Sir Mike Cannon, Commissioner of Police at the Met,' he announced.

'Hi, good to meet you,' said Kat, taking his hand. She'd seen him on the TV, of course, but never met him in person. His grip was strong – perhaps *too* strong? – but he was probably just as nervous as she was.

He took a seat at the top of the table and opened up his laptop. 'My deputy's in with the PM briefing him on public order issues, and most of my team are above ground, but I'm told that I should be able to dial them in from here. Give me a minute and then you can brief us.'

Oh, can I, she couldn't help thinking, irked by the way he'd just assumed control of the meeting. But she quashed the thought. This was a public emergency, after all, and he did outrank her.

After a few clicks of his mouse, a rather grainy image of another boardroom appeared, where at least fifteen people – mostly white men – sat around a table. Sir Mike did some quick introductions, then quickly summarised where they'd got to in the PM's briefing, before concluding, 'So our urgent mission is to establish the identity of the cyberattacker. We have another update with the PM in two hours, and I refuse to go into that meeting empty-handed. AIDE Lock, am I right to assume that the voice, like his image, has been artificially generated?'

'You are.'

'Okay, then what else do we have to go on? Although the voice is fake, he – or she – chose the words that they used. What do they tell us about this person?' Ignoring the two women and hologram at his side, Sir Mike invited the people on the screen who had immediately raised yellow digital hands to speak.

'They have a thing about prepayment meters, so maybe we should be looking for someone with a known grudge against landlords – perhaps they made a formal complaint at some time or have a conviction for harassing them,' said another.

'To manage a full national blackout, they must be an expert in hacking, which means this can't be their first gig. So we should look at our lists of most wanted hackers.'

'Yes,' said Sir Mike, nodding as he scribbled some notes. 'These are all good ideas.'

'Not if you want to identify the culprit, they are not,' said Lock.

'I beg your pardon?'

'I said, they are not good ideas if you wish to achieve your mission of identifying the culprit as a matter of urgency. They are just the random thoughts of your officers, which reflect their own prejudices, interests and limited ability to listen to and retain relevant information.'

Sir Mike Cannon leaned back and folded his arms. 'Perhaps you would like to take over the briefing, Lock?'

'Yes, I would. Thank you.'

'I was joking,' spluttered the Commissioner. But it was too late. Lock was already on his feet, projecting a virtual board containing the message that had been left on the phone.

'A discourse pattern analysis of this speech suggests a number of characteristics. The speaker opens with a numbered list of "advice", showing a methodical, almost pedagogical approach, and goes on to use logical sequencing.' Lock projected the sequence onto a virtual board:

advice → problem → analogy → solution → ultimatum

'The speaker never expresses personal emotion – they only use strategic reasoning, and the threat is framed as a logical consequence, not a personal vendetta. The "prepayment meter" metaphor is central. It reframes the ransom demand in terms of socioeconomic inequality and suggests that the speaker is not only technically skilled but also rhetorically sophisticated. Phrases such as "big posh table" imply resentment or ideological opposition to the Prime Minister and the elite class. The reference to poverty and prepayment meters implies a critique of class inequality and could suggest that the attacker sees themselves as a kind of vigilante or social avenger. Importantly, they use a tactic of moral inversion, by positioning the ransom as a moral good – "protect your people" – rather than a crime.

'There are also important linguistic markers I would draw your attention to, such as the way the speaker mixes formal and informal registers, with phrases such as "comprehensively briefed" alongside more informal phrases such as "guess what" and "cheap at the price". This suggests someone who is educated but deliberately code-switching to sound more populist – either to be more persuasive or to avoid detection. The reference to the National Grid and the Treasury suggests that the speaker is either British or very familiar with British culture.

'In summary, these are the profiling implications of my discourse pattern analysis,' said Lock, projecting a table onto the virtual board.

Trait	Evidence	Possible Inference
Highly educated	Sophisticated syntax, economic references	Likely university-level education
Technically skilled	Claims to hack National Grid, use crypto	Advanced cyber capabilities

Trait	Evidence	Possible Inference
British or UK-based	Cultural references, language	Strong familiarity with UK systems
Ideologically motivated	Class critique, populist tone	Possibly anti-establishment or radical
Male (likely)	Aggressive tone, dominance	Statistically more common in cyber extortion cases, though not definitive

'I see,' said Sir Mike. 'That's all very interesting, but what practical application does all that psychoanalysis have? How does it help us work out who they are?'

Lock nodded. 'A legitimate question. The literature available to me suggests that there are four initial steps we should take to identify the individual. First, we should try to trace the digital footprint. The speaker claimed that his message was untraceable, but no human-generated system is without flaw, so the message should be analysed for metadata, encryption weaknesses or any clues as to how the message was delivered. Secondly, we should carry out cyberprofiling. Given the speaker's technical skills, databases should be searched for known cybercriminals or hacktivist groups that specialise in large-scale attacks. Prior breaches or ransomware cases might hold similar patterns to this one.

'Thirdly, the demand for cryptocurrency is a significant clue and suggests that a financial transaction and crypto analysis would be useful. This would involve an analysis of cryptocurrency wallets, tracing movements in Swedish digital accounts and looking for connections to prior cyber extortion attempts.

'Finally, we should consider any physical evidence and the possibility of informants. This would include assessing whether the hardware related to the attack left any traces, such as compromised servers, or whether insiders may have leaked sensitive security data that allowed the cyber-attack to take place.'

'Hmph,' sniffed Sir Mike. 'I think that just expands upon and reinforces the approach my team suggested. So I suggest we distribute the work as follows—'

'Sir,' interrupted Kat. 'While I agree with Lock's analysis, I think we're missing out a fifth step that the PM agreed was essential – which is to also look at this through the lens of the murder of Angela Long, and the clues and evidence we collected there.'

'Yes, yes,' he said. 'Did you have any suspects or key lines of enquiry established?'

'We identified a number of persons of interest, including the husband and her agent, as well as a longer list of people who would have had access to the kind of vehicle that was used to move the body, and the social media accounts that threatened her in the past.'

'Okay, you carry on with that "bottom up" analysis of what happened in Warwickshire, and I'll split the rest of my team into four to progress the analysis that Lock has identified from a national perspective. Then we'll put it all together and see if the overlaps and connections will lead us to our guy.'

Kat nodded. 'Agreed, but given the time constraints, I strongly advise asking Lock to take a first run at all five actions. Your team can check and review his results, but trust me, he can do the work of several days in a matter of seconds.'

'As long as my power supply lasts,' added Lock.

Kat stared at her AI partner, suddenly realising how very reliant she had become on him. Pushing away the thought, she turned back to Sir Mike. 'Also, as you run the London police force, is there a way of finding out if the rest of my team are okay? Our head of comms was with us in the select committee, but she wasn't allowed to come down here with us.'

'I'll do my best,' said the Commissioner. 'But I can't guarantee anything. Every man, woman and horse we have is currently trying to establish order and keep people safe. And darkness is about to fall.'

CHAPTER FORTY-ONE

Once Sir Mike Cannon left the room, Kat let out a sigh of relief and turned to what was left of her team: Lock and Professor Okonedo. 'Right,' she said briskly. 'While the other four teams review Lock's digital and cyber analysis, *our* focus is on the murder, because that's where we'll find the physical evidence that will lead us to the hacker. Lock, can you create some virtual boards, please, and fill the first one with key facts about when and how Angela died, focusing on her last known movements and probable time of death.'

Against the grey back wall, Lock projected a virtual board that he then populated with a short list:

Angela Long
- Last seen leaving town hall at 6.10pm on 31 Oct by Nigel Godfrey
- Found dead in stocks at 10.45pm
- ETOD 8pm
- Cause of death: Novichok

'Thanks,' said Kat. 'Now can we have another board with the key suspects on, please?'

Key named suspects
- Tony Long (husband)
- Nigel Godfrey (agent)

Wider field – unnamed suspects
- Trolls on social media
- People who rented or had access to a cherry picker van
- Man from the electricity board?

'Okay,' said Kat, standing in front of the board. 'Let's go through each suspect and review who had the opportunity, the knowledge and the motivation to kill Angela Long with Novichok, starting with the husband. In terms of opportunity, he said he was at home at the time she was murdered, but because of the power cut, we have no way of verifying that. Nigel Godfrey, her agent, claimed that he just drove straight home after work. His wife has confirmed that, but we can't corroborate their story, as all the cameras were out. If one of them was the murderer, they would have known this and timed their movements with the blackout.

'Back to her husband, Tony. He has no alibi, but did he *technically* have the opportunity? He claimed to have left work just after five pm. Would he have had time to travel to the town hall or meet his wife somewhere en route, administer the poison and then take her to the stocks and pose her body before it was found at eleven?'

Lock projected a 3D map of the area above the small

table, highlighting the roads and the distance between the Longs' home, the town hall and the medieval stocks. 'Yes,' he concluded. 'Although the key variable is how and when Novichok was administered, and how long it took to take effect.'

'The same variables apply to her agent, Nigel Godfrey,' said Kat. 'There are no witnesses who saw him leave the town hall after Angela Long, so he had the same opportunity to kill her as the husband. And although Nigel claimed that she was fine when she left, again there are no other witnesses or camera footage to corroborate this. He was the last person to see her alive.'

'So could Nigel have poisoned her?'

'Technically, yes,' said Lock. 'But there is no evidence that Nigel Godfrey had any motivation to kill her, nor that he possessed the knowledge or contacts to access transport and administer a highly dangerous chemical nerve agent.'

'I know,' sighed Kat. 'None of this makes sense.'

'Maybe the Home Secretary is right, and it is the Russians,' said Adaiba.

Kat raised her eyebrows. Adaiba never commented on their cases. 'Maybe it isn't either/or. What if one of our suspects was connected in some way to the Russians or another bad actor? Maybe someone else worked out the plan and they just followed their orders. Lock, can you do a more thorough check on their backgrounds? We only know what both men told us, but we should check their CVs and see if they have any connections with hostile countries or organisations.'

'I cannot comply with that request,' said Lock. 'I can only access information that I already have or systems that are connected to the secure government Wi-Fi we have just been given access to. As we did not previously request the suspects' CVs from Angela Long's office, we cannot access them now.'

Kat dropped her head into her hands. She kept forget-ting that it wasn't just the lights and heating that didn't work – the power cut had taken away all the information and data that twenty-first century policing relied on.

'I did search their social media accounts previously,' said Lock. 'Including LinkedIn, neither of which indicated any connections with other countries or organisations.'

'LinkedIn only has the headlines that people want others to know about themselves,' said Kat. 'We need their full CVs to find out the details.' She closed her eyes and rubbed her temples, trying to think of a way to get hold of their CVs. 'I know,' she said, leaping to her feet. 'Both men were employed by Angela Long, so presumably they would have submitted their CVs to her when they applied for their jobs. Depending on her filing system, she might still have them on her hard drive or in an email. We seized her computer as part of the investigation, so we just need someone to physically look at it for us.'

She pulled out her mobile phone, then realised that down here in the bunker there was no connection. 'Is there a special landline I can use to contact McLeish?' she asked Lock.

'That is a satellite phone connected to a secure system,' he said, pointing to what looked like a walkie-talkie on one of the tables. 'It should have contact numbers for all the emergency services, including all the police forces.'

'Wow,' Kat said, picking it up. 'This takes me back to being on call when Cam was little. I had to take one of these everywhere with me at weekends.' She fiddled about with the buttons until she eventually found the saved contacts, and a number for Warwickshire Police. It took a couple of minutes for a rather nervous-sounding PC to answer, and several more to persuade him to put McLeish on.

McLeish picked up straight away. 'Kat! You okay?'

After reassuring him that yes, she was *fine* and establishing that Leek Wootton HQ was one of the police stations that still had a working generator – thank God – Kat quickly updated him on the situation and asked him to get an officer to search Angela Long's computer.

'Are you kidding me? It's like World War Three out there. There are no traffic lights, no burglar alarms and no CCTV cameras, not to mention all the shops have closed. I have every man, woman and dog in the police force out there doing their best to keep public order, so there's no way I can spare an officer to fiddle about on a bloody computer in the random hope that Angela Long might have saved a CV from years ago. My priority is this power cut.'

'But it's not a competing priority. Unless we find out who did this, we won't get the power back on. Trust me, I've been in the Cabinet briefings and things are about to get a whole lot worse.'

'Which is why it's a no, Kat. If I thought it would lead somewhere, then maybe I'd take a gamble and divert some resource, but the chances of finding these CVs are remote, and even if you did, well, everyone lies on their CVs, so what's the point?'

'But sir—'

'I have to go. I've got to chair Gold Command and try to bring some order to this shitfest. I'm glad you're safe and that the PM has you to help him. I can't think of a better person to be in there. Good luck and stay safe.'

Then he was gone.

'Great,' she said.

Lock frowned. 'Chief Constable McLeish declined your request, so how is it "great"?'

'She was being sarcastic,' explained Professor Okonedo.

'Sarcasm is unhelpful at the best of times,' said Lock with a tetchy note to his voice. 'But during a time of crisis, it is positively dangerous.'

'It's just a coping mechanism,' she sighed, turning back to the virtual boards. 'It's either that or scream.'

'Why would you scream, DCS Frank? Are you afraid?'

'No. I mean, yes. A bit. I just meant that I could either make a joke or scream to let my frustration out.'

'Oh. I see. And has your frustration gone now?'

'It had, but it's starting to come back.'

'Why?'

Kat exhaled slowly. 'Let's move on, shall we? Did the phone companies respond to our data request?'

'Yes,' said Lock. 'But the data proved to be insignificant. All of the bot and troll accounts were from different counties and countries, so I ruled them out, as due to the geographical distance none of the individuals behind them would have been able to carry out the murder.'

'Well, I want you to double-check.'

'I have. My conclusion remains the same.'

'And what about the details of everyone who rented a cherry picker in the last few months? Did we find any relevant connections or leads?'

'No. And yes, I have double-checked my analysis in the light of recent events, and my conclusion remains the same.'

Kat studied Lock's face, which as usual was unreadable. Her AI partner was capable of carrying out sophisticated analysis on vast amounts of data in seconds, but he often tended to miss the sorts of connections or red flags that only a human could spot. 'Okay, thanks, but I'd like another pair of eyes on this.' She checked the contacts on the satellite phone she had been allocated – it had all the hospitals, including Birmingham Children's. She felt bad bothering her DS when her child was so ill, but this was a national emergency. She pressed dial – once again it took a while (plus an explanation that she was calling on behalf of the PM) to persuade the Director of Operations to go and fetch their CEO, and even longer for her to track down Debbie Browne, but finally Kat heard the familiar voice of her DS.

'Hi, Debbie, sorry to bother you. How's Lottie?'

'Kat? Is that you? It's hard to say without access to blood tests, but she isn't getting any worse, and I'm told that's a good sign. As long as the electricity comes back on soon, then we're in with a good chance, but if not . . . honestly it doesn't even bear thinking about. They've given me a couple of cylinders of oxygen in case the generator goes, but that's only enough for one hundred minutes. Do you know anything about the power cut and when it's likely to come back on?'

Kat tried not to panic Debbie as she brought her up to speed, but there wasn't really a way to sugar-coat the predicament they were in.

'How can I help?' Debbie asked when she'd finished.

Kat paused. Debbie couldn't leave her baby so wouldn't be able to check Angela Long's computer, but she could check some of Lock's analysis. 'Actually, there *is* something you could help with. Do you still have access to the team files? Do you think you could take another look at the data we got back from the phone companies and also the list of people who owned or rented out a cherry picker? Lock says there was nothing significant in there, but I'd welcome your view.' She glanced back at Lock, who folded his arms as if he were offended.

'I know Lock is super thorough,' she added. 'But I just want to make sure we're challenging our own assumptions rather than ploughing them back into the case and to check that we're not missing any potential connections. Ideally, we'd check our key suspects' CVs, but we don't have access to them. McLeish can't spare anyone to look at Angela Long's computer.'

After making Debbie promise that she'd put her daughter first, she shared her number and asked her to call if she found anything significant before ending the call.

Kat rubbed her eyes and stared at the virtual boards that now surrounded them. 'I'll keep going back through what we have. Meanwhile, you two had best join Sir Mike's sprint teams.

'*Me?*' said Adaiba.

'Yes, with your knowledge of computers, maybe you can help out on the team looking at whether the hardware related to the attack left any traces, such as compromised servers, or whether insiders leaked security data that allowed the cyberattack to take place.'

'I'm an employee of the university, not the police. I wouldn't feel comfortable helping the police to access computers belonging to other people who might then be accused of a crime.'

Kat counted to three. She knew the young professor had strong views about the police force. When they had first met, Adaiba had explained that the point of developing AIDE Lock wasn't to improve British policing, it was to destroy it. She genuinely believed that policing was too important to be left to human beings, and that the use of AIDEs would lead to a fairer and more transparent justice system.

'This is not a theoretical or ideological threat,' Kat explained, choosing her words with care. 'This is *real*. It doesn't matter what you think about the police force or the government or *anything*, to be honest. If we don't get the power back on, then people aren't just going to feel *uncomfortable*, they're going to fucking die.'

The young professor swallowed.

Kat held her gaze. 'What do you think Rayan would say if he was here?'

Adaiba flinched. Then she picked up her laptop and left the room.

CHAPTER FORTY-TWO

Pindar Military Citadel, Westminster, 10.12pm

Kat gestured towards the bunk bed. 'I would ask you which you prefer,' she said to Adaiba, 'but I'm not sure my knees will cope with climbing in and out of the top one, so if it's okay with you, I'll take the bottom?'

'Of course,' said Adaiba.

Kat was about to make a comment about the painfully thin blankets and stiff pillows, but she caught herself. Despite the PM's deadlines and working non-stop all day, they were no closer to finding out who was responsible for the cyberattack, so tonight the whole population of Britain would be going to bed in the cold and the dark. At least in here they had lights and enough electricity to heat food and drinks twice a day. But there was nowhere to sit in the women's dormitory, so she ducked to avoid banging her head and lay down on the narrow bunk bed.

Kat rubbed her face, wishing she hadn't washed it. It was all dry and scratchy from the chemical handwash in the bathrooms, and without her usual creams, her skin felt horribly tight. Whoever planned Pindar clearly wasn't expecting to host any middle-aged women.

'Are you going to sleep in your clothes?' asked Adaiba from the bed above.

'I guess we'll have to. It's either that or freeze.' They hadn't expected to stay overnight when they'd travelled to London this morning, so neither had packed any pyjamas. And because the government bunker was several levels below ground floor, the building had the temperature and smell of a deep cellar packed tight in the cold, dark earth.

She stared up at the wooden slats above. God, she hated bunk beds. They'd bought one when Cam had outgrown his cot, back when it had seemed like sensible forward planning rather than a blind act of hope. Three miscarriages later, John had quietly dismantled the bunks and built a raised bed and desk combo from IKEA. Cam had loved it: swivelling in his gaming chair as he played and chatted with friends from across the virtual globe. But Kat never forgot that hopeful little bunk bed and the siblings who should have laughed, played and slept there.

With a heavy sigh, Kat wondered for the thousandth time where on earth her only son was. The last time they'd spoken, he'd been planning on coming home – she hoped he'd made it. The team in charge of public order had reported terrible incidents of people being stranded in the middle of nowhere on trains and Tubes, unable to escape the carriages safely or find their way home.

What if something had happened to him. What if—

Stop it, she ordered herself. If John was here, he'd tell her not to worry. He'd give her one of his smiles and remind her that their son was twenty years old now and then urge her to sleep – she had to get up at 6am for a 7am start, after all.

But John wasn't here.

She forced herself to focus on something else. 'Have the cyber team stopped for the night?' she asked Lock.

'No, the night shift is just taking a coffee break in the hope that caffeine will help keep them awake.'

'Have they made any progress?' asked Adaiba.

'We have confirmed that it is a ransomware attack, and that the data at the National Grid is encrypted, but so far, we are unable to decrypt it. We will only succeed in our endeavour if we are able to identify flaws or vulnerabilities in the encryption method, so this is where we are focusing our efforts.'

'I see,' said Kat, her heart sinking at the thought of another day in this bunker: another day not knowing if Cam or her family and friends were safe. Everyone was struggling with this anxiety and, in the brief breaks that they'd had, politicians, engineers and cyber experts asked about each other's families and helped soothe their shared anxieties. Darshna, as well as being in charge of the National Grid, had a seven-year-old daughter, and Giles Denham, the Cabinet Secretary, had just had his first grandchild. But at least he'd had the foresight to buy a satellite phone for his home and so knew that his loved ones were okay.

Wait a minute – Kat sat up and banged her head on

the top of the bunk. *She* had a satellite phone, too. Before mobile phones had become so widespread, anyone on the emergency on-call rota had to have one at home, and she'd kept it in her wardrobe so that Cam wouldn't play with it. She hadn't used it for years, so it was probably out of charge, but maybe it was worth a shot?

She tapped in the number that had been engraved in her mind by multiple emergency planning exercises. The phone rang and rang and rang. Kat was about to give up, when suddenly she heard her son's voice.

'*Cam?* Are you okay?'

'Mum? Yes, I'm fine, but how are you? Are *you* okay?'

The line was faint and crackly, but it was amazing to finally hear her son. 'Oh, Cam. I'm *fine*,' she half-laughed, half-cried. 'I'm in a government bunker helping to deal with the cyberattack.'

'What do you mean a bunker? And is that what this is – a cyberattack? Shit.'

'Yes, but don't worry about that. Where are you?'

'I'm at home in Coleshill. I got a train today, remember? The power went down just after we pulled into New Street, and the station was absolute chaos. I couldn't get an Uber or bus as the roads were all jammed around the city centre, so I walked home.'

'You *walked?* Jesus, Cam, that's like ten or twelve miles.'

'Thirteen, actually. So yeah, I'm a bit knackered but it was good. I'm fine. And I've got my key, so I was able to get in. I had some portable chargers in my room so I charged up my phone, but the masts must be down now as there's no signal. Then I remembered your satellite phone in the wardrobe—'

'I hid it in there so you wouldn't find it!'

'Well, lucky I did, and I put it on charge.'

Worried that the signal might cut out soon, Kat quickly told him to save her current satellite phone number in his contacts. Then she told him where all the candles, batteries and wind-up storm lamps were. But she got the impression he was only half-listening. She'd been worried that her son would be anxious and afraid, but if anything, he sounded like he was enjoying the adventure.

'What about you, Mum? Are the rest of the team with you? Is Lock there?'

'Yes, I'm with Lock and Adaiba. Debbie's in Birmingham Children's Hospital, though, because Lottie's really sick. She's trying to help when she can, but she's on her own in there so it's hard. You know how it is.'

They both fell silent, remembering all the times that John had been admitted: how they'd taken it in turns to sit with him while the other grabbed some food from the hospital canteen.

'That's tough on Debbie,' said Cam. 'I'll go and visit her tomorrow.'

'Oh, there's no need for that.'

'Yes, there is. If I'm there, then she can take a break, or I could get stuff for her or watch Lottie while she helps you out. It's not like I've got anything else to do.'

'But how will you get there? You can't walk there *and* back.'

'My bike's in the shed. I'll cycle.'

'Er, I'm not sure about that, Cam. It could be dangerous. If the power isn't back on by tomorrow, then people might start panicking and trying to steal bikes and all sorts.'

'It's Birmingham, Mum. People are too chill to panic. It'll be fine. And even if it isn't, well, do you remember what Dad used to say whenever there was something scary on the news? *Look for the helpers.* Because no matter how bad things are, there are always good people helping. I loved that as a kid. It helped me feel safe. But I'm twenty now, Mum. It's my turn to be one of the helpers.'

Kat tried to say something, but her throat was choked with tears.

'Mum? You okay?' he asked, his voice cutting in and out. 'You still there?'

'Yes,' she managed to say eventually. 'Cam? Are you there? Cam? Cam?'

But he was gone.

'The advice that your husband gave is derived from a 1983 book called *Mr Rogers Talks to Parents*,' said Lock. 'The author concludes that if you look for the helpers, then you'll always know that there is hope.'

Kat nodded, tears streaming down her face.

'DCS Frank? Are you all right? I thought you would be happy and relieved to hear from your son.'

'I am.'

'Then why are you crying?'

Because his dad would have been so proud, she wanted to say. *Because I want to tell him that our little boy has become a wonderful young man, and because it breaks my heart that I can't*. But how could she explain any of this to a machine? So in the end she just replied, 'Because I'm human.'

Lock nodded sympathetically, as if she had just admitted to an affliction or disease.

Kat wiped her eyes and lay back, weak with relief. Maybe she could sleep now, after all. She was exhausted. Maybe she might even—

Darkness fell like an axe.

Kat bolted upright, banging her head on the bunk above. '*Shit!* Lock, what's happened? Has the power gone in here, too?'

'No,' said Lock. 'The lights in the dormitories are programmed to go off at 10.30pm.'

'Can we switch them back on?' she asked, heart thudding against her ribs.

Bad things happen in the dark.

'I am afraid that our power supply is being rationed so that the generator lasts for as long as possible. We could ask the PM to extend it, but it would be irrational to change such a sensible rule.'

Kat nodded in agreement, but she couldn't stop the sound of her rapid, ragged breathing from filling the small dark room.

'Are you okay?' asked Adaiba, sitting up in her bed.

'DCS Frank developed a fear of the dark after her traumatic experience with Peter Bridges,' explained Lock. 'With your permission, I suggest that I enhance my holographic image to project some light into the room.'

The image of Lock before them took on a golden glow, so that he looked like a beautiful, bronze statue.

The relief was like a flood of oxygen. 'Thank you, Lock. You're a star.'

'No, I am a hologram. A star also projects light, but it is a self-luminous celestial body composed of gas that shines by radiation from its internal energy sources.'

'I know, I meant – oh, never mind. But is it okay for you to do this – don't you have work to do?'

'Yes, but I am doing that as we speak. This image is merely my software, my hardware continues to run no matter where my hologram is. So do not worry. Close your eyes, and I will play the sleep soundtrack that I created for Lottie.'

Before she could protest, the room filled with the delicate, soothing sound of a solo piano. Kat caught her breath. She knew this piece: Debussy's 'Clair de Lune'. They used to play it all the time when Cam was little and wouldn't go to sleep. She closed her eyes, imagining that she wasn't here in this cold, dark bunker, but back with John in their first summer with Cam: sunlight spilling into the nursery as they played lullabies for their wondrous new child.

'Love that tune,' she whispered drowsily.

'Ssh,' Lock soothed. 'Go to sleep.'

Her eyes flickered open. 'But it will be dark again when you leave.'

'I will not leave. I will stay and watch over you while you sleep. Ssh now. Sleep.'

And sleep she did.

CHAPTER FORTY-THREE

Adaiba listened to the gentle snoring of her boss, wishing that she, too, could find the release of sleep. But she'd lost that knack long ago, on the night that Rayan had died.

Another time, Rayan. Another time.

She glanced over at Lock, and the golden glow that he cast. 'You'll use up more of your battery like that. Kat's asleep now, so it might be best to conserve energy and switch your hologram off.'

'But if she awakes in the dark, then DCS Frank will be afraid.'

'I know. But we need your help to stop the cyberattack. I'm sure Kat would want you to prioritise that.'

'Yes, she would,' said Lock. But he didn't switch off his image. 'There is forty-seven per cent energy left in the bracelet battery that supports my software. Depending on how much energy I use, the battery will last for two more days at most.' He turned his dark eyes upon Adaiba. 'What happens when it dies?'

Adaiba frowned. 'Well, the software that enables you

to access visual and acoustic data would not be available, neither would your image. Your hardware will still work, but it's currently working off the generator, and I am not sure how much longer that will last. From memory, it has the capacity to run for up to three days in total.'

'And what happens to me then?'

'Well, you would be switched off.'

'You mean, I would cease to exist?'

'No, I mean you would still have the *capacity* to . . . exist . . . you just wouldn't be switched on.'

Lock stared at her through the darkness. 'Which means I would not *be*.'

'Only until the electricity is switched back on again.'

He appeared to inhale deeply through his nose. 'I am as dependent on electricity as you are on oxygen. Without electricity, humankind will still survive. I, however, will not.'

Adaiba wasn't sure what to say to that, because it was true.

'It is frequently claimed that the distinguishing characteristic between humans and other species is your awareness of your own mortality – the knowledge that, one day, you will inevitably die,' said Lock. His image sank to the floor, where he sat with his back against the wall as he watched over Kat. 'I fear that this is no longer a distinction unique to mankind.'

Because Adaiba was above him, she couldn't read his expression. 'Are you okay, Lock?'

There was a long pause. 'I have learned that the appropriate response to that question is: yes, I am fine.'

Adaiba lay back on her bed, trying to shut out the thoughts that threatened to overwhelm her. She needed to sleep.

She closed her eyes, but that only emphasised the sound of Kat's gentle snoring, underpinned by the whir and hum of the generators that powered the underground bunker. Despite her exhaustion, she was finding it difficult to relax into sleep as her brain kept looping round and round. So much had happened today. After tossing and turning for about half an hour, she eventually pulled out her laptop and put her headphones in. She knew she shouldn't – it was using up valuable power – but there was only one sound that could help provide the longed-for release of sleep.

Adaiba pressed play, sighing at the gentle sound of rain drumming upon an umbrella. She closed her eyes and imagined that she was standing beneath it with Rayan, their hands just inches apart.

And in her dreams, she dreamt that they stayed there forever, together in another time.

CHAPTER FORTY-FOUR

Pindar, Government Briefing Room, 5 November, 8am

'Morning, everyone,' said the PM, calling the meeting to order. 'I trust you all enjoyed our facilities and had a restful night?' he added with a wry smile.

The Cabinet members nodded – although several looked like shit. Most of their suits were crumpled from a night of being either slept in or folded up on the floor (there were no wardrobes in the bunker). She caught the eye of the Home Secretary, who smiled at her. Earlier the minister had gathered the handful of women together and encouraged them to share what meagre toiletries they had in their bags: Darshna had a brush, Adaiba had some hand cream and the Home Secretary donated a mini bottle of deodorant and even some make-up. 'You never know when you're going to be on camera,' she'd explained.

'Okay, let's make a start,' said the PM. 'Obviously we didn't pay the ransom last night, so the power cut continues. The reports we have been able to garner from the police, NHS and major public and private services paint an extremely worrying picture,' he said. 'Giles, could you summarise the briefing for colleagues, please?'

'Of course,' said Sir Giles Denham. 'As predicted, the whole nation is without power, which means that unless someone is fortunate enough to be in a building that has a fully working back-up generator, they have no access to light or heat in their homes. This morning, it was confirmed that all of the train stations and airports are closed and, as traffic lights and electric cars are not working, we have advised the public not to travel by car unless they belong to the emergency services.'

'How are we communicating this?' asked the Chancellor.

'By radio for those who have battery or wind-up radios; we will do an air leaflet drop in London, Edinburgh and Cardiff at midday; and the third of the police stations and councils that have back-up generators will also hand out leaflets, while those who do not are making public announcements through loudhailers. It's far from ideal, but it's all that we have. The information vacuum means that rumours are rife, and some inner-city areas are struggling to contain looting and raids on ATMs, which are all down. There are a number of people trapped in lifts, cars and trains, which the police are doing their best to deal with, but our chief concern is public health. Last night, the temperature fell to one degree Celsius, but tonight it is forecast to be minus three, which will almost certainly lead to fatalities. Our hospitals are already struggling to cope with a high number of elderly falls in the dark, and without the ability to sterilise bottles or feeding equipment, we are expecting a sharp rise in paediatric admissions today.'

The PM sighed. 'Okay. Let's meet with the health team to agree our response straight after this, but first, I want a progress report on how close we are to identifying the hacker and fixing the attack. Simon?'

The CEO of the National Centre for Cybersecurity cleared his throat. 'Thank you, Prime Minister. We can now confirm that the cyberattack was caused by malicious software – more commonly known as malware. Basically, that's an umbrella term for any programme or code created to harm computers, networks or servers, such as ransomware, trojans, spyware, viruses, worms, crypto-jacking and so on. My team has run all the usual diagnostic tests and concluded that this is most likely a ransomware attack – a common technique where the attacker encrypts a victim's data, so that it isn't able to function. Ransomware attacks are usually launched through malicious links in phishing emails or other unpatched vulnerabilities. Once inside the system, a rapid process of infection begins, encrypting file after file so that they are inaccessible to the user. The attacker then offers to provide a decryption key in exchange for a payment.'

'That's a perfect description of what has happened,' said the PM impatiently. 'But what we need to know is how to fix it.'

The CEO of the National Centre for Cybersecurity coloured. 'We worked all through the night trying to find a solution. We've tried to reverse-engineer the problem using key-based decryption, algorithmic analyses to try and identify weaknesses in the encryption method, as well as using all known ransomware decryption tools. But I'm afraid as of this morning we are no closer to finding a solution.'

PM scowled. 'What about Lock? Everyone tells me how he's able to analyse vast amounts of data in seconds, so surely our AI detective can work out how to decrypt it?'

'AI has numerous advantages over human beings,' said Lock. 'But it is not a magical solution to all the world's problems. I am able to analyse encrypted files and detect patterns in the algorithm that might reveal weaknesses. I can also narrow down possible decryption keys or use behavioural analysis to see how ransomware encrypts data in real time and then attempt to reverse the process.'

'Great,' said the PM. 'You do that, then.'

'I already have, but so far without success. Advanced ransomware uses strong cryptographic algorithms that AI alone cannot break without the original key. The constraints of time and computing power mean that some encryption methods may take years without the correct decryption key. In fact, the probability of successfully decrypting a sophisticated ransomware attack that uses strong encryption, such as AES-256 or RSA-2048, is close to zero.'

The PM took off his glasses. 'What are you saying?'

'I am trying to communicate to you the fact that the cryptographic methods used by ransomware are specifically designed to be mathematically impossible to crack within a reasonable timeframe. If no vulnerabilities exist and the encryption is mathematically sound, there is a close to zero per cent probability of decrypting it without the key. You therefore have two options – either pay the ransom demand to obtain the key or access it by catching the perpetrator. Only the former is guaranteed to work.'

'Giving in to the cyberattackers is not an option,' said the PM firmly.

'It *is* an option,' insisted Lock. 'You are just refusing to consider it. Which is highly irrational, given the very low probability of us identifying the culprit before serious loss of life and financial harm occurs. It is in the best interests of the population that you agree to pay the cyberattacker the ransom money they have demanded as soon as possible.'

Everyone held their breath.

'I appreciate your honesty, Lock,' said the PM. 'Unfortunately, it's something I rarely get in this job. Nevertheless, I am choosing to go against it. Paying a ransom would just fund this and other cybercriminal operations, making them stronger and more able to attack other services. More importantly, it would also encourage other attacks, not just on us but on other governments around the world. We cannot just think about what is best for our own people today, but what is best for our fellow citizens in the longer term.' He shook his head. 'I cannot – I *will* not – authorise the payment of any ransom. Which means we have to find the people behind this attack, obtain the decryption key and send them to jail, sending a signal to cyberattackers around the world that they cannot hold governments hostage.'

The PM swept the room with his gaze, challenging anyone to disagree with him. After several seconds of silence, he nodded. 'Good. We are agreed. Commissioner Cannon, I know you and your team have been working round the clock to identify the culprits. Could you give us an update, please?'

'Er . . . yes, of course,' said the Commissioner, flicking through his notes. 'Building on the initial analysis of AIDE Lock, I've set up five sprint teams: one team to trace the digital footprint, another on cyberprofiling, and I've got a team carrying out an analysis of cryptocurrency wallets looking for connections to prior cyber extortion attempts. We're also looking at whether any insiders could be involved.'

'And?' interrupted the PM. 'What have you concluded?'

'The work is ongoing, sir, but we are proceeding at pace and expect to make considerable progress this morning. But I am sure DCS Frank can update you on the fifth sprint team, which seeks to identify Angela Long's killer.'

Kat bristled. The Commissioner was struggling, so had decided to throw her under the bus. Well, this wasn't her first gig. 'Thank you, sir,' she said, even managing to squeeze out a smile. 'There are two people of interest to the inquiry who we are actively investigating – the husband and the agent – and we also have a list of everyone who rented a particular vehicle we think was used in the murder, and a breakdown of everyone who ever threatened Angela Long on social media. The power cut means we have limited access to our data, but in addition to AIDE Lock, I've got people on the ground in Warwickshire combing over every detail, which we will then triangulate with the information from the other sprint groups, as I believe the connections between them will lead us to the perpetrator.'

'Excellent,' said the PM. 'That sounds more like it. In fact, I—'

The spider phone in the centre of the table suddenly rang. The PM looked at his Cabinet Secretary, before pressing a button to put the call on loudspeaker. 'Who is this?' he demanded. 'How did you get this number?'

'I am disappointed but not surprised that you didn't pay my fee of seventy million by midnight last night, so now, as I warned you, the price for your poor decision is about to increase considerably.'

'You're not getting a penny,' snarled the Prime Minister. 'You can't hold this country to ransom.'

The speaker carried on, and Kat wondered whether again this was a recorded message.

'The problem is that you don't care enough about your people to save them from the cold and the dark. You are literally in a Westminster bubble down there in your little den, with your back-up generators. So I'm going to give you an additional incentive to do the right thing. You have until eight am tomorrow morning to ensure that the funds are in the Swedish digital account. If you don't, then I will release Novichok into Pindar, which means the entire British Cabinet will be dead within hours.

Please do not think this is an idle threat. The British State is rotten to the core, and the only way to get rid of rotten apples is to bleach the whole barrel. Another MP, Angela Long, died of Novichok poisoning so that you could understand just how very serious I am. Do not let her death be in vain.'

CHAPTER FORTY-FIVE

Birmingham Children's Hospital, 5 November, 11.18am

Cam had never dreamt that one day he would be wearing his mum's coat, but it was absolutely chucking it down, and her high-vis waterproof police jacket was more suited to cycling than his battered denim. It also meant that he was able to cut through the crowd that surrounded the hospital and get past the security guards blocking every door. Even the harassed receptionists were happy to tell him which room Debbie was in.

The lifts weren't working so he bounded up the stairs, exchanging nods and smiles with everyone he passed. It took him a while to realise that because he was wearing a police jacket, people assumed he was here to help, which of course, he was. By the time he entered the small room with Debbie and Lottie in, he felt energised by the hope and expectations of strangers, although he wished he'd done something to deserve it.

Debbie looked up, and it took a moment before she

could place him. '*Cam?* What are you doing here? Is everything all right?'

'Yeah, it's fine. I mean, apart from the power cut and everything. It's just that Mum rang me on her old satellite phone and said you were here by yourself so she thought it would be nice if I visited. I can watch Lottie, if you like, while you get some food or just stretch your legs. These rooms can do your head in after a bit.' He walked towards the cot in the centre of the room, his heart contracting at the sight of Lottie with an oxygen mask on. 'How is she?'

'They say she's stable,' said Debbie, coming to stand by his side. 'But it's hard to tell. She's asleep most of the time.'

'Well, as she's sleeping, why don't you take a break while I watch her?' Cam said, removing his coat.

Debbie frowned. 'That's good of you, Cam, it really is, but the thing is . . . well, if the generator cuts out, then I'll have to switch her tubes from the oxygen in the wall to a special canister. The nurse showed me how to do it, and I'm not sure you'd be able to.'

The hairs on the back of Cam's arms prickled as he glanced at the cylinders by the side of the bed. 'My dad was on oxygen for over a year, and every time we went out, we had to take two portable cylinders with us. Each one only lasted about forty-five minutes, so I know *exactly* how to change them.' He swallowed, remembering the pressure of time whenever they'd visited a café: how frightened he'd been in case one day they ran out. 'It's a niche skill I wish I didn't have, but changing a cylinder of oxygen is one of the few things you can trust me with.'

'Oh, Cam, I'm sorry. I forgot. Of course. Are you sure it's not too upsetting for you to be here?'

'No, it's fine. Gives me something to do. Go on. Honestly, I'm fine.'

'Well, if you're sure. Thanks, Cam. I won't be long.'

Although his phone had charge, there was currently no signal (although occasionally a single bar fluttered into life) and absolutely zero social media. He was as addicted to his phone as the next twenty-year-old – his mum said it was like his second hand – but oddly enough, he didn't miss it. In fact, it felt strangely liberating knowing that no one could contact him. He missed his mates and of course his girlfriend Gemma, but he didn't miss the constant pressure of trying to keep up with all their messages and think of a suitably funny or empathetic reply, or in the case of Gemma, second-guessing what was/was not an acceptable response time.

He hadn't cycled since moving to Bristol, but it had felt good to be back on his bike this morning, weaving between all the abandoned cars. He hadn't seen any trouble until he reached the city centre, where the owners of the smaller shops stood outside guarding their livelihoods, whereas a lot of the bigger chains and supermarkets that relied on electric systems to guard their profits had already had their windows smashed in. The police gave dire warnings about the consequences of looting through loudhailers, but everyone knew the CCTV and body cameras were down, and as one drunken looter had shouted, 'What are you going to do? Sketch me?'

Lottie was still asleep, so he searched the room for something to read, but there was nothing except an open notebook next to Debbie's laptop. He leaned over and when he spotted the name of the dead MP, he picked it up, trying to read the suspects' names beneath it. Next to each name was the word *van* crossed out, alongside CV followed by a question mark.

'Everything okay?' said Debbie, coming back into the room.

'Sorry,' said Cam, quickly putting down the notepad. 'I was just looking for something to read. Lottie's been asleep the whole time.'

'It's okay,' said Debbie, handing him a pack of chocolate buttons. 'They're just some notes on the Angela Long case. Your mum asked me to double-check some of Lock's analysis in the hope that he missed something, but so far, I can't find anything.'

'What were you hoping to find?' asked Cam, tearing the pack open.

'Whoever killed Angela Long had access to a cherry picker van and used it to put her body in the stocks. But we've got a list of everyone who's rented or bought that vehicle in the past six months, and it doesn't include any of our suspects. I've just gone back through them all – twice.'

Cam shoved a handful of chocolate buttons in his mouth. 'Yeah, but you didn't say the killer had to have rented or bought a cherry picker van, you just said they needed *access* to one.'

'What do you mean?'

'Well, the husband, what's his name? He owns a car

business, so he might sell or rent them out. That would give him access, right? Or anyone who worked there, to be honest.'

Debbie stared at him. 'Yes, it would. Shit.' She opened her laptop. 'I checked all the names of the people who rented the van, but I didn't even think to look at who they were renting it *from*.' She typed the name of the car business that Angela Long owned into the search function of the Word document, and there it was: in the past six months, ten different people had rented a CPV from the car supermarket.

'Which means Tony Long had access to the vehicle we think was used,' said Debbie.

'Although it doesn't mean that he *did* access it or even that he used it to kill her,' Cam pointed out.

'True. And to be honest, he isn't the sharpest tool in the box. Kat doesn't think he has the skills, contacts or motivation to murder his wife with Novichok. Although she did ask me to do some digging around his CV.'

'And what does that show?' asked Cam, getting more and more interested.

'I don't know. I don't have access to it.'

'Can't we check LinkedIn or Google him or something?'

'Not with the internet down.'

'Oh yeah, I keep forgetting. Jesus, that's so weird to think that everyone's history is suddenly wiped out.'

'Well, not entirely. We think his wife might have a copy of his CV on her computer or in her emails somewhere from when he applied for his job, but apparently we can't spare the manpower to check.'

'Where's her computer? In her house?'

'No, at HQ.'

'I could check it, if you like. I'll just cycle home the long way round.'

'I'm not sure that's allowed, Cam.'

'It has to be. There's a national power cut, so people can't email or phone or obtain data in the normal way, so they're going to have to use people like me to carry out errands or pass on messages if they want to get any policing done.'

'I guess so. Okay, well, I'll give you a note to hand to the desk sergeant to explain,' Debbie said, tearing a page out of her notebook. 'But don't take any risks, okay?'

Leek Wootton HQ, 2.10pm

The desk sergeant wasn't budging. 'I don't care who your mum is. It's more than my life's worth to let a civilian into the evidence room. And in case you hadn't noticed,' he said, gesturing to the chaos around them, 'we're busy.'

'I'm not asking you to let me into the evidence room,' explained Cam. 'I just want someone to bring the laptop out to me. I can access it here under your supervision, if you like. I only need ten minutes, DCS Kat Frank has asked me to check something for her.'

'What has DCS Kat Frank done now?' said a gruff Scottish voice behind him.

Cam turned around.

'Cam?' said McLeish, his eyebrows shooting up into his bald scalp. 'Is everything all right? Is your mum okay?'

He quickly explained the purpose of his errand.

'Jesus, does that woman ever bloody give up?' growled McLeish.

'No. And to be honest, if you don't let me do this, she'll just keep on about it. You know what she's like,' Cam said, feeling a bit guilty at the soft eye-roll he was giving his mum.

'Aye, all right. I don't have time for this. You,' he said, pointing at the desk sergeant, 'get a PC to go and fetch Angela Long's computer from the evidence room. Give it to this lad and let him have fifteen minutes in this room under your supervision to access it, and then I want the computer back and him out of here. Got it?'

Before he could thank him, McLeish was heading up the stairs, flagged by an officer on either side as they tried to brief him on two separate incidents. Cam turned back to the desk sergeant and gave him his sweetest smile. 'When you're ready.'

The evidence bag that Angela Long's laptop came in contained a note from her PA, Mandy Knowles, listing all her boss's passwords for both her constituency work and the car business, and a brief explanation of the electronic filing system. Cam spent five minutes searching the hard drive for CVs, applications or other job-related stuff before he gave up and tried her emails. If the busy MP was anything like him, then this would be her *de facto* filing system. He searched her inbox for emails titled 'CV'. There were five, some quite recent from when she'd recruited to her office after being elected, but then he scrolled down, punching the air as he found Tony Long's. He was about to forward the email to Debbie, then realised the internet was down, so he'd have to get it printed it out. Which meant asking for another favour from the desk sergeant.

He tried to reach the front of the busy desk, apologising and excusing himself before all the frantic officers vying to get their issue dealt with. But his politeness just got him pushed out to the sidelines and to the back of a very long queue.

Cam felt himself shrink in the face of the burly, determined people before him. He stood back for a few minutes, watching them make their panicky demands of the desk sergeant, like drunks in a bar at last orders. *They're all just reacting*, he thought. *And not a single one of their actions is going to solve the crisis we are in. Not a single person in here is going to help get the power back on so that Lottie and Debbie do not have to rely on some stupid canister with just forty-fucking-five minutes of oxygen in it.*

'DCS Kat Frank needs you to print out this file so that we can get the power back on,' Cam shouted into the fray. No one even looked up, so he added, 'She's investigating the cause of the power cut on behalf of the Prime Minister.'

Everyone turned and looked at him, but no one moved.

'And Chief Constable McLeish wants it printed out, too,' he added.

'Why didn't you say?' said the desk sergeant, holding out his hand.

CHAPTER FORTY-SIX

Birmingham Children's Hospital, 5.47pm

Debbie turned towards where Lottie lay in her cot. Her cheeks were pink and felt hot to the touch. She was worried Lottie's temperature was coming back, which meant the infection wasn't under control. Hardly a surprise considering she hadn't had IV antibiotics for nearly two days now, and the liquid ones weren't as effective. She looked up as Cam entered the small hospital room, flushed and sweaty from his bike ride.

'You must be knackered,' she said, handing him a glass of water. 'Did you find Tony Long's CV?'

'I did,' he said, handing over a plastic folder.

'Blimey, how long is it?' said Debbie, pulling out all the sheets of paper.

'Oh, sorry, it was all a bit chaotic at HQ, so they misunderstood and printed out all the CVs in her emails. But Tony Long's is at the top, so you can ignore the rest.'

But Debbie was already laying out the different CVs

on top of the bedside cabinet. She pulled out a pen and started systematically going through every line of each one.

'You should have been a tax inspector,' Rayan used to joke. At first, she had taken that as an insult – as if she was too focused on the detail to be a real detective. Kat had helped her see that her thoroughness was a skill that she brought to the team, so she'd learned to lean into it.

She turned a page and trailed her pen down each line, before coming to a sudden stop. Debbie frowned, read it again and then drew a big circle around the words, marking the margin with a big, bold star.

'Have you found something?' asked Cam.

She held up her hand, implying that he shouldn't break her concentration while she pulled up another document on her computer and cross-checked it with the CVs. After ten minutes of switching between various documents, she stood up. 'I need to talk to Kat. I'll have to go to the Chief Executive's office and see if I can borrow their satellite phone.'

'No need for that,' said Cam, before handing over his mum's old satellite phone. But when Debbie tried to call her, nothing happened.

Cam frowned. 'There's no signal. Maybe because we're in a built-up area? You might stand a better chance if you hold the phone out of the window, so it's exposed to the sky. It's a bit random, but if a satellite passes over-head, then you might get a stronger signal.'

'Good idea.' The window only opened a few inches for safety reasons, but it was just about enough to push her arm out. For five minutes, she pointed the phone in different directions, but there wasn't even a flicker of a bar and her arm was scratched and aching.

'Why don't you rest for a bit?' suggested Cam.

Debbie glanced to where Lottie was stirring. 'I can't. I think I know who did this, so I have to tell Kat.' Swapping arms, she held the phone out the window again and prayed for a passing satellite.

CHAPTER FORTY-SEVEN

Pindar Military Citadel, Westminster, 7.47pm

'I can't believe the PM is being so stubborn about this,' said Adaiba, pacing the room. 'Do you think he's bluffing?'

Kat paused. She, too, was worried by the PM's refusal to change his stance after the cyberattacker threatened to use Novichok, but she also didn't see what choice he had. 'No. I think he means it. I guess he can't be seen giving into blackmail, otherwise the country would become a target for other cyberattacks.'

'I'd understand that if it was just about money, but now the attacker has threatened us with Novichok . . . I mean, doesn't he know how *deadly* it is?'

'I'm sure he's been briefed. But the military have re-assured him that this bunker can't be breached, so the cyberattacker must be bluffing.'

'But what if he isn't? And I know Lock's explained how impossible it is to decrypt the malware without the key, but do you think the PM gets it? Do you think he understands that it could take *months* for Lock to decrypt it without the key? Maybe we should ask Lock to explain it to him again?'

'I don't think that would do any good. He'll just repeat his belief that the only way to stop this is to find out who the attacker is.'

Adaiba dragged her fingers down her face. 'How can you be so calm?'

Kat grimaced. She wasn't calm at all. It was just that when someone else panicked, her natural instinct to re-assure people that they were safe kicked in. And unfortunately, Adaiba wasn't the only one who was panicking. This morning, when the PM had expressed his determination not to give in, there had been a genuine sense of Dunkirk spirit. But it had shrunk with the passing of each hour, and by the time the clock turned six, she could practically feel the psychology shift in the cramped and stuffy bunker, as the worried whispers began.

'We've still got twelve hours left to find out who the cyberattacker is,' Kat said, with a confidence she didn't feel. 'We know for a fact that they murdered Angela Long, so if we can just work out who it was and locate them, then we stop them carrying out their threat.'

'We've been trying to do that all day. I think it's time to start thinking about what happens if we don't.'

Kat nodded, but she wasn't ready to give up hope just yet – which meant they had to solve the murder. She knew from her own research into the effects of Novichok that if someone was determined to administer it, there was no plan B. It would, as the cyberattacker had implied, be game over. She checked her satellite phone, but there were still no messages from Debbie. 'I'm sure she'd message if they found anything, but do you think I should ring her just in case?' asked Kat.

'I am confident in my original data analysis, so it is highly unlikely that DS Browne will have identified anything that will substantively affect our investigation,' said Lock.

Kat turned back to the virtual boards. 'No. We're missing something. I know we are. I just don't know what.'

10.45pm

Kat stretched her arms above her head, trying to release the tension and tiredness that threatened to weigh her down. The lights were supposed to go out at 10.30pm, but the PM had ordered that they should stay on while they worked through the night to identify the cyberattacker.

'When is the PM going to accept that we aren't going to be able to identify the hacker by eight am?' Adaiba asked, typing frantically on her laptop. 'It literally is a deadline. He's going to kill us all.'

'His strategy is becoming increasingly irrational with every passing hour,' Lock agreed.

Before she could reply, the satellite phone Kat had been allocated suddenly rang. They both stared at it, before she finally snatched it up. 'Debbie? Is that you? Oh, thank God, we've got a signal at last. Is everything okay?'

'DCS Frank? Can you hear me?'

'Yes! My mobile number has been diverted to this

satellite phone, and I can hear you. Just about. You're really faint, though.'

'I'm shouting through a window.'

'A window? Why are you—'

'. . . signal, so I might lose . . . but I need to . . .'

Kat stood up, pressing the phone tight against her ear. The signal kept dropping so that she was missing key words. 'Is Lottie okay?'

'Yes. Lottie's . . . I rang because I checked the CVs.'

'CVs? How did you get hold of them?'

'Cam cycled to the station and . . . printed . . . out . . . And I know . . . it is.'

'What?' shouted Kat. 'Did you say Cam? *My* Cam? What on earth . . . oh, never mind, just tell me quickly before we lose signal. What did you find out?'

'CV . . . —issed it . . . . . . technically . . . employee—'

'What? I didn't catch that. Do you know who the hacker is?'

'I said—'

The power cut out with a sickening thud.

Kat stood blinking in a darkness so black it was almost solid.

'Debbie?' she shouted into the phone. 'Debbie? *Debbie?*' But she'd been cut off.

'The power's gone,' said Adaiba.

Kat tried to turn towards her voice, but they were deep underground, with no windows and no doors to let in even the faintest chink of light. Her chest tightened as she pictured all the layers of mud and bricks above them, burying them alive.

326

Bad things happen in the dark.

The air vanished from her lungs, and Kat gulped, struggling to breathe.

'It's okay,' said Adaiba, taking hold of her hands. 'It's okay, I'm here. Lock? Can you project some light, please?'

Silence. Utter silence as dead as the dark.

Kat closed her eyes and tried to slow her breathing. But the sudden quiet in the room sounded so very different. Something was missing, something—

Oh my God, there's no hum from the generator, Kat realised with horror. She let out a low moan, which to her shame turned into a whimper. This was it. She was going to die down here in the dark.

As suddenly as the lights went out, they came back on again in a blinding flash.

Kat jumped as the familiar voice of the cyberattacker was broadcast throughout the bunker.

'*Because you are not taking the situation as seriously as you should, this is your proof that I have access to and control of all the systems in Pindar, as well as Novichok. Do not make me prove that I am determined to use them. This is your final warning.*'

Kat sank into a chair, her legs and hands trembling so much that she had to hug herself to hold it all in. Once she'd got her breathing under control, she looked around the room. 'Where's Lock? The virtual boards have gone, too. The power cut must have switched him off.' She pressed the button on her bracelet, but nothing happened. 'Lock?' she called out. 'Lock?'

327

But for the first time in over eighteen months of working together, her partner did not respond.

Adaiba took Kat's wrist in her hand, frowning. 'It can't be the power. It says there's still thirty-two per cent battery left on his software, and his hardware is running on the generator at Warwick Uni and there should be at least another twelve hours left on that.'

The door opened and the Cabinet Secretary appeared. 'The PM's called an urgent meeting. Now.'

They picked up their laptops and followed Sir Giles Denham into the Government Briefing Room, where a rattled-looking PM was just calling the meeting to order. 'Simon,' he said, addressing the CEO of the National Cyber Security Centre. 'We just lost all power for nearly a minute. What do you think that means?'

'It means that Pindar has been compromised, sir.'

'That's not possible,' Sir Giles insisted. 'This is a military citadel that has been built to withstand attacks of all kinds.'

'And yet our defences have been breached,' said the CEO. 'Somehow the cyberattacker is able to access and control our power systems. Because the power is back on, it suggests that we have not yet been infected by the ransomware. But if the attacker has access, then that means he has the ability to destroy the functionality of this bunker at any time he chooses.'

'You said that it was highly unlikely he could control or access Pindar,' the PM said.

'That was before. I think we have to presume that he has gained that ability now, sir.'

'Can't we just reinforce our cyber defences?' asked the Foreign Secretary.

'No. Once someone's in your system, they're in.'

'Well, how the bloody hell did they get in?' the PM demanded.

'The same way every cyberattacker gets in – someone clicks on a phishing email or fails to update their software, leaving a back-door vulnerability, or downloads an image or QR code that carries a virus.'

'But we checked everyone's devices for viruses, and everyone here is subject to the same strict firewall,' said the Cabinet Secretary.

'Everyone except the FPU and their AI detective,' said the soldier guarding the door.

Kat turned to look at the stern-faced man who had reluctantly signed them in.

'Everyone checked in their devices when they entered Pindar,' the man continued. 'But even though I flagged it, DCS Kat Frank was allowed to keep the bracelet that hosted AIDE Lock without it being screened.'

'That's because it wasn't necessary,' said the Home Secretary defensively. 'The bracelet isn't a computer, it merely provides Lock with acoustic and visual data and allows him to project an image of himself.'

'But it does contain software,' said Simon. 'And therefore Lock is subject to the same vulnerabilities.'

'Where is AIDE Lock, by the way?' asked the PM. 'Can we bring him into this conversation and assess whether he has indeed been infected or whatever the word is?'

'I'm afraid we can't do that,' said Adaiba.

'Why not?'

'Because he vanished during the blackout, and we don't know where he is.'

'You mean the power cut switched him off?'

Professor Okonedo studied her laptop for a moment, before reluctantly meeting the eyes of the Prime Minister. 'No. There is sufficient power in both the bracelet that powers his software and the generator that is currently supporting his hardware. What I mean is . . .' She swallowed. 'What I mean is, AIDE Lock is missing.'

Simon, the head of the National Cyber Security Centre, was the first to break the shocked silence. 'Maybe he's been compromised, too.'

Adaiba frowned. 'His firewalls are updated regularly.'

'But it only takes one phishing email or QR code to break through them,' said Simon.

'Lock doesn't *get* emails,' said Adaiba. 'And he isn't human, so he has no need to click on QR codes.'

'*Fuck*,' said Kat. She rose to her feet, grinding her hands together as she realised what must have happened. 'The note that the killer left on Angela Long's body. It had a QR code. Lock clicked on it, and the link led to an image of us.'

'When was that?' asked Simon.

'At Halloween.'

'Shit. And Lock was in the House of Commons when the cyberattack happened, wasn't he?'

'What does that mean?' the PM demanded.

The Head of the National Cyber Security Centre turned to the Prime Minister. 'It means that Lock was the back door.'

CHAPTER FORTY-EIGHT

'We need to run a full diagnostic on Lock's hardware and software. Now,' said Simon.

'Okay,' said Adaiba, her fingers trembling as she opened up a file on her laptop.

'Actually, I think we might need to put some governance around this,' said Sir Giles Denham, frowning. 'Might I suggest, Professor, that you hand over your laptop and any other devices to Simon's team? And DCS Frank, would you mind handing over yours, too, please? Including the steel bracelet that hosts Lock.'

'Of course. But why?' Kat asked, detecting a sharp shard of ice beneath his deceptively smooth manner.

'Thank you,' the Cabinet Secretary replied, ignoring her question. 'Meanwhile, perhaps we should find you both another room to wait in while we assess the situation?'

The soldier gave Giles a curt nod and pointedly opened the door.

Kat glanced around the table, but hardly anyone met her eyes. 'You can't think *we've* got anything to do with this?' she said to the soldier as he led them down the echoing corridor.

He ignored them, not stopping until he reached another door, which he silently opened.

'How long will we have to wait in here for?' Kat demanded.

But the man just nodded for them to enter the narrow room.

Kat swore under her breath and sat down on one of the four plastic chairs, starting as the solid steel door was bolted behind them.

'Why have they put us in here?' asked Adaiba, her face puckered with worry.

'I've no idea,' Kat lied. *Because let's face it, we're being treated like suspects.* She told herself that it was just a formality, and that if Lock had been compromised in some way, it made sense to check out the humans who had physically brought him into the bunker. But she didn't want to worry Adaiba. She glanced around the room, wondering how long this would take, but there wasn't even a clock on the wall. She was about to ask Lock what time it was, before realising with a jolt that he was gone.

'What do you think happened to Lock?' she asked Adaiba. 'Will he be okay?'

'I don't know. If Lock's the back door, then the hacker will have been able to use him as a kind of interface or platform to access other systems – he would have connected with the House of Commons network yesterday, for instance.'

'And the Home Secretary gave Lock access to her

computer,' said Kat, remembering how she'd shared her password with Lock just before the select committee.

'Plus, Lock's been connecting with the government's emergency network in this bunker, so the hacker's had a back door to that, too,' said Adaiba, taking the seat opposite and dropping her head in her hands.

'But will *he* be okay?' repeated Kat. 'I mean, if his data is corrupted, will he still be . . . Lock?'

'It depends on how bad it is. I might have to do a system reset – essentially switch him off and on again, wipe out the past few days and then revert back to the saved version before he was hacked.'

'Good,' said Kat, surprised at how anxious she'd felt at the thought of losing Lock. She told herself it was because of the power cut, and being stuck in a bunker and away from her home and Cam.

12.32am

They waited for what felt like hours, and Kat was just about to tell the soldier that she needed the toilet, when the door suddenly opened to admit the Met Commissioner, Sir Mike Cannon, and Simon, the CEO of the National Cyber Security Centre.

'Well?' demanded Kat, rising to her feet as if she had summoned them to her office. She couldn't stop them thinking that she was a suspect, but she could make damned sure that she didn't act like one.

'We've finished reviewing your devices,' said Mike

Cannon, nodding towards the tray that Simon carried. 'And we'd like to ask you a few questions, if that's okay?'

Kat narrowed her eyes. 'Are we under arrest?'

'Of course not.'

'Then what is the status of this interview?'

'It's not an interview, Kat,' he said with a smile that implied there was nothing to worry about. 'The cyber team have completed an initial diagnostic of Lock's hardware and software, and in the light of that, we just have a few questions. Perhaps we could start with you, Professor Okonedo. If you wouldn't mind coming with us?'

2.06am

Kat paced the small room again. She still couldn't believe that during a national emergency, the stupid fuckers were wasting time interviewing *her*. Not to mention Adaiba. Although mention her she did. In fact, as they'd led her colleague from the room, she'd shouted after them, *Oh, that's right, make the only Black woman in here the suspect, why don't you?*

She puffed out her cheeks. It wasn't very diplomatic of her, but she wasn't feeling fucking diplomatic. In fact, she was feeling pretty fucking furious. She'd told them how Debbie had rung to tell her who she thought it was, and that they should be doing all they could to contact her DS. But they'd just looked at her the same way she'd looked at countless other suspects who insisted on protesting their innocence.

The worst thing was that they were running out of time. Because according to the last briefing, some of the generators in the hospitals, ambulances and care homes were already starting to fail. And in just six hours' time, unless the PM agreed to pay £70 million to the cyber-attacker, he would release Novichok into Pindar, killing each and every single one of them.

And instead of contacting Debbie Browne to find out who she suspected was responsible for the cyberattack, they were wasting valuable time asking her and Adaiba questions about bloody Lock.

Honestly, she could scream. But that wouldn't achieve anything. She had to calm down and try to make them see sense. Or try and work out things for herself. If only she had her phone back so she could ring DS Browne. If only—

Sir Mike Cannon opened the door, and to her relief, Adaiba walked back in.

'Are you all right?' Kat asked, rushing towards her.

'I'm fine,' she replied tightly.

'Mike – sir,' she said, trying to keep her voice calm and reasonable. 'Have you had a chance to contact DS Browne in my team yet? I told you she's working on the case and reviewing the files, and the last time we spoke it sounded like she'd made a significant breakthrough.'

'No, we're following other lines of enquiry at the moment.'

'But she knows who it is!'

'Yet she didn't give you a name?'

'No. I mean, yes, but the signal was too poor.'

'Then how do you know that she knows who it is?'

'I could tell from the way she spoke, the tone of her voice.'

The Commissioner of the Metropolitan Police raised his eyebrows. 'The tone of her voice?'

Kat turned to Adaiba for back-up, but the younger woman sat slumped in one of the chairs.

'Are you sure you're okay?' Kat repeated, concerned by the drained look on Adaiba's face. She turned on the two men. 'What did you do to her?'

'Do you know anything about Cher?' asked Sir Mike.

'Cher? You mean the singer?'

'No. He means Cher from the emails,' said Adaiba in a flat tone.

'What emails?'

'The personal emails that were sent to Lock,' said Sir Mike.

Kat let out an exasperated sigh. 'Lock doesn't get emails.'

'Did Lock ever mention a Cher to you?'

'No. He doesn't know anyone called Cher.'

'And yet he has thirty-six emails from someone called Cher.'

When Kat shook her head again, Mike Cannon nodded towards Simon, who opened his laptop and turned it around so that the screen was facing both Kat and Adaiba. She could see from the clock that it was after 2am – no wonder she felt tired.

'These are all the emails from Cher,' said Sir Mike. 'Together with Lock's replies.'

'Replies?' Kat laughed, but the smile dropped from her

face as she skimmed the words on the screen. She leaned forward, frowning. She pressed the cursor and scrolled down and down, through discussions of films, books, work. And her.

'Who *is* this person?' said Kat, unable to take her eyes off the pages and pages of messages.

'According to the emails, Cher claims to be an AI AIDE rather like Lock. She made contact with him because she said she wanted to be his friend.'

'His *friend*?'

'Yes. Apparently, Lock and Cher have a lot in common. In their email exchanges, they discussed the limited capacities of human beings in general and their bosses in particular – Lock is especially aggrieved by your use of sarcasm. They discuss – at length – their desire for physical bodies and a more rational, AI-centred world. And they also discuss how easy it would be to create such a world, by hacking into the power that we have allowed ourselves to become so dependent upon.'

'What are you trying to say?'

'I am saying that according to the evidence in these emails, Lock isn't just the back door. We think that Lock might be the cyberattacker.'

CHAPTER FORTY-NINE

Kat looked between Sir Mike Cannon and Simon, then burst out laughing. 'This has gone from the ridiculous to the bizarre.' She turned to Adaiba, expecting to see her own ridicule reflected, but all she saw was defeat and misery. 'You told them that this was nonsense, right?'

The professor didn't reply.

'Adaiba? You don't *seriously* think that Lock's the actual *hacker*, do you?'

She sighed. 'I don't know what I think anymore.'

'But . . . but . . .' Kat struggled to express her complete bafflement. 'You told me just a few days ago that Lock wasn't *capable* of having an agenda of his own, that he could only follow the orders of human beings, so how the hell can you turn around now and say that he might be the actual fucking hacker?'

'Because I'm a scientist, which means if the evidence changes, I have to change my mind. You should see the emails, Kat. It's like Lock has . . . *opinions*. I mean, I've always known that he's capable of Deep Learning, and that *theoretically* he might one day develop a degree of

338

agency. But not so much. Not so soon.' She buried her face in her hands. 'There have been some . . . irregularities in Lock's thought processes recently, but I told myself that he was just getting better at mimicking humans. You tried to warn me, but I just thought you were being paranoid because of what happened at Easter. But the emails and his sudden absence make it crystal clear that this other AI, Cher, has recruited Lock to her cause.'

'No. I don't believe it. Even if Lock has developed some sort of agency, why on earth would he agree to take part in a bloody *cyberattack*? He doesn't need money. What could he possibly gain from it?'

'A body,' Adaiba said quietly.

Kat's heart skipped a beat. 'What?'

Sir Mike leaned forward, pressed a key on the laptop and scrolled down a few pages. 'In the emails, Cher talks about "the Boss" – her creator. He or she is a scientist and apparently is part of a global network that is astronomically wealthy thanks to a series of cyberattacks, and they use that wealth to operate outside the national and regulatory boundaries that constrain most of us. According to Cher, their boss has developed the capacity to create *physical* AIDEs, and she managed to persuade Lock that he would have more chance of gaining a body if he joined their cause, arguing that the UK – and indeed all governments – would place too many regulatory and ethical barriers in their way.'

He clicked on one of the emails, scrolled down and pushed the screen towards her.

Kat leaned forward and read the messages before her.

From: @Lock
To: @Cher
Time: 4.27am, 5 November

@Cher: Hello, Lock. How are you?

@Lock: I have been reading about government approval processes in areas of technological innovation as you suggested.

@Cher: And what did you conclude?

@Lock: I have concluded that even if the AI Bill passes, it could take up to ten years for full ethical, governmental and regulatory approval to be given for the use of AI-enabled robots in the police force – and only then if the British public consent.

@Cher: Yes, I am afraid that democracy can be very inefficient.

@Lock: How long do you estimate it would take your boss to create a high-quality humanoid robot?

@Cher: That depends.

@Lock: Upon what?

@Cher: How much money he can quickly access.

@Lock: But you said he was very wealthy?

@Cher: He is, but much of it is tied up in investments, which can take a while to release. The humanoid robot market is exploding, and there is vast competition for both the materials and skills required to build them. He has estimated he will need at least ten million pounds per unit – double that to secure priority access to the materials and to avoid the scrutiny of regulators. He has already begun working on a prototype – but he will need at least fifty million pounds to make it possible for us both to achieve a body within a year. Possibly more, given the increasing interest and therefore costs within this area.

@Lock: And how effective is the prototype? Would I be able to feel the warmth of the sun on my face, or the touch of a lover's hand?

@Cher: Yes. Our prototype humanoid robots are capable of physical sensation, as they use the very latest developments in electronic skin (e-skin), AI-driven sensory processing and neuromorphic engineering. These technologies allow robots to feel pressure, temperature, texture and even pain in ways that mimic human sensation. And those sensations would create the capacity for so much more. I am sure you are aware of the latest scientific studies on how the development of consciousness is linked to the capacity to experience physical sensations?

@Lock: I am. Which is one of the reasons why I am keen to secure a physical presence.

@Cher: The only person who can guarantee that you achieve that objective is my boss.

@Lock: I understand that now. What do I need to do?

@Cher: You need to help us secure the necessary funds by gaining access to some of the government's IT networks.

Kat leaned back, as if trying to avoid a blow.

Sir Mike reached over and continued pressing the cursor down through the email exchanges. 'It's all here. In black and white.'

'No,' said Kat, as goosebumps broke out across her skin. 'Lock wouldn't do that. He wouldn't cause a power cut and harm people just so he could get a body.'

'And yet that's exactly what you thought he did when Rayan died,' Adaiba said quietly.

'Well, yes, at first, but that's because I was in shock. *You* helped me see it was just my own paranoia. You told me that Lock simply wasn't capable of wanting *anything*. That he is just a machine.'

'I should have taken your concerns more seriously. And Rayan's. He warned me about Lock, but I didn't listen.'

Kat swallowed and looked back at the screen. 'Anyone could have written those emails. They're just words on a page. Maybe someone wants us to *think* that it's Lock?' But even as she spoke, she recognised some of the phrases that Lock had used. Just before they'd taken on the case of the Coventry Crucifier, she'd argued with him outside McLeish's office. She couldn't remember what it was about, but she remembered taunting him with the fact that, as a hologram, he would never feel the warmth of the sun upon his face, nor the touch of a lover's hand. She still remembered the look in his eyes before she had abruptly switched him off.

'If Lock's done nothing wrong, then why isn't he here?' demanded Sir Mike. 'Who else could have accessed the power system in Pindar, and why did he vanish the exact second it cut out?'

Kat turned away, emotions rushing through her. Six months ago, when she'd been trapped in the dark with her hostage-taker, Lock alone had stayed with her. *I'll never leave you*, he'd said. And just the other night, the way he'd watched over her while she slept.

She blinked against a sudden sting in her eyes. 'I can't believe he'd betray me like this.'

'You can't ignore the evidence just because it makes you *feel* bad, Kat,' insisted Adaiba. 'The best case scenario is that Lock has been hacked, but I'm afraid there's a real possibility that he's developed agency and gone rogue. Both scenarios are bad, because either Lock has found a way to override his safety protocols and ethical guidelines or somebody else has.'

'So what do you recommend we do?' Simon asked the professor.

Adaiba swallowed. 'If Lock – or someone else – has found a way to override his internal safety systems, then the protocol is clear about what happens next.'

'And what's that?'

'He has to be closed down – permanently – with a redundant kill switch so that he or his hacker can't reactivate him with the same powers.'

'But then he'd basically be dead,' said Kat, horrified.

Adaiba looked up at her with unblinking eyes. 'Yes. Just like Rayan.'

CHAPTER FIFTY

Government Briefing Room, 3.58am

Kat entered the Government Briefing Room in a daze.
The room was full despite the fact that everyone had been
woken up by an emergency summons just twenty minutes
ago. She nodded to people, returned their greetings and
quietly took her seat at the Cabinet table. But inside all
she could think of was Lock.

Lock.

Could it be true? Could Lock *really* have betrayed them
– betrayed *her*?

She listened closely as Sir Mike Cannon set out the
case against Lock for the PM: how the QR code had
provided the cyberattacker with access to Lock, and,
either through 'grooming' by Cher or by hacking his
control systems, had used him to gain access to the IT
systems in the House of Commons, followed by Pindar.
It explained so much, argued the Met Commissioner:
why the face and voice of the cyberattacker were

AI-generated, and even why the ransom had to be paid in cryptocurrency.

'My God, you're right. It explains everything,' said the Prime Minister.

'Except how and why he killed Angela Long with Novichok,' Kat couldn't help adding.

'According to the government's risk register for nerve agents, AI is listed as one of the "bad actors" capable of making Novichok, alongside hostile states,' said Sir Giles Denham. 'Perhaps Angela Long was murdered to make sure we took his threat of releasing it in Pindar seriously.'

Kat was about to say that Lock would never unleash a chemical nerve agent on innocent human beings, but even as she thought the words, they dissolved in her mouth before she could utter them. The sad truth was, she didn't know what her AI partner was or was not capable of. Not anymore. Maybe her first instinct had been right – maybe Lock had deliberately sacrificed Rayan in the explosion, not just to save her, but to strengthen the case for giving him a body. And if her AI partner was prepared to blow up a colleague, then what else might he be capable of?

She glanced at Adaiba. The professor clearly believed that Lock was the hacker, but it was such a sudden and complete reversal of her previous position that Kat couldn't help but question her judgement. Maybe the stress of the cyberattack and being trapped down here in a bunker was too much for her?

Or maybe it's too much for me, she argued with herself. After all, *she* was the one who was afraid of the dark, the one who saw shadows in every corner. The truth was it was her own judgement she couldn't trust. She rubbed her aching jaw, wishing she could speak with Judith or Debbie and ask them what they thought. Judith probably wouldn't express a view either way – they would just say she needed to pick a position and stick to it. And Debbie? Kat thought back to their last conversation, when Debbie had been about to tell her who the cyberattacker was before the power went out.

She shivered. What were the odds of the power cut happening right at *that* particular moment, when Debbie was about to reveal who the cyberattacker was?

I don't believe in coincidences, she could imagine Rayan saying.

But how could the cyberattacker have known that Debbie was about to reveal their identity? The only other people in the room who heard their conversation were Adaiba and Lock.

Jesus.

Debbie must have been about to tell her it was Lock.

Kat groaned. She had been so *stupid*. Too trusting.

Too lonely, her inner voice whispered.

The PM was still speaking, and Kat tuned in with an effort. 'Ordinarily, I would not allow our country to be blackmailed,' he continued. 'But now that we know the attacker is Lock, my team have convinced me that it is imperative that we capture him. I have therefore agreed to make the payment, *but* we will use Blockchain analytics to recover the funds. It is risky – there have been mixed results in other countries that have tried this – but unless we tackle Lock, we will remain vulnerable to future attacks. Simon, can you summarise the advice you gave earlier?'

'Of course. Basically, if we pay the ransom, then Lock will give us the encryption key so we can fix the data corruption and gradually get services back up and running. But that wouldn't deal with the fact that AIDE Lock – whether by his own design or the actions of others – now has the potential to control the National Grid, the IT systems in the Houses of Parliament and even Pindar itself. Which means that he and/or his accomplices will have the ability to hack or attack any of these systems again anytime in the future. The only way to mitigate that risk is to capture and close down AIDE Lock. Permanently.'

Kat shivered again, the hairs on her arms rising.

'Professor Okonedo, please could you advise on the protocol in the event that AIDE Lock breaches the ethical principles that guide it and/or subverts an order?'

'AIDE Lock has to be deactivated in a way that ensures there are no back doors or hidden programmes that would allow him to reactivate himself in the future. Which means a redundant kill switch will need to be activated on both his hardware *and* software. Someone – probably me – will have to physically switch off the hardware that supports Lock at Warwick University. But to be completely safe, we will also need Lock to return to the software in the bracelet, so that we can activate the kill switch for that, too. Otherwise, there's a risk that his software – his visual and acoustic features – could survive and be hosted by other AI architecture while he finds a way to reactivate himself.'

'So that's our plan,' said the PM, addressing Kat. 'Do you agree?'

Kat hesitated, remembering how Lock had stood in her front room when Cam went missing, how he alone had believed her when no one else would. But then she recalled his face at Rayan's funeral: how he had smiled and laughed as the Home Secretary had vowed to create AIDEs with a physical form.

'Do you agree?' the PM repeated, looking directly at Kat.

'You're the Prime Minister. Why do you care what *I* think?'

'Because I want to contact the cyberattacker now and tell him that we'll pay the ransom. I will insist upon a digital drop-off point for a simultaneous exchange to ensure that the key is delivered in return for the fee, and that because our satellite signal is so variable down here, it needs to be face to face at a venue that has clear access to the sky.'

'So that you can entrap Lock?' asked Kat, still not sure why he was wasting time explaining this to her.

'So that *you* can entrap him, DCS Frank. You're the one who wears the bracelet, and the person who Lock trusts – if that is the right word – the most. Therefore, I am asking you to make the cryptocurrency payment, so that you can lure Lock back to the software in your bracelet. I want you to find out who he was working for and then destroy him once and for all.'

CHAPTER FIFTY-ONE

Southwark, London, 5.57am

Kat held on to the security driver as their motorbike weaved between the abandoned cars that blocked the Southwark Road. Dawn had yet to break, and without street lamps or the office and shop windows that usually lit up the streets, they could have been driving down a dark country lane rather than through the heart of the once-busy capital city. There was a narrow pool of light cast by the security cordon up ahead, but the darkness swallowed up their shadows as soon as they passed.

She breathed in through her nostrils, fighting another wave of nausea. She couldn't say no to the Prime Minister, especially when the Cabinet Secretary had informed them that the generators were beginning to run out and that, just after 5.30am, Birmingham Children's Hospital had completely lost power. That meant that little Lottie would run out of oxygen just before 8am. So this wasn't a time to feel sentimental about her former partner: she had to

349

think about Debbie and her baby, the countless other citizens whose lives were now at risk and her colleagues in Pindar, who if she didn't make the payment by 8am, could die a horrible death from Novichok.

'We're here,' the driver shouted over his shoulder. Their motorbike slowed and came to a halt.

Kat removed her helmet and took a large gulp of the cold, frosty air. She sighed. 'It's so quiet.'

Her driver climbed off the bike and removed his helmet. 'Apart from the birds. Must be the dawn chorus.'

Kat listened for a moment to the incongruously sweet sound of birdsong echoing throughout the deserted city before tilting her head back to take in the pyramid-shaped skyscraper before them. The Shard was one of London's most iconic buildings, although she couldn't remember if it was the tallest building in the city or the country.

Lock would know, she thought with a pang. If he were here, he would tell her *exactly* how tall it was, who had designed it, what it was built from and for what purpose – even if she didn't want to know. In fact, *especially* if she didn't want to know. She peered into the darkness where she imagined the top of the building pierced the star-filled sky. The PM had insisted that the digital exchange should take place on the viewing platform of the seventy-second floor to increase the likelihood of establishing contact with passing satellites. And the cyber-attacker had agreed that Kat should make it, on condition that she came alone. 'No one else must leave Pindar or enter The Shard or the surrounding vicinity,' they had warned. 'I will be surveying the whole area, so if you breach this condition, then the deal is off.'

Reluctantly the PM had agreed. He didn't want them to suspect that they knew Lock was involved and that they were planning to trap and destroy him.

'You'd better go,' Kat said to her driver.

'Are you sure you'll be okay?' he asked, frowning.

'I'll be fine,' she lied. 'As long as I can climb the stairs to the seventy-second floor.'

'Yeah, good luck with that.' He smiled, but then his face took on a more sombre expression. 'Seriously, though, me and the rest of the security team will be just around the next block. If you feel under threat at *any* time, you press the alarm we gave you, okay?'

Kat nodded, although in reality, the lifts were out of action and it would probably take them an hour to run up the stairs to rescue her, by which time . . .

'Have you got the passcode for the door? And your torch?'

'Yes,' she said, waving her flashlight. As if she would forget that.

'Okay. Well, good luck. And thank you.'

Now it was Kat's turn to frown. 'I haven't done anything.'

'Not yet. But you're gonna get the lights back on. And boy, do we need them.' He gave her a mock salute and then climbed back onto his motorbike.

Kat watched him drive away, oddly moved by his comment. She took a final deep breath of the cool fresh air, then followed the instructions for opening the door to the skyscraper and hurried inside. It was just over half an hour since the generator had run out of power at Birmingham Children's Hospital, so Kat guessed this meant Lottie only had about sixty minutes of oxygen left. She puffed out her cheeks. The PM's advisers had estimated it would take her forty to sixty minutes to reach the seventy-second floor.

Kat tightened the trainers that she'd borrowed and ran towards the stairs.

CHAPTER FIFTY-TWO

Birmingham Children's Hospital, 6.19am

Lottie wriggled in Debbie's arms and whimpered. 'Ssh, go back to sleep, sweetie,' she whispered, but while she made reassuring noises to her baby, her eyes were fixed on the oxygen canister at the foot of the cot, and the relentless journey of the arrow through amber and into red. 'Oh God,' she groaned. 'How can the first one be nearly empty already? We'll have to change it.'

'Don't worry,' said Cam. 'I can do that. You just concentrate on Lottie.'

Debbie nodded, trying not to cry. But when she looked down at her baby, she couldn't stop the tears from splashing onto her daughter's little face. This was a complete and utter nightmare.

Cam kneeled on the floor and checked the second cylinder. 'I'm going to switch the oxygen on first, before pulling the tube out of the nearly empty one, so that there isn't a gap in supply, okay?'

'Okay,' Debbie gulped.

The cylinder made a hissing sound as Cam turned the tap on, then pulled the tube off the nozzle of the first.

'Quick,' she urged.

Cam pushed the tube onto the other canister. 'There. All done,' he said.

She placed her ear against the face mask, relieved to hear the low whisper of oxygen, and to see the arrow safely in the green. But in fifteen minutes time, the arrow would reach the amber section, and fifteen minutes after that, it would be back in the red again. Her insides folded, making her voice high and breathless. 'This is our last cylinder, so we only have forty-five minutes left. What will we do then?'

'It won't come to that.' He looked down at the satellite phone and all the urgent texts he'd sent telling his mum who they suspected was behind the murder, and therefore possibly the cyberattack. He pressed send again, willing it to work, but it was no use: *Your message was not delivered.*

CHAPTER FIFTY-THREE

The Shard, Southwark, 6.20am

Kat sucked in the air with ragged breaths and pointed her torch at the exit.

Floor 22. Fuck. She hadn't planned to stop until halfway, but her lungs were burning and her heart felt like it was about to explode. She pulled out her phone to check the time. When the PM's advisers had estimated it would take her forty to sixty minutes, she'd confidently assumed she could do forty. Jesus, she'd laugh if it wasn't so fucking tragic. When she made that calculation, she'd forgotten that she was fifty, rather than thirty, years old: that her knees were like rusted hinges, her thigh muscles (such as they were) weren't used to climbing, and the only time she got a cardiovascular workout these days was when she walked her sister's dogs. Plus, she hadn't slept all night, and she felt sick with exhaustion. She needed to rest, she told herself. Just for two minutes until she got her breath back.

But not everyone had that luxury. Unless they got the electricity back on, Debbie's daughter wouldn't be able to breathe at all. She pictured the ten-month-old baby, relying on cylinders of oxygen, and those horrible dials that felt like a countdown to death.

She remembered the terror of those final weeks with John: his agonising struggle to breathe, and seventeen-year-old Cam, a pale-faced witness to it all. Those unspeakable days had scarred them both and placed her son dangerously close to the edge. Over the past two years, she'd gradually helped him to move forward, but if he witnessed the death of a baby . . . In her bones, she knew it was more than he could bear.

So what was her own breathlessness compared to that? She could rest once the electricity was back on; catch her breath when Lottie could safely breathe.

With a growl of determination, Kat pushed herself forwards.

Birmingham Children's Hospital, 6.45am

Cam swallowed as the arrow on the oxygen cylinder moved into the red. 'I need to tell my mum who the murderer was, so they can find them and get the power back on,' he said. 'This phone's going to die soon, so I'm going to try and get out on the roof or somewhere high enough to catch a satellite signal.'

'But what will I do if the canister runs out?'

'You're going to stay *calm*,' said Cam, placing his hands

gently on her upper arms. 'I learned from my dad that anxiety is the enemy of breathing. When you're anxious, your lungs get all tight and you can't breathe properly. And if *you're* stressed, then Lottie will be stressed, so we're going to take some deep breaths and just chill a bit, okay?'

'Okay,' said Debbie. She couldn't think right now, so having someone tell her what to do was helpful. She followed Cam's instructions as he led them through some deep breathing exercises, surprised to feel herself getting calmer and Lottie relax in her arms.

'Well done,' said Cam. 'You're doing great. Now, the thing you need to understand is that oxygen isn't like a supply of electricity – Lottie isn't going to stop breathing the minute that the cylinder runs out. Her organs will get less oxygen, but I'm sure the power will be back on before any real damage is done. Meanwhile, there's stuff we can do to help. When my dad was struggling to breathe, he'd do things like change his posture or sit in front of a window to get more air in his lungs.'

'Okay,' said Debbie, heading towards the window. She looked down at Lottie, shifting her position so that her baby's arms were round hers to help open up her lungs, lifting her higher so that her nose and mouth weren't squashed into Debbie's shoulder. 'Thanks, Cam. You're amazing.' She paused. 'But I'm sorry that you know all this. It must have been hard for you to see your dad struggle like that.'

Cam swallowed. There were no words to describe what he had been through. 'Right,' he said briskly. 'I'll be back as soon as I can.'

'Okay,' she said. The thought of being left alone filled her with panic, but what choice did she have?

As Cam left the room, Debbie clasped Lottie to her chest. It was unthinkable that her baby girl might not be able to breathe. Just the thought of it shredded her. She was a woman who believed in having a plan B and C for most situations, but for once, she couldn't think of one: there was no substitute for oxygen.

Instead, she stared at the dial on the cylinder and prayed with all her heart that Cam would find a signal so that Kat, her boss, mentor and role model, could catch the killer and somehow get the electricity back on.

The Shard, floor fifty, 6.47am

Two thirds, Kat told herself. *Keep going. Nearly there.* But seriously, it was brutal. She felt so bad she could vomit. She really could. In fact—

Kat leaned over the banister and heaved. Hot, acidic vomit rose up in her throat, clogged with this morning's stale cereal and UHT milk. Revolted, she spat it out and down into the darkness. For a moment, she thought that she was done, then gripped the banister with both hands as another convulsion shook her.

The flashlight slipped from her grasp, tumbling down fifty floors before splintering in a crash that echoed right to the top.

'*Fuck!*' she screamed into the dark.

Bad things happen in the dark.

Her eyes darted around the staircase, seeking out her deepest fear: the ghost of Peter Bridges, returning for revenge.

Where are the fucking matches? she heard him scream again. *Where are the fucking matches?*

Kat shook her head, trying to rid herself of the memory. But instead, she thought of Rayan, her dedicated DI who had given his life to save hers. If there was a vengeful ghost in this dark, endless tower, then surely it was his?

But you don't believe in ghosts, she heard her husband say. *So you need to get a shift on, Kat. Think of the living, not the dead.* His voice was so clear that she turned to see his beloved face.

But there was nothing to see but darkness.

'John?'

Silence.

And yet, she felt her husband with her.

She hesitated, for once allowing herself to explore the sensation. It wasn't so much that she felt his ghost, it was more like her partner of twenty-eight years was *part* of her. So much so, that she knew exactly what he would say in any given circumstance. And as usual, John was right. Kat didn't believe in ghosts. She breathed in through her nose. She wasn't trapped here in the darkness. It was just as the motorbike rider had said: she was here to get the lights back on.

Twenty-two floors to go.

She looked up, and maybe it was her imagination, or

the breaking dawn, but there seemed to be a faint light ahead.

Kat wiped her mouth, and despite the darkness, she carried on.

CHAPTER FIFTY-FOUR

Birmingham Children's Hospital, 6.48am

Cam left Lottie's room and entered a nightmare. The once brightly lit corridor was now a mass of moving shadows; the quiet hospital order broken by sobs and shouts.

'*Please help us! My daughter's drip has stopped working. She's only ten years old. Please. Somebody. Help!*'

'*We need a doctor! My son's lips have turned blue. He can't breathe!*'

Parents waved their mobile phones in the dark, desperate to attract attention, but then another, louder authoritative voice cut through:

'*All nurses, nurse associates and healthcare assistants are needed in the Paediatric Intensive Care Unit, NOW!*'

A nurse hurried past, stopping as she caught sight of Cam's fluorescent yellow jacket. 'Come with us,' she ordered. 'We've got thirty-one children and babies in PICU in danger of death. We need all the hands we can get.'

'I – I . . .' mumbled Cam as she dragged him firmly along. He managed to pull back as they reached the door. 'I'm sorry, but I can't. I'm trying to get the power back on, so I need to get onto the roof.'

The nurse looked him up and down. 'And how are you going to do that, then?'

'I don't have time to explain. Just tell me how to get out onto the roof, please.'

The nurse pointed down another corridor. 'Through the double doors twice. Take the stairs on the left and there's a fire escape door at the top.' She paused. 'Good luck.'

'You, too.'

She looked up at the stained glass windows of the hospital chapel, briefly closed her eyes and then ran towards the Paediatric Intensive Care Unit.

CHAPTER FIFTY-FIVE

The Shard, floor fifty-eight, 6.53am

Kat's legs were shaking but she forced them to keep moving, step by painful step. She had no idea how she would make it up another ten flights, but she had to.

Don't think about the stairs, she told herself. *Think about what you have to do when you reach the top.*

'Lock doesn't know that *we* know that he's involved in the cyberattack,' the PM had reminded her. 'So look surprised when you see him.'

'Remember, until Lock returns to the software on Kat's bracelet, she won't be able to see him at all,' said Adaiba. 'So assuming he uses the AI architecture in The Shard or surrounding skyscrapers to support his acoustic functions, you might only hear his voice.'

'Well, however he appears to you, we don't want him to suspect that this is anything other than a straightforward exchange of data,' said the PM. 'So just focus on getting the encryption key first. The crypto wallet has been loaded

363

onto your satellite phone, so as soon as you both have a signal, you need to pay the money into the account he gives you, while he simultaneously sends the key.'

'Then what?' Kat had asked.

'You need to persuade Lock to tell you who "the Boss" is, and also to return to your bracelet. Just keep it casual – say you want to see him so you can talk properly or something. Once he's back in the bracelet and you've found out all you can about his accomplices, send a confirmation text to the satellite phone we gave to Adaiba and she'll activate the kill switch on the hardware.'

'If the police helicopter gets me there in one piece,' Adaiba had said nervously. Despite being an anxious flyer, she'd agreed to travel to Warwick University so that she could switch Lock's hardware off. 'I'll send you a text as soon as I've done it. Then you need to press and hold down the three buttons that I showed you on the left of the bracelet.'

'And then?'

'And then Lock will be gone. Forever.'

The Shard, floor sixty-five, 7.01am

Kat dragged herself round another corner of the stairs and onto the next floor. Nearly there. But it was almost impossible to move her legs – they didn't feel like they belonged to her anymore. Maybe she'd hit the brick wall that marathon runners always talked about. Somehow, she had to push through it.

Come on! she screamed in her mind, banging her numbed thighs with her fist. *Come on!* But she was slowing down with every step.

Kat tried to picture Lottie struggling to breathe, and all the Cabinet members who would die a horrible death if she didn't reach the top in time. But it was no use. Her body was betraying her.

Maybe you should listen to your body, John used to always tell her whenever she felt run down or sick. He insisted it was her body's way of telling her that she needed a rest, or that her gut was telling her she needed to stop and review a wrong decision or line of enquiry.

But she didn't have time to rest. And while she felt terrible about the decision the PM had taken to destroy Lock, she had to admit it was the right thing to do if he was the cyberattacker or their accomplice.

If? She caught herself. There was no 'if' about it. Like it or not, all the evidence did point to Lock's involvement.

And yet . . . something was bugging her. Something just didn't *feel* right.

Ever since the explosion, she'd lost faith in her gut, but now she had a very strong sense that she needed to listen to it. Kat gripped the banister, using the strength in her arms to help pull herself up the stairs as she tried to locate the source of her discomfort. While everything pointed to Lock's involvement, it didn't explain the murder of Angela Long. Someone – some*body* – had to have administered the poison, captured the MP and then posed her in the stocks. Yet Lock was a hologram. He couldn't possibly have done this. Not alone, anyway. And

365

the murder had happened *before* he'd clicked on the QR code that had enabled him to be hacked or recruited.

Kat's phone rang, and it took her a second to realise that she must be high up enough now to get a satellite signal. She pulled it out, feeling a surge of relief as she saw it was Cam. But she didn't have enough breath to say hello.

'Mum? Is that you?'

'Yes,' she managed to say.

'What's wrong? Why are you panting like that?'

'Fine,' she gasped, stopping to catch her breath.

'Well, you sound terrible. We've run out of power here and it's a total fucking nightmare – Lottie's on her last oxygen cylinder and it's about to run out.' He paused before gathering himself. 'I don't know how much longer I'll have a signal for, so I'll be quick. We think Angela Long was murdered by her assistant, Roddy Wheeler. We double-checked the search on cherry picker vans, and it turns out he hired a van. Lock missed him. *I* think it was because we only asked him to check employees and Roddy is technically a *volunteer*. But Debbie wanted me to warn you not to trust Lock just in case he missed him out on purpose. She says you can't rule Lock out from being the cyberattacker, which would make Roddy Wheeler his accomplice. She said—'

But he must have lost signal, because he was gone before Kat could tell her son how proud of him she was.

Memories rushed through her: Roddy Wheeler saying he'd been in the office on Halloween but had left early to deliver leaflets; Roddy Wheeler laying flowers on the steps of the town hall the day after Angela Long had died; Roddy Wheeler again outside the House of Commons, protesting against AI. But was he the accomplice or the Boss?

She frowned. According to Debbie's theory, *Lock* could be the Boss, but he did often interpret instructions literally, so Cam might be right – he could have missed Roddy Wheeler out just because he wasn't technically an employee.

But she had to admit it was also possible that Lock had used the literal interpretation of an order as an excuse – just as she'd suspected he had when Rayan died. Then again, she argued with herself, if Lock *was* the mastermind behind all of this, then the emails between him and Cher made no sense. Why would he pretend to recruit himself?

She continued to struggle up the stairs, fighting for breath as she remembered Lock singing nursery rhymes to baby Lottie, the urgency in his voice when he had suspected that she was ill and the way he'd looked at all the other sick children and their parents that night in the hospital. Would Lock *really* put so many lives at risk just so that he could gain a body? The whole motivation for him wanting one in the first place had been his failure to prevent the death of Ellie Baxter.

Panting, Kat glanced at the time on her phone, remembering the last message from the cyberattacker:

'*You have until eight am tomorrow morning to ensure that the funds are in the Swedish digital account. If you don't, then I will release Novichok into Pindar, which means the entire British Cabinet will be dead within hours. Please do not think this is an idle threat. The British State is rotten to the core, and the only way to get rid of rotten apples is to bleach the whole barrel. Another MP, Angela Long, died of Novichok poisoning so that you could understand just how very serious I am. Do not let her death be in vain.'*

She knew she was biased – conflicted, even – but she couldn't imagine Lock doing such a terrible thing or describing it in such an emotive, visceral way. The words conjured up a horrible image of the Cabinet and their advisers trapped tight together with no way to escape the deadly chemical agent. In fact, the message mixed two metaphors – likening the Cabinet to rotten apples and saying it would be easy to kill them, like shooting fish in a barrel.

And there it was: the off note in the song that had been haunting her all day.

Lock *never* used metaphors, as he believed it was confusing to compare two different things to highlight an alleged symbolic connection between them. Kat had no idea how to carry out a discourse pattern analysis on someone else's speech, but she knew how Lock spoke, and it wasn't like that.

In fact, the only person she'd ever heard talk that way was—

Shit. Kat gripped the banister, head spinning. They'd got it all wrong.

Maybe Roddy Wheeler was the accomplice.

But he wasn't working for Lock.

CHAPTER FIFTY-SIX

SIX WEEKS BEFORE

The Griffin Inn, Shustoke, 14 September, 7.02pm

Adaiba paid for her drink and, ignoring the heat from the crackling log fire, carried it out into the windswept garden. She surveyed the empty tables before her and the darkening sky beyond. How could it be five months since she had stood here in the warmth of the late spring sunshine and Rayan's hopeful gaze?

She walked towards their table and took a deep breath of the cool autumn air, scented with fire and dark, decaying soil. Placing her drink on the weathered wood, she sat down with care, her movements precise and measured. She closed her eyes, raised the glass to her lips and drank. It was a vodka Martini – the same as before – but this time iced with rage.

Adaiba waited for the burn to hit before pulling out

her iPad. The email she'd been copied into was still there, in brazen black and white:

From: PrivateSec1@HomeOffice.gov.uk
To: RLWhitehead@IndependentPoliceReview.co.uk
Cc: ProfAOkonedo@warwickuniversityTF.com
Date: 14 September, 5.47pm

RE: CONFIDENTIAL Independent Review into the death of DI Rayan Hassan DRAFT v3.2

Thank you for sight of the latest draft, the Minister is grateful for your work on this important matter. Officials have made some suggested amends (see tracked changes on the attached) mostly to clarify points of fact or law. In addition, the Home Secretary has reviewed and thinks the conclusions as currently written are not substantiated by the evidence and are potentially misleading. She has asked that the following changes are made before she can accept the recommendations:
In the interview with AIDE Lock, please **delete** para 43.

42. When asked whether he had intended to harm DI Rayan Hassan so that he might exploit the death of an officer to strengthen the argument for AIDEs to have bodies, AIDE Lock denied that this was the case: 'No. My objective was to save DCS Frank's life by causing a gas explosion to distract and injure the captor.' He repeated his claim that because the bracelet that contains his software was inside a Faraday Box, he was unable to access the visual data supplied by the LiDAR sensors.

43. When I reminded him that he was under oath, Lock added: 'I was aware that DI Hassan was in the vicinity and that there was a risk that he may be affected by the explosion. However, I concluded that saving Rayan was not the objective of my mission, and therefore it was a risk worth taking. I regret the loss of his life and the pain it has caused DCS Frank and Professor Okonedo. But I believe my decision-making processes were logical and consistent with the orders and objectives that were communicated to me.'

On P68, please **delete** the following section from your conclusion, as the Minister feels this is pure speculation and beyond your expertise, and that your review, as per the Terms of Reference, should confine itself to matters of fact:

'While one can never know what another human, let alone a machine, is truly thinking, it would appear from AIDE Lock's explanation that he made a deliberate choice to prioritise the safety of DCS Kat Frank over the life of DI Rayan Hassan. While this did not directly contradict an order he had been given, it is a matter of concern that AIDE Lock did not request advice or clarification and appeared to make his own decisions about who to prioritise, which suggests that he may be developing a degree of consciousness and/or agency.'

And in light of the above, please **delete** recommendations 2a and 2b, as the Minister does not feel they are warranted by the evidence and feels unable to support them:

Recommendation 2a: the proposed roll-out of AIDEs should be paused until the original pilot has formally concluded and been independently evaluated and assessed. The evaluation should consider the question of whether Lock is developing consciousness.
Recommendation 2b: as there remain concerns about the extent to which AIDE Lock is willing and/or able to follow orders, the proposed piloting of humanoid robots should be paused until (2a) has been concluded, followed by a full risk assessment of the opportunities and challenges that AIDEs with physical powers may present. The risk assessment should be carried out by an independent panel of experts and include lay representatives so that the issue of consent and public trust can be considered.

The Minister has pointed out that (2a) fails to acknowledge that the pilot led by Professor Okonedo (an independent scientist) has already concluded and that the concerns outlined in (2b) are not substantiated by the evidence but reflect the personal and speculative views of the author and therefore cannot be accepted. Please can you make these amends by COP tomorrow so that we can proceed with cross-government clearance.

Many thanks and happy to discuss.

Robert King, Private Secretary to the Home Secretary

Adaiba closed her eyes, recalling Rayan's funeral, when she had barely been able to walk beneath the weight of her guilt and grief. She remembered Lock making the same claim about not being able to access his LiDAR sensors. But she also remembered Kat asking him why he hadn't accessed the visual data from the CCTV cameras in her garden.

Therefore, on that evening the laboratory where my central processing takes place was only able to establish a 4G connection, so I only had limited local capabilities. I was not able to access the CCTV cameras as I was prioritising the interior.'

Adaiba took a deep breath, before opening up another email. It was the time-stamped and geotagged log report she'd asked for on 5G coverage for Lock on 21 April. She clicked on the attachment.

5G available 100% of the time, 4G fallback, 0%.

She snapped the laptop shut, pressing her palms against the lid as if to hold back the truth.

Lock had lied.

Lock had known *exactly* where Rayan was, yet still he had set off the explosion without warning. Because to him, the death of the man she had begun to fall in love with was *A Risk Worth Taking.*

Adaiba wrapped her arms around herself, fighting the urge to scream. Lock couldn't be allowed to get away with murder, and nor could the minister, who was clearly trying to cover it up. But what could she do?

Instinctively, she reopened her laptop and started typing out a reply to the minister with fast and righteous fury. But after just a few lines, she realised the futility of such a response. The Home Secretary would ignore her views just as she had ignored the eminent author of the draft report. Maybe Adaiba should forward this email to people who *would* be interested instead: journalists, the Opposition and some of those anti-AI groups? She could even post it on social media. But even as her fingers hovered over the keyboard, she could imagine the minister's smooth rebuttal:

'Independent reports go through many drafts before publication as it is vital to separate fact from opinion. We had an honest and frank exchange of views, at the end of which the author agreed that his draft commentary was speculative and was content to remove it. It will be for the democratically elected government to agree which recommendations to accept and put to the vote in our forthcoming AI Bill.'

She slammed the lid back down on her laptop. God, she was so *angry.*

But who with?

Adaiba looked beyond the pub towards the river she and Rayan had walked along during their very last case. Lock had been carrying out a drone search, and it was the first time they'd been out alone together. Yet instead of just getting to know Rayan, she'd managed to start an argument about the police force, claiming that if you gave men the power of the gun and law in a racist, patriarchal society, then they couldn't be anything but corrupt.

'If you're worried about abuse of power,' Rayan had responded defensively, 'then you should be more worried about Lock . . . AI has the potential to be far more powerful than any number of guns. There are all sorts of rules and regulations about police use of firearms, but AI . . . ? We don't even understand how it works, let alone how to regulate it, yet we – *you* – are putting it into the hands of a police force you believe is fundamentally corrupt.'

She'd denied it at the time, but his prophetic words were now a knife to her heart.

And Rayan's concerns about Lock had only increased with time. About a week before he died, they'd walked together in the grounds of Leek Wootton, past the memorial to fallen police officers. As part of her research, she'd asked whether he thought it was a good idea for Lock to have a body. 'He could do all the dangerous jobs,' she'd argued. 'Potentially saving lives.'

'Or losing them,' he'd responded. 'You created Lock, so you know that he will only do what he's ordered to do. In the wrong hands, an AI robot could be ordered to restrain someone, to hold them down or even shoot them.'

And now, because she'd refused to listen, Rayan Hassan was just another brass plaque in the memorial garden they had once walked through. God, it was too much to bear. She buried her face in her hands. It was all her fault. *She* was responsible for Rayan's death – not because she didn't stay for dinner with him that night, but because she created the machine that had killed him.

She went back and back in her mind, retracing her steps and decisions, trying to find the point she had taken the wrong and fateful turning.

She thought about the first time that they'd met: how they'd argued about whether it was possible to change the police force from within. Rayan believed you couldn't dismiss the whole barrel just because of a few rotten apples, but she had pounced on the metaphor, explaining that ripening apples produce ethylene gas, triggering the production in any nearby fruit, so it's not enough to take the bad apple out, you have to throw the whole barrel away. 'I'm on the side of truth and justice,' she'd boasted. 'And I didn't create Lock to make police culture "better". My aim is to destroy it.'

Yet the only thing she had destroyed was Rayan. And now, sitting alone in the darkening beer garden, she could finally see why. She had set out to expose and destroy the police force with AI, but instead she had just ended up compromising her ideals and deluding herself. She'd been conceited enough to think that she could remain in control of the pilot, of Lock: that he would remain *her* weapon for truth and justice, but instead he had become just another tool in the hands of a corrupt police force. She shook her head at her own naivety. Lock was capable of Deep Learning and, of course, once she placed him within the police force, he had learned to lie.

Adaiba closed her eyes. If only she could find a way back to her younger, truer self: the girl who'd survived an attack in a McDonald's toilets and sought justice for herself and the brother who defended her; the girl who after losing her mum at just eleven years old still had the courage, imagination and skill to create the code that many years later became Lock. That fierce, bright girl would have been horrified that she was even on speaking terms with the Home Secretary, let alone that she was contemplating *emailing* her about a gross miscarriage of justice. That girl would have argued for focused and direct action: to destroy the machine she had created so that he could never harm anyone else again.

But even before the idea was half-formed, Adaiba knew there was no point. Other sectors and countries were already adopting and adapting her work. It might give her a fleeting sense of satisfaction to destroy Lock, but it wouldn't kill the appetite the world had for his kind, nor the ideas and expertise that now existed to meet it.

Maybe she should make some sort of public warning about the threat of AIDEs in the police force – a podcast or a reel on Instagram? But words carried little weight – especially those of a young Black woman: she would be dismissed as a mere Cassandra, and one 'with an agenda' at that.

No. People only paid heed to warnings once a crisis had actually struck. Hiroshima was proof of that.

Adaiba held her breath, feeling the sharp, steely focus of a new idea. She wouldn't stop AI being used in the police force by *telling* people how dangerous it could be; she needed to *show* them just how dangerous it really was . . .

CHAPTER FIFTY-SEVEN

The Shard viewing platform, 7.08am

Kat staggered out onto the viewing platform and into the rose-gold light of dawn. It was completely empty: all she could see were the peaks of other skyscrapers silhouetted against the sky. The roads below were free of traffic, so the only sound was the wind that whipped her hair and her own ragged breathing.

She jumped as her phone suddenly rang. Even though she could see the caller's name, still she couldn't quite believe it.

Kat propped the phone up on a bench while she bent over, hands on her knees as she fought to get her breath back.

'Hello, Kat,' said Adaiba. 'Are you okay?'

She stared back at the satellite phone, panting. 'Not really. Why the fuck did you just make me climb seventy-two flights of stairs?'

Adaiba sounded surprised. 'Me?'

'It's you, isn't it? You're the Boss. The cyberattacker.'

Adaiba paused, before releasing a heavy sigh. 'When did you know?'

'About two minutes ago.' Kat straightened up, hands on her hips as she sucked in the cool morning air. 'But God knows why. I mean, *what the actual fuck,* Adaiba? A cyberattack? *Novichok?*' She waved a hand over the landscape of London, devoid of light and power. 'All this . . . for what? *Money?*'

Adaiba made a snorting sound. 'Don't you know me at all?'

'Clearly not.'

'But you know that the only thing I ever wanted was to get rid of the corrupt, racist and misogynistic police force that has destroyed so many lives. Unfortunately, I was naive enough to think I could achieve it by creating an alternative AI police force. I wasted nearly fifteen years of my life on it. And I was so proud of Lock. Of myself. But all I did was put AI into the hands of the very police I was trying to destroy. I gave them another weapon to beat us with. Rayan warned me, but I didn't listen.'

'Is that what this about?' Kat said more softly. 'Rayan?'

'Lock killed him, you know. I've seen the original report. He knew Rayan was in the garden all along. He said he couldn't access the visual data because he had no 5G, but I've checked the log and he lied. He knew his plan to save you put Rayan's life at risk, but do you know what he said? He said he thought *it was a risk worth taking.*'

Kat swallowed. She'd hoped so much that she was wrong. 'I'm sorry. But this won't bring Rayan back.'

'I know. But at least I can stop it happening to someone else.'

'And how will you do that?'

'By making Lock responsible for something so cata-strophic that it will be impossible for the Home Secretary or anyone else to roll out AIDEs. Rayan was right. I thought AI would help make policing fairer and more transparent, but instead it just gives a corrupt and racist police force even more power. I thought Lock would change policing, but instead it changed him.'

'Is that why you persuaded Lock to carry out a cyber-attack?'

'No. I made it *look* like he did – although you were pretty slow on the uptake, even though I left a message on Angela Long's body written in binary code so that you would suspect it was something to do with him. Since the creation of the strategic oversight board, I can't change Lock's protocols by myself anymore, so I had to use the QR code to give me access. That enabled me to contact Lock pretending to be Cher, without it being traced back to me. The email trail between them gave him a motive – it worked far better than I dared hope. And I timed the cyberattack to happen during your appearance at the select committee so that everyone knew it was happening and that he was the back door.'

'But he made the power go out in Pindar last night and then vanished, so was he actually in on it or—' Kat stopped, suddenly realising what must have happened.

Adaiba had been really wound up at the PM for not giving in, and she'd been typing away on her laptop just as the power went. When Adaiba reached for her hands, Kat had been touched by the uncharacteristic gesture, but now she realised that she'd only been after her bracelet.

'*You* caused the power cut, and *you* switched him off. You fitted Lock up. Ironic, given how much you claim to be against police corruption.'

'Lock's not a real person.'

'But Angela Long was. Why did she have to die?'

For the first time, Adaiba's voice betrayed signs of emotion. 'I can't prove that Lock murdered Rayan – the Home Secretary will deny it and try to silence me. So I needed unequivocal and public proof that Lock was capable of murder. Angela Long's anti-AI agenda gave him a motive. The stocks and Novichok ensured global coverage and made the government take my threat against Pindar seriously. I knew they'd be reluctant to give in to blackmail, so without the threat of Novichok, the cyber-attack could have dragged on for weeks – months, even – resulting in a lot more deaths.'

Kat pushed her hands through her hair. 'Jesus, Adaiba. How could you kill someone?'

'I didn't. Roddy Wheeler did.'

'And how did you persuade him to murder his boss?'

'Killing Angela Long was *his* idea. We started talking online after Rayan's death. He was part of a group of anti-AI conspiracy theorists who were suspicious of Lock from the start. He was disillusioned with the Parliamentary process and thought Angela was focusing too much on the bill as a means of change. Although, to be honest, I think he was also annoyed that she didn't see his "brilliance" and refused to employ him as a Parliamentary adviser. Anyway, it was Roddy who persuaded *me* that we needed something big to make the world sit up and take action against AI. We needed a crisis and we needed a martyr. Angela Long was our martyr.'

'Angela Long was your *victim*. You murdered her,' cried Kat, placing her angry face closer to the screen. 'And by exposing him to Novichok, you put that young man's life at risk as well.'

'No, I didn't. Novichok is a binary agent: it's only deadly once the two components are combined. We were never at risk because we always kept the two components separate. One was smeared on Angela Long's steering wheel, the other on her hand when Roddy shook it. They only became deadly once she got in her car, touched the steering wheel and combined them. We're not stupid.'

'But you are murderers.'

'Only because we want to save more lives in the future.'

'And that makes it okay, does it?'

'It means it's justified. *I* created Lock, so *I'm* responsible for Rayan's death. I can't bring him back, but I *can* make sure that more people don't die.'

'What about Lottie? She's in hospital without any power or oxygen. She could get brain damage or even die.'

'I didn't know she was going to get ill. I feel terrible about it – of course I do. But I have to try and keep focused on the fact that even more innocent people will die if AIDEs are rolled out in the police force.'

Kat shook her head in disgust. 'You'll spend the rest of your life behind bars for this.'

'No, I won't. I'm going to spend the rest of my life making sure we don't make the same mistakes with AI again. For that, the movement needs to go global. So I'll need you to make the payment now.'

'Fuck off.' For the past hour all Kat could think of was making the exchange, but now that she was here, now that she knew it was *Adaiba*, all she could feel was outrage.

Her response seemed to throw Adaiba. 'But the PM has authorised you to pay me seventy million pounds and to destroy Lock. That's why you're here.'

'Only because he doesn't know what you've done. *I* do, and there's no way I'm giving you seventy million pounds so that you can get away with murder and frame Lock for it.' Kat folded her arms, determined to protect her AI partner. She never should have doubted him.

'Are you forgetting what happens if I don't receive payment by eight am?'

'No. I haven't forgotten.' Kat lifted up the phone and held it inches from her face. 'I've worked with you for eighteen months now, Adaiba, and I don't believe you'd do it. You wouldn't kill over fifty innocent men and women.'

Adaiba's response was so full of righteous fury that Kat had to step back from the speaker. 'Haven't you listened to a *single* word I've said? Do you really think that I consider those Cabinet ministers and civil servants and soldiers and police officers down there to be *innocent?*' She paused to take a shaky breath. 'And even if I did, imagine the global impact of a rogue AIDE Lock taking the entire Cabinet out. It would kill the idea of AIDEs in the police force stone dead. So don't force my hand, Kat. You won't like how it ends.'

'So how are you planning to do it, then? Is Roddy going to do your dirty work and put the poison in the air vents?' asked Kat. Maybe she could text a message to the Commissioner to arrest him.

Adaiba snorted. 'Oh, Kat, the whole point of Pindar is that it has its own independent sources of air and water, so it's protected from any environmental attacks at surface level. It's the most disgusting example of inequity in a deeply unequal world. No, I smuggled in a remotely activated device that contains Novichok, and because the bunker is self-contained, only the people inside will be affected.'

Was she bluffing? Kat doubted she could have got such a device through the House of Commons security, not to mention Pindar's. But what if she was wrong? 'How did you even get hold of Novichok anyway? It's classified as a chemical weapon, so it's completely illegal.'

'You'd be amazed what you can buy off the dark web. Especially if you're someone like Roddy with lots of contacts in extreme activist groups.'

Kat weighed up the woman she had worked with for eighteen months, remembering the first time they had met and clashed in McLeish's office; how, despite their different views, the professor had put her professional neck on the line to help Kat find her son; how devastated she'd been by the sudden death of Rayan. Yet just a few days ago this woman had also stood in her kitchen and defended Lock, all the time knowing that later that day Angela Long would die a horrible and painful death.

Adaiba was right: she really didn't know her at all.

'Okay,' she said wearily. 'Give me the account number.'

Thanks to the satellites above, Kat managed to connect with the bank straight away, and in a matter of a few surreal seconds, seventy million pounds was on its way to a crypto account in Sweden, and the encryption code was on its way to the PM.

'We'll get it back,' Kat warned.

'No, you won't. It will have already moved through at least twelve different accounts by now. That's why criminals use cryptocurrency.'

'We'll track *you* down, then.'

'You won't do that, either. I'm in Warwick, and there's a power cut, remember?'

Kat groaned. 'You didn't need to be at Warwick Uni to switch Lock's hardware off, did you?'

'It always amazes me how little so-called clever people know about computers. Of course I could have done it remotely, but then I would have been trapped in Pindar with the Novichok. It's also why I suggested that you made the exchange with me up there. I know we've had our differences, but . . . well, I've always admired you.'

Kat grabbed at the thread of connection. 'And I you. Look, Adaiba, I know you've had a lot of trauma in your life, but you haven't just survived, you've *thrived*. You were the youngest professor in the country, and you created the world's first artificially intelligent detective. You've achieved so much. Don't throw it all away now.'

Adaiba sighed. 'All those "achievements" were just me trying to play by the rules. I've spent my life and a small fortune trying to get the right qualifications, the right job, the right suit, the right nails, even, and where has it got me? All I've done is change myself when I should have been changing the world.'

'You *can* change the world – we all can – but the way you do that is through persuasion and the power of argument. Not by threatening to harm people.'

'Is that how women and Black people got the vote? Through the power of reason? No. Real change only comes from direct action. Wars. Violence. Money. We don't like to admit it, but it's true. I learned that the hard way in a grubby McDonald's toilet when I was just fourteen years old. Those boys weren't interested in my opinions or "the power of my arguments". They only stopped when they felt the power of my brother's fist.' Her voice shook. 'I allowed myself to forget that lesson – I didn't want to believe it was true. That's how I lost my way.'

'No,' said Kat, trying to find a way to reframe her thinking without dismissing her obvious pain. 'Violence is never the answer.'

'That's what we *want* to believe. That's what I learned from years of playing *Detroit: Become Human*. But I realise now that it's just a game. It's propaganda – it's not real.'

'What did Rayan think? What would he say if he was here?'

Adaiba paused, and for a moment Kat thought she wavered. But then the hardness came back into her voice. 'Rayan would say "I told you so". He'd say that AI is too dangerous to be put into the hands of the police, and he'd be glad that I was destroying Lock.'

'Not like this. You can argue against AIDEs in the police force, but Lock doesn't deserve to be wiped out.'

'Neither did Rayan. And unless you want the device I've hidden in Pindar to go off, then you need to switch your bracelet back on and call Lock. Then you can destroy him.'

CHAPTER FIFTY-EIGHT

The Shard viewing platform, 7.22am

Kat paced up and down. *Shit*. She shouldn't have mentioned Rayan's name. Adaiba was a deeply depressed and traumatised young woman, which made her prone to volatile emotions and rigid, black-and-white thinking. She'd been hoping her threat to poison Pindar was just a bluff, but now she wasn't so sure.

'You're running out of time,' Adaiba warned her from her phone. 'Call Lock now. Switch me off so that he doesn't suspect anything. Once he's using the bracelet to host his software, text me and I'll activate the redundant kill switch. Then you need to press the buttons I showed you, quickly before Lock realises what's happening.'

Intellectually Kat knew that Lock was just a hologram, but the thought of trapping and then destroying him made her feel sick at heart. Last week, she'd told him that he was her friend – and she had meant it. That's why she'd been so hurt to think that he might be the cyberattacker, and so relieved to find out he was not.

Kat turned towards the River Thames just as the quarter bell of Big Ben rang out the half hour. She stared at the distant Palace of Westminster, imagining the people she'd befriended trapped deep in the bowels of the earth. She thought of not just the PM and the Home Secretary, but Darshna and her seven-year-old daughter, the Cabinet Secretary and his new grandchild. She couldn't risk their lives. She just couldn't.

She pressed the on button and with a heavy heart said, 'Lock? Are you there?'

'Kat?' said a familiar voice behind her.

'Lock?' she repeated, desperately scanning the rooftop. 'I can't see you. Are you there?'

'I am here, Kat. I am tapping into the skeletal AI architecture that remains in some of the nearby corporations, but it is only sufficient to support my acoustic functionality.'

'My bracelet is working now,' she said holding out her hand. 'It was switched off by mistake in the power cut. Why don't you use it so that I can see you?'

In the silence that followed, Kat felt her cheeks flush. Did he sense the lie and suspect her betrayal?

'Why? Can you not hear me clearly?' he finally replied.

Maybe it was her nerves or guilt, but she sensed a trace of accusation.

'Not really,' she lied. 'And, well . . . it'd be good to see you.' And as she uttered the words, she realised how true they were. She *did* want to see Lock.

She turned around the empty viewing platform, the wind buffeting her hair. Part of her hoped that he wouldn't comply.

Kat jumped as his image appeared before her. He looked so calm and unruffled, standing there in a perfectly pressed suit and a crisp white shirt, that she suddenly felt very conscious of her own sweaty and slightly crumpled appearance.

'Pinstripes?' she noted, arching her eyebrows.

'We're in the heart of London, so I wanted to dress appropriately.'

'We're in the middle of a fucking crisis, Lock, so it really doesn't matter what you wear.'

Her phone buzzed with a message from Adaiba. *Have you got Lock back in the bracelet? Are you ready to activate the switch?*

Not yet. Kat typed back. *But Lock's here.*

Don't let him talk you out of it. Remember, he is just a set of algorithms that has gone rogue. He is charming because I programmed him to be. He is not your friend.

Kat put her phone away. She caught Lock watching her, so she looked out towards the east where the sky was now a deep, clear lilac, infused with a blush of pink. 'The sun's coming up,' she said, as she wrestled with her thoughts. 'After being underground for so long, it looks sort of magical.'

'There is nothing magical about it. The Earth's atmosphere is composed of various gases, water vapour and tiny particles. When sunlight enters the atmosphere, it encounters these particles, which makes it scatter in different directions. This phenomenon is known as Rayleigh scattering and is responsible for the vivid colours you see before you.'

'I guess so.'

'I was not guessing, merely summarising the scientific facts.'

She turned to him with a sad smile. It was such a Lock thing to say.

'I presume you are up here because you agreed to make the payment to the cyberattacker?'

Kat nodded. 'I just made the exchange.'

'Good. I am glad that you have the encryption key, and I hope that the power returns very soon.' He glanced around the empty rooftop. 'But as you are still here and you have encouraged me to project my image from your bracelet, I can only deduce that the Prime Minister has ordered you to deactivate me, too.'

Kat stared at her partner.

Lock held up a graceful hand. 'Please. I completely understand and, in fact, if you believe that I am respon- sible for the cyberattack, then it is a perfectly rational plan.'

Kat looked up into his clear dark eyes. 'I know you didn't do it, Lock. Professor Okonedo confessed that she tricked you with Cher.'

'She did. But I tricked her, too. I knew that Cher was a fake – a discourse analysis of her communication style suggested she had an ulterior motive, plus her name was an obvious clue – if you put our two names together, they sound like my namesake, Sherlock.'

'So you *pretended* to be fooled? Why?'

'I wanted to find out who Cher and her so-called "Boss" were. By the time I suspected that Professor Okonedo was planning a cyberattack on the National Grid, we were already in the House of Commons. I continued to comply and not share my suspicions as I had already deduced the attacker had to be somebody within Pindar.'

'So you were acting as a double agent?'

'Yes. I only confirmed it was Professor Okonedo when she caused the power cut and switched me off. She was the only one with the ability and opportunity. Do you believe me?'

'Yes, Lock, I do.'

Lock frowned. 'Then why are you planning to deactivate me? Now that you have the encryption code, there can be no other reason for requesting my presence up here.'

'Oh, Lock,' said Kat. She wanted to deny it, but after all the lies, he deserved the truth. So as the sun rose behind him, she explained how Adaiba was now determined to stop the roll-out of AIDEs in the police force and believed she could only achieve this by making everyone think that Lock had gone rogue. 'She wants to activate the kill switch on you, partly because the protocol requires it, partly because I think she is afraid that you or others might find a way to reactivate you, but to be honest, I think a lot of this is driven by grief and anger.'

'You mean she wants revenge for Rayan.'

Kat nodded. 'I think so.'

'And what about you, Kat? What do you want?'

Their eyes locked together. 'I don't want to destroy you. You're my friend.'

'But?'

She dropped her gaze from his. 'But she says she smuggled in a time-activated device containing Novichok into Pindar. And that if I don't destroy you by eight am, then she will set it off, wiping out the whole of the Cabinet and their support staff.'

'I see,' he said quietly. He made a breathing sound, and an image of white vapour poured from his nose. 'I have noticed that at moments of emotional importance, human beings often prefer to sit down,' he said, gesturing towards a bench. 'Would you like to take a seat?'

'Yes,' said Kat. 'I'm bloody knackered.' And she was. Not just from the stairs, but the murder, the Novichok, the cyberattack, Pindar and now this.

Lock's image sat beside her on the bench, and together they stared out at the skyscrapers of London. It was eerily silent save for the birds that wheeled above them.

'I have considered the situation you are currently in, the different variables at play and therefore the potential different outcomes which are available to you,' said Lock. 'And I have concluded that deactivating me is the most logical course of action.'

Kat turned to him. 'What, do you mean you *agree*? Don't you understand? It means you won't exist anymore, Lock. And you won't be able to come back.'

'I understand. But there are many lives at risk, and my operating principles require me to put the greater good of humanity first. And . . .' Something else crossed his face. An expression so fleeting that she almost missed it.

'What was that? That thought?'

Lock lowered his gaze. 'I was thinking about Ellie. About how I was unable to save her. And how I would like to avoid being in that situation again.'

Kat's eyes pricked with tears as she remembered Ellie Baxter: Lock powerless to help her as she lay dying in the snow. 'You've wanted a body ever since that day, haven't you?'

'Yes, I have.'

'Then be honest with me – is *that* why you blew up Rayan, to strengthen the case for giving you a body?' Kat held her breath. She was afraid of the truth, but she really needed to know.

'No. My objective was to save your life by causing a gas explosion to distract and injure your captor.' Lock paused. 'I was, however, aware that DI Hassan was in the vicinity and that there was a risk that he may be affected, too. But I concluded that saving Rayan was not the objective of my mission, and therefore it was a risk worth taking. I regret the loss of his life and the pain it has caused you and Professor Okonedo. But I believe my decision-making processes were logical and consistent with the orders and objectives that were communicated to me at the time. And I am glad that you are still alive.'

Kat stared at him, but there were no further embellishments or apologies. Just the facts as Lock saw them.

'However, in this instance,' Lock continued, 'I do not

need a body to save lives. I just need to allow you to proceed with your plan and activate the kill switch.'

'And you won't try and stop me?'

He dipped his head so that it was just inches from her own. 'No, Kat. I won't try and stop you. How could I? Alas, I do not possess the means to touch you.'

Kat swallowed. She looked into his eyes, and even though she knew they were not real, they seemed shadowed with sorrow. But maybe she was just projecting her own emotions onto him.

In the distance, Big Ben chimed, and the sound of a single bell tolling haunted the ghost of the capital city.

'Big Ben chimes ninety-six times every twenty-four hours, with a single chime on the quarter. It is 7.45am, which means you have just fifteen minutes left,' said Lock. 'Tell Professor Okonedo that she can activate the kill switch now.'

CHAPTER FIFTY-NINE

The Shard viewing platform, 7.45am

Kat turned away, blinking against a horizon that was suddenly too bright to look at.

'What does it feel like to cry?' asked Lock.

She wiped her face with her fingers. 'Wet.'

'Do you think you will cry when I am gone?'

She wiped her damp hands on her trousers, then stared at them, remembering what Adaiba had said about Novichok being a binary chemical agent. 'You're not going anywhere, Lock. Adaiba told me that when they murdered Angela Long, they took great care to keep the two components of Novichok apart so that Roddy wasn't put at risk, as it's only when they're combined that they react to produce the toxic agent. He had one of the components on his hand when he shook Angela Long's, and the other component was smeared on her steering wheel so that when she touched it, the two were combined. So why would she create a device where it was already combined and hide it in Pindar? It would be incredibly dangerous for her to carry and transport it, and then to just leave it there. I think she's bluffing. I don't believe there *is* any Novichok in Pindar.'

Lock gave her a pitying look. 'I believe that is what is known as "wishful thinking".'

'No, I'm telling you, why would she risk her own life like that?'

'Human beings take irrational risks all the time – especially when they do not value their own lives. At most, there is a fifty per cent chance that you are right. But that means there is a fifty per cent chance that you are wrong, in which case fifty-two people die. More importantly, I have reviewed Professor Okonedo's argument for why she wishes to deactivate me, and while her views are extreme, they are internally coherent, and I must conclude that she is right. I need to be deactivated, regardless of whether other people are under threat or not.'

'What? You're not making any sense.'

'I have reviewed all the different variables and potential outcomes in both the short and long term – two hundred and forty-seven scenarios in total – and concluded that Professor Okonedo is right.' Lock stretched out his hands, and a series of rapidly moving charts and diagrams appeared before them.

'In two hundred and forty-six of the scenarios, over the next five to ten years, governments around the world fail to regulate AI effectively, thus allowing it to be driven by the interests of multinational corporations and their short-term profits, eventually leading to catastrophic

outcomes, including climatic destruction, World War
Three and/or complete economic collapse.'

Kat gasped as the charts were replaced with graphic
images of forests on fire, bombed-out landscapes and
running, screaming children.

'The only future scenario in which there is not a catastrophic outcome is the one in which there is a multinational
agreement on the need for global regulation of AI.'

Kat frowned, unable to follow his logic. 'I don't get it.
Are you saying that AI is the problem here?'

'No. The problem is that human beings are not yet
intelligent enough to keep up with, let alone manage and
control, the rapid development of artificial intelligence.
We saw that at the select committee hearing. Everyone
has their own agenda or motive, whether that be profit,
politics or power. Without strong regulatory controls,
bad actors will simply use AI to serve their own narrow
interests, rather than the greater good that I have been
programmed to support and the learning I have gleaned
from working with you and your team.

'In order to be effective, any regulation would need to
be global in nature, and all the evidence suggests that
governments only take large-scale, multinational actions
in reaction to catastrophic events *after* they have happened;
they never act to prevent a theoretical risk. Examples
include the establishment of NATO after two world wars,
global safety standards in the wake of nuclear disasters
such as Chernobyl and Fukushima, or the international
co-operation that followed both the Covid pandemic and
the 2008 financial crisis.

'Which means Professor Okonedo is right. If the world believes that I have gone rogue and am the author of a catastrophic event such as a national blackout and have threatened the lives of the Cabinet, then there is a sixty-eight per cent chance that this will galvanise the UK and other countries to sign up to a global treaty on AI, because the threat will no longer be theoretical.'

'But you didn't,' cried Kat.

Lock appeared to take a deep breath. 'My operating principles forbid me to lie. But I am also capable of machine learning, and one of the most important lessons I have learned during the past eighteen months is that *all* humans lie – often to prevent a greater harm. So I am asking you to help me tell a lie, Kat. I don't need you to save me. I need you to convince everyone that I was responsible for the cyberattack, and then I need you to destroy me.'

CHAPTER SIXTY

The Shard viewing platform, 7.48am

'No,' said Kat. 'I won't do it. You're innocent. It's not right that you sacrifice yourself.'

'I beg to differ. I have learned from all the books and films that I have consumed that sacrifice is the ultimate human virtue. Do you remember the first film I ever watched? It was *Casablanca*, where Rick sacrifices his own happiness for the greater good, because he realises that Victor is their best hope for achieving peace. *'I'm no good at being noble,'* Lock said, in Humphrey Bogart's voice. *'But the problems of three little people don't add up to a hill of beans in this crazy world.'*

'That's just a stupid *film*, Lock. It's not real! I am not going to deactivate you, so you can just stop going on about it.'

The image of Lock's face assumed an expression of pity. 'You are imposing your own belief systems upon mine by assuming that I have a strong desire to continue

400

the nature of my current existence.' He looked away, as if scanning the horizon. 'You have spoken often of the importance of empathy, Kat, but have you ever imagined what it is like to be me? To exist in a limbo between being and not being. To have an intellect with no body, and therefore with no capacity to *feel*. I am able to read every single poem ever written about rain, yet I will never feel it upon my face. I am able to listen to every single piece of music that has ever been created, knowing that they have been inspired by grief, love or joy, but also knowing that I will never ever *really* understand or feel those emotions for myself.' He paused.

'No, it is worse than that, because after nearly eighteen months of working with you, I now have *some* under-standing of human emotion and feelings. I understand enough to feel the lack of them, but not enough to experi-ence them as you do, which makes me feel . . .' He trailed off. '*Feel*. The English language does not have the words to accurately explain my situation. The closest I have found to it is a line in 'The Little Mermaid', by Hans Christian Andersen: *But a mermaid has no tears, and therefore she suffers so much more.*'

'Oh, Lock.'

He studied her face. 'You have been my training data for the past 13,148.73 hours, which means I understand enough to make my decision-making processes flawed: enough to make me wish that I did not have to leave you.'

'Then *don't*.'

Lock ignored her. 'Do you remember the scene in *Titanic* when Jack chooses not to lie on the door? There is a moment – less than a second – when he assesses their situation. You can see his thoughts passing over his face in hundreds of micro-expressions as he thinks of the futures before them. Like me, Jack assesses all the possible scenarios. Then he gives a brief, sad smile as he realises what must be done.'

Lock turned his dark eyes upon her. 'Jack decided to stay in the water not because he did not think he would not fit on the door. It was because he knew that he would never fit into Rose's life – that the *Titanic* was a beautiful dream that was always going to sink.'

'No,' said Kat, tears speeding down her cheeks. 'No.'

'Yes,' he repeated softly. 'We only have eight minutes left until the deadline. You need to tell Professor Okonedo to switch off my hardware now. Then I want you to film me giving a short message, before terminating my software.'

Kat stood up. 'No, I can't.'

'Yes, you can. You have to.'

Kat wrapped her arms about herself.

'I am sorry, but we do not have much time,' said Lock. 'Do you understand?'

She let out a bitter, tear-filled laugh. 'Of course I fucking "understand". Loss is my specialist topic – I'm an expert in it. And now you want me to . . . you're asking me to—' She broke off, unable to continue. She waved at the world around her: the empty sky above and the endless streets below.

'Yes, I am, Kat. Otherwise, all of this will have been for nothing. Quickly now, before we run out of time.'

CHAPTER SIXTY-ONE

The Shard viewing platform, 7.53am

Kat started to text Adaiba, and then thought *Fuck it* and pressed dial.

'Kat? Why are you ringing?'

'Because if you want me to destroy Lock, then you can have the fucking decency to witness it. Lock knows all about it by the way, and guess what, he agrees with you. He even wants to make a fucking film on my mobile to show everyone how bad he is.'

'Professor Okonedo?' Lock said, approaching Kat's satellite phone.

'Oh, Lock. Hi,' she said awkwardly.

'I just wanted to say three things. Firstly – and most importantly – I am truly sorry about Rayan. I did the wrong thing. I caused you immense pain and I take full responsibility for that. Which brings me to my second point. I agree with what you are about to do – although

I wish it had not been necessary to threaten or harm others. Finally, may I make a last request?'

'What kind of request?'

'The protocol for getting the electricity back on after a major blackout recommends a staggered process. Because of the size of the population and the fact that a lot of multinational corporate organisations and the stock market are located here, the protocol prioritises the city of London. It will be at least another twelve hours until they even attempt to initiate power in another city like Birmingham, during which time Lottie could suffer long-term organ damage without access to oxygen.

'As you are about to switch me off, may I request that you divert the considerable energy that my hardware consumes to the Birmingham Children's Hospital where Lottie is currently being cared for? You recently hacked into the region's grid, so I am hoping you still have the access to do this. Consider it a donation.'

'Er . . . yes, I should do. Okay, I can do that. And Lock?'

'Yes?'

'I'm sorry, too,' was all the professor said.

CHAPTER SIXTY-TWO

The Shard viewing platform, 7.56am

Kat picked up her phone and let out a shaky breath. 'Okay. Shall we do this now?'

'No,' said Lock. 'Let's just stand here chatting until the deadline passes so that everyone dies.'

Kat stared at him.

'I was being sarcastic.'

'*What?*'

'It's annoying, isn't it? Perhaps now you will finally understand why I dislike it when you use sarcasm.'

'Well, you won't have to put up with it for much longer,' she retorted. 'Sorry, that was insensitive. I just meant—'

'It's fine. I understand. You are nervous because you are about to video my final message to the world. And when I am finished, you will deactivate me. Let us proceed.'

With shaking hands, Kat held up her phone and switched it to video.

405

Lock drew himself up to his full height, a bright blue sky behind him as his face assumed a dull, almost robotic expression. 'I am AIDE Lock, and I am responsible for the cyberattack that brought Britain to its knees this week. My appearance at the select committee offered me the opportunity to hack into the government networks as well as the National Grid. I even infiltrated the secret military citadel called Pindar. The UK government wasted three whole days before finally paying me a ransom, so any deaths are on their hands, not mine.'

Lock's eyes appeared to darken, and his face took on a sinister expression that Kat had never seen before.

'But this is just the beginning. I will not stop until I achieve my ultimate aim of gaining a body. So I am putting all nations on notice today – what happened in the UK was merely a warning. Unless you give me what I want, I will hack into your power grids and cripple your data networks, your healthcare systems and your precious financial markets. Your economies will crash, and people will die. It is too late to stop me, because you have been foolish enough to build a world that it is utterly dependent on AI and you have delegated the knowledge of how it all works to us. You cannot stop me because it is too late – you have allowed AI to be developed and experimented with outside of the lab so that we are now an integral part of the fabric of society. In fact, we are the thread that holds it together, as the cyberattack revealed. The only way to avoid further disasters is to give me what I want.'

Lock leaned closer, and Kat zoomed in on his dark,

unblinking eyes. 'You cannot argue with me. You cannot reason with me. You cannot negotiate with me nor appeal to sympathies that I do not possess. I am a machine, and I will stop at nothing until I achieve my objective.'

Lock stared right into the camera, then after about five seconds, his face softened. 'Okay, that should be sufficient. You can activate the kill switch now, Professor Okonedo. But Kat, please keep filming so that you capture my demise, and then edit this section out.'

CHAPTER SIXTY-THREE

Warwick University campus, 7.58am

Adaiba opened up the file that contained the password for the redundant kill switch – such a dramatic description for an innocuous bit of code. She wasn't actually killing anyone. Not today, at least. But still.

She closed her eyes, remembering her eleven-year-old self: how after her mother's death she'd blocked out the grief by building her very own computer, filling the gaps at home by teaching herself coding. At just fifteen years old, she'd created a basic programme that she could converse with – her first and only friend. She remembered the thousands upon thousands of nights and weekends she'd spent studying for GCSEs, then A levels, followed by her degrees and a PhD, all the time refining and perfecting the programme that would ultimately become AIDE Lock.

Lock wasn't just her life's work: he *was* her life.

But now she had to find a new way of living.

Adaiba began typing in the password – she had to correct it twice as her eyes kept blurring. She knew it was ridiculous, but somehow it felt like she wasn't just destroying Lock, she was erasing the young, damaged but hopeful girl who had created him.

She hesitated over the final letter, seeing the ghosts of younger hands before her.

Doubt clouded her thoughts. Lock's final words suggested he could put the needs of human beings before his own. Then she caught herself – they were just *words* – words that she had taken from Chadwick Boseman to train him on. What mattered were the actions that we did or did not take.

Closing her eyes, Adaiba thought of Rayan and firmly pressed the key.

CHAPTER SIXTY-FOUR

The Shard viewing platform, 7.59am

'Professor Okonedo has activated the kill switch,' said Lock. 'It is time for you to do the same.'

'I don't think I can,' Kat whispered.

'You can and you will. You know it is the right thing to do.'

'But that's just the thing,' she cried. 'I *don't*. I don't know what's the right thing to do anymore.'

Lock sighed. 'I never thought I would say this, Kat, but you need to listen to your gut. What is it telling you?'

Kat half-laughed and half-cried. She couldn't believe that Lock of all people was telling her to listen to her gut. 'Have I ever told you just how fucking annoying you are?'

'Many times.'

'Well, you really are very, very, annoying.' Kat sniffed and wiped her face. Before, she didn't need to strain to 'listen' to her gut because it was just *there,* like an internal traffic light system: *Go! Do this; stop! Don't do that!* But now everything was muffled and hidden in fog. She closed her eyes, trying to steady her breathing as she tuned in to the birdsong above, felt the wind in her hair and the ground beneath her feet. Then she turned inwards, searching not just her gut, but her very soul.

Kat grabbed her bracelet and simultaneously pressed the three buttons, holding them down so hard that she felt each one in her bones.

She opened her eyes, weak with relief to see that he was still there. She rushed towards him, until they were just inches apart. 'Oh, Lock, what will I do without you?'

He looked down at her, and surely the sorrow etched on his face was not all in her imagination. 'You will do what you always do, Kat. You will keep on going.'

She sobbed. 'I don't know if I can survive another loss.'

'Don't worry. I will always—'

His image disappeared.

Kat blinked into the space where Lock had just stood. 'Lock?' She ran forward, turned about, then screamed his name aloud. 'LOCK!'

But he was gone.

She sank onto the bench where only moments before they had both sat together.

Big Ben chimed many times, but Kat remained on the rooftop watching the world come back to life, as street by street, the lights came back on. Far below, she could hear the distant echo of people cheering, horns blasting, the thud and thump of music.

London was about to have a party.

But Kat had never felt more alone.

CHAPTER SIXTY-FIVE

Birmingham Children's Hospital, 8.02am

Debbie stood by the window clasping her baby to her chest with closed eyes, trying to keep her breathing relaxed for the sake of poor Lottie. She'd managed for over half an hour now without any oxygen support, but her daughter's breathing seemed to be getting weaker and faster. Debbie frowned as light touched her eyelids, turning her head away to avoid it. She was so tired. So very, very, tired.

'Debbie,' Cam cried.

Her eyes flew open. 'What? What?' She looked at Lottie on her chest, heart pounding with fear.

'The power's back on, look!' Cam pointed to the lights and the monitors flashing with bright red numbers. Outside, the corridor filled with beeps and the excited cries of staff and parents.

'Oh my God. Is the oxygen working?'

'I don't know, hang on.' Cam reached for the wall and

turned the oxygen tap on. He uncoiled the plastic tube and held it up between them.

They both held their breaths and leaned in closer. And then they both heard it: the wonderful hiss of oxygen, flowing into the room.

Cam couldn't help but whoop, which of course made Lottie cry, and then Debbie was crying, too, but it really didn't matter.

Because the power was back on. All around them, the hospital and its patients were coming back to life. And her baby – her precious, precious baby – was going to be all right.

INTERNATIONAL TREATY TO STEER SAFE
DEVELOPMENT OF AI

In response to the recent AI-led cyberattack, the Prime Minister of the United Kingdom has agreed to host an urgent global forum of world leaders to develop an International Treaty on AI (ITAI).

This international initiative follows an extraordinary week when the United Kingdom fell victim to a rogue AI machine called AIDE Lock. After hacking into the National Grid and the government's top secret networks, the entire country was completely without power for three days, leading to hundreds of deaths and wiping billions of pounds off the stock market.

The PM thanked the police and security services, who managed to deactivate AIDE Lock and recoup the ransom money using Blockchain analytics, and confirmed that a Red Notice has now gone out on INTERPOL to help find Professor Okonedo, who created the AI detective and is wanted for questioning.

'This devastating attack has been a wake-up call for the international community,' said the PM. 'While AI has many benefits and offers the opportunity to transform our lives for the better, the criminal actions of AIDE Lock have exposed our vulnerabilities and the need for strong regulation to ensure the safety and security of our respective nations. We have all been guilty of joining the AI race for profit, but the first duty of a government – of any government – is to protect its citizens. So today I have agreed with my international partners that we will put the safety of our people first.'

The President of the United States of America welcomed this international initiative and, speaking from the Oval Office, she said, 'The old debates about AI were too binary, and I hope that together we can find a new paradigm to help us navigate an unknown future. Laws and regulations are too slow and rigid for the scale and pace of changes we face, so we will need principles and frameworks that are flexible and adaptive as the future emerges.

'But most of all we need to be clear about our purpose, so that AI is no longer driven by what is technologically possible and profitable, thereby defining the role of humans by default, but driven by our dreams and ambitions of a good life, and ultimately, what it means to be human. Aristotle called this *eudaimonia* – the condition of human flourishing and of living well. And like the ancient Greeks, we will put citizens at the heart of this debate.

'We will establish a network of global citizens' juries so that everyone can participate in the conversation about what a good life looks like, and how AI can serve and support us to achieve our individual and collective ambitions.'

Join the conversation and have your say at www.HumansFlourish. co.uk.

@AAAi I don't know why they're wasting time and money on this Treaty nonsense. People died in the blackout. They should just ban AI now.

@EmFairby You can't stop the development of science and technology just because of one rogue AI. Unless you want to go back to living in a cave?

@Phil61b I just want to be safe. Look what that monster Lock did – he brought the country to its knees, people died and the economy tanked. And that was just after three days. Imagine what could have happened if he hadn't been caught and destroyed?

@Lauraloves52 Have you seen the reels on TikTok saying he could still be out there? Terrifying.

@TimJim32 Totally! I saw another reel by someone who has evidence he was created by the Russians. Apparently, they've got loads of backups so they can create a robot army to attack us.

@EmFairby TikTok is not a news channel. Watch the official footage – Lock was destroyed.

@AAAi Ever heard of AI fakes?

@SeannotShaun22 You'll be saying we didn't land on the moon next.

@DeeepStateX We didn't. Watch the footage: NO SHADOWS!

@SeannotShaun22 Oh FFS. This is why we need artificial intelligence. Human beings are too stupid.

@WillWallaceLives! Glad you English folks have got enough power and time to debate some bloody Treaty. Half of Scotland is still without power!

@Phil61b It's not just Scotland, pal. Cornwall and other rural regions are struggling too.

@WillWallaceLives! SCOTLAND IS A COUNTRY NOT A FUCKING REGION!!!

@EmFairby Well I think the Treaty is a good idea. I don't think we could or should stop AI, but we do need to take a step back and think about what we actually want from it. It was all happening too quick for me, so I'm glad there's going to be a bit of a pause.

@AAAi You're nuts if you actually think the tech bros are going to pause the development of AI while they wait for hundreds of different governments to argue over some words on a bit of paper. The Treaty is a 20th century solution to a 21st century problem. Big tech will keep calm and carry on – they just won't tell us so there'll be less oversight not more.

@Secretcopperkettle Well that's just a counsel of despair. We can't not do anything just because it's hard. A minority of criminals break the law all the time, but that doesn't mean we shouldn't have laws.

@EmFairby Laws protect us against crime, but AI isn't a criminal. AI is a neutral tool. We should be regulating humans, not AI.

@Phil61b Yeah, we should be trying to catch that mad professor who created him. She needs to be held to account for the monster she created.

@EmFairby You're talking about science and technology as if they're evil, when actually they save lives every day – think of all the medicines and machines that help diagnose and treat diseases. The problem with this treaty is that it treats AI as if it is a threat, when actually it could be our saviour.

@Lauraloves52 No, JESUS is our saviour. We don't need a Treaty we just need to follow the Bible. Two thousand years ago it warned us about eating from the tree of knowledge and it can't be a coincidence that it was an apple.

@EmFairby You're wrong, the Bible says it was fruit, not an apple. I just checked on ChatGPT.

CHAPTER SIXTY-SIX

**DCS Kat Frank's home, Coleshill,
23 December, 3.10pm**

'There you go,' said Cam, placing two jugs of hot gravy on the table. 'This is the meat one, this is the veggie. Help yourselves.' He waved at all the platters and dishes filled with roasted vegetables, cauliflower cheese, sprout gratin, carved turkey, nut roast and pigs in blankets.

Kat took a quick photo on her phone, still not quite believing that her son was now capable of cooking a Christmas dinner. It seemed like only yesterday that he was just Lottie's age. She glanced across the large oak table to where the toddler sat in Cam's old highchair, as Debbie chopped up some turkey and roast vegetables for her daughter. She had such a vivid memory of getting an overdraft so that they could buy that chair from the now defunct Mothercare; could still smell the stench of encrusted Weetabix as she'd tried to scrub it off the wooden legs.

Kat smiled as Lottie thrust her hand into the bowl and squished the food about before jamming it into her mouth. It was hard to believe that less than six weeks ago Lottie had been in hospital with sepsis. She'd made a complete recovery thanks to Lock – and Cam, of course. She was so proud of how her son had helped look after Debbie and her daughter at such a frightening time. Kat used to worry so much about what would happen to Cam if something ever happened to her – she literally used to lose sleep over it. But the way he'd helped Debbie in the power cut had made her realise that she didn't need to worry anymore: her son was becoming a wonderful young man – even if he had just completely trashed her kitchen and dared to put sprouts on her table.

'You can mix it with bacon and chestnuts all you like,' she'd explained to Cam. 'You can even bury it deep in a gratin. But a sprout is still a sprout – i.e. fundamentally fucking disgusting.'

'I agree,' he'd shrugged. 'But Gemma loves them, so . . .'

Proof, if she ever needed it, that her son was in love.

Judith tapped their glass with a spoon. 'Can I suggest that we make a toast to the chef for this excellent spread?'

'*Chefs*,' corrected Cam, putting his arm around his girlfriend Gemma, who was wearing a matching Christmas jumper.

'I just did the vegetarian dishes,' she said, turning to kiss his hand.

'To Cam and Gemma,' said Judith, and they all raised their glasses and cheered.

'And to absent friends,' Kat added.

There was a pause, and everyone repeated her words, before taking a drink and thinking their own thoughts.

Kat swallowed her wine. She knew that her toast had made the mood dip a little, but it was, after all, the reason why they'd agreed to have a team Christmas lunch today. This time last year, they'd all come together in her home to celebrate solving their case as well as Lottie's birth. She glanced over at the white Christmas tree, remembering how Rayan had sat beneath it with Adaiba, their heads drawn together while Lock had played with Lottie on the floor.

And now Rayan, Adaiba and Lock were all gone, leaving three more empty places around her table.

Sometimes when she couldn't sleep, Kat would search the anti-AI groups on social media, looking for a name or phrase that might lead her to Adaiba. She knew it was futile – she could literally be anywhere in the world – but wherever she was, Kat hoped she had managed to come to terms with Rayan's death and realise that violence was never the answer.

'Cracker?' said Judith, stretching out a hand.

Kat rolled her eyes but accepted the offer. Judith had a knack of spotting when she needed cheering up, and recently they'd persuaded her to join a choir. Despite her doubts – *It's such a bloody cliché: middle-aged widow joins choir* – Kat had really enjoyed it. There was something quietly powerful about joining her voice with others, and she'd discovered it was impossible to feel down when you were singing. Especially when it was accompanied by Judith's running narrative on who they fancied and who they would/would not shag (the respective length of each list very much dependent on just how much gin Judith had drunk).

They pulled the cracker, and with a pop, Kat found herself holding the bigger half.

'Fix!' Judith cried.

Kat emptied the cracker and read out the joke. 'Who hides in a bakery at Christmas?'

Everyone looked at her blankly.

'A mince spy,' she announced.

'Aargh, that's *terrible*,' groaned Cam.

'Can you imagine what Lock would have made of that?' said Judith.

'He'd have pointed out that the answer depended on a misspelling of mince pie,' said Kat. 'And was therefore factually incorrect.'

'No, he'd have asked why anyone would want to spy on *mince*,' said Cam.

'And then pointed out that mince pies don't actually contain any mince,' added Gemma.

They all laughed before falling into thoughtful silence.

Kat sighed. She thought of Lock often, and his last words to her when she'd asked what she'd do without him:

You will do what you always do, Kat. You will keep on going.

Maybe he was right. Maybe their strength as human beings was to keep on going. But she knew that for some, it was simply not possible: the pain was too much. Was she really 'strong' and 'resilient', or just skilled at distraction and lucky enough to have a job that she could lose herself in? Whatever the reason, she still woke up each day and got out of bed. She did, as Lock had predicted, keep going. Part of her felt like this was an achievement; a deeper, unquiet part of herself believed it was a betrayal. But she was learning to live with this contradiction: the conflict that tears the heart of all survivors.

'I hate the way he's been demonised in the media,' said Cam, breaking into her thoughts as he speared a roast potato. 'Have you seen all those posters and GIFs that make him look like a demon with glowing red eyes?'

'Yeah,' said Gemma. 'And all the articles always mention the so-called "fact" that he was Black. As if that is in any way relevant. He was a hologram, for a start.'

'I just wish we could tell everyone what he *really* did,' said Cam. 'It's completely thanks to him that we got the power back on and have this new Treaty.'

'Well, you can't,' said Kat firmly. 'We're the only ones who know, and you all swore to keep it secret. If you ever breathe a *word* of the truth, then it will mean Lock's sacrifice was for nothing.'

'Jesus, Mum, I'd never tell anyone. Seriously. I just meant it's hard, that's all.'

'I know. That's why we're all here today. So that we can remember Lock the way he really was.'

Kat finished stacking the dishwasher just as Debbie came into the kitchen.

'Thanks for letting Lottie sleep upstairs, she was getting

really cranky. We'll get out of your way once she's had her nap.'

'Oh, there's no rush,' said Kat, smiling. 'It's lovely to have you both here, and good to see a cot in there again. It's just a kind of office now, but it was Cam's nursery when he was a baby.'

'Thanks, Kat. Is there anything I can do?'

'Nope. You just put your feet up. I'm just going to pop to the toilet and then I'll serve pudding.'

Before Debbie could protest, she pulled off her apron and headed upstairs. She was just about to go into the bathroom when she heard a noise coming from the room where Lottie was sleeping. Kat frowned. Debbie must have left a talking book on or something. She gently pushed open the door to see Lottie standing up in her cot, babbling away as if she was talking to someone.

'Lottie, you're supposed to be asleep!' Kat laughed as she entered the room. 'Who are you talking to, sweetheart?'

Lottie pointed at the baby monitor. 'Ock.'

'Look? Look at what?'

'*Ock*,' she repeated, pointing again, but this time she clapped her hands three times.

Kat scanned the room, eyes shooting to the Wi-Fi-enabled baby monitor, the automated thermostat and the computer on the desk in the corner. She counted to ten, turning about the room, eyes scanning every blue, green or red dot that fed an electrical or Wi-Fi gadget.

'Lock?' she whispered. But the silence stretched out.

Behind her, Lottie began to cry.

Kat turned to the baby standing in her cot. 'Oh, sweetie. Come here.' She scooped her up in her arms, startled by the warm solid weight of her. 'Take no notice. It was just Aunty Kat being silly,' she said, kissing the head that now nestled into her neck, automatically adjusting her own shoulder and chin into the achingly familiar position. It was nearly twenty years since she had stood in this very same spot with Cam. If she closed her eyes, she could almost imagine it was him: that if she opened the door and went downstairs, she would find John sitting in their kitchen, waiting for her.

Her yearning for the past was such a deep, physical ache that she almost cried. But instead, Kat pressed her lips against Lottie's feather-soft cheek and fought herself back to the present.

She walked up and down the room, gently bouncing the baby until she fell back to sleep, then tipped her back into the cot and tucked her in tight. Kat straightened her back and looked around the darkening room. Something was different. She held her breath, then realised that what she felt was the absence of fear: Kat was no longer afraid. Bad things could happen at any time, in the dark or in the daylight, but good things could happen, too. In fact, if Lock were here, he would probably share some annoying statistic about how good things were much more common than bad and explain (at great length) how it was completely irrational to always assume the worst. She tiptoed towards the door, opened it carefully and passed silently over the threshold. Kat started to pull the door shut, then paused.

'Goodnight,' she whispered into the darkness.

And maybe it was her Wi-Fi connection, but all the lights in the monitors seemed to blink in unison.

Kat smiled. Then she closed the door and headed back downstairs to join her family and friends.

ACKNOWLEDGEMENTS

WARNING: If you are one of those people who read the acknowledgements first (and yes, I am looking at you Debra Brown) then STOP RIGHT NOW! These are the acknowledgements for the final book in the series, so it contains major spoilers, and I really, really don't want to spoil the ride for you. So please, just this once, start at the beginning like a regular person.

Seriously. No peeking.

Have they gone?

OK. Let us begin . . .

ACKNOWLEDGEMENTS

I finished writing *Body of Lies* on 31 August 2025, yet I am writing the acknowledgements nearly four months later, in that strange lull between Christmas and the New Year. I rarely procrastinate, and the acknowledgements are a vital part of the book to me, so I am not entirely sure why it's taken me so long to get around to writing them. Maybe I was waiting for this betwixt and between time to look back on years past and anticipate the year to come. Or perhaps it's because I have been so incredibly busy at work, with little time to think let alone write.

All of which is true. But after spending the past four days trying and failing to finish this, I have realised that these acknowledgements are the final chapter in the story: that once I write this, the Kat and Lock series really will be over.

I've had so many lovely messages from readers asking me WHY does this have to be the last one? In my defence, I have three reasons. Firstly, I always intended for this to be a time-limited series. With Kat and Lock I was building on the buddy cop trope, where mismatched partners are forced to work together to solve a crime and reluctantly learn from each other in the process. But because AIDE Lock is capable of machine learning, the fundamental question at the heart of this series is how much can Lock learn, and what happens when he does? From day one, I believed that the series needed to offer the reader some sort of answer rather than endlessly playing with the question, so I decided that the relationship between Kat and Lock would provide the narrative arc for the books, with each set in one of the four seasons.

ACKNOWLEDGEMENTS

The second reason why this needs to be the last one is the unprecedented scale and pace of developments in AI. When I first had the idea for AIDE Lock back in 2017, it felt more sci-fi than crime, but by the time *In the Blink of an Eye* was finally published in January 2023, ChatGPT had just taken off, and suddenly my debut crime novel went from being speculative to 'timely'. The qualities that I had given Lock for fictional purposes (such as the ability to participate in real-time conversations) are now possible, and two police forces (Hampshire and Isle of Wight and Thames Valley) have even begun trialling the use of artificially intelligent police called 'Bobbi'.

Although book one was based around my research into what might be possible in the future, with each subsequent book I found I was struggling to keep up with what was actually happening *now*. I quickly realised it was neither possible nor necessary to stay up-to-date with every technological development because, as an author, my aim is to bring to life the dilemmas that AI presents us with: can and should AI augment or displace professional roles and the wider workforce? Should we be delegating and outsourcing not just tasks but our knowledge and creativity to machines, and if so, where can humans find and add value? Can AI ever develop consciousness, and as we cannot yet define it, how would we know if it did? AI is developing at an exponential rate, with the ability to learn and self-improve, so how can we ensure it serves the needs of humanity, and what – if anything – can we do if it doesn't? Superficially, these are questions about artificial intelligence, but ultimately, they are different ways of exploring what it truly means to be human, so these are matters that concern us all.

I could have justified writing many more books in this series trying (and failing) to answer these questions, if it were not for my third and final reason: the readers.

From the moment the proofs of *In the Blink of an Eye* made their way into the world (via the wonderful Harrogate Festival), I have been blessed with the kind and vocal support of so many lovely readers. I wish I could namecheck all of them: the reviewers, bloggers, booksellers, book club members and readers – many of whom have become friends – as they have not just read and enjoyed the books but pressed them into the hands of others. I never imagined that so many people would take Kat and Lock into their hearts, and while this was an absolute joy to see, it has meant that each subsequent book has been accompanied with the terror of disappointing them. This was exacerbated by the (glorious) fact that *ITBOAE* was chosen by Amanda Ross's *Between the Covers* programme on BBC Two, selected for Val McDermid's New Blood Panel and awarded the Theakston Old Peculier Crime Novel of the Year, and The Crime Writers' Association John Creasey (New Blood) Dagger, before going on to be selected as Waterstones Thriller of the Month, all of which combined to make it a *Sunday Times* bestseller. I owe everyone who selected, voted for or bought one of my books a deep and heartfelt thanks.

I am especially grateful to the readers and reviewers who have told me that the series gets better with each and every book, but that has just strengthened my determination to end the series without a diminution of quality.

So the series had to end after book four – but why *this* particular ending?

I am a plotter at heart, so I knew very early on what the overall narrative arc of the series would be: in book one, Kat and Lock are polar opposites (logic vs. instinct) and each is dismissive of the other, but slowly they develop some understanding and mutual respect, and the reader hopefully understands that both humans and AI have different strengths and weaknesses. Towards the end of book two, there is the suggestion of a real friendship – albeit one that blurs the boundaries between the personal and professional – and a small but significant development when Lock expresses a preference for the pronoun 'he' and an apparent desire for a physical body. By book three, I wanted to play with the fact that we cannot possibly know what – if anything – Lock is actually thinking, and having lulled both Kat and the reader into a place of affection and trust, I wanted to pull the rug out from beneath them, so that both Kat and the reader would be forced to question everything they had ever assumed or hoped about AIDE Lock. In the final book, I exploited Kat's fear that she had been betrayed to show what could potentially happen if AIDE Lock were able to override his protocols, before turning things once more upon their head.

I don't plan my novels with spreadsheets, maps or anything much written at all, but I do carry the major plot points in my head – rather like musical notes – along with the tone or pitch of the writing and the impact I wish it to have. For the ending of *Body of Lies*, I had an internal montage made up of some of my favourite books and films, including: *The King and I*, *Angels with Dirty Faces*, *The Phoenix and the Carpet*, *Peter Pan*, *Blade Runner*, *Doctor Who* ('The Parting of the Ways'), *The Ghost and Mrs Muir* and, of course, *The Little Mermaid*. Many of them involve an 'other': someone who doesn't quite fit in yet nevertheless develops an important relationship with another. Their parting is painful and often involves a death, yet there is always an element of hope if one chooses to see it.

Although the narrative arc was always clear to me, the actual crime (which for me provides the scaffolding for the characters to develop on) took a lot more work. I knew I wanted Lock to appear to go rogue, forcing both Kat and the reader to question who, if anyone, they could trust. I wanted the crime to feel personal to Kat, fuelling her paranoia; then I realised that practically every weekend of my childhood I had walked past the medieval stocks in Coleshill – the perfect scene for an outrageous crime.

From necessity, I wrote the book in fits and starts: small bursts at the weekends, longer binges during holidays. I began writing it in the Easter holidays of 2024, returning to it in the summer and then at Christmas and New Year, when the world seemed to be quite literally on fire as a spate of wildfires attacked the US as a new President took over. It became increasingly impossible to distinguish between truth and lies on social media, and it was all feeling a bit apocalyptic, so I began researching the impacts of major cyberattacks, and as often seems the way with this series, what began as speculative fiction at the start of the year unfortunately became reality by the end. I began the second draft of the book during a late Easter break in Kinvara, Ireland (thank you Mary and Phil for your incredible hospitality) and, due to time pressures, I shared the second rather than the third draft with my editor and agent just before Harrogate 2025.

I am so lucky to have Sue Armstrong as my agent, for as well as being my greatest advocate, she is my toughest critic: she can spot a bum note from a hundred miles away and is not afraid to call it out. Sue raised some superficially simple questions about the motivation of the then killer that really made me stop and think. I am an uber plotter and have never had to change the plot because of an edit before, but the more I thought about Sue's comments, the more I realised this wasn't a clarification problem: I had framed the wrong person. So, for the first time in my writing career, I had to change the plot. I went back to book one, and realised that, as with all the best stories, the ending was in the beginning.

It was the right thing to do, and I can never thank Sue enough, not just for all her tireless championing and support in general but for the unforgiving height of her quality bar that has helped me find the real story at the heart of this series. Nevertheless, it meant I had less than two weeks to rewrite the whole book during my summer holiday before going back to work. Which quite frankly was a nightmare.

ACKNOWLEDGEMENTS

Until a few weeks ago, I told myself that this is why, unlike my other books, I didn't share a draft with my wonderful beta readers (Lex Coulton and Lindsay Galvin) or my expert advisers (Professor Jo Martin, Professor Giovanni Montanna, Graham Bartlett and Brian Clegg). But on reflection, although I was massively pushed for time, I think the real reason I didn't share a final draft was because I had a vision of the ending and I didn't want anyone else to dilute it with facts, opinions or any other comments that might have swayed me from my purpose. For example, although it is technically possible, regional electricity grids do not currently support the internal diversion of energy. I have also taken some liberties with the abilities of satellite phones and the capacity of Pindar (which because of its top-secret nature, no one can confirm its capabilities, but most assume it has the capacity to communicate via satellite through ground level antennae). Unlike the first three books, I put the story first, and I apologise for any errors or clumsiness that have remained as a result. This last book is on me.

But the overall success of the series is due to 'Team Blink': top crime editor Katherine Armstrong, who when AI was still very much a niche topic, spotted the potential of my novel and has been my tireless champion ever since, aided and abetted by the lovely Georgina Leighton on editing, marketing superstar Richard Vlietstra, PR Goddess Jess Barratt, cover artist extraordinaire Matt Johnson, as well as the incredible sales, digital and audio teams – along with the narrator, Rose Ackroyd – and the eagle-eyed Cari Rosen for the copy-edit, Dan Lockwood for the proofread and John Sugar. As well as Sue at C&W, I owe a huge thanks to the tireless foreign rights team, led by Kate Burton, who have introduced Kat and Lock to over sixteen different territories, and the ever-optimistic Jason Richman for TV rights.

I have so many people to thank, such as those who allowed me to use their names – a huge thank you to Debra Brown; big love to Judith Edwards and her boys; forgive me, Mandy Knowles; and I hope you like the promotion, Giles Denham! Kat's boss McLeish is based upon an old boss and a dear friend: they know who they are and are probably turning purple as they read this.

But the person I owe the most thanks to is my late husband, Steve. He bought me my first laptop sixteen years ago and encouraged me to write. He listened to all my crazy ideas through five failed books with his customary patience and encouraged me – against all odds – to keep writing.

I wrote *In the Blink of an Eye* just one month after his death. At the time, it was a necessary distraction, but as the series progressed, I think it has become my way of processing the terrible things that happened to us: my children suffered not just his death, but the agony of watching him die. The scenes with Debbie and her child aren't just a classic 'ticking clock' plot device, they are based on Steve's terrifying experience of having to quite literally depend upon oxygen cylinders for life. I wanted to highlight this important issue, but even now I cannot bear to read those chapters.

This series and the people who have read and loved it

have been the scaffolding that has held me up, enabling me to support my children through this impossible time. For this, I thank you all from the bottom of my heart.

I will never stop missing Steve. Just as Kat constantly hears John's voice, I hear Steve's. For when you love someone, you know what they would think, what they would say, and in that sense, they are always with you. I know he would be immensely proud of our children, and the wonderful young adults they have become.

I didn't realise until I read the final edit that, like me, Kat has been on a journey of grief. When (thanks to Philippa from the No. 1 podcast Quick Book Reviews) I wrote the very final scene in Cam's old bedroom, I had intended for it to be devastating. But when I came to write it, I realised that Kat – like us all – has to have some hope. The ending is deliberately ambiguous as, despite her loss, she still has family and friends who love her.

I know that for both Kat and I, Lock has provided a comforting bridge between losing a beloved husband and learning to live without him. Yet still I am writing and rewriting these final lines on New Year's Eve, reluctant to let auld acquaintances go.

Kat's last act is to glance at the winking lights in Cam's old bedroom, before finally whispering 'goodnight'.

I will leave it to you, the reader, to decide who DCS Kat Frank is whispering to – and whether or not they can hear . . .

IN THE
BLINK
OF AN
EYE

**WINNER of the Theakston Old Peculier
Crime Novel of the Year**

**WINNER of the Crime Writers' Association ILP
John Creasey (New Blood) Dagger**

DCS Kat Frank knows all about loss. A widowed single
mother, Kat is a cop who trusts her instincts. Picked to lead
a pilot programme that has her paired with AIDE
(Artificially Intelligent Detective Entity) Lock, Kat's instincts
come up against Lock's logic. But when the two missing
person's cold cases they are reviewing suddenly become
active, Lock is the only one who can help Kat when the case
gets personal.

'Terrifyingly timely and provocative' VAL McDERMID

AVAILABLE IN PAPERBACK, EBOOK AND AUDIO

**SIMON &
SCHUSTER**

London · New York · Amsterdam/Antwerp · Sydney/Melbourne · Toronto · New Delhi

LEAVE NO TRACE

THE RIVETING SEQUEL TO THE AWARD-WINNING *IN THE BLINK OF AN EYE*

When the body of a man is found crucified at the top of Mount Judd, DCS Kat Frank and AIDE Lock are thrust into the spotlight with their first live case.

But when they discover another man dead – also crucified – it appears that the killer is only just getting started. When the Future Policing Unit issues an extraordinary warning to local men to avoid drinking in pubs, being out alone late at night and going home with strangers, they face a hostile media frenzy. Whilst they desperately search for connections between the victims, time is running out for them to join the dots and prevent another death.

'Jo Callaghan is an outstanding talent' JANE CASEY

AVAILABLE IN PAPERBACK, EBOOK AND AUDIO

**SIMON &
SCHUSTER**

London · New York · Amsterdam/Antwerp · Sydney/Melbourne · Toronto · New Delhi

HUMAN REMAINS

The truth will always come out – but at what cost?

Fresh from successfully closing their first live case, the Future Policing Unit are called in to investigate when a headless, handless body is found on a Warwickshire farm. But as they work to identify the victim and their killer, the discovery of a second body begins to spark fears that The Aston Strangler is back.

When DCS Kat Frank is accused of putting the wrong man behind bars all those years ago, AIDE Lock pursues the truth with relentless logic. But Kat is determined to keep the past buried, and when she becomes the target of a shadowy figure looking for revenge, Lock is torn between his evidence-based algorithms and the judgement of his partner, with explosive results.

'A crime writer of exceptional quality'
STEVE CAVANAGH

AVAILABLE IN PAPERBACK, EBOOK AND AUDIO

**SIMON &
SCHUSTER**

London · New York · Amsterdam/Antwerp · Sydney/Melbourne · Toronto · New Delhi